The Steerswoman

"We'll handle the steerswoman, girlie. Calm down!" Bel subsided, looking at the woman with a wild eye. "You done good," he assured her. "Probably a promotion in this for you."

"So, we take her to Druin?" The man spoke close behind Rowan's ear. Her heart stumbled. Druin would remember that the women had come in together; the ploy would fail.

"Not this one." The servant approached and viewed Rowan with a self-satisfied, superior air. "She goes straight to Themselves, and no delay." He nodded to Bel. "You come, too."

But when the servant emerged from the room to which they had been led, Bel was instructed to return later to make her report. Rowan exchanged one glance with her before passing through the door the servant held wide. The Outskirter's expression was stony, with what emotion Rowan could not guess. Accompanied by two of the guards, the steerswoman stepped in to meet the wizards.

When she saw them, her first reaction was: *Gods below, they're children!*

ROSEMARY KIRSTEIN

The Steerswoman

PAN BOOKS
London, Sydney and Auckland

First published 1989 by Ballantine Books, New York, as a Del Rey Book
First published in Great Britain 1990 by Pan Books Ltd, Cavaye Place,
London SW10 9PG
9 8 7 6 5 4 3 2 1

ISBN 0 330 31348 7

Printed in England by Clays Ltd, St Ives plc

This is dedicated to

SABINE KIRSTEIN

Who taught her little sister the music of language,
and the dance of ideas.

Umber
Terminus
The Wulf
Lake Cerlew
The Wulf
Kiswan
Archives
Wulfshaven
The Crags
Inland
(Ships vanish)
Southport
Shoreline Uncertain

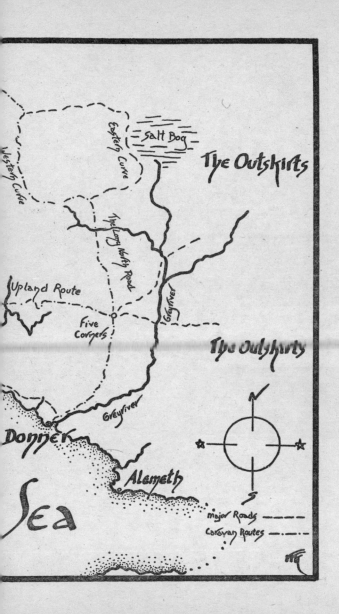

CHAPTER
One

The steerswoman centered her chart on the table and anchored the corners around. A candlestick, a worn leatherbound book, an empty mug, and her own left hand held the curling parchment flat. The lines on the paper seemed to be of varying ages, the ones toward the center drawn with cracked, browning ink, those nearer the edges sharp and black. Extent of detail also showed progression. A large body of water, labeled "Inland Sea", dominated the central portion. The northern shore was depicted with painstaking precision. Farther north and farther east lines became more general, and there was a broad blank space on the right-hand side of the map.

The innkeeper regarded the woman a moment, then turned his attention to the chart. "Ah, look at that, now, all laid out just like we were birds and all." He tilted his head for a better vantage. "Here we are, then." He placed a chubby finger down on the parchment, on a spot north and east of the sea, midway between precision and vagueness. "Here's this very crossroads, see, and the town, and the tavern itself." This last was not depicted. The steerswoman made no comment.

The finger moved northeast, leaving a faint, damp mark. "There, that's where me and my brothers used to live. Right there; I know that river, see."

"And that's where you found the jewel," Rowan the steerswoman said.

"Yes, lady, that's right. Felling trees, these great big ones here." With a sweep of his arm he indicated a vast supporting beam visible in the ceiling of the narrow sitting room. "There we were, cutting these great things down – they did the worst of it, I'm not so strong as my brothers." The innkeeper was an immense square block of a man, of the sort whose padding generally concealed considerable muscle. "So I spot this smaller one, more in my range, like. And I heave back my axe, give it one great bash – and there it was."

Rowan reached across the table and picked up the object that lay there, an irregular lump of wood about the size of her two fists. As she turned it over in her hands, something glinted inside the hollows and depressions carved into its surface: rich colors that fractured and shifted as the light shifted, opalescent – now blue-black, now sky-blue, now a flash of purple, recalling amethyst. The surface was laced with tiny veins of silver. Rowan touched one of the visible faces and found it perfectly smooth, far smoother than a jeweler could have cut it, and with a faintly oily feel.

Putting the object down on the chart, she reached into the neck of her blouse and drew out a small pouch, hung by a leather cord. She slipped the cord over her head, opened the pouch, and slid its contents out onto the table.

The innkeeper smiled. "Ah, you've got one, too, though not so large and fine as mine." He picked up the blue shard, about half the size of the thumb he rubbed across it. "Oh, it's the same, yes." But it seemed less a jewel than a slice of a jewel. It was flat and thin as a knife blade. Only one surface showed, the other sheathed in some rough-textured, silver-colored metal, as if it had been pulled from or broken from a setting.

The steerswoman made a vague gesture. "We can't tell how large yours is, imbedded in wood. All the others I've seen are like my own, small and one-sided. I suspect that what you have is actually several jewels, nestled together." She turned back to the map. "Can you recall which side of the tree it was found in?"

He was surprised. "Side? No side, lady. It was inside like I said."

"Yes, but wasn't it closer to one side than the other?" She tapped the object. "It wasn't directly in the center, or the pattern of the grain would run around it in a circle. It was off-center. I need to know in what direction."

"Ten years back? Who can tell one side of a tree from another, ten years back?"

Rowan leaned back in her chair, contemplating a moment. She was an unprepossessing figure, of average height, and of average build for her height. Her traveling clothes, a rough linen blouse and trousers, were dusty and perhaps a bit tattered. Her hair, cut short for convenience, was the color of dark wet sand, save where the sun had bleached pale streaks. She possessed no outstanding beauty, and yet her face fascinated, not by any great perfection of feature but by its intelligent, constantly shifting expression. It seemed as if the actions of her mind were immediately reflected on her face, giving her a strange air, part vulnerability, part arrogance. One could not tell if she was helplessly incapable of guile, or if she simply considered it beneath her.

"The jewel showed at the first strike of your axe?" she asked the innkeeper.

"Yes, lady."

"Which way were you facing? Were there landmarks about? What did you see?"

"See?" He was blank a moment, searching his memory; then his face lit up. "I saw the Eastern Guidestar. The sun was just setting, see, the stars just showing, and as I get ready to swing, I look up and see the Eastern Guidestar shining through the branches like an omen. I remember thinking that."

Rowan laughed, slapped her hand down on the table, and rose.

"Does that tell you something, lady?"

"Indeed it does." She had gone to where her pack lay against an armchair, and was opening her tubular map case. She pulled out another chart, smaller than the first, and brought it back to the table. "Here." She pushed the lump to one side and spread the new chart on top of the first. "Do you see that this is a more detailed map of this small area?" She indicated the land around his finger-smudge.

"Yes . . ."

She nodded. "Here's the river, as you said, and it must have been around here that you felled the tree."

He squinted along her finger. "Could be, yes . . ."

"Were there any other landmarks? What did you pass on the way there?"

"We crossed a brook . . ."

"Could it be this one?" With a series of questions she narrowed the possibilities until both she and the innkeeper were satisfied. She marked the position with a small star. Next she questioned him closely about the terrain and the other types of vegetation nearby, adding symbols and notes. At last she said, "And you were facing the Eastern Guidestar, which is southeast from there," and drew a small arrow by the star, pointing southeast. The innkeeper saw that there were perhaps a dozen such stars on the map, three of them accompanied by arrows. All the arrows pointed southeast.

The steerswoman picked up the wooden shape again, giving her attention not to the jewels but to the wood itself. She ran her fingernail lightly along the grain. "Did you use the tree that held this in constructing any part of this building?"

"Why, yes. The great mantelpiece over the fireplace in the common room."

She tossed the lump to him. "Show me." The terse command was tempered by her evident delight. The innkeeper could not imagine why the prospect of examining a mantelpiece would please her so. He led her down the short paneled corridor, passing a wide-eyed chambermaid who hastened to get out of their way, either out of respect for her master, or for the woman who followed him.

The common room was a wide low chamber that ran the entire length of the inn. In the far corner, a door led to the kitchen and service area, with kegs of various brews and wines nearby. Rowan and the innkeeper entered from another door in the same wall. A massive fieldstone fireplace filled the area between the two doors. The opposite wall held the entrance and a rank of windows, all flung open to admit the weak spring sunlight. As an attempt to dispel the native gloom of the chamber, this was a failure, and only served to offset the dark comradely warmth that prevailed.

The confluence of several bands of travelers had provided the inn with a crowd of surprising size. In one corner, a caravan guide was regaling a merchant who had three lovely young companions – daughters, by the merchant's evident disapproval of their bright-eyed attentiveness. Nearby, some of the other caravan members were conversing with five soldiers in red surcoats, apparently in the service of some or another wizard currently aligned with the Red. Close by the fire, a group of pilgrims were receiving an impromptu lecture from their leader; a local wag stood close behind his chair, parodying the man's pontifical gestures and expressions, while the pilgrims watched in a dumbfounded fascination that the unknowing leader seemed to attribute to his own rhetorical brilliance.

Far to the left of that group, Rowan identified a band of no less than a full dozen Outskirters. War-band size, she realized with some concern. But they seemed, at the moment, cheerful and unthreatening, oblivious to the ring of silent watchfulness around them, a ring that was slowly being frayed by the friendly, the brave, and the simply curious.

Seeing that nothing undue was about to transpire, she turned her attention to the fireplace and the mantelpiece, which was high up, safely out of casual arm-reach. It held a display of oddments and fancy mugs.

Rowan found a tall stool by the fire. She tested it with a fingertip, and it wobbled perceptibly. Seeing her intent, a local farmer leaped up. "Here, lass, I'll give a hand." He moved it to where she indicated and patted the seat, saying, "Up you go, lass, be glad to hold you," with a grin and an overly familiar wink.

"A little respect, man. That's a steerswoman," the innkeeper protested. The farmer backed off in surprise.

"It doesn't mean I couldn't use a hand," Rowan said, half annoyed, half amused. She climbed to the top of the stool while the farmer carefully steadied it, his friends chortling at some expression on his face, invisible to Rowan.

Ignoring them, she turned and carefully examined the squared-off end of the mantel, her face close to the wood, her hands moving over the grain.

The innkeeper watched in perplexity, then eyed the group around the fire, as if debating whether to betray his ignorance with a question. His quandary was solved by a serving girl, who, bustling by, noticed the steerswoman for the first time. "Here, what are you doing?" she called.

Rowan looked down. "Counting rings," she said with a grin, then returned to her work. The innkeeper's flapping gesture sent the girl back to the customers, and then he cleared his throat experimentally. His comment was forestalled by an explosion of loud voices from the near corner, and heads turned in the direction of the Outskirters.

One of the barbarians, a particularly burly specimen with a shaggy red beard, had risen and was leaning across the table to reply to a local who had joined the group. But he spoke with laughter and had leaned forward to pour more wine into the man's cup. "Ha! Stories! We've tales enough, and more than enough. I shouldn't wonder you'd ask, living in these soft lands. Sit in a tavern with good wine and good ale, and hear someone else's miserable adventures."

The band of Outskirters was becoming more infiltrated as surrounding people edged a little nearer at the possibility of a story.

"As for us," the barbarian continued, sitting down, "when we want something unusual we come to small taverns and sit under dry roofs, drink wine, and gawk at the local dullards." He spoke good-naturedly; certainly none of his comrades seemed to find the present company objectionable. One Outskirter woman at the end of the table sat shoulder-to-shoulder with a handsome field hand. He spoke to her in quiet tones; she gave occasional brief replies, a small smile on her face, eyes looking now to the left, now to the right.

"We'll bring a goblin, next time," a second barbarian volunteered, speaking around a mouthful of roast venison. "He'll have stories, or perhaps he'll do a clever dance."

"I've seen the goblins dance," said a farmer with brooding eyes. "I don't care to make closer acquaintance."

"Nasty beasts," the first Outskirter agreed. "Singly and in troops. Only last month our tribe was beset by a troop, and at night, too, the worst time to deal with them. Garryn's pyre, remember?" His friends nodded. "We had to burn him at night. Ha, there's a story— " He received a shove from his comrade.

"What!"

"Let Bel tell it."

The man was outraged. "I was there!"

"For only part."

"I never left!"

"You slept."

"Never! Well, yes, with the help of a goblin's cudgel . . ." But the cry had been taken up by the other Outskirters. The woman at the end of the table rocked indecisively a moment, then rolled her eyes and got to her feet. Somewhat shorter than expected, she climbed to stand on her chair so she rose above the listeners, her head up near the low rafters.

She gazed up at the air for a while, as if choosing her words. Though small, she looked strong and able. She kept her balance on the chair easily, feet planted wide in shaggy goatskin boots which were met at the top by leather leggings. Her sleeveless shirt was equally shaggy. Her cloak was made of the unmatched skins of seemingly dozens of very small animals, crudely stitched together. Rowan wondered if she was not too warm.

With a gesture that commanded instant silence, the barbarian began to speak.

"Silence and silence; the battle stilled.
The outcome delivered, foes dispersed:
Garryn's gift. His was the guidance,
Warrior's wisdom, and heart of wildness."

Distracted, Rowan returned to her counting. The innkeeper finally spoke up. "What does it tell you, lady?"

"A moment." She finished, then gestured for him to pass the wooden lump. She placed it on the edge of the mantel and turned it this way and that, comparing it to the beam. "It tells me the age of this tree."

"The age?"

A grizzled elderly local spoke up. "One ring every year, on a tree." He was seated on a stool by the hearth's edge, his hands busy knitting a large square of off-white wool. Beside him, in a deeply cushioned armchair, an even older woman worked at needlepoint,

15

her nearsighted eyes perilously close to the flashing needle. The old man grunted. "Don't need a steerswoman for that. One ring a year." The woman nodded, her work nodding with her.

"You can see the center of the tree, here. I can count all the way out to the edge: forty-three rings." The innkeeper and the farmer peered up. "And this— " She turned the glittering wood object again. "See how close the grain is? It came from about this area. Where the tree is perhaps fifteen years old."

Across the room, the quiet grew deeper as more people turned their attention to the Outskirter.

"The sun sank, urging us speed,
For in deep darkness, fire calls to Death,
To furies fouler, more fearsome than Man— "

Goblins were attracted by fire, Rowan remembered, only half listening. She clambered down from her perch, thanked the farmer, then settled on a lower stool. "Forty-three years old when it was cut down, ten years ago. And the jewels appeared at the fifteen-year mark, about. Roughly, then, thirty-five years ago, these jewels and the tree came together."

"Came together? But surely they grew there, magic and all?"

She smiled. "Possibly they grew there. Likely they were put there, that is, driven into the bark, just at the surface. Later, the tree grew outward, and the wood engulfed the jewels."

"The tree didn't grow them, then?" The farmer spoke up, indicating the innkeeper with a thumb gesture. "Like he's always telling?"

Rowan looked apologetic. "I have one, found in a spadeful of dirt from an irrigation ditch, far from any tree. If trees grow them, then the earth does, as well."

The old man spoke to the farmer. "She's going to find out about them. That's what they do, you know. Always asking questions, the steerswomen."

"I thought they answered questions."

"Of course!" he laid a finger aside his nose. "You and me, we ask the steerswomen. And they ask themselves. Answer themselves, too, they do, in the end."

Rowan made to speak to the innkeeper, but found him distracted by the Outskirter's poem. Apparently the goblins were attacking:

> "The cries of the crazed ones, hefting cudgels,
> Driving from darkness, drawn by fire,
> Hunting heat, and knowing no hindrance
> Of men, matter, arms, or means . . ."

The steerswoman went to the innkeeper and got his attention. "Might I possibly borrow this piece of wood for a time? It would be good if I could show it to some people at the Archives."

He was dubious, but reluctant to deny her. "Well, lady," he said, "I'd hate to part with it. I mean, how I found it and all . . . I'm sure it must be magic, and as it hasn't done any harm yet, I suppose it must be doing some good."

"I don't really need it," she admitted. "But it would be helpful." A change in the reciting Outskirter's voice made Rowan glance her way.

> "Faltered finally, felled by this sword— "

Bel stood straight and slapped the hilt with a gesture that tossed back one side of her cloak. Her movement revealed, below the edge of her shaggy vest, an eye-catching belt of silver, decorated with flat blue gems.

Rowan handed the jeweled lump back to the innkeeper blindly and forgot about the man as completely as if he had vanished. Edging her way through the tables, she approached the crowd around the Outskirter woman.

> "—held by this hand. So passed horror."

Bel paused, then shifted her weight slightly, and the informality of the movement made it clear that the tale was over. There were murmurs of appreciation from those gathered and some table-pounding on the part of her Outskirter cohorts. She hopped down from the chair, with an unnecessary but clearly welcome assist from the field hand. He made a comment that Rowan could not discern but that made Bel laugh with plain happiness.

Rowan approached them, torn by reluctance and necessity. "Warrior?" she called, using the barbarians' preferred form of address. The woman turned to her, curious, not annoyed by the interruption. "Might I speak to you?"

"You're doing it."

"I'm curious about your belt."

Bel looked down at it herself, appreciating it afresh. "My father made it himself, a long time ago. So, there's not another one like it, if that's your interest."

"Not quite. I wonder about those jewels, where they came from." She saw suspicion rise in the other's eyes. "I'm a steerswoman," she hastened to explain.

Suspicion changed to interest. "Ha! I've heard of such before, though I've never met any. It means I can ask you anything I please, can't I? And you have to answer?"

"If I know the answer, I have to give it," Rowan admitted.

"That's not always sensible. There are some answers one may need to keep to oneself."

Rowan laughed. "The situation arises less often than you might think. Still, I'll answer anything you like, but I'd first like to ask, if I may. Can you— " She tried not to glance at the field hand. "Can you spare some time?"

The barbarian considered, weaving minutely. Then, with an apologetic look toward her friend, she led Rowan to a table to one side.

Rowan briefly recounted her interest in the jewels and displayed her own shard. "I noticed the first as a charm in a witch-woman's hut in Wulfshaven. She told me where she'd found it; I was only interested because of its beauty. But when I came across another, in some arid farmland on the western curve of the Long North Road, I became more curious. There's no similarity in the types of terrain where they're found, as there ought to be. And they're never found in a natural state; always polished, with some metal setting."

Bel listened, then, with a new curiosity of her own, removed her belt and studied it. Rowan leaned forward.

The belt consisted of nine jewels shaped as rough disks, thickly edged with silver and connected by large silver links. The whole was finished with a heavy clasp in back. The jewels themselves varied more widely than any Rowan had seen before. Some had silver veins running from a central vein, as a leaf might; others had the same fine parallel lines as Rowan's. There was one type totally new to her: not blue at all, but a solid rich purple, with rough veins so thick as to stand in high relief on the surface. "How old is the belt?"

The Outskirter calculated. "My father gave it to me some ten years ago, when he joined a war band in another tribe, for love of the woman who led it. I heard he was killed in a raid later. But he had it before as long as I can remember, which I admit is not many years. Twenty-one." Something occurred to her. "No, here; there came a man looking for my father some years ago. He named him as the Outskirter with the blue belt, and said he'd heard of him from a tribe we had passed." She paused, then shook her head. "Many years ago, well before I was born, my kin told me. So that he had it twenty-five, perhaps thirty years ago."

"Did he say where he found the jewels? I have some maps; perhaps you can point it out?"

"I'll be glad to try."

Rowan led the barbarian back to her chamber, then drew out and displayed her charts. The small-scale map proved useless, as no part of it was familiar to Bel. The large-scale map was of limited use.

"My father told me he found them on Dust Ridge, out on the blackgrass prairie," the Outskirter said. "But I don't find that here."

"What direction does it lie from where we are?"

"Due east. At a guess, I'd say two months' march."

Rowan measured out a distance with calipers. The location was situated in the vaguest part of the map, solidly in the Outskirts. She had no information about the area.

She sat back, silent. Bel watched her with interest, making no comment. "I'll have to go there," Rowan said finally.

"My war band returns tomorrow, in that general direction. They won't take you all the way, but you'll do well to travel with them as far as you can. It's no place for casual visitors."

Rowan proceeded to put away the charts. "A good idea, but I have things to attend to first." She gave a small grimace. "I'll have to return the Archives and tell the Prime my plans. I've neglected my usual route as it is, following the lead on that charm the innkeeper keeps."

"This Prime is your leader?"

"Not in any usual sense. She doesn't command. She's . . . central. She keeps things in order; she's a final source. Her opinion carries weight, and her suggestions are usually followed. But she doesn't completely control me, or any steerswoman. Still, I don't think she'll be happy to hear I want to spend all my attention on this one problem . . ."

Bel watched as Rowan organized her possessions with practiced efficiency, packing away those things not necessary in the morning. Presently the Outskirter spoke. "Where do these Archives lie?"

"West," Rowan said. She discovered a clean mug and with a gesture offered Bel some wine from an open jug. "North of Wulfshaven." She poured for herself also, and sat. It came to her that Bel probably had no idea where Wulfshaven was, or what lay to the north of it. "I'm sorry, did you mention that you had a question?"

"Yes," the Outskirter replied. "You're going back? Farther into the Inner Lands?"

"That's right. Three weeks' journey, perhaps, considering the spring rains I'm likely to meet. Or, I may do better to go south on the Long North Road, to the sea. I can halve the time, if I happen to meet a ship traveling in the right direction."

The Outskirter sipped. "I've never seen the sea." She raised her cup a little. "Nor tasted wine as good as this. None has made it out as far as my tribe's lands." She looked at Rowan, her head tilted to one side. "What's it like, the sea?"

Rowan settled herself into an explanation. "Large," she began, but Bel spoke again before she could continue.

"May I travel with you?"

Rowan was taken aback. "That's not your question?"

"No. I'm curious, the Inner Lands sound so different. I was going to ask you what life is like there, but if I travel with you, I'll find my own answers."

The steerswoman looked at her again, studying her anew. Dark eyes, large eyes full of intelligence. An Outskirter with curiosity.

Rowan considered her usual displeasure in traveling with company. She had done it before, for convenience or added protection in difficult regions, but she had never found it comfortable. There were always compromises, the need to consider the other's personality and quirks. Such things tended to accumulate, eventually requiring major adjustments in Rowan's natural behavior. It became irksome.

But this barbarian, this warrior, seemed somehow cleaner, more direct than other people Rowan met. But not uncomplicated, not without depth. Rowan considered the improvised poem. A woman with such a talent was certainly no common barbarian. Also, she seemed genuinely friendly and was manifestly no fool . . .

Her request made sense; an Outskirter, even traveling alone, would be considered a threat by any people she might meet. Steerswomen, on the other hand, were usually welcome everywhere.

Rowan found herself intrigued, interested, and suddenly pleased with the idea. "We leave in the morning."

Bel laughed happily, an honest, cheerful laugh. They spent the evening discussing routes.

In the morning the innkeeper breakfasted with them, resting from the duties that had roused him well before dawn. "Feast or famine, see. A week of good business, then they all leave at once. Those barbarians were out early."

"It's a long march back to the Outskirts," Bel said, examining her gruel as if she had never before seen the like. "It's best to cover as much ground in the morning as possible. It makes for a longer rest in the evening." With a discerning eye she studied the row of little condiment jars on the table, experimentally combined two on her meal, and seemed pleased with the effect.

"Did everyone leave?" Rowan asked the innkeeper.

He jerked his head in the direction of the back rooms. "The pilgrims are snoring – and making an unholy racket of it, as well. The caravan was gone before light, and the soldiers just left. Scattered every which way, they did, on some wizardly errand, I suppose."

21

They stood at last before the door. The air was cool with mist, and the sky was white with the cloud-diffused sunlight. The road south was deserted, the few shops and houses just beginning to come to life. The jingle of a donkey cart could be heard, hidden by the mist, and the air was still in the way that always presaged furious heat for the afternoon.

The yawning serving girl handed them packages of trail food and Rowan reached in her pocket for some coins for the innkeeper. He pushed back her hand. "No, lady, business has been good; and I'd have to be doing poorly indeed to make a steerswoman pay for lodging."

Embarrassed, she thanked him quietly and put her money away. She was always disturbed by such moments, always gratified and always vaguely ashamed. She felt she would never get used to it.

Bel stood expectantly silent a moment under the innkeeper's gaze, then resignedly pulled out a small silver coin and handed it to him. "Tell your cook to put tarragon in the stew," she advised, then ambled off without a backward glance. Rowan hurried to catch up, then fell in step beside her.

CHAPTER
Two

Bel and Rowan had chosen to travel south from the inn at Five
Corners, down to the mud flats and the dreary port of Donner
on the mouth of the Greyriver. The road was broad and well
established, as it represented the southern end of the Long North
Road, one of the few major caravan routes. It was presently
deserted, and the travelers walked alone as the darker north forest
gradually gave way to a wood of silver birches, bare but for handfuls
of tiny bright green leaves at the very ends of the branches. The
Outskirter watched everything about her with lively interest.

"Is this very different from the land where you live?" Rowan
asked.

Bel nodded, a broad movement. "Mostly in the color. The
farther into the Outskirts you travel, the duller the colors grow.
Trees are green, while they last, but they thin out quickly. And the
animals are fast to find any greengrass that makes its way that far."

A clearing appeared on the left-hand side of the road, and they
found themselves passing a meadow aburst with dandelions. On
the far edge stood a small cabin, a corral nearby holding a crowd
of white goats.

There was a faint rustling in the greengrass nearby. The
movement caught Bel's eye. "Ha!" A stone was in her hand and
out of it in an instant; it contacted with a faint thump.

She went to the spot and came up with a small rabbit. She waved it happily at Rowan and laughed. The steerswoman found herself laughing, also; Bel's pleasure was neither innocent nor childlike, but it was wonderfully direct. They continued on, Bel expertly gutting their dinner as she walked.

"What kind of dangers do you meet here?" the Outskirter asked.

"Wolves," Rowan said. "But they're not common, and they tend to stay clear of the road, save at night. On the other hand, bandits are attracted for the same reason the wolves stay away. The road's not well traveled this time of year, so we've less danger of bandits."

"But more of wolves?"

"Somewhat. Rarely, a goblin band will find its way to these parts. When we get to the mud flats we may have to watch for dragons; it's a breeding ground. Still, they'll be small ones. I understand the local wizard considers them his job. Unusual responsibility on the part of a wizard."

Bel digested all of this. "It's a very rich land, and a soft one. A raid wouldn't risk much, and could stand to gain a lot."

Rowan stopped dead in surprise. In her enjoyment of Bel's company she had forgotten what the woman was. She hurried to catch up again. "Of course, the people cooperate against any large dangers. They can be surprisingly well-organized."

"We'll deal with that if it comes up."

"They'll hardly extend their hospitality to you if they think you may be an advance scout for a war band."

"They won't hear of it from me."

Rowan stepped in front of her. "Steerswomen are trusted. I can't let you abuse my goodwill. I can't guide you around the countryside if you'll be using my assistance to find the best way to destroy what you see."

Bel looked up at her with nothing more than mild surprise. "Oh, very well. I won't use what I learn." She stepped around Rowan and continued down the road, leaving the steerswoman behind again.

Confused by the barbarian's nonchalance, Rowan caught up once more. "I don't know if I made myself clear. I'm going to need some kind of assurance from you. I don't know anymore if I should trust what you say."

Bel studied her face for a long time, great dark eyes unreadable. At last she said with careful casualness, "I'm interested in traveling to different lands and seeing things I haven't seen before. I suppose that includes local customs. Now, when I say a thing, I mean it. But that may not hold true for others I meet. I suppose I must . . . make allowances for differences in customs . . . and manners." She smiled benignly up at Rowan. "So I won't kill you for that insult."

As they walked along together, Rowan tried to dispel the feeling that she had tossed stones into the den of a wildcat, and that the cat had greeted her with purrs. She might not be forgiven so easily on another occasion.

Bel settled to the ground by the fire, pulling her piebald cloak around her. "I think," she said without preamble, "that they're part of the moon."

Rowan looked up from her writing, saw that a long conversation was afoot, and carefully put the lid on her ink jar. She had found during the day's march that Bel's times to talk neatly coincided with her own – or possibly the Outskirter was sensitive to Rowan's moods and never started a conversation when she knew Rowan had no interest. "The moon," Rowan countered, "was white."

"Sometimes it was blue."

"Rarely."

"Yes, but think about it; the moon changed sizes. It was bigger sometimes, and smaller at other times."

"That's known." Rowan studied Bel across the fire: a small bundle of various furs, a thatch of dark hair, dark eyes bright with firelight and starlight. The Outskirter was wearing an odd little smile, as though she found the workings of her own mind entertaining. "That's known, as much as anything about the moon can be said to be known," Rowan continued.

"What do you mean?"

Rowan poked the fire with her hiking stick. "Only that no one's ever seen it. We don't know for certain that it ever existed."

Bel was outraged. "Of course it existed! How can you say the moon never existed? I've been hearing of it all my life. The eldest person of my tribe recalled hearing of it. And he told me of when he was young, and the eldest then told him about hearing of it. The tales have existed forever."

"But no tale tells of where it went."

"Ha! That's what I'm speaking about." She leaned back, and her belt caught the firelight, glinting. "Things look larger when they are close, and smaller when they're distant. If the moon changed size, then I think it must have been near sometimes, and far away at others. Perhaps it came too close, and fell down."

The idea surprised Rowan. "It would explain a great deal." She considered. "No. The moon's been gone for a long time, hundreds of years, perhaps thousands. If it had shattered into jewels, many more would have been found by now. And the innkeeper's jewels – if they were imbedded at the time of their fall, they would have been deeper, in a far older tree. No, they're recent."

After more discussion Bel reluctantly agreed. "My father was hardly the first person to visit Dust Ridge, only the first for many years. No one before him found any jewels. He told me they were in plain sight, scattered across the face of a cliff."

"Which direction did the cliff face?" Rowan asked.

"I don't know. Does it matter?"

"Possibly. In every case where the jewels were found on one side of a thing, it's always been the northwest face. It's as if a giant flung them across the land – and the giant faced southeast."

"That may be the answer."

Rowan laughed, amused by the image. "No, it couldn't be, of course. He'd have to be far too tall, and far too strong."

"But why not, if it's just a question of size? There are more strange things in the world than you or I have seen."

Rowan felt a strange chill fall on her. She became aware of the space around and above her: the distance to the road, the edge of the forest close at hand. She sensed the area that the first line of trees defined, heard the wind whistling in the space that curved over their tops. She saw two women huddled by a fire, in a place that lay equally distant from each horizon, in the center of a circle. And she knew, with a mapmaker's eyes, how small that circle was.

The world was a very large place, and might well contain such things as giants large enough to scatter objects with a single toss, from the Long North Road to the heart of the Outskirts.

And yet . . .

"Well, let's see." Rowan shifted back a bit from the fire, leaving a wide clear area in front of her. She picked up her pen and, using the blunt end, sketched in the dirt. "We'll simplify. Instead of thinking of a scattering of jewels across a whole range with a single throw, let's consider two points." The piece of ground transformed into a rough chart of the terrain surrounding the jewels. "Assuming that he threw in a southeasterly direction, the shortest limit would be here— " She marked a point with her pen end "—and the farthest here." She made as if to mark that point also, then saw that her scale was off. She got up and backed farther away from the fire, finally guessing at the position of the Dust Ridge in the Outskirts. "And if we make it as easy for him as possible, we'll have him stand right on top of the first point. All he needs to do is drop his jewel, and we've established the first finding.

"Now to throw, from there, all the way to the Outskirts . . ." She squinted a bit, thinking. "He's throwing well past the horizon. I wonder how he aims, or if he aims? And his jewel has to move very fast, to cover that much ground before it falls." She stepped to one side, and stooped down, quickly drawing a complex of interlocking lines.

Rowan discovered that Bel was beside her; lost in her calculations, she had not noticed when the Outskirter had left her seat across the fire. "What is that?"

"A graph," Rowan began. She prepared to elaborate, but her thoughts ran ahead, leaving her explanation somewhat abbreviated. "It charts the time it takes an object to fall. The horizontal distance traveled isn't a factor. We look at distance traveled here— " And she sketched a second figure beside the first. "Moving objects fall in a curve. The harder the object is thrown, the faster it moves, and the farther it can travel before falling. And, of course, it helps to start from high up."

She looked up and saw that Bel was not looking at the sketches at all, but was studying Rowan's face. The steerswoman realized she had left her friend behind. Bel could understand maps of a terrain, but she obviously had no means to interpret a map of an event.

"Here." Rowan picked up a white pebble and tossed it into the road. "You saw that it fell in a curve?"

"Of course. How do you think I hit that rabbit?"

Rowan found another, tossed harder.

"Another curve," Bel said.

"A flatter curve," Rowan pointed out.

"Yes . . ."

Rowan turned back to her graph. "Think of this as a chart of the route traveled by the pebble. This line could be the ground, and here's where we start to throw it. This line shows how the pebble travels along, curving back down to the ground . . ."

Bel nodded. "But the ground isn't flat."

"True, but for now we'll pretend there are no hills or valleys— "

"No, I understand that. But your line doesn't show that the ground curves, too. The earth is round."

Rowan stopped short. Bel continued. "You don't need to think about it, normally, but if you're pretending the giant is throwing past the horizon, it seems to me that it would make a difference."

"True." Rowan felt faintly embarrassed for having underestimated the level of Bel's knowledge. She knew aristocrats in Wulfshaven who doubted that the earth was round.

She tried to adjust her explanation to a more sophisticated level, then realized that was a mistake, also. There was simply no way to guess how much knowledge Bel possessed, and of what kind. Instead, Rowan resigned herself to being constantly surprised by the barbarian.

"True, it would make a difference," she repeated. "You have the curve of the earth's surface— " She drew a long arched line. "And the curve of the jewel's path." She drew a second, wildly out of scale, intersecting the first. "And of course, the harder he threw, the more the arc flattens." She drew a flatter path, reaching farther past the curved "horizon".

She looked at the three lines for a long time. "That's odd."

"What?"

She reached out and added one more line to the out-of-scale sketch. Abruptly, she started laughing. Bel watched her in perplexity.

"I'm sorry," Rowan said at last. "Call it a steerswoman's joke. Charts like this can fool you sometimes."

"What do you mean?"

Rowan pointed. "According to this, if he threw something hard enough, it would never come down." Bel looked at the sketches, tilting her head.

"It's ridiculous, of course," Rowan continued. "There's no way to throw that hard, not even with a catapult. But if you could, then the path of the object would curve less than the curve of the earth. When the object fell, it would— " She laughed again. "It would miss the earth."

"And then?" Bel asked easily.

"And then nothing." Using her foot, Rowan rubbed out the drawings. "It doesn't happen that way, of course. It only seems so, because I haven't drawn accurately, I haven't used real distances. Nothing can throw that hard, and nothing thrown can move that fast. It's amusing, but nothing can be learned from it." She sat down again and reached for her map case.

Bel dragged another dead branch toward the fire and began breaking it, standing on the center of the limb and pulling up on the thinner end. It cracked noisily, and she repeated the process. "No giants?"

"Not in this case." Rowan pulled out the smaller map of the jewels' distribution and began measuring with her calipers.

"That's too bad. What about magic?"

"It's beginning to look like that's the answer. Which means no answer at all."

Bel tossed the wood onto the fire. The flames diminished, damped. Picking up Rowan's abandoned hiking stick, she pushed the new pieces into better positions. "Why don't you ask a wizard?"

"A steerswoman ask a wizard? Not likely. Or rather, not very useful. They don't answer."

"I thought everyone had to answer a steerswoman."

"Nobody has to answer anyone; people answer because they want answers in turn. If you deny any steerswoman's questions, no steerswoman will ever answer yours again."

Smiling, Bel sat down next to Rowan. "And wizards don't care."

"Exactly."

Bel's eyes glittered. "There's more than one way to ask a question. And more than one way to find answers." She made a stretching reach and dragged her small pack closer to the fire. "Here's a way I understand." She pulled out a square cloth-wrapped object somewhat larger than her hand. The cloth was silk, Rowan saw, and she wondered briefly how the Outskirter had acquired it. Bel unfolded it, revealing a varnished-paper box, and inside the box—

Rowan laughed. "Cards!"

"Do you know the cards?" Bel began to sift through them, tilting their faded faces to the firelight.

"Well enough, I suppose. But I don't believe in their accuracy."

The barbarian gave her a sad look of reproach but said nothing. She found the Fool and placed it on the ground before her. After a moment's hesitation, Rowan pulled the jewel from its leather pouch and laid it atop the card.

"Shall I shuffle, or will you?" the barbarian asked.

"I don't see that it matters. The jewel can hardly shuffle for itself. You go ahead."

The cards were of the traditional size, large and awkward in anyone's hand, especially unwieldy for Bel. She shuffled them thoroughly, though clumsily, cut them three times with her left hand, re-formed the pack, and pulled the first card.

It was the two of rods, reversed. Bel moved the blue gem to one side and placed the card on top of the Fool. "The situation," Bel began, "is controlled by others, a domination that causes suffering."

"Well, the jewel certainly suffered. See? It's shattered."

Bel glowered. "Are you going to take this seriously?"

"I'm afraid not."

The second card was the Priest, and Bel placed it across the first two. "The way to counter this is by conforming to expected behavior."

30

"The jewel doesn't do that at all."

"Perhaps if it had, it wouldn't have shattered," Bel retorted. "Now, be quiet, please." She placed the next card in position above the first two. "Fortune, reversed. A bad turn of luck." She threw Rowan a warning glance, and the steerswoman held her peace, reminding herself that it was impolite to mock another's religion, and simply bad tactics to anger an Outskirter.

The next card was the nine of cups, reversed. "At the root of the matter, an imperfection in plans." The Hanged Man. "Suspension. There has been a period of waiting, of suspended decision, but this is now ending." Rowan found herself thinking of an object hurled into the sky and not falling down; suspended, somehow, but that period of suspension over. Suspended like – like what?

Encouraged by Rowan's serious expression, Bel continued. "The queen of swords, reversed. Narrow-mindedness, intolerance . . . these are the influences now coming into effect."

Rowan broke off her chain of thought and leaned closer, interested. "I learned that card differently. Don't you read a face card as representing the influence of a person?"

"Not at all. The person on the card stands for the attributes." Rowan wondered which interpretation was the original, what aspects of life led the more primitive society to take a more symbolic point of view. One would expect the reverse, but it seemed the cultured Inner Lands had either clung to or developed the literal interpretation. It was an interesting observation.

The cards now formed a cross on the ground, and Bel placed the next one to the left of the figure. The five of cups, reversed. Bel squinted at it, thinking. "A new alliance, or a meeting with an old friend, bringing hope."

"But which?"

"Perhaps both. And at this point— " Bel placed the next card above the previous. "Four of swords, that's a period of rest, or recuperation, a withdrawal." Bel looked dissatisfied, then brightened. "Of course! You're going back to the Archives, where you'll rest, see old friends, then gather your forces again."

"Is this reading about the jewel, or is it about me?"

"Your fate is interwoven with its," Bel said confidently. She turned up the next card and put it in position. She looked at it for some moments, puzzled.

"Poor workmanship," Rowan prompted. "Pettiness, mediocrity."

"Yes, but it's in the Spirit position . . . How can the spirit of the jewel be pettiness, or poor workmanship? Poor planning, perhaps? It's very mysterious."

And very vague, Rowan thought. But if the jewel was magical, or part of a magic spell, perhaps it had been poorly made? So that in use, it would fail, resulting in that period of inactivity Bel found in the cards?

Here was the very nature of the cards' appeal, she reminded herself. Presenting symbols, emotionally powerful archetypes open to wide interpretation, they were immensely seductive to any pattern-seeking mind. And above all else, steerswomen were adept in the skill of detecting patterns amid seeming chaos.

In any chaos of symbols, patterns, if none existed, could be easily created. Rowan took a moment to admire the pattern her mind found, to enjoy it in a purely aesthetic fashion – then, with no regret, discarded it. It was fantasy, disguised as information. Nothing could be learned from it.

Much could be learned, however, about Bel and the attitudes of the Outskirters, and Rowan shifted her interest to her new friend and the culture that shaped her. "What's the last card?"

Bel turned it up: the Emperor, reversed. "Dependence," Bel said. "And danger. Either physical danger, or a threat to possessions." Bel thought carefully for a while, obviously casting about for connections, that same search for patterns that Rowan had briefly followed. "I don't see how the jewel itself can be in danger, so it must be that it carries danger. I think we should be very careful."

Rowan picked it up and returned it to its sack. "I'm surprised you don't tell me to simply discard it." That would have been the advice of a true believer in the cards.

"Oh, no," the Outskirter replied, and she smiled as she gathered her cards. "This is more interesting."

Much later, Rowan was still poring over her charts. At last she rose, and not wishing to disturb the sleeping Outskirter, she crossed to the opposite side of the fire. Using her hiking stick, she began again to draw the same graphs, but carefully, accurately. All sense of her surroundings faded. She was like a swimmer, exploring by touch alone the bottom of some rocky pool, trying to create a chart for something that could not be seen, a chart not for the eyes, but for the touch of the mind.

CHAPTER
Three

"Never just duck," Rowan's old swordmaster had instructed her. "Bad idea! If the enemy comes up behind, how can you tell what his move is? An overhand blow, and you die on the ground instead of standing. Duck and move! Gamble! He's probably right-handed. If he's not striking straight down, he's sweeping from left to right. That's his strongest stroke. Move to the right, fast! Roll! Face him as soon as you can, so you can see what he's doing. Instinct will say roll to the left, keep your own right arm free. Fight it! You'll be rolling into his blow."

The memory brought with it the feeling of sawdust underfoot and the unfamiliar weight of the sword in her right hand. She was aware of the fellow students in line beside her, all of them shifting uneasily at the fervor of the instructor's delivery and his nonchalant acceptance of the existence of enemies who would seek blood. And later, the strain and ache after hours of practicing some single, isolated move under the swordmaster's shouts and curses. Over it all, the sharp tang of sea air that crept over the high walls of the courtyard.

Unbidden, all those things flashed into Rowan's mind in an instant – flashed and were gone in the space of time it took to hear Bel's shout: "Duck!"

Rowan ducked and rolled to the right. The sword came straight down, striking mere inches from her right arm. She kept moving, scrabbling, her left hand searching for some weapon. The man drew back again. Suddenly Bel was on his back. She scratched at his eyes with one hand, one arm around his neck, and he staggered back a step.

Where was her sword? It was by her pack. Rowan sensed the fire behind her head. The pack was beyond it.

The man shrugged Bel off, then whirled. The Outskirter bobbed neatly beneath his blow, eyes aglitter. Rowan's hand touched something: her hiking stick. In an instant she was on her feet. She smashed at the attacker's head with a weak left-handed blow.

He turned back. She shifted her grip, holding the stick like a quarterstaff. Misguided instinct; useless, she realized. The sword shattered the stick in two. She jumped back to keep clear.

Two pieces of stick were in her hands; the one in her right was short and balanced. She flung it like a knife into the man's face. It struck him in the right eye and he shrieked hoarsely.

Rowan turned and dove over the fire toward her sword. She heard the hiss as Bel drew her own sword, then the ring as it met the attacker's.

The guard of Rowan's sword hilt had fouled in one of the thongs on the scabbard. She struggled with the binding and glanced back in time to see Bel's second blow, a two-handed sweep that began over her head and forced the man's point to the ground by sheer momentum.

The upstroke that followed split the man's chest and ended in his throat.

The barbarian stepped aside to avoid the last move of the attacker's sword and watched him fall, his chest a ruin of blood and bone, drained of color by firelight.

Rowan moved to Bel's side, surprised to find her own sword finally in her hand, unused. She looked down at the man. His face worked with strange emotions. His voice wailed and burbled.

"Who are you?" Rowan asked uselessly. But he was silent at last.

They stood together wordlessly; then Bel shifted. "That's a bad place to keep your sword, so far from your hand."

Rowan nodded vaguely, still gazing down. "He was at the inn."

Bel was astonished. "Are you certain?"

"Yes." She turned away from the dead man. Her throat was dry; she felt light and empty. That could have been her, she realized. She could have been the one to end staring blankly at the sky, under blood. She looked at Bel. "Thank you," she said.

The Outskirter eyed her. "Have you never seen a dead person?"

"Yes, I have. But I never so nearly was one. Had you not been here – but I think he was counting on that. He didn't know we were traveling together. He left before we did."

"You're sure he was there?"

She nodded. "He was one of the five soldiers. He was wearing Red then."

Bel looked back. "Well, he's wearing red now."

CHAPTER
Four

It was the sea at last.

They had spent the last two days trudging along the damp road that traced the edge of the mud flats, and when the road turned in and became too undependable they found rides on various rafts and flat barges that wandered among the estuaries. Those waterways widened imperceptibly until it finally became clear that the travelers had reached the shallows of the Inland Sea.

Rowan found herself standing taller, looser, her legs prepared to adjust to changes in footing, even though there were yet no perceptible waves. She was home. She had never been to this port before, knew of it only from her maps. It did not matter; she was home, as the sea was the home of every steerswoman.

The sea had shaped the order, defining the necessary nature of Steersmanship by its own variable nature. The need of precision in knowledge, adaptability in action, clarity in thought, and always the need to know more, to complete one's understanding – all these grew from the dangers of the changing sea, and from the endless sky. They lodged in the hearts of the steerswomen and stayed however long they might travel dusty inland roads. Rowan herself, born on flat dry farmland on the edge of the Red Desert, on the far northern limit of every map drawn – Rowan, who never saw the sea for the first eighteen years of her life – still knew it as her home, the home of her heart and mind.

Bel sat quietly on a bale of wool, carefully erect and unmoving. She watched the wide spaces around the barge as if they might sprout enemies; not nervously, but warily. Rowan could not tell how much of the scene the barbarian was assimilating. Finally they rounded a curve of the shoreline, and the wharves and buildings of Donner came into view.

Donner made a poor port, but it was a necessary one. The Greyriver was a natural road to the sea, allowing easier and cheaper shipment than the caravans provided. But there was no deep harbor there, and the ships anchored far out from the river's mouth. Barges shifted cargo and people from the town to the sailing vessels, providing ample though intermittent local employment, and a certain amount of congestion on the water. The barges competed for greatest speed and capacity, so that as their boat neared the docks, Rowan and Bel found themselves surrounded by great masses hurtling in every direction. The air was full of voices clamoring warnings, curses and demands of right-of-way. The cause of all the turmoil, a mere three ships, stood off in the distance, calm and almost disdainful.

Ashore, Rowan wove through the busy longshoremen. Bel followed in her wake, watching everything with cheerful caution.

They made their way into the thickest part of the crowd and found there a short squat woman directing the action with sharp shouts. She carried a slate that she consulted and marked regularly.

Rowan called to her. "What ships are those?"

"Go away, I'm busy!"

"I'm a steerswoman."

"Damn! Wait, then." Rowan and Bel waited as the woman laboriously simplified a complex set of orders for a blank-faced trio of beefy men, all the while making marks with a black crayon on various boxes and crates carried to and from the place where she stood. The three men wandered off dubiously, and she wrote on her slate.

Without slackening her activity, she spoke to the two women. "That's the *Beria*, out of Southport, for one – and their navigator jumped ship; you'll be welcome there."

"Where bound?"

"Southport again. Then The Crags."

"By way of the Islands?"

"No." She spared an instant to eye the steerswoman. "Sailing west from Southport. Wizard on board; he promises protection. I wouldn't risk it."

For a moment Rowan's heart cried to take that trip; to travel, protected, into that small corner of the sea from which few ships returned.

"Is this wizard Red?" Bel asked.

As she remembered the Red soldiers at the inn, and the attack of the night that followed, Rowan's dreams froze in midflight. "Blue. Our wizard, Jannik, he's Blue. Someone saw him talking to this fellow."

Rowan nodded. The Crags had been Blue for as long as anyone remembered. Still, where wizards were concerned, that was no guarantee of permanence.

She called to the woman again. "We're looking to get to Wulfshaven."

"The *Morgan's Chance*. And calling at no other ports on the way. They'll be heavy laden, and the cabins all booked."

"Who's the captain?"

"Morgan. At the Tea Shop." She pointed without looking up.

They found the establishment overlooking a weedy estuary, the patrons dining and socializing on a broad veranda with dark-stained rails, under the hazy off-white skies. The noise of the distant docks was a faint clamor, and sea gulls swooped above, alert for opportunities for poaching. The clientele was cheerful and chatted quietly over the music of a lap harp played by a tinker who occasionally raked his audience with a gaze of infinite disdain. His opinion went completely unnoticed.

Rowan asked a few quiet questions, and presently she and the Outskirter found themselves standing before a table where two men were poring over a navigational chart. Beside this stood two mugs, a pot of peppermint tea, and a small pottery carafe labeled "Brandy" in fanciful script.

The man seated on the left examined the women dubiously. He was lean, almost gaunt, with glossy black hair and sea-blue eyes. He and his mate were relaxed, comfortable, and dressed in clean clothes. By contrast the two women were travelworn and somewhat bedraggled, and more than somewhat unscrubbed. They still carried their packs and wore their swords. When Morgan noticed the silver steerswoman's ring Rowan wore on her left hand, he smiled and pulled two wicker chairs from a nearby table. The women seated themselves. "How can I be of assistance?"

Rowan drew a breath. "We need passage to Wulfshaven."

He raised his eyebrows and looked off across the water. "My ship is booked. Possibly I can ask one of my officers to shift in with another." The other man winced; evidently one of those officers would be himself.

Rowan gestured negatively. "I don't want to inconvenience anyone. Perhaps there's room to sling another hammock among the crew members?"

"You wouldn't be offended?"

She laughed. "Not in the least."

"There are some who would be." He rubbed the side of his nose, still gazing into the distance. "We'll do well on this trip, but I have some debts," he said carefully. "I can't afford at this point to lose any money. I'll have to ask you to pay for your food, or bring your own."

Rowan made a rapid calculation involving the prevailing winds, the local weather patterns, and the size of Morgan's ship. She compared the resulting length of voyage to the number of coins in her pocket, with a guess at Donner's market prices. "That's not a problem."

"Good. If you can bring food that doesn't need preparation, all the better. Our cook's shorthanded as it is. We've never had so many passengers."

"Spring," his companion suggested. "Wanderlust."

"Perhaps that's the explanation." Morgan turned his glance on Bel.

"Can this be done for two?" Rowan asked.

"No."

"I can pay full fare," Bel said easily.

"We haven't the room."

"I'll pay full fare for a berth with the crew members."

40

"We'll be crowded enough with the steerswoman."

Rowan said to Bel, "His cook's shorthanded."

The barbarian smiled beatifically. Morgan made to protest, but Bel spoke up. "And since he can't afford to lose money, I'll generously work for no wages. And I don't suppose he'll need the extra help after the passengers for Wulfshaven leave, so I'll relieve him of myself at that point. How lucky for him that we happened by."

The captain sighed, then raised a finger. "In good weather, you sleep on deck."

"Ha. I prefer to. Why crowd in when it's not necessary?"

"I'll do so myself," Rowan said. She had a sudden vision of nights on deck: warmly wrapped in blankets, cold sweet air on her face, watching the constellations slowly shift behind one or another Guidestar, the comforting creak and shift of the ship beneath her. The prospect made her smile.

Morgan regarded the pair speculatively, then nodded, resigned. "We leave at dawn. You'd best be aboard three hours before, to settle," he pointed at Bel, "and get introduced to your duties. Go along." He dismissed them with a wave of the hand and turned back to his charts.

As they wove their way out through the tables, Rowan said, "I know you can cook for two; you'll be called on to do so for a great many."

Bel smiled her small smile. "It's just a question of numbers. You can help with the calculations."

The two women found a public bathhouse down a narrow street, and Bel made acquaintance with the superiority of hot water over cold for bathing, and wooden tubs over pools or brooks. Later, on the justification that she was saving money on her passage, she treated herself and Rowan to an elaborate meal in a well-appointed inn. Bel gave careful attention to the different dishes, seeming to study each with interest, and finding none she did not like.

As they conversed over dinner, Rowan found that the impression she had gained of Bel on the road proved equally true in more civilized surroundings. The Outskirter remained both curious and adaptable, her comments again that intriguing combination of ingenuousness and perspicacity. Rowan found herself ever more comfortable in Bel's company, recognizing in the other not a like mind, but a complementary one.

Their conversation was overheard by a merchant at the table next to theirs, a long, thin man with a beaked nose and a fastidious expression. He was accompanied by a pudgy blond boy, about ten years old. When the merchant discovered that Rowan was a steerswoman, he began to toss her occasional questions: insignificant details about the port of Donner, other points of geography, facts about sailing ships. He asked these as asides in his own conversation with the boy, whenever a convenient point of curiosity arose. He effectively ignored Rowan when not asking a question, and ignored Bel altogether. Although he was elaborately polite, beginning each question with "Tell me, lady," and responding to her answers with an unctuous "Thank you, lady," he seemed to care little when Rowan sometimes did not know an answer. Bel's annoyance increased with each interruption. Finally she said in exasperation, "He's treating you like a servant!" She made no attempt to conceal her comments from the merchant.

Rowan used her fork to push a bit of bread around in a dollop of vegetable paste, keeping her gaze carefully on her plate. "Some people are like that." She knew that she looked meek and subdued, perhaps a bit pale. In fact, the paleness was from fury; the merchant's offhand imperiousness made her seethe with hatred for the man. She discovered herself wishing him dead in a thousand unpleasant ways. The force of her anger and her inability to act fed on each other until she felt dizzy.

"Can't you refuse to answer?"

Rowan looked up at her, attempting to keep her expression neutral. "Under certain extreme circumstances, and this is not one. But I'm familiar with his type. It's usually easier to go along, or simply to leave."

The Outskirter studied the steerswoman's face for a long moment, and Rowan found that she could read in Bel's expression all that Bel could read in hers, through her poor attempts at control. Bel had the look of one seeing a helpless creature victimized. Rowan was surprised; it had not occurred to her that her occupation would ever put her in a position of helplessness, but as soon as she saw it, she realized that it was sometimes true.

But Bel was free to act as she chose. She turned to the merchant. "You. You're bothering me. Shut up or I'll slit your throat." The man dropped his fork.

A serving man was at their side in an instant, carefully polite. "Is there a problem?" Near the entrance to the kitchen, two other servers exchanged words briefly. One hurried off in one direction, one in another; the second soon returned with a calm elderly woman who scanned the room with a proprietary concern. The first came back with a very large young man in tow. The four then stood quietly on the side, watching.

Rowan put her hand on Bel's arm and spoke to the serving man at their side. "We'd like a different table, please."

Presently they were led through the center of the room to a table on the other side. The other diners silenced as they passed through, conversation reviving in their wake, more subdued in volume but livelier in tone.

The new table, in an alcove off the main room, was quieter, flanked by a row of low windows. The shutters were open a crack; Rowan pushed them wider, and the dock noise drifted in faintly. She saw that the haze was clearing as dusk approached. She wished herself on the *Morgan's Chance* and under the stars.

She turned back to find Bel studying her. Rowan smiled thinly. "It has two sides," she admitted.

The proprietress appeared with three mugs of wine and seated herself with them. "My apologies, lady; some people are crass. Reeder always puts on airs." With a tilt of her head she indicated the merchant across the room. "I hope you haven't a poor opinion of our establishment."

Rowan sipped her wine. "Not at all."

"And you, Freewoman?"

Bel made a gesture with her mug, indicating the room and its contents. "I think the establishment is fine; but I find my sense of honor affronted by that what passes for civilized behavior in the Inner Lands. If people had to defend their attitudes, things would be simpler."

"Perhaps. But think of the violence that would result!"

Bel smiled.

The woman continued. "Stay the night, as my guests. Tomorrow, you won't be bothered by Reeder again; he's leaving at dawn."

Rowan sighed; Bel narrowed her eyes. "On the *Morgan's Chance*."

"Why, yes."

The two travelers chose to forgo the entertainment in the common room. A waiter directed them through a door at the end of their alcove, and they were met on the other side by a chambermaid with an oil lamp, who led them down the short corridor.

"How long will our trip last?" Bel asked Rowan.

"It depends on the weather. Perhaps five days."

Bel grimaced. "Five days with that Reeder creature."

The corridor ended at the foot of a short staircase, leading up. Instead of ascending, the chambermaid turned left, leading them along a stone wall with a plastered section in its center. They were in a square open area, rising three stories to the raftered ceiling, each storey presenting a narrow balcony along its three inner sides. The doors of the guestchambers were visible, overlooking the central well.

Out of habit, Rowan oriented herself in an imagined map, the probable floor plan of the inn. They had entered under one end of the first balcony, then crossed the well to the opposite end.

Rowan considered the stone wall. "There was a fireplace here, once?"

"Yes, lady." The girl had opened a closet and was pulling out a collection of bed linens. Bel held the lamp. "This used to be the old common room, I'm told, before business was so good. They added the new dining room, built extra stories here, and sleeping chambers. The other side of the hearth still works."

"The other side being in the kitchen?"

"That's right."

Looking up, Rowan saw a wooden chandelier suspended from the ceiling, unlit and cobwebbed. The arrangement of the building was visually impressive and extremely inefficient. Like much of Donner, Rowan realized.

44

Closing the door, the chambermaid bundled the linens under one arm and accepted the lamp again. There were no stairs to the first floor on this end, and Bel and Rowan followed her back across the cold open area.

"You shouldn't worry too much about Reeder," Rowan told Bel as they ascended. "Close quarters can be an advantage. He'll come to see me as a person, eventually." But Bel was occupied in peering nervously over the railings as the three women rose higher.

The room was spacious, the beds warm and comfortable after the days on the trail, but Rowan found herself waking over and over, as each doze took the edge off her tiredness. Each time she enjoyed the luxury of sinking into sleep again, but at last she found herself following her thoughts into wakefulness.

They were on the third floor, in a corner chamber. One window faced north, the other east, and the surrounding houses were low-built on the flat land. There was little to obstruct the view. Rowan turned in her bed to watch the Eastern Guidestar, shining in one corner of a window, slightly more than a quarter of the way up from the horizon.

She saw that Bel had pulled the blanket from her own bed and arranged it haphazardly on the floor. She lay on her stomach, in her usual sleeping attitude, with her face away from Rowan. She stirred, then turned, and Rowan saw that she was also awake.

"You're uncomfortable?"

"A little. It's so closed-in." Rowan found the room luxuriously wide. "And high. I keep feeling I might fall."

"You'll have less space on the ship. And it will move, rock."

Bel made a face in the gloom. "I suppose I'll adjust. I'll have to; I can't walk away from a ship."

"There is that."

The Outskirter sat up. "You're not sleeping anymore?"

"No. My mind wants to be busy." A problem was nagging her for attention.

"I can't sit still."

"Let's walk, then."

They rose and dressed, Bel donning, instead of her shaggy vest, a yellow cloth blouse she had purchased in a shop by the bathhouse. If her change of costume was an attempt to fit her surroundings, it was immediately negated when she added her cloak and goatskin boots. Both women buckled on their swords.

Once outside the chamber door, Rowan led Bel to the end of the landing and down the stair. Along the way they passed rooms silent with sleep, or raucous with snores. One room on the ground floor leaked the mutters of two women in argument, punctuated by an amused masculine rumble.

Seeing no other exit, Rowan found their way through the passage to the dining area. "It's like a maze," Bel remarked, surprised when they reached the large room. "Your sense of direction is better than mine."

"Part of my training."

Outside the night was clear and dusted with stars, the Guidestars nearly balanced opposite each other, the Eastern slightly higher than the Western. Stable points in the sky, they told Rowan her exact position by their angles, and the precise time by the constellations that lay behind them.

Saranna's Inn fronted on a round court where a decorative fountain had been erected with much ornamentation and little skill. Beside it, more prosaic, were a simple well and watering trough, constructed with straightforward efficiency. Around the court the houses were dark and quiet, save one flickering candle in a baker's shop. A breeze replaced the smell of sea wrack with that of fresh bread.

The two women circled around the fountain and paused on the far side by the watering trough. Bel leaned back on the edge, regarding the dwellings. "How can they live so close, for all their lives? They must tread on each other constantly."

"You don't live completely alone in the Outskirts, do you?"

"No, but the tribe, that's different. It's one's own kin, and comrades. When we cross another tribe, then there may be trouble."

"The proximity can be useful. People can barter work, or trade objects . . ."

"We trade, when we have something to trade." Bel jingled the coins in her pouch.

"Where do you get what you trade? Do you sell part of your herd?"

The Outskirter was outraged. "The herd? Never, the herds are life!"

"For a goldsmith, gold is life."

Bel considered this.

Rowan moved to sit beside her. The open court pleased her, its edges crowded with shops, now silent, a pause filled with the imminence of the next day's activity. Events to come; movement.

"What is life for a steerswoman?"

Rowan looked at her in surprise. She had never heard the question posed in that way. Related questions, questions direct and easy to answer, she had often considered, but she saw that those were only pieces of this one. She took a long time to think. Bel ventured, "Is it your books? Those charts you take such care at?"

"No . . . The books and charts are just the means to hold on to what you learn, in a way that makes it easier for others to learn from you. They're a way to— " She thought carefully. "To add up learning, to accumulate it past your own lifetime."

"The learning itself?" The barbarian watched her with wide dark eyes, patient and curious.

"No . . ." Rowan saw that in some way the things she learned were also only pieces. She moved her hands, shaping a space between them, tilting the space as though investigating what lay there. "Facts, ideas fit together. It's the fitting, the paths that connect them, that matters. The pieces can change, but the fitting lies beneath it all. The world is made of such fittings." Then she had the answer, but it seemed too large, and it sat strangely in her mind, like an important childhood memory that explained things that had seemed not to need explanation. "It's the world, I suppose."

Bel accepted this, and a large peaceful silence ended the discussion.

Rowan watched the Western Guidestar shining between two roofs in front of her. As she was watching, it went dark. "It's not long before dawn," she observed.

Bel checked the Guidestar herself and nodded. "Let's go, then." They rose and crossed back to the inn.

CHAPTER
Five

The ornate double doors of the dining area were locked, and the windows that looked out on the square were shuttered tight. Rowan knocked lightly, hoping to get the attention of the servant who had been sweeping earlier. There was no response.

Bel was amused. "Do we break in?"

Rowan shook her head, then beckoned. "The common room is this way." She led the Outskirter around the building to the left, to its opposite side, where they found a single low door and four shuttered windows facing the small side street. As they approached, the door opened, and a stout woman in an apron leaned out to peer at the sky, with the attitude of a person guessing the time.

"Three o'clock," Rowan supplied.

The woman shook her head aggrievedly. "Late again, and there'll be plenty of early breakfasts, what with that ship leaving this morning." She examined Bel and Rowan. "Up early, or coming in late?"

"A little of both, perhaps," Rowan replied.

They entered the common room and declined the woman's offer of guidance to their chamber. Carrying a single candle, Rowan led Bel to one of the two doors flanking the fireplace, and passing through, they found themselves back in the deserted dining area.

"How did you know this was here?" Bel wondered.

"It stands to reason. If a large fireplace doesn't back on an outside wall, then it's two-sided." She led Bel around the tables, dimly visible in the gloom. "The other side would serve either the kitchen or the common room. The closed-up fireplace in that open area by the stairs backs on the kitchen, so I knew the common room had to connect to the dining room." Bel bumped into a table; they had left the lighted doorway to the common room around a corner. Holding her tiny flame higher, Rowan took Bel's hand and guided her through the alcove and the door to the sleeping chambers.

Bel stopped suddenly at the foot of the stairs. "Listen!"

Rowan heard a faint scrabbling. "Rats."

"So many?" The sound intensified briefly, then ceased.

The two women continued up. "Any large town is bound to have a lot of them. They're attracted by the garbage." The rooms along the second floor were quiet, but dim light showed beneath the doors of two.

As they turned the corner and approached the stairs leading to the third floor, the scrabbling returned, behind them. It was punctuated by a human squeak. "It's only a rat, woman," Bel mumbled derisively.

Rowan looked back across the balcony to the two lighted rooms. Now another room on the left was also lit. "It sounds like they're climbing on the east wall."

The scrabbling turned into a patter of small feet. From the newly lit room the voice sounded again, a faint, weird wailing.

Bel was halfway up the stairs. Rowan grabbed her furskin cloak to stop her. "No. Wait."

"What?"

Rowan looked across the central well, and in that moment all her training, all her skill in perception, observation, integration, and reason, came into play in perfect coordination. She was aware of the space around her, the wall to her left, the staircase behind her, the balcony rail, and the open area beyond. She sensed the chandelier above, the distance from floor to roof. She knew the direction of the sounds, the three lit rooms along the east wall, how they stood in relation to the building as a whole, as clearly as if by some sense of touch. The air around her was alive with meaning.

"We have to get out of here," she said.

"Right now?"

Rowan let loose Bel's cloak. "Yes. Now."

"We'll want our packs." Bel continued up.

"No!" Rowan clattered up the stair after her and, as her head cleared the stairwell, reached out and buried her fingers in Bel's shaggy boot. The Outskirter fell sprawling.

Bel turned over and wrenched her foot away. "Rowan!"

Rowan looked past her to the door of the third floor corner room. White light was spilling out beneath it, growing brighter. "That's our room," she said.

The door burst open, splintering, driven by three gouts of white flame.

"Down!" Rowan shouted over the sudden roar of fire. "Go down!" Then, as loud as she possibly could, she yelled, "Fire! Get out, everyone! Fire!"

Bel stumbled down the stair after Rowan, colliding with her. The now-useless candle fell and rolled off the balcony. "Come on!" Rowan hurried along the landing.

Two doors on the east wall burst outward, flinging with them a woman, a woman in flames. She fell against the railing, clawing at some dark shape that clutched her thigh. The railing broke, and she fell.

Heat, and wreckage; Rowan and Bel paused for an instant. Rowan began to pick her way across the burning rubble.

Around them, doors were opening, voices were shouting, people were running. One man recklessly pushed past Rowan and rushed toward the stairs. The wall beside him opened like a flower, gushing smoke. The landing above collapsed. He was buried in burning timber.

The way was blocked.

Rowan turned back toward Bel, seeing half a dozen stunned faces behind her, Reeder and his boy among them. "Windows!" she told them, and ran back the way she had come.

The group followed, and as she opened one of the doors, they pushed past, fighting in panic to reach the window. A half-dressed dark-skinned man reached it first and, with a blow of his fist, smashed out the shutters. He scrambled up the sill, and then a white lance of flame caught the side of his face. His hair was burning.

He fell back, shrieking. "They're loose! They're swarming!" Someone caught him and threw a blanket over his head, smothering the flames.

"What's loose?" Bel shouted, but Rowan knew.

Over the edge of the windowsill, weaving its flat head, came a glittering cat-sized creature. Its hide was shimmering green and silver, its faceted eyes bloodred. Flailing its tail as it sought balance, it emitted a two-toned whistling shriek, an infant version of a dragon's scream.

It froze like a lizard, studying them with one of its side-set eyes. Rowan stepped forward as it swung to face them, pulled the blanket off the man's head, and flung it at the beast. The blanket burst into flame, and the creature squealed in fury.

Two more small forms appeared in the window. "Out," Rowan said, pushing people before her. A pale woman urged the now-blinded dark man, pulling at his arms.

Bel was already at the railing. "We can't go out the windows, and we can't reach the stairs that lead down."

Rowan looked across the central well and saw that the east and south sides of the top floor were burning wildly. On the second floor, the balcony along the east wall had collapsed to the ground. Directly across, the lower south wall showed spots of fire.

Two people clattered up the stairs to the top floor. How they planned to escape, Rowan had no idea.

"We go over," Rowan said. "Drop down." She swung herself over the balcony, shifted her grip to the bottom of the balusters, hung by her hands, and dropped the last eight feet.

The boy imitated her immediately, followed by Reeder; they hung, dropped, then ran toward the exit to the dining room. The pale woman shouted instructions to the blind man, guiding his hands to the railing.

Bel stood frozen on the landing, staring in shock at the distance down.

The sounds of fire and the crack of weakening timber surrounded Rowan as she looked up. "Skies, no," she cursed in anguish. "Bel! Bel, do it!"

Out of the wreckage along the east wall, small writhing shapes began to emerge from the fire.

The blind man came down in a twisting sprawl. His woman began to follow, and as she hung by her hands Bel suddenly moved. She grit her teeth, grasped the rail, and swung herself over the edge.

The pale woman reached the ground and led her man stumbling to the exit. Under the landing where Bel hung, a door opened, and a burly man and two women in nightshifts emerged. The man wore a sheet. They gazed about in confusion.

Bel looked down once, and Rowan cried, "Don't look, just hang and drop!"

Bel dropped. Behind Rowan, the landing cracked, splintered, and fell.

Bel landed on her feet and made to run. Rowan stopped her.

The exit was buried under the fallen landing.

Rowan turned to the man. "Your window."

One of the women answered. "It's all animals, spitting fire, like. Outside."

Rowan looked around quickly, seeking an option, any option. The east wall looked as though it might collapse inward. Along the south wall, the fire was moving along the rubble of the fallen balcony. The smoke, rising, had completely filled the upper half of the central well; the air Rowan breathed was hot, getting hotter fast, but still clean.

There was a sudden movement in the ceiling of smoke, and Rowan pushed Bel and herself against the wall as the chandelier came down with a screeching crash, shattering on the stone floor. A pair of small forms tumbled out of the wreckage. One landed at Rowan's feet, writhing, trying to right itself. It was the size of a rat. Rowan stepped on its head; it was like standing on a stone. The creature struggled wildly; then suddenly its skull popped, and it lay twitching, emitting a brief shower of sparks.

Bel shouted in fury, and Rowan turned in time to see her swing her sword against the side of a larger beast. The blow injured it not at all, but the force sent it sprawling aside, and it tumbled into the open door of the just-vacated room. The burly man stepped forward and pulled the door shut.

"That won't stop it for long," Rowan said. Instinctively, she began to back along the wall, away from the heat, toward the old fireplace.

Bel came up beside her, looking back at the wall of fire. "We're trapped. We're truly trapped."

"Yes." Rowan looked at the mortared-up hearth and raised her voice to be heard more clearly. "We'll stand up against the fireplace. Perhaps when the wreckage falls, the configuration— " She stopped short, suddenly remembering. "Yes!" She ran to it.

The others followed quickly and found her searching the right-hand edge of the hearth. "It has to be here— "

Bel had not understood. She brought her face closer and shouted, "What?"

Rowan faced her. "A door! There has to be a door!"

One of the other two women had collapsed in terror. The man was trying to pull her to her feet. The second woman pointed at the rubble on the other end of the fireplace. "Door's buried!" she shouted.

"There was another. I saw it!" Rowan turned back, and saw how the wood paneling overlaid the stones. She moved right, and found the door she had seen the chambermaid open. She pulled it wide.

A linen closet. One of the women made a sound of anguish. Bel let out a single, near-inhuman shriek of fury, gripped her sword tighter and swung around to face the inevitable attack of dragons.

Rowan began pulling out linens, throwing them blindly behind her, shouting as she did. "This area was a common room! The fireplace backs on the kitchen; did you ever see a common-room hearth like that, that didn't have doors on *both* ends?" The fronts of the shelves were bare. The left wall of the closet was stone; the right was wood. Rowan could not see to the back.

She smashed the heels of her hands against the underside of a shelf, and the plank lifted and clattered onto the one beneath it. Using both hands, she tugged at the right edge of the second shelf, and it tilted up, then slipped off its supports to the floor.

Rowan stumbled over the shelves, tripping, and fell against the back wall. It was wood.

She regained her feet, pulled out her sword, and put all her strength into a two-handed underhand stab. A half-inch of the point wedged into the wood. She twisted it as she pulled, then checked the result with her fingers: a shallow gouge.

"Bel!" Rowan came out of the closet and gripped Bel's shoulder. "The back wall is wood. We have to break through!" Bel stared at Rowan blindly, her face that of a warrior's during battle. Then her expression changed, and she understood. She pulled away and scrambled over the scattered linens into the closet. She was stronger than Rowan; her sword was heavier. Shorter, she had room to swing overhand.

The burly man was standing against a wall, one of his women clinging and sobbing, the other standing free and watching Rowan with desperate alertness.

The man was huge. Rowan extended her sword hilt to him. "Take this. Help Bel."

He extricated himself, stepped to the closet, and pulled out the planks of the fallen shelves. Lifting one, he tested its heft. He said to Rowan, "You keep the sword," and pointed past her with his chin.

She turned and saw the shattered chandelier, and on it, three dragons. They crawled over it and over each other, indiscriminately, heads weaving and searching, tails writhing. The largest was as big as a dog.

Behind her, Rowan could hear the thumps as Bel and the man set to work. She stood with her back to the closet, knowing it was only a matter of time before the dragons sighted her. Wondering if, like frogs, they could only see moving objects, she stood as still as she could.

She sensed a presence beside her. Glancing to the side, she half expected to see Bel, but found instead one of the two other women, the self-possessed one. The woman was holding another plank in her hands, dividing her attention between the chandelier and Rowan's face.

One of the dragons sent a random gout of flame splashing against the center of the fireplace.

Rowan searched her knowledge, seeking information about dragons. She found little, next to nothing. She had only her eyes and her reason.

She watched for a few moments, then spoke to the woman beside her. "The larger they are, the slower they move. They'll cover ground quickly, because of the length of their stride, but these don't react as fast as the tiny ones. Those flat heads have no room for much brain; they're not very smart. Their eyes are set on the sides of their heads, but the flame comes from their snouts. So, if they're looking at us, they can't burn us; when they're trying to burn, they can't see us well."

The woman nodded; one of the dragons froze, studying her with its right eye.

Rowan said, "I think they're attracted by motion," and then the dragon swung to face them. Rowan shoved the woman to the left and moved to the right. The flame spouted to where the woman had stood.

Rowan was up against the fireplace. The woman had fallen against one of the pillars supporting the balcony overhead; the closed door of the room behind her began to burn.

Rowan found herself pinned in the gaze of another dragon. She prepared herself to dodge, but a falling piece of timber in its opposite field of vision distracted it. It sent white flame in that direction, then pulled itself off the chandelier to investigate. Rowan hoped it would find enough to occupy itself.

Two remained: the dog-sized dragon on the left, and one slightly smaller on the right. Rowan realized that the woman by the pillar would shortly be trapped between the dragons on the chandelier and dragons that would emerge from the room behind her.

The two beasts were weaving again, searching. The larger shrieked in frustration, tilted back its head, and spat a fountain of fire straight up. Rowan watched the second, and at the instant its weaving brought its face toward her, she ran straight at it.

She brought her sword down on its flat head. The blow drove its head against the stone floor, and it was like striking an iron bar.

The larger creature noticed the movement, took an instant to study Rowan with its left eye, then the edge of a wooden board was driven against its throat. Aim ruined, the flame it spat caught the left side of Rowan's cloak.

The dragon beneath Rowan's sword twisted free, uninjured, and began spitting at random. Rowan dropped to the ground, writhed out of her burning cloak, rolled to the right, and froze. The flames on her cloak snuffed against the stone floor.

The woman's plank had splintered down its length. She flung one half overhead past the dragons, one half to the left. She stood motionless, as the dog-sized dragon cocked its gaze left toward the clattering board.

She was standing some three feet in front of its blind snout. Her face was an agony of terror, but she did not move.

The smaller dragon had sent its flames at waist level, passing over Rowan's head. It subsided and began searching again.

Rowan knew that the tableau could not last. When the dragon on the right was facing her again, she moved forward, in full view of the larger one, and with a sweeping blow, she struck the smaller creature across the neck. Her sword skidded harmlessly up its length, then caught the edge of one garnet eye. The eye shattered with a weird merry sound, like breaking china. The dragon did not cry out but twisted, trying to find her with its remaining eye.

In the moment the larger beast turned its snout toward Rowan, the woman in front of it took three steps back, then broke and ran. The dragon turned back and swept her with fire. Her night-shift flared like a lamp wick.

Rowan scuttled back, grabbed her cloak, dashed to the left and threw the cloak around the burning woman. Then she moved right again, distracting the dragons as the woman rolled on the ground.

Her feint was not sufficient. The dog-sized dragon heaved itself off the chandelier toward the cloaked figure.

"Damn you!" Rowan rushed it, struck at one eye, and shattered it.

The east wall collapsed inward from ceiling to floor, settling like a dropped curtain. Heated air struck Rowan like a blow, and she was thrown back against the wall and to the ground.

Someone was tugging on her arm. She could not breathe. She felt herself pulled to her feet, opened her eyes, then closed them against searing smoke. "This way!" a voice shouted. It was Bel. The Outskirter pulled her along.

Rowan fought. "No, wait!" She stumbled and fell. Bel pulled her up again. "That woman," Rowan cried. "Is she all right?"

Bel pushed her forward. "There's no one."

In blurred vision, Rowan saw the closet door and found the presence of mind to make her way into it. Out of the back wall, two huge hands grabbed her under the arms and pulled. Wood splinters scored her scalp and her back; then she was through and into a pitch-dark room. The man released her and turned back to help Bel.

Rowan groped and found shelves of crockery. Plates crashed to the floor. Bel was behind her again. "Out. Straight ahead."

They were in the kitchen. Rowan regained her bearings and hurried through into the dining room. There, orange light from the courtyard led them to the open double doors.

Two lines of people were passing buckets to and from the well. The water was being poured not on the inn but on the walls and roofs of adjacent houses. Rowan and Bel were pushed aside by the man who had helped them. He broke through the bucket line and ran to the edge of the crowd surrounding the courtyard, and into the arms of his surviving woman.

As Rowan and Bel reached the crowd, there was a shout, and a milling motion off to the left. A word was being passed from person to person. "Jannik!" "Look, there's Jannik!"

"About time," Rowan muttered, wiping soot from her face. She and Bel moved deeper into the crowd.

On the left, the mass of people parted, and a small man emerged and walked across the courtyard. He was no taller than Bel and somewhat round, dressed in silver and green. His hair was white and short, his beard a trim white point. He had the face of a habitually cheerful man.

Halfway across, he paused and looked up at the disaster with an expression of vast annoyance. He raised his hands, and the crowd hushed.

Rowan slipped farther back among the people, urging Bel with a hand on her arm.

Bel resisted. "Don't you want to see this?"

"I want to get out of here."

They left the crowd behind and found their way out and down a twisting street that ended by the lamp-lit docks. Rowan heard a voice exhorting, "Move, man, or Morgan'll skin us." She followed the sound.

They came to a heavily loaded barge where a narrow blond man was cursing at a pair of dockhands, who were viewing the glow above the buildings with interest.

"You're going to *Morgan's Chance*?" Rowan asked.

He eyed her. "Passengers? Come later, there's a barge at dawn."

Rowan indicated Bel with a tilt of her head. "She's crew."

"What, her?" The crewman examined Bel. "Don't know her."

Bel spoke up. "I'm the cook's new assistant. And she's a steerswoman."

He conceded a bit grudgingly. "All right then, get in. But don't rock, mind. We're riding low."

CHAPTER
Six

It took the better part of an hour to cross the shallows from the loading docks to the *Morgan's Chance*. Their boatmates were all members of the ship's crew, returning before the onslaught of passengers due at sunrise. Most were silent, watching the subsiding glow above the buildings that lined the shore. One tipsy fellow, oblivious to the chaos they were leaving behind, was singing a crude song, most of the words of which seemed to have escaped him. He improvised.

The barge was crowded with crates. Additionally, there were three goats and two wooden cages of ducks. The ducks showed great interest in the proceedings, extending their necks out through the slats as far as possible. The cages, abristle with yellow beaks, emitted a constant natter of avian complaint.

The barge rode low on the water. Where Rowan and Bel sat in the gunwales, Rowan brooding, Bel looking at the surroundings, the calm surface of the water was a handsbreadth away from swamping aboard. Bel leaned over and trailed one hand into the cold, starlit darkness. Then she pulled it out and tasted. "I heard it was salt," she said to Rowan. Then she affected Reeder's condescending tone. "Tell me, lady, why is the sea salt?"

The Outskirter seemed remarkably resilient; for her own part, Rowan found it impossible to take her mind off the disaster

59

they were leaving behind. "No one knows," she answered, half-indifferently.

"Ha!" Bel returned to her own voice. "I can tell you. A wizard had a magical box that delivered him salt whenever he called for it. But while he was out, his apprentice tried to impress some friends by demonstrating its magic. The apprentice forgot the words that halted the spell, and the box kept spewing out salt, until the whole house was filled. In desperation, the friends dragged the box to a cliff and tossed it into the sea. And there it lies, to this day."

Rowan looked at her friend and smiled despite herself. "A possible explanation."

Eventually the barge sidled up to the ship. Cables were tossed down for the cargo. Meanwhile, the returning sailors dragged themselves wearily up rope ladders.

Rowan noticed Bel watching the technique with a grim studiousness and realized that the barbarian had no intention of letting unfamiliarity slow her down again. When her turn came, Bel pulled herself up carefully, clearly considering every step. Rowan followed close behind, with complete ease, keeping an eye on her friend. At one point, a small swell caused the ship to tilt; for a moment, the ladder swung away to one side, hanging unsupported save at the top. Bel looked up in startlement, then down at Rowan and the dark water, then at the ladder itself. Recognizing her safety, she laughed in delight, then ascended faster.

Morgan was at the railing, shouting questions to the arriving crew. "What's the problem ashore?"

Reaching the top, Rowan answered him herself. "Dragonfire."

"What!"

"Saranna's Inn was attacked by nestlings. It's destroyed."

He leaned farther past the rail's edge, gazing out at the shore. A reddish orange glow marked the former location of the inn. "Gods below," he muttered. He turned away, then came storming back. "It's ridiculous, the dragons haven't got out of hand for years. And the breeding grounds aren't even near there. Where was Jannik, fast asleep? Are those fools ashore afraid to wake a wizard?' He cursed again, viciously.

"He came," a crew member answered. "A bit too late, but he came."

A voice spoke from behind Rowan. "You look as though you were in it yourselves." She turned and found the officer they had seen at the Tea Shop with Morgan. "Tyson, ship's navigator," he introduced himself. "We'll talk later." It was customary for any sea-traveling steerswoman to consult with the navigator, to update the ship's charts. "But you're not injured?"

"No." She brushed her hair away from her forehead. The hand came back sooty. "Singed, perhaps."

Bel spoke up. "But we lost our possessions in the fire. Our traveling packs. We have our clothes and my sword, that's all."

"I'll have the provisions I brought for the voyage," Rowan pointed out. "I arranged yesterday for a crate that I left at the cargo docks."

Tyson looked distressed. "But your notes and your charts?"

"All gone."

His brow furrowed. "I have some chart paper you can have. I'll buy some new at Wulfshaven. And some old pens I don't use. Some ink powder . . ."

"You're very kind."

"And look at you, you haven't even got a cloak. Can't have you catching a chill; I've a spare you can use."

Rowan was taken aback. "You're too generous."

"Nonsense, you're one of us, and we take care of our own." Tyson was referring to the solidarity of spirit that sailors shared with the steerswomen. He stopped a passing crewman and directed him to bring the items from the navigator's cabin, then excused himself to oversee some of the preparations at hand.

"A pleasant fellow," Bel commented. "Perhaps I'll become a steerswoman, so that everyone will be nice to me."

"Then you'd have to deal with the Reeders of the world."

Bel made a face. "True. It's hardly worth it."

When the crewman returned with Tyson's donations, Bel asked for directions to the galley. Unable to explain clearly enough for the Outskirter, he finally led her personally. Rowan remained on deck and presently noticed her crate of provisions being hauled aboard. A few questions to the purser determined the best place to stow it; Rowan made sure she knew how to find it again. Then she wandered forward, keeping out of the way of the work being done.

A handful of crewwomen jogged past her to clamber up the rigging. They tugged at the mainsail halyards, readying them for the command to set the sails. The women waited at their ease, chatting softly to themselves, calling up to a pair of men working the main skysail, all of them visible to Rowan only as distant forms blocking starlight, shifting against the sky as the ship rocked slowly.

Rowan went back amidships, where the passenger barge was expected.

The ship's activities slowly came to a standstill, and crew members became idle. Morgan regained his composure and sauntered about the deck, exuding a carefully assumed nonchalance. Tyson watched him with something like amusement. Eventually the east brightened.

The light revealed a vertical line of smoke onshore where the glow had been. Rowan was standing at the starboard railing, facing shore. Looking around her, she saw that most of the people on deck were on or near the starboard side: deckhands, a few officers, and three early-boarded passengers.

Presently a barge separated itself from the general harbor traffic and poled along toward the *Morgan's Chance*. The sun had cleared the horizon by the time it came alongside.

The passengers took their time negotiating the rope ladders. Morgan approached when a purser's mate clambered aboard; Rowan moved nearer and joined them.

"A whole bloody swarm of them dragons, they say," the purser's mate was complaining. "About fifty, tall as your waist, and smaller. Spitting and hissing, sending fire all over. Never heard of anything like it."

"The passengers," Morgan prompted.

"Oh. Yes, sir. None lost, sir, just all of them upset, especially the ones who'd been staying at the inn."

The witnesses were easy to identify; they were quiet, and the purser and purser's mates had trouble getting their attention. They tended to gaze around them as if a sailing ship were the strangest wonder in existence, and death by dragonfire were the usual human fate, escaped from only by luck. They were filled with what they had seen. Rowan decided to wait to ask them for the details she wanted – perhaps several days, until they were past their shock.

She stopped the chief purser as he hurried by. "You'd do best to tend to the people from Saranna's Inn first. Get them into their cabins and comfortable, and most of all, away from each other. They're standing in a clot together here, do you see? They're just feeding each other's distress. People can become hysterical in situations like this."

He paused, annoyed. Morgan forestalled his protest. "She's a steerswoman, and she's making sense. Do as she says." The purser hurried off.

Rowan eyed the mate who had been ashore. The man threw up his hands. "Not me, lady, I'm fine. Of course, I didn't watch anyone die, either."

Morgan dismissed the man, who went back to the still boarding passengers. The captain and the steerswoman watched the activity for a while. Then Morgan regarded her a moment, looked off to shore, out to sea, and gazed up at the rigging. He said reluctantly, "If you have any more suggestions, lady, I'll be glad to hear them."

Rowan had many questions, but only one suggestion. "I suggest," she said, "that we leave."

It was some time after noon that Bel shambled on deck. The ship was well underway, finally past the shallows of Donner and into bluewater. Bel lurched a bit on the shifting deck, from unfamiliarity or her obvious weariness. Blinking in the bright light, she found Rowan and dropped herself down to sit on the deck. She leaned back against the rail and closed her eyes, giving herself to the sunlight. She had shed the boots and was still wearing the loose yellow blouse she had purchased in Donner. Barefoot, in shirt and trousers, she could have been any sailor, but for the silver-and-blue belt. She was small and wiry and tan. She looked able, nimble, and not at all dangerous.

Rowan had spent the morning arranging her matters as best she could. She had taken the large chart papers Tyson had given her, folded them to smaller size, and cut the folds with a knife. After a visit to the sail locker, and the loan of a needle, sail-maker's palm, and some cord, she had a pamphlet-sized coverless book of thirty-two pages. Some canvas scraps were transformed into a small shoulder-slung pouch to contain the new book and pens.

While testing her hastily hung hammock in the women's crew quarters, she had noticed that the gum soles of her steerswoman's boots had worn down to the leather. The gum was the same type used by sailors everywhere, to aid in gripping the deck when not working barefoot. She had found the quartermaster, laid down a new surface on the soles, and brought the boots on deck to dry.

Then she had stopped to talk to a pair of crew members new to the trade, to show them the best way to coil a rope so that it stowed in the least amount of space but payed out easily. She hoped to find several such odd jobs to ease the duties of the officers and make herself useful. Done with her lesson, Rowan sent the two men off and sat next to Bel.

"How are you taking to your work?"

The Outskirter opened her eyes, squinting against the sunlight. "Well enough. The food is strange, but interesting. The cook knows his job, but he lacks any sense of adventure. He won't let me experiment."

"His loss. You seem to have an instinct for such things."

Bel made a sound of disinterest and closed her eyes again. "Do dragons carry disease?"

"No. Why do you ask?" Rowan was briefly concerned, then quickly realized Bel's problem. "Here. Stand up."

"No, please . . ."

Rowan pulled her up, against little resistance. "Trust me, it's better this way. Here." Rowan positioned her by the railing and demonstrated. "Stand with your side to the rail and hold with one hand, so." The ship was crossing the swell of the waves obliquely. "No, open your eyes; you need to balance."

"I can balance with my eyes closed," Bel said through her teeth, "when the ground doesn't move beneath me."

"Well, it's moving now." Rowan stood facing Bel, with her back to the bow. "Look past me, to the horizon. Unlock your knees . . . there. Bend them a little. Have you ever ridden a horse?"

"How will a horse help me on a ship?"

"It might be a little easier to explain . . . never mind. You have to get rid of the idea that the ship's deck is the ground; you mustn't try to align yourself to it. You need to find your own center of balance. Don't make the mistake of just trying to keep your head level— "

"I have to keep my head level!"

"Yes, but don't bend your neck to do it. Don't put your head at odds with your body. Use your legs. Bend your knees to compensate for the change in the deck's position . . ." She demonstrated as the approaching swells altered the deck's angle, exaggeratedly bending her left knee as the ship rose on the wave, then straightening and shifting the flex to her right as they rode over the crest.

Bel imitated Rowan's movements stiffly. "That's better," Rowan told her. "Keep your body relaxed; keep your head centered over your torso. Look past me at the waves as they approach."

Bel kept her eyes grimly on Rowan's face. "Must I really?"

"That's how you can tell what changes to expect." Bel shifted her gaze, her tan complexion graying. But as Rowan continued her coaching, the Outskirter eventually began to look more comfortable, whether from gained skill or from the distraction of learning the technique, Rowan could not determine. "Weren't you seasick when you were belowdecks?"

"I was too busy with the cook. I had too much on my mind to notice."

Rowan stopped exaggerating her leg movements and shifted back to her own more natural sea stance. "Then here's something to occupy your mind: at Saranna's Inn, what section did the dragon nestlings attack first?"

Bel attempted to make her own physical adjustments match the subtlety of Rowan's. "Do you mean, north or south? I lost all my direction, inside the building."

"Think about it."

"Well . . ." Bel loosened her death-grip on the railing and tested her ability to balance without support. "As we entered the guest-room section, the corner they attacked was across from us, diagonally. On the opposite side of the open area."

A trio of crew members jogged past aft to where a mate stood, exhorting them to some minor adjustment in the sheets. Rowan prompted Bel. "And?"

"And up. Toward the roof. The corner where our room was."

Rowan said nothing.

Bel considered for a long time. "Did we do something to attract them? What sort of thing attracts dragons?"

"I have no idea. Very little is known about dragons. I don't know what they like; I don't even know what they eat." She looked off to the side, thinking. "But I know that in Donner, the dragons are kept in check by Jannik's powers."

"But sometimes they get loose."

"Sometimes. They chose an interesting moment to do so." Around the two women, the ship's activity rapidly increased. Without thinking, Rowan noted that the wind had shifted, and a major readjustment of the sails was imminent. More passengers had come on deck, either to enjoy the brilliant sunlight, or to observe the crew's movements. Rowan stepped closer to Bel and, with a hand on her arm, directed her closer to the rail, away from the action. "And here's something else to think about: the first night out of Five Corners, we were attacked by a soldier who turned out to be in the service of a wizard."

"So you said. But he wasn't wearing a surplice or a sigil. How could you be sure he belonged to a wizard?"

"I saw him at the inn at Five Corners, remember, and he wore a Red surcoat then."

"Perhaps he just resembled one of the Red soldiers at the inn."

"I don't forget a face." Rowan saw Bel's dubious expression. "I don't," she stressed. "It's part of my training. I could sketch his portrait, right now."

Morgan himself had come on deck and was sending out a steady stream of shouted directions, relayed by mates to all quarters of the ship and up the rigging. Bel had to raise her voice to be heard. "Can you really think that a wizard is responsible?"

"It's a possibility"

"But why would a wizard care about us?"

"I've never attracted one's attention before. And there's been only one change in my activities, one new thing that I'm doing."

Bel looked at her. "You mean that jewel. Of course, it's magic— "

"We don't know that— "

"But I've had my jewels for years, and no one's cared. And that innkeeper at Five Corners, he's never been bothered."

"There's a difference." Oblivious to the noise around her, Rowan reviewed her speculations in her mind. "Several people have the jewels," she said, "but I'm the first person trying to find out about them."

Bel took a few pacing steps and found she had to grab the railing when the ship hit a sudden uneven swell. She moved cautiously away from the rail and leaned her weight against a vent cowling farther amidships. "Are you certain about this? Is this something . . . something your training tells you?"

Rowan came out of her reverie. "No, my training tells me not to be certain, not yet." She smiled. "The steerswomen have a saying: 'It takes three to know'."

"Three of what?"

"In this case, three instances. In the first instance, it's possible that the soldier was performing a little independent banditry, for his own profit. In the second instance, the dragon's attack may have been pure coincidence. But if anything else of the sort occurs . . ."

"Then you'll be sure."

"Exactly."

Bel made a derisive sound. "Much good it'll do, if the third instance kills you."

"Being unconvinced is not the same as being foolhardy. The possibility alone is strong enough to make me cautious."

Bel's gaze narrowed as she considered the situation. "I don't like this. It feels like we're running away from our enemies. If we stayed in Donner, we could have found out more about that dragon attack. It would have been much simpler."

Rowan found herself agreeing. "But I want to get to the Archives, and this is the only ship to Wulfshaven at the moment."

"So we sail."

"Yes."

There was a small burst of activity, a thumping of leather-soled shoes – no sailor hurrying, but Reeder's boy, dashing to the starboard railing, followed more sedately by a crewwoman. "There!" he cried excitedly. "It was out there!" He pointed. "But I don't see it anymore."

Rowan moved aft, Bel following carefully, unsure of her new sea legs. The crew member, a strong, brown, middle-aged woman, peered out to sea. "Don't see it."

"It was dark-colored, and small. It went up and down, on top of the water."

"Him. Piece of driftwood, maybe."

"I think it was a mermaid."

The woman suddenly dropped to the boy's height, grabbed his shoulder with her left hand, and covered his mouth with her right, roughly. "Don't say that! That's bad luck on a ship! They're evil creatures, murderous. Do you want to call one?"

"The boy spoke in ignorance," Rowan said gently.

The sailor looked up at her. "Aye. But you know the saying, lady: 'What you don't know, can kill you'." She released the boy but shook her finger in his face, once, admonishing.

Rowan looked out to sea, seeing nothing. "Perhaps it was a dolphin."

The sailor brightened. "Aye, perhaps." She scanned the waves again.

"Dolphins aren't real," the boy said. "They're . . . they're just heraldic beasts. Like lions."

"Dolphins certainly are real," Rowan told him.

"Lots of sailor's tales of dolphins," the crewwoman added.

"And the steerswomen have verified it, as well." Rowan saw that Bel had come closer, listening to the conversation with interest. Rowan continued. "More than two centuries ago, a steerswoman went swimming off the bow of a becalmed ship. Dolphins came up to her, pushing her like children at play. They danced on top of the sea, standing on their tails."

"It sounds like a wondrous sight," Bel said. She had found a seat on the roof of the pilothouse. "Lady, what's a dolphin?"

Rowan gathered her information. "A fish, large, nearly as long as a man is tall. They leap in the air as they swim along, and have a hole in the top of their heads. They sing through that hole, as you would through your mouth, but their song is like all the different birds of the air. Their tails are flat, opposite to other fish," she demonstrated the configuration with her hands, "and they are so strong that they can balance on top of the sea's surface by moving only that tail in the water. They possess great curiosity, and have never been known to injure a human."

"Are they good to eat?"

The sailor threw her hands in the air. "More bad luck!" she cried.

Bel spoke quickly. "Sea woman, I beg your pardon. I come from a far land and know nothing of the sea. If there is any ritual or obeisance I should make, please tell me now, so I can fend off the evil of my words. And, please, I ask you to teach me what I should know, so that I will never offend the sea god again."

Rowan looked at the Outskirter in admiration. A barbarian in birth but not in attitude—or, again, there seemed to be more to the Outskirters than rumor credited.

The sailor nodded, mollified. "That was well spoken. Aye, I'll teach you, if you need it. Between me and the steerswoman, we'll see you safe."

The boy sniffed disdainfully. Rowan looked down at him and recognized trouble on the way. He said, "Tell me, lady, what's a mermaid?"

The sailor made a grab for him, but Rowan stopped her with a hand on her chest. The woman wavered, agitated, trapped between two customs of equal force.

Rowan dropped to her knees in front of the boy and spoke eye-to-eye. "Child, I will be glad to answer your question, but first I will give you information for which you did not ask. Sailors live on their ships, care for their ships; a ship is a sailor's home. The beliefs of the sailors are like a religion. Now, when you're in a person's home, it is bad manners, it is inexcusably rude, to scoff at his or her religion, whatever your own beliefs. The person has offered you kindness and protection, and you cannot offer insult in return. It is outrageous, uncivilized— " She thought of Bel and amended her comments. "It is crude. It would be kinder, and inoffensive, to wait until we reach Wulfshaven, when we are in no sailor's home, to ask that question. So tell me again, boy, do you have a question for me, at this time?"

The child stared at her, wide-eyed, and the sailor leaned close to his ear. "Say that word again, and I'll throw you overboard."

A voice came from behind them. "What's this?" Reeder's boy broke and ran, clattering down a companionway into the ship.

The crewwoman straightened, startled. "Ah. Sir. You shouldn't sneak up on one like that."

It was Tyson, the navigator. "Now, Marta, I can't help if my boots are silent. You know I would never sneak up on you."

"Aye, sir. Right, sir. Officers never sneak up on the crew."

Bel spoke up. "The boy might have seen a dolphin."

Tyson laughed and clapped his hands together. "Then that's good luck!" He took a few moments to make a methodical examination of the sea off to starboard. Rowan did the same, but neither found any encouraging signs. The sailor, Marta, peered out dubiously; then, with a noncommittal grunt, she returned to her labors.

"Ah, well." Tyson turned back, leaving one arm resting along the railing. As he tilted his head back to view the new set of the ship's sails, Rowan discovered that she rather liked the way his auburn hair looked against the pale sky, how his light eyes contrasted with his broad brown face. She found herself watching herself watching him, a little amused.

Bel roused out of deep thought. "I like what you said," she told Rowan. "About respecting other people's religions. That's very sensible."

Distracted from her distraction, Rowan considered her answer. "I'm sorry, Bel, don't misunderstand me. I don't necessarily respect other people's religions, or any religion. But the people – I respect them, and I give them the honor they deserve, whatever they believe."

"And that boy – would you have answered his question?" Bel turned to Tyson. "He was asking about ill-omened creatures," she explained.

Rowan leaned back against the railing and studied Tyson's and Bel's expressions. "Yes. I would have, had he asked again."

Tyson nodded, with the understanding of long association with steerswomen, but Bel shook her head ruefully. "You. I don't understand you at all, sometimes. Just when you finish saying a hundred things that are incredibly wise, you turn around and act like a plain fool."

Rowan felt a flare of anger. In all the Inner Lands, no one spoke to a steerswoman so insultingly. She was about to retort in kind when, by reflex, her training stepped in. Everything she knew about Bel, in all her short experience with the Outskirter, came to her mind in ordered array: the patterns of Bel's behavior, what Rowan surmised about Bel's context of knowledge and habit, the occasional sudden swordlike thrusts of Bel's quick mind . . .

To everyone's surprise, including her own, Rowan replied with a laugh. "And you," she said to Bel. "Just when I'm convinced you're nothing but a plain fool, you turn around and say something incredibly wise."

Bel wavered, uncertain of how to interpret that. At last she said reluctantly, "Then perhaps between the two of us, we make one very clever person."

"Perhaps that's the case."

Tyson had watched the exchange with some perplexity. "You're an odd pair of friends," he said. "You are friends, aren't you? Traveling together?"

"Yes," Rowan clapped Bel's shoulder in a consciously over-acted gesture of hearty camaraderie. "And very advantageous it's been, for both of us."

Bel caught her mood. She said to Tyson, aside, "She covers for my ignorance, and I cover for her flaws of personality."

Tyson smiled. "Flaws of personality?"

"She's difficult to convince."

"True," Rowan admitted.

"She has no gods."

"Also true."

"She's too serious."

"A matter of opinion."

"There's not enough magic in her soul."

"Well, I'm not at all certain about magic," Rowan admitted.

Bel dropped her bantering attitude and stopped short. "What can you possibly mean?"

Rowan regretted the change in mood; nevertheless, she considered carefully before speaking. "The few times I've been faced with something called magical, it seemed . . . well, simply mysterious. As if there were merely something about it that I didn't know. Understand, I'm not giving you a steerswoman's conclusions, here. As a steerswoman, I have to withhold my decision, out of ignorance. But the fact that I can be this unsure . . . that seems to indicate something, to me." She shrugged roughly, uncomfortable with her uncertainty. "Sometimes I feel people call it magic, because they want magic."

"Perhaps Rowan feels that way because steerswomen are immune to some kinds of spells," Tyson said to Bel.

She looked at him in astonishment. "Immune? Can that be true?"

Rowan made a deprecating gesture. "So it's said. It's supposed to be true of sailors, as well."

"Sailors and steerswomen," Tyson nodded. "We're much alike. The sea in our blood, you see."

"That's hard to believe," Bel said. "I know there's real magic in the world, but would it be so . . . selective?"

"I don't know. I haven't enough information," Rowan replied. "But it seems unlikely."

Tyson clapped his hands together and laughed. "Simple way to prove it. There's a chest in the hold; belongs to a wizard. We're shipping it through Wulfshaven."

Bel was suspicious. "So?"

"It's guarded, by a simple spell. Nothing major, so I'm told. But we had to take precautions loading it. Come and take a look." He looked at Rowan, eyes crinkling in humor. "Come, lady, let's look at a wizard's magic; and perhaps we can show your friend something surprising of our own."

After pausing for Rowan to don her now-dry boots, the two women followed him. He led them down a forward hatch to a series of narrow companionways that carried them deep into the hold, far below the waterline.

The air acquired a contained feel, and the slap of waves came from somewhere overhead. They went back along a cramped passage created by the crates and bales that crowded the hold. Following last, Rowan found herself distracted by the variety of shapes, and the odors hinting at what each contained. There were dusty kegs of wine, others sending out a tang of brine, chests of some sharp spice; one bale of wool exuded a cloud of fine powder when Rowan's hand touched it. She sneezed.

She heard another sneeze and, looking up spotted Reeder's boy perched on top of the bale. His eyes were wide with distress at being caught, his jaw slack. Rowan only smiled and waved, and he watched dumbly as she followed Tyson and Bel.

Tyson brought them to a corner where several chests were stacked less precisely. He leaned back against a column of crates made of some rough pale wood. With a sweep of his hand he indicated rather vaguely the general area of the chests. Rowan and Bel looked at them.

"Which one?" Rowan asked.

"Perhaps Bel can tell."

"What, me?" Bel gave him a cautious, dubious look.

He spread his hands. "It's a minor spell, I know. Won't harm you, it'll just . . . warn you. Rowan pointed out, when people expect magic, they sometimes find it when it's not there. I'd like to see if you can find it if you don't know where it should be."

Bel raised her eyebrows and rocked a moment, intrigued. She scanned the area, then cocked her eye at one chest of dark wood, ornately carved and inlaid with a pattern of lighter wood. She approached it and, standing at the farthest distance possible, stretched out her left hand to touch it with index finger extended.

Rowan glanced at Tyson and found him watching Bel with controlled amusement. He so carefully kept his gaze steady that it was obvious that he was avoiding looking at the correct box. Rowan guessed from the stance of his body that it was one of a pair off to the right.

Bel's finger contacted the chest in question. She held the pose a moment, then slapped the box disdainfully with her palm. She turned to the others.

One in the center was unadorned, but bound about with iron chains and padlocks. It was perched rather sloppily across two others. Bel stepped up more confidently and rapped it with her knuckles. "Ha!" Nothing remarkable happened, but the action caused the chest to rock back slightly, then forward. Bel took a step back, caught her bare heel on an uneven plank, and threw out her right arm for balance. The back of her hand brushed one of the chests on the right.

With a very unwarriorlike squeak she yanked the hand back violently. The sudden change of motion caused her stance to unbalance completely, and she landed on the deck, narrowly missing a small puddle. She pressed the hand against her body with her left arm. "It *bit* me!"

Tyson laughed without mockery and strode over to the chest. He stepped into a space behind it and, keeping his eyes on Bel and Rowan, laid his hand flat upon its lid, fingers spread.

The women watched a moment. He showed no sign of discomfort.

Rowan gave Bel a hand up, and they approached.

The chest was about half as long as Rowan was tall and would have come to her knee if stood on the deck; it was standing on a wooden framework that raised it as high as Tyson's waist. It was covered with intricately tooled leather decorated with a swirling meshlike pattern of worked-in copper. Some of the copper lines came together to consolidate into clearly marked but unreadable runes and symbols. The whole chest was strapped about loosely by plain leather bands with loops on the side, and the wooden stand was padded with leather.

Bel studied Tyson, then touched the surface with one cautious finger. She snapped it back instantly, shaking it as if from a bee sting. Rowan thought that at the moment of contact there had been a brief, faint noise, like an insect buzz, and a thin odor that disappeared immediately.

Rowan stepped up, seeing amusement and challenge in Tyson's eyes. She carefully laid her own hand next to his. The leather felt rich, the copper discernibly cool. Automatically she ran her hand across the lid, part of her appreciating the workmanship. She turned to Bel, speechless.

Tyson tilted his head. "Try to touch Rowan."

Both threw him glances of surprise and suspicion. Unable to resist the opportunity to learn, Rowan reached out with her left hand. With vast reluctance, then forced bravery, Bel put her hand in Rowan's.

Quickly they pulled away from each other, Bel cursing. This time Rowan had felt it, but not from the box. It had passed between Bel's hand and hers, not painful, but strong and unpleasant – an eerie stinging vibration.

Rowan was suddenly reminded of the feeling one got from gripping a mainsail sheet under a stiff wind: how the wrist-thick rope would be rigid as iron, yet pass into one's hand the massive tension of the fight between wind and canvas, between sea and wood. The ship was a live thing, and holding that rope was like holding a tensed muscle.

The magic of the chest's guard-spell was sharper, violent but somehow similar. Something living had seemed to pass between the hands. Rowan had been like that rigid rope: whatever it was had passed into and through her to reach Bel. Appalled, she stepped back from the box.

There was no apparent reason for the sensations. The power was near-silent and invisible. For a moment her thoughts swirled, automatically sifting, searching for any information that might connect to give hints or theories about the effect. But when her mind came to rest, the only possibilities that remained involved spirits and spells.

Bel was delighted. "How did you load it on the ship?"

Tyson indicated the leather straps and loops. "We had to slip wooden poles into these, then carry it by the poles."

"It's not a bad spell. But even though I didn't know which chest had the spell, I knew that one of them must. For a real test, we ought to try someone totally in ignorance."

Rowan doubted that would make any difference. Although she was immune, after a fashion, she had felt something real. She was certain she would have felt nothing, if it had been at all possible to do so.

And what was her attitude now? She introspected and found that she still possessed no solid opinion. That surprised her, until she realized that she still had not enough facts to come to a conclusion. But, with the facts and new experience she did have – all the tentative ideas and half-formed theories had reformed on the opposite side of the issue, pointing to exactly opposite possibilities. She felt a mild internal vertigo.

Tyson stroked his beard thoughtfully. "Wait, now." He stepped into the main passage and looked down it both ways. Something caught his attention. He called down the passage. "You! Yes, you, come here a moment, you'll do. Come on!" Reeder's boy rounded the corner hesitantly, his face full of apprehension.

Tyson went back to the chest and beckoned to the boy. He patted the lid. "Put your hand on this, boy."

The lad froze. His gaze flickered among them, from Rowan to Bel, to the chest, to Tyson. His eyes widened. He glanced at the exit, then back to the chest. He clearly had no idea what was planned and just as clearly knew that it meant nothing pleasant for him. He seemed unsure whether to attempt an escape, or to obey the order of the navigator, who was, after all, a very large man. His turmoil immobilized him. He paled. He began to pant.

The three watched his performance; then Rowan laughed despite herself. The others joined in, and Bel clapped him on the back. "Go on, boy." He fled.

Bel turned to Rowan. "What do you think, now?"

"I think . . ." Rowan reviewed her thoughts again. "I think that there is a great deal that wizards know, that I don't."

When they reached the open air again, night had fallen. A jumble of clouds in the west were still faintly underlit by the departed sun, and were crowding toward the zenith. No land was visible, but with a glance toward the Eastern Guidestar, Rowan offhandedly located herself in her world with perfect precision. She automatically noted the westward progress they had made since morning.

When she looked at Tyson, he was doing the same, although she suspected that his accuracy would be less than hers. Then he scanned the horizons. "Wind'll come up before dawn. Rain, as well." She nodded.

Bel sighed. "The crew will be crowded tonight. Well, we'll be warm and dry, at least."

"Overhead leak somewhere down there," Tyson commented. "I hope you're not under it."

"Damn."

He spoke to Rowan. "Lady, does this upset your theories?"

"I had no theories. Only the possibilities of some theories. There are still possibilities, just somewhat different ones."

The three stood by the rail for an hour, watching the progress of the clouds and enjoying inconsequential conversation. Presently the first mate scurried down into the aft cabin and emerged with Morgan in tow. The captain viewed the scene, then issued orders to adjust the sail positions, watching with affected disinterest as he slowly paced the poop deck.

Eventually Bel decided it was time to turn in and made a few good-natured insults about the cook's particularity for early hours and promptness in assistants.

Rowan and Tyson remained, talking idly and companionably. Presently Tyson put forth an invitation, which Rowan considered carefully, then declined. Uninsulted, Tyson stayed with her for another hour; then he wished her good night and retired.

Rowan wandered the deck alone for a while, enjoying the feeling of the deck as it shifted beneath her feet, the subtle changes of wind strength and direction. Eventually her mood shifted a bit, and she found herself regretting her refusal of Tyson's suggestion. This she remedied by knocking softly at his cabin door at midnight.

In the morning Reeder's boy was found dead, lying blue-faced in a puddle of water next to the wizard's chest.

CHAPTER
Seven

"Stupid," Morgan pronounced, shifting through the papers on his worktable. "Foolish. Stupid. He was looking for trouble, or he was too stupid to know when he'd found it. Damn!" He slammed down a fistful of notes and receipts. "Why bother a wizard's chest? There was a warning spell on it; he must have noticed it."

Rowan sat in a low chair across the cabin, legs stretched out in front of her. "It wasn't particularly unpleasant. It can't have killed him."

"No, of course not." He pointed a finger at her. "He tried to open it. He ignored the guard-spell and met the protecting spell. I can't be held responsible for the idiocy of a boy."

Her face was impassive. "He was curious. Intrigued." To herself she added, Challenged.

Morgan grunted noncommittally. Shifting his papers into apparently arbitrary piles, he calmed visibly. "Have you gone over the charts with Tyson?"

"Yes." The hiss of rain overhead grew louder. Someone walked on the deck above, steps slow and heavy.

"Were there many corrections?"

She shook her head. The steps above paused, apparently at the taffrail. "There was nothing incorrect on them, but you'll find quite a few additions. Some areas where not much was known before."

There was a creak as the person above shifted. Morgan nodded. "Good. I'd like to review them with you. Where's Tyson, do you know?"

"On deck."

"In this? Have someone find him. And bring the charts." He caught himself. "Pardon me, lady. I'll get them."

Rowan rose. "No, Captain, I'll go. Excuse me, please." She exited, closing the door on his surprised expression. Wrapping her cloak around her, she climbed the short companionway to the deck.

The wind was strong but not storming. Rain fell in a solid pour, weighing down like a hand on Rowan's head and shoulders. The deck was near-deserted. Through the shifting gray she could faintly make out the back of the helmsman, not far from her, placidly manning the wheel. She turned and went up the steps to the raised poop.

As she came to the top, the wind caught her borrowed cloak and whipped it about like a loose sail. She grabbed at the folds and pulled it close. Its protection closed about her like the walls of a room, water running off her hood in streams before her face. She had to move her whole body to direct the hood opening. She saw a lone gray cloaked figure motionless at the taffrail, looking off astern, and she moved toward it.

She spoke, but the noise of water covered her voice. She touched his shoulder; he seemed not to notice. Using both hands, she turned him to face her.

It was Reeder. His face was pale with cold, slick with rain. Sparse hair lay wet against his forehead, like lines drawn in ink. He looked at her expressionlessly, eyes blank and bright. His eyes were a beautiful pale green color; she had never noticed that before.

Startled, she stepped back. She made to speak, but he turned away.

Rowan left him and searched every part of the deck for Tyson. The downpour limited her vision to the length of her reach, so that her scope was small, her search detailed. She began from the poop deck, where she left Reeder, and worked forward, and so at last found him up by the bowsprit.

He stood far forward at the angle in the railing. Where the rest of the ship was only dreary, there the violence of the elements showed itself. The seas were not very high, but the ship moved heavily, and the bow smashed each crest, with a noise like the absent thunder.

Tyson faced the seas. Each time the bow met a wave, the impact sent a stinging sheet of spray over the rail; he did not flinch, but only blinked against the water. His cloak was soaked through, and he wore his hood down. He was as wet as if he had been underwater. Rowan guessed he had been there since dawn.

She called out to him, but the hiss of rain, the whistle and rattle of rigging, and the jarring crash of waves covered her voice. She moved closer and shouted.

Some sound, if not words, reached him. He turned and she saw him recognize her – recognize and withdraw, his face a closed door.

A dash of spray slapped across his back and into Rowan's face. She winced and wiped her eyes with her fingers. When she could see, his expression had changed, and he seemed surprised, as though he had thought himself alone despite her presence. It was the cold water on her own face, his realization of her pain and discomfort, that brought him back.

He grabbed her arm, put his face close, and shouted. The words came faintly. "Get out of the weather!" Beads of water hung in his beard like crystals. The cold he had absorbed drew the heat away from her face, out through her hood.

She tried to explain. "The Captain," she began, but she could not make her voice loud enough. At last she put her hands on his arms and looked him full in the face, letting him see her utter refusal to leave him there.

Thoughts moved behind his eyes. He let her lead him away.

They went below, down to the galley. Bel was there, dealing with an immense kettle hung over the brick stove. She looked up in astonishment. "What happened to him?"

Rowan brought him into the warmth. Tyson muttered protests. "Don't fuss, I'm all right."

"You are soaked." Rowan took his cloak. The shirt beneath was as wet as his face. "And frozen." His face was white; he shivered. Bel ladled soup from the kettle into a mug and passed it to him. He wrapped his hands around it but did not drink. His eyes found the fire and rested there.

Bel watched him silently, then turned to Rowan for answers. Rowan told her about Reeder's boy, and Bel listened, eyes wide.

"People should be careful with magic," the Outskirter said. "He ignored the warning. It was a stupid thing for him to do."

"Boys are stupid," Tyson said bitterly. "It's in them to be stupid, and to do stupid things. That's how they learn. Adults should know better."

"It's not your fault." Rowan put a hand on his shoulder and studied his face. "He was down there already. He was looking for mischief. It's horrible, but he found it himself."

He turned to her. "He would have left it alone, after the guard-spell warned him. But he saw us. And I – I dared him."

She had no answer. It was true.

"Perhaps he thought he'd be immune," Bel said. "Perhaps he fancied himself a sailor." The idea set off in Tyson some chain of thought that forced his eyes closed in pain.

The room was thick with dampness and cooking scents. The air was dark and close. The fire painted their faces with warm light.

Rowan remembered such a light, such air, such faces.

She had been a very young girl, perhaps five years old. The harvest was in, and it was very late at night. There was still much to do, and the family had brought their work by the firelight.

Her mother and father were husking fist-sized ears of maize. A morning rain had soaked the ears, and they gave off a visible steam in the heat. Her aunt, a narrow, fragile-looking woman, was sorting beans, and her uncle sat close to the firelight, squinting as he carefully repaired a wicker basket.

Young Rowan was shelling peas, very bored. She absently counted the number of peas in each pod, wondering if they would go past ten. Ten was all she knew.

The adults' conversation seemed not to pertain to her, and she accepted it as a dull background to a dull job. Presently there was a lull, and her aunt began to sing a little song in a high thin voice. Rowan became more interested and stopped counting to listen.

The song was about a bird. Rowan liked that, as she was fond of birds, and there were so few around. The bird, a swallow, flew alone in an empty sky. In the morning it came close to earth and flew very fast, skimming the fields. Later it began to rain, and the swallow passed a barn. Looking inside, it saw that all the animals were in their stalls, warm and safe. At night, it flew high above an empty castle and looked down on the towers, circling around. At last it found a nest and slept, while the mysterious moon crossed the skies. Rowan thought it was a fine song.

But when it was finished she happened to look over at her uncle and saw that he was silently crying. He had stopped his work and closed his eyes. Tears ran down his weathered cheeks.

Rowan was surprised. There was nothing to cry about. The only thing that had happened was that her aunt had sung a song. The other adults ignored her uncle. That upset Rowan; someone was unhappy, no one was paying attention, and it was not right.

Then it came to her that somehow the song was not about a bird but about sorrow. She was confused. There was nothing in the song except the bird, and what it had done. Still, she knew it was so.

Later, after she had been put to bed, she crept outside and stood alone in the back yard. With her back to the house, she could see out to the edge of the cultivated land, past the funeral groves, where the desert began. The sky above was wide and empty; she thought of a tiny bird high up in that sky, looking down on her. She tried to remember the song and sang it to herself. As she sang it, her own eyes filled with tears, although she could not see why they should.

It came to her that there were reasons behind events, reasons she did not know, and that the world contained many things that were other than what they seemed. She thought that perhaps if she could fly very high, she might see a great deal.

Rowan still knew the song and sometimes sang it to herself.

She took off the cloak she was wearing and wrapped it around Tyson's shivering shoulders. He did not look at her, but he leaned back slightly, accepting its warmth.

With a glance toward Bel, Rowan stepped out of the galley into the passageway. She wound her way among the passages, back to

Tyson's cabin. Inside, she went into his sea chest and found a warm shirt of white wool. With that, and her arms full of his charts, she emerged to encounter a very surprised purser's mate, his hand raised to knock. Offering no explanation, she told the man about Reeder, doubtless still at the taffrail in the rain. He hurried off, and she went back to join her friends.

CHAPTER
Eight

The first sign of the approach to Wulfshaven was not a view of the mainland itself, but of one and then a series of small islands that swept south from the still-distant mouth of the great river Wulf. The islands were mostly unclaimed, bare earth and rock, but as the *Morgan's Chance* neared the port itself, there were more signs of human hands. Occasionally an island would actually be inhabited, usually by a lone fisherman feeding the land by the offal of his or her trade. More often one of the regularly planned dumps of garbage or a deposit of other fertilizing substances had brought to life some still-deserted island, creating isolated spots of green, lonely but promising.

Rowan and Bel found a place on the poop, out of the way of the increasing activity. Bel sat comfortably on the deck with her back against the aft railing. She had donned her shaggy boots and cloak, to ward off the chill sweeping down from the windy gray sky.

The previous day Rowan had made her farewells with Tyson. After the death of Reeder's boy, he had become ever more distant and solitary, shunning Rowan and conversing with the captain and crew only at need. Rowan could find no comfortable way to approach him, no way to learn why the child's death had affected him so personally. They parted as strangers.

Now Rowan stood near Bel, watching the maneuvers with interest. Although Morgan strode about the deck with an air of nonchalance, his glance was sharp, and his orders quick and precise. The heavy ship wallowed with all the grace he could muster and, in one lovely, astonishing move, sidled up to the wharf, its sails luffing the instant it barely nudged the dock. Morgan allowed himself a small smile, then turned away as if the matter concerned him not at all.

Wulfshaven was a deep harbor, and unloading and disembarking was a far simpler affair than at Donner. A railed gangplank bridged the shifting gap between the wharf and the ship's starboard side. With no luggage to unload, Rowan and Bel simply walked across the plank, and so arrived at last in Wulfshaven.

The steerswoman led the way, skirting a small crowd consisting of a well-dressed portly man leading a nattering group of less elegant fellows: a merchant, with clerks in tow. A number of smaller vessels were docked along the length of the wharf, some of them sailboats in such bad repair that their status had clearly been shifted from transportation to permanent abode. Children hooted and chattered and clattered past to investigate the *Morgan's Chance*.

The wind picked up briefly as they reached the end of the wharf. Rowan had returned Tyson's cloak; she shivered.

"Do you want my cloak?" Bel offered.

"And leave you with just that blouse? No, I'll get another soon enough." She led Bel left, along a broad, weather-beaten esplanade.

"How soon? Are we going somewhere in particular?"

"I have friends here. We'll spend the night with one of them – Maranne, a healer. I lodged with her during my training. I think you'll like her." Shops lined the shore side of the esplanade. They passed a chandlery, a sail loft, and a ropewalk.

"I thought the Archives were north of here."

"They are. One doesn't train at the Archives." Rowan stopped suddenly beside a filigreed iron pole. "What's this?" The pole stood twice as tall as a man and was surmounted by a translucent white sphere. Bel paused while the steerswoman circled, studying it.

Rowan pulled aside a passerby, a fisherman by his dress, and put a question to him. He replied with surprise. "You're new here? That's a lamp. They're all along the harbor."

Rowan looked down the street and saw another at the next corner, and the next; they lined the business street along the harbor, clustering around the open square that fronted the Trap and Net tavern farther down. "But there's no opening," she said. "How can they light the wicks?"

The fisherman beamed with an air of civic pride. "No wicks. They're magic. A gift from Corvus." He hurried on his way. "Come see them at night!" he called back. "There's nothing like it!" The women watched as he continued down to the Trap and Net, where he noisily greeted a crowd of cronies outside.

"Corvus?" Bel asked.

"The local wizard," Rowan said, turning back to the lamp. "Blue. Though he was Red when I was here last." Abandoning her inspection, she led the Outskirter down the street, brooding. "Why would Corvus give Wulfshaven such a gift?"

"Out of friendship?" Bel's gait had naturally acquired a bit of a roll during their voyage, and she weaved slightly as she tried to compensate for nonexistent waves. "I know the steerswomen don't like wizards, but surely the wizards do a great deal of good? This Corvus, doesn't he help the town at all?"

Rain sprinkled the street briefly, then stopped. A woman pushing a pastry cart paused and viewed the shifting sky with annoyance. "Yes," Rowan admitted, angling around the cart. "He'll predict the weather, sometimes, and always if there's a heavy gale. And if the fishing is poor, he'll give advice that's always true. Still— " Spotting something ahead, she walked faster to the next corner.

A small man was working at the next lamppost, stooping down to deal with something at its base. On the ground beside him lay a leather shoulder satchel, and he periodically removed and replaced items in it with an air of confidence and satisfaction.

Rowan spoke as she approached him, but he cut her off cheerfully. "Hold on a bit, now, this won't take a moment," he said, and continued with his work. Rowan could see that he had opened a small panel, disguised by the filigree, and was involved with something inside.

"There." He shut the panel and locked it with a tiny key dangling by a cord from his wrist. Looking up, he appraised the two women. "Now, how can I help you?"

"I'm wondering about these new lamps," Rowan began.

"Lovely, aren't they?" He slapped the pole familiarly. "You must be strangers." He gave Bel's clothing a second, squinteyed inspection.

"We just arrived by ship," Bel explained. "From Donner."

"Donner, is it?" His face lit up. He stood and dusted his hands on his trouser legs. "Well, I have family in Donner. My little niece, of course she's not so little now, she married a fellow who— "

Rowan interrupted. "I'm sorry, I'll be glad to give you any news I have from Donner, but first I'd like to ask you about these lamps."

"Well, Corvus, that's our wizard, he gave them— "

"Specifically," Rowan continued, "I'd like to know how they work."

"Oh, no." He clicked his tongue. "I can't help you there. Guild rules, you see."

"Guild? What guild is that?"

"Why, the new Lamplighters Guild. See, when Corvus gave them, he had to teach us the spells to make them work. All very secret, sworn to secrecy, every one of us— " His eyes caught the glint of her gold chain, and his speech ended with a trailing "T. . . ." He sent a confirming glance toward the silver ring on her left hand, then winced. "I'm sorry, lady, truly I am. But I can't tell you."

Rowan gazed at him for a long moment. At last she said, "As I don't have much time to spare, you needn't go into detail. The general idea will suffice." And she waited, suddenly quite still.

The man agonized. "I just can't."

Rowan simply stood, silent. Bel looked from her face to the lamplighter's in perplexity. Finally Rowan turned without a word and began to walk away.

"Lady, please, wait a moment— "

She stopped, then slowly turned around, but did not approach.

"I need to know something— " he began.

"No."

Understanding dawned on Bel's face, and she watched the man with interest.

"Not for myself," he continued, "but for the Guild. I, that is, they ought to know, is your ban now just on me, or will it hold for the whole Guild?"

Rowan took her time replying. "The ban holds for any individual who refuses questions." She made to turn away again, but Bel called to her.

The Outskirter was viewing the lamplighter with concern. "Rowan, this man has family in Donner." Rowan said nothing, and Bel went on. "They might have been in the fire at the inn— "

"A fire?" He said in shock, "My niece, she works in an inn. And her son, too— "

"Do you know the name?" Bel asked.

"No, no I don't." His face showed agony. "But I know the street, Tilemaker's Street." He looked helplessly at the steerswoman, who waited patiently for Bel, saying nothing.

At last Bel said, "Rowan, do you know if Saranna's Inn was on Tilemaker's Street?"

"Yes, I do know," Rowan replied. "I'll wait for you at the next corner."

Down the street she found a street vendor's stall and interested herself in a display of bone flutes and pipes. They were of remarkable workmanship. Rowan tested a flute but lacked the skill to produce any sound at all. She had better luck with the pipes, managing to elicit a mellow hoot from the low register.

Eventually Bel joined her, and Rowan led them along a cobbled street that climbed and twisted up one of the hills above the harbor. They walked in silence, and when Rowan glanced at her, she saw that the Outskirter was deep in angry thought. Finally Bel said only, "Family is important. Rowan, that was cruel!"

They turned up a side street so narrow that the overhanging second stories sometimes had planks laid from one window to the opposite neighbor's. Some were decorated with bright flower boxes. "Bel," Rowan said carefully. "Suppose you discovered that another tribe had stolen half your herd and refused to give you what was yours?"

Bel stopped in outrage. "We'd kill them!"

Rowan turned back to her. "Kill them? How cruel." And she continued on her way, leaving Bel to catch up.

The street doubled back on itself, and when they rounded one last corner, suddenly the area before them opened up. The sea was visible, patched with light and dark by the heavy clouds that moved above. Before them, the roofs of Wulfshaven were a confusion of green-tiled shapes sweeping down to the harbor below.

Rowan stopped before a house on the corner, a haphazard construction of whitewashed brick. Suddenly all the previous unpleasantness was swept away in a river of bright memories. The handful of years in the life of a taciturn farm girl from the northlands, years of struggle and confusion lanced with sudden comprehension and delight, years that ended with the arrival at the Archives of a young woman of confidence, depth, and inner strength – those years were contained in this town, these streets, and one little attic room in this very house.

"Are we going in?"

Rowan smiled. "Give me a moment," she said. "It's been a long time."

Inside, the ceiling was festooned with tied bundles of dried herbs sending out dozens of evocative odors. The room was dark, the shutters pulled to against the coming rain, and a small fire flickered in the hearth. A heavyset blond woman approached them. "How may I help you?"

Rowan quelled her disappointment. "Is Maranne about? I'm an old friend."

"No, she's off in the east quarter. Pulling a tooth and delivering some coltsfoot tea. I'm afraid she'll be quite late."

"Do you mind if we wait and sit by the fire? There's rain on the way."

The blond woman looked at the pair uncertainly: one slightly damp woman, not dressed for the weather, and another in outlandish garb.

"Rowan used to live here," Bel said.

The woman brightened. "Rowan? Maranne speaks of you often – you're that steerswoman. Come, I'll make us some tea." She closed the door against the distant clatter of hooves on the cobbles and led them to the fire. Chairs were drawn and a kettle hung. The blond woman scanned the ceiling for likely candidates. "I don't remember you, but I remember when the Academy was here. Oh, that was a time! People from all over, all those teachers, and experts in this and that. It takes the strangest mix to make a batch of steerswomen." She found some peppermint hanging by the window, then added a tiny sprig of comfrey.

"I remember you," Rowan said. "You're Joslyn. Your father was the cooper."

Joslyn was pleased. "There's an example of steerswoman's memory." The sound of hooves outside became audible again, and with it a shouting voice. "Now, what's that?" She opened the window.

The sound stopped, and an instant later the door slammed open and a large form filled the doorway. "Rowan! I knew it!"

The man crossed the room, and suddenly Rowan found herself engulfed in strong arms and the sweep of his cloak. Joslyn said faintly, "My word, it's the duke!"

Rowan tried to extract herself. His hug was no comradely embrace, as he had often given her, nor even a lover's embrace, but something full of desperate relief. "I knew it couldn't be true!" he railed. "Damn Corvus and his scrying!"

"Artos!" She managed to pull away. "What is this?"

Bel eyed them from her chair. "You know this duke, then?"

He spun aside and pounded a nearby table violently. "That lowborn bastard! How could he tell me such a thing?"

"Tell you what? Artos, calm down," Rowan pleaded, knowing well that the duke was one man who could never be calm.

But he did stop, all his native energy held still for a moment while he looked at her and said in a smaller voice, "He said you were dead."

She was astonished. "Corvus?"

"Yes!" He spun away and paced, more quickly than a man his size ought to in so small a room. "He said that he was scrying and saw that you'd been killed. In Donner, by dragons! He said, 'I'm sorry to tell you, but your pet steerswoman is dead.'" Artos stopped and held up his hands to ward off a reaction. "I know, I understand, you're nobody's pet. Those were his words, not mine. But it looks like his scry-stone was mistaken."

He paused, then smiled. "Did I mention how glad I am to see you?"

Rowan laughed happily. "Yes, I'm glad to see you, too."

Bel spoke from her place by the fire. "The scry-stone was not far off, at that. We very nearly were killed by dragons."

Artos turned to her, seeing her for the first time. He took in her clothing, her sword, and the piebald cloak draped on the chair behind her, with a speculating gaze. "This is Bel, my friend, an Outskirter," Rowan explained. She turned to Bel. "You should stand when the duke enters."

"He's no duke of mine, and he's already entered." Bel did stand, but it was to swing the bubbling kettle out of the fire. "Perhaps this duke would like some tea?"

Joslyn recovered some of her composure and nervously sidled over to deal with it.

Bel approached. "Well, I'd like to know how to address a duke, and also, how he knew where to find us, and when." She looked up at him.

"I came as soon as I heard there was a ship arrived from Donner, with a steerswoman. If it was Rowan, I knew she would come here; she couldn't be in Wulfshaven and not visit Maranne." He paused. "And the proper address is 'my lord'."

Bel considered, then shook her head. "That won't do."

"Bel— " Rowan began.

"Outskirter," the duke mused. He had finally placed the term. "That's a warrior, a barbarian."

"True."

"You're small for a warrior."

Bel acknowledged it. "I'm closer to the ground, and harder to knock over."

"That's a large sword for so small a woman."

"I swing it two-handed."

He nodded, his wariness tempered by interest. He leaned back against the table. "That's good. But then you can't carry a shield."

"Ha. My sword is my shield."

"Bel has been traveling with me," Rowan said. "She's an honorable person and has given her word not to lay waste to the Inner Lands while she's in my company."

The duke laughed. He had a huge laugh, as big as his person, honest and uninhibited. "Then you'd best not separate. I believe this woman could do more damage than her size might suggest. Let's sit by the fire and wait for Maranne, and you can tell me the story." He looked around and found Joslyn standing uncertainly by the fire. He dropped into graciousness easily. "I hope this is no inconvenience to you. Pour some tea, and please sit with us."

Joslyn complied, hesitantly, and pulled up a stool, but Rowan noted that the herbalist kept a bit of distance between herself and the visitors. Joslyn found the situation uncomfortable, and Rowan realized with regret that at some point in the past Artos had ceased to be a frequent casual visitor to Maranne's house.

But Bel was completely at ease and settled into a chair, tucking up both legs as if she were seated on the ground. "I've heard something about these dukes and barons and squires you have in the Inner Lands," she said. "How is that a steerswoman knows one so well? Are you all of the same class?"

Artos gave a half smile. "They say that the steerswomen are the only aristocracy open to the common folk."

"That's not true at all, and it's a bad saying," Rowan put in with some vehemence. "We come from all classes before we join, and belong to no class when we're accepted."

"You're certainly well treated by the people," the duke pointed out. "And they defer to you, grant you certain privileges. . . ."

"The people treat us well of their own accord. There's no law that compels them."

"Custom can have the force of a law."

"Not at all. There's no punishment, no soldiery involved— "

He held up a hand. "Now, let's not get into one of our discussions. We'll be at it all night."

Remembering, Rowan laughed. "Talking until dawn . . ."

"Often, right by this very fire . . ."

Joslyn looked about the room in wonderment. Rowan said to Bel, "The Academy's not a place, it's an event, and the year I trained it was held here in Wulfshaven. Artos was forever haunting our classes."

"So many strange people," he said, and his gaze turned inward at pleasant memories. "From all the Inner Lands. Candidates from far-off towns, teachers, experts in the most peculiar things. So much to see and hear about. I never knew the world held so many things, such strange thoughts . . ."

"He looked so fascinated, and so lonely, that I took pity on him at last and started a conversation. It was easy to become friends. He has a quick mind, as it turned out, and I practically recited my daily lessons to him, most evenings . . ."

"A steerswoman can take pity on a duke?" Bel was amused.

"I wasn't a steerswoman, yet . . ."

"And I wasn't a duke," Artos said. "But my uncle died near the end of the training, and I," he made a deprecating gesture "ascended to my position." Then he looked a bit regretful. I'd like to have seen it all you know. I learned a lot in my haunting, as Rowan calls it. I know I'm better for it.

"Well." He slapped one knee and leaned forward. "Now you must tell me how our Corvus can be so far off the mark. What happened to you?"

At the duke's insistence, Rowan began with the fire at the inn. As it was not the true beginning of the tale, she found she had to keep backtracking and filling in, responding to peripheral questions as they occurred. The story wound its way through events almost haphazardly, but at last Artos had the whole tale of her jewel, and of her suspicion about the interest of a wizard. She showed him the glittering fragment.

He fingered it, musing. "I've seen this before. That witch-woman, at the edge of town."

"Yes, you were with me. That was the first one I'd seen."

He nodded vaguely, his eyes on the fire. From the depth of his concentration, Rowan suddenly realized that he was thinking in his areas of greatest expertise: violence and defense. Her thoughts ran ahead of his. "You can't be serious," she said.

He looked up. "You could always read my mind."

"The wizard could hardly harm me at this distance."

"How can we know? Corvus saw you all the way off in Donner. And those dragons – that must have been done at a distance. Unless your Red wizard followed you." He returned the jewel.

"Or," Bel put in, leaning forward, "unless it was done by Jannik."

"Help a Red? Not likely. The Blues and Reds hate each other, only the gods know why." And with that, the duke grew silent.

Rowan watched his face, suddenly disturbed. "Something has happened?"

He nodded. "A nasty little war, last year." Avoiding Rowan's face, he addressed his explanation to Bel. "Corvus turned from Red to Blue, and six months later someone's trying to establish a new Red holding just northeast of us. And our helpful Corvus requested— " He spat the word, and abruptly his composure vanished. He slammed the arm of his chair and was on his feet, pacing like a beast. "*Requested!*"

"Requested how many soldiers?" Rowan asked.

He flung his arms wide. "All of them! All of my regulars, all of my reserves, and" his mouth twisted "as many impressed from the citizenry."

Rowan made a calculation against her estimate of the area's population. "And how many came back?"

"I lost twenty of my regulars. Of the rest— " He paused for effect. "Half returned." He watched the steerswoman's reaction, then continued in a flat tone. "Wizards. Sometimes I think they're all insane." He brought himself back to his chair but did not sit; he gripped the back with his large hands. "Did you know, one of them even brought a basilisk onto the battlefield? Can you imagine it? The damned thing killed as many on their side as ours."

Bel looked at Rowan. "What's a basilisk?"

"A magical creature, usually disguised in some fashion."

"That's the thing of it," Artos said to the Outskirter. "If it looks at you, you die, sooner or later, and how can you tell if it's looking at you when you can't recognize it? It wiped out a squadron on their side, and one on ours. And the ones that lingered, they had it worst. We brought some of them here, no one else wanted to help them. That Red captain, what was his name?" he asked Joslyn.

"Penn," she supplied quietly.

"You should have heard him curse his masters. The poor bastard scarcely looked human at the end."

Joslyn was sitting silent on her stool by the fire, her cup in her lap, her head bowed.

"Your father?" Rowan asked.

The woman looked up slowly. "Tell me," she said carefully. "Have you seen the magic lamps by the harbor?"

Artos spoke through his teeth. "A gesture of thanks."

Bel sipped her tea. "It's trouble if you cross a wizard, trouble if you help a wizard, and trouble if you don't have a wizard, for things like dragons and hurricanes." She put down the cup. "That's altogether too much trouble."

The duke sat down again abruptly. "Rowan, who else knows you're in Wulfshaven?"

"I've made no secret of it."

"Of course not. But Corvus thinks you're dead, and probably Jannik, too. With any luck, your Red wizard does, as well."

"So there's no reason for him to look this way, to scry or try to divine my fate."

"Word may reach him. There may be spies – I'll let it be known that the steerswoman on the ship from Donner turned out not to be you."

Rowan was offended. "Artos, I won't have you lying on my behalf."

There was a shift in his demeanor. Suddenly he was not only a friend, but a duke, a man who gave orders and who chose his own behavior. "I'm no steerswoman. I'll lie if it suits me, to protect whomever I damn well please." He thought briefly. "You're going to the Archives?"

"In the morning."

Artos stood. "Leave now."

"We'll have to wait. It's a full day's journey, and this rain— "

"Take my horse. You'll be there by midnight."

"Artos— "

"No, he's right," Bel said. "The sooner we get to where we're going, the better."

He looked around, and found Joslyn. "Pack them a meal for the journey. And does Maranne have an extra cloak for Rowan?"

"No. Take mine." She went to make the preparations.

"I hardly think this is necessary— " Rowan protested.

"Rowan," Bel said. "Shut up and let your friends help you. The duke knows more about such things than you do, and so do I."

It was true. Rowan was familiar with violence; it was part of the world. But the violence she had met had been random, small-scale – the occasional road bandit, a fleeing criminal. She had defended herself and even killed in defense.

But this: if in fact there was a pattern to the recent events, if there was a single will behind them, then it pointed to the existence of an enemy. She stopped to absorb the idea: *I have an enemy.*

Bel and Artos understood enemies.

CHAPTER
Nine

Rowan awoke to find a wood gnome regarding her from the foot of the bed. He was perched on the footboard, peering down with droll interest, munching some bit of fruit. When he saw she was awake, he stretched out one long arm to offer her a taste. She accepted politely but only gave the piece a token nibble, as it seemed to have been dragged through several different kinds of dirt. It proved to be a slice of winter apple, identifiable only by flavor. Wood gnomes had no more than a vague recognition of cleanliness.

She looked around the room. The other four beds were empty, but Bel's fur cloak lay on the floor next to one. Bel herself was nowhere in sight.

They had ridden through the long night, with storms gathering around them, gathering, then breaking. They ran Artos's fine war-horse through rain along the north-going river road, a smooth clear track, until the rising hills forced them to walk. Bel rode behind Rowan, clutching her waist. Though the Outskirter never complained, Rowan felt the tension in her arms at each jolting misstep. But when the sky cracked lightning, the horse remembered battle and cried out challenge to the sound, and Bel, in kindred spirit, sat straighter, balanced, and echoed with a warrior's laugh. Later they wearily dismounted and guided the horse in booming thunder and dancing wind up the rocky, wooded path to the stables nestled under the overhang of the Archives' stone walls.

The wind snatched the stable door from Bel's hand as Rowan brought the horse in, and the slam summoned Josef, the groom, from sleep to amazed discovery of the exhausted women. He led them upstairs to the transients' dormitory, lit a fire, then left them to collapse into the chilly beds.

Now spots of sunlight climbed the far end of the room. Rowan turned back to the wood gnome and addressed him in the language of hand signals that his people shared with humans. "Where woman?" she gestured.

"Woman in bed," he replied, obviously meaning Rowan.

"No. Other woman." She pointed to the bed with Bel's clothing.

"Fur-woman. Noisy woman, gone. Throw rock at me." With an expression of vast melancholy he indicated a spot on his shoulder. Rowan made sympathetic noises. She could easily imagine the Outskirter's reaction on waking to find a strange creature on her bed.

She rose and rummaged through a wardrobe until she found a clean shirt that fit her, then added her trousers. The wood gnome watched, rocking on his perch, long toes gripping the bedstead as easily as if they were fingers. He munched his apple. "Time for breakfast, hurry," he advised.

"I go to find fur-woman first."

He eyed her sadly. "Watch out for rocks."

At the door, Rowan paused. Slanting beams of light from the high, small windows fragmented the corridor into shapes and angles of alternating light and dark. If Bel was wandering out of curiosity, in which direction would she go? Right led to more residences – another transients' dormitory and the permanent quarters. Rowan guessed that if Bel found that those were private rooms, she would double back. The steerswoman went to the left, retracing the path they had taken the previous night; around a corner, then up again to the gallery. Bel might sensibly have done the same, to impress a known route on her memory in a strange place.

The gallery led her back to the entrance hall. A quick check of the stables downstairs showed them to be deserted. Rowan climbed the narrow stairs up to a lookout room above the entrance: empty, the dusty close air cool and motionless, windows still shuttered against the previous night's rain.

She descended and entered the informal hall on the left. A series of great double doors filled the wall on the right. When open, they communicated on a cool stone courtyard. They were closed now, and the high-ceilinged room stood in darkness but for the far end, where a door stood open to the next chamber; a rectangle of light, where faint voices could be heard.

Crossing to it, she entered the map room. The room was tall and long, slanting at an angle away from the entrance where she stood. Cool, clean air circulated freely through the tall open windows. Morning sunlight fell on the three ranks of long tables, whose surfaces tilted up to take advantage of the illumination.

On two walls, between the windows, the stones had been plastered, then papered and transformed into huge maps. One was a rough working chart, drawn as accurately as current information permitted, but hastily, with much amendment and many hand-scrawled notes. The opposite wall was currently blank, freshly papered; it served as an alternate when the first needed to be redrawn more concisely. Usage switched between the two with predictable regularity.

But it was the great master chart at the far end of the room that drew Rowan. Her eyes went to it as she approached, passing between the worktables.

The map ran from floor to ceiling. The wall there was curved concave, so that a person standing at a certain point could see all the map's expanse without the distortion of visual foreshortening. The point of best vantage was outlined on the stone floor in a brass rectangle.

The floor was slightly raised in the area before the master chart. Rowan climbed the three steps and moved to the rectangle.

In a single glance, she saw the areas of change: positions corrected, details where none had been before. For a moment she felt an internal shift, as if she were on a deck that tilted to a wave too small to change her direction but large enough to alter her perspective.

"What do you see?"

She turned. Below her was a woman twice her age, dark-haired, dark-skinned, blue-eyed. Keridwen, the chartmistress.

Rowan laughed happily. "I see lakes in the mountains. A stream runs from one – that contributes to the Wulf. Another fjord south of The Crags."

"And three new towns on the Shore Road." Keridwen climbed the steps. "You're not due back until next year, Rowan. Is there trouble?"

"Perhaps," she replied. "But I've found something. I need to talk to the Prime."

"She heard you were in. Someone was sent to wake you."

"I woke before she arrived. Or perhaps I missed her in the corridors. Unless it was a wood gnome that was sent?"

Keridwen laughed. "They returned early this year. A very mild winter."

"Not where I was traveling." Her mind returned to Bel. "But I'm looking for a friend of mine, who woke before me."

"I've seen no strangers today. Perhaps she found the kitchen and breakfast?"

"Or upstairs?" There was a high, bright chamber above the map room, used in fair weather to copy charts for storage.

"I came from there."

"I'd better continue, then. She may find this place . . . strange."

Rowan left by the door opposite to the one she entered. It gave onto a short passage whose right wall held tall doors. She swung them open and looked out; the courtyard revealed was empty.

Rowan found herself pausing, struck by a feeling that had been growing, unnoticed, in her. She stepped into the courtyard and then realized: it was familiarity. She felt like a person returning to a place of her childhood, finding it familiar yet strangely altered. But the place was the same, and some subtle change was in herself.

It had been well over three years since last she had been at the Archives. She had traveled long and mostly alone, over lands unknown to her when she met them, then well known to her through scrupulous observation. Her logbooks had returned to the Archives by other hands, and news of the place had reached her through the words of others. And yet, across that distance, she knew where every room lay, knew the names of all who dwelt there. She could walk into the Greater Library and place her hand immediately on the shelf where her own writings were stored.

This small courtyard had been a particular favorite of hers. It was cool even in high summer, and always sheltered on windy days. She remembered bringing old logbooks there to study, and reading them with fascination; then, sensing a presence behind her, turning to see the smiling wrinkled race of the very steerswoman who wrote them. She remembered an evening celebration not long after the arrival of herself and her fellow trainees from Wulfshaven; nine of them gathered in the courtyard, Janus playing flute, herself talentlessly struggling with a mandolin, Ingrud plying her squeeze-box with gusto; others laughing and conversing, sound echoing off the ancient walls . . .

On an adjacent side another door opened, then another, and the passage on that wall was transformed into a veranda on the courtyard. A woman peered at her, then approached: Berry, tall and dark-haired, recognizing her nearsightedly. "Rowan, is it? The Prime is looking for you."

Rowan smiled at her. "Fine greeting. You're looking well. Yes, I want to see her too, but first, have you noticed an Outskirter going by, or perhaps in the libraries?"

"An Outskirter? What, a shaggy barbarian here?"

"Not too shaggy; she's a woman. Well, shaggy perhaps, if you consider her clothes. But you haven't noticed her, then."

"Hardly! Is she dangerous?"

Rowan considered. "Under certain circumstances."

She left by the doors Berry had opened and looked down the passages. The one on the right led to the Prime's study and residence. After a moment's consideration, Rowan went left.

She passed a study and paused to check inside. Two women and a stocky man of middle age were gathered around a worktable. Graphs, some of startling configuration, were pinned up haphazardly around the walls of the room.

Rowan made to leave, but the man caught sight of her.

"Rowan! You're back before your time. Come take a look at this."

"I'm sorry, Arian, I'm looking for a friend who may be lost in the passages." But she found herself intrigued and stepped inside. "Are you making progress?"

"None to speak of. Still, surprises keep coming up." One of the steerswomen with him looked up suddenly, as if remembering something. "Henra is looking for you," she told Rowan.

"Yes, I've been told." But she suddenly recalled the calculations she had made on the road to Donner. "Wait, I have something." She came to the table and found a blank sheet of parchment. "Look at this." Sketching quickly, she briefly explained the problem of the dispersal of the jewels.

Arian tapped the rough chart. "With an area that wide, your imaginary giant would have to stand very far back."

"And be very tall indeed," one of the steerswomen noted.

Rowan laid a straightedge across the scales, indicated a number.

"That's too tall," Arian said.

The other steerswomen spoke up. "The ground would never support him, do you see?" "He'd sink in." "He couldn't eat enough to live."

Rowan was annoyed at the digression. "It needn't be a giant, a tower will do. It's a giant for the purposes of the problem." She turned back to the chart. "So. He stands this far away, he's this tall, and throws parallel to the ground. The area his throw covers, assuming, shall we say, twenty objects in his hand . . ." She read off two numbers from the right-hand scale and made a simple calculation.

Arian looked at the result. "Straightforward enough."

Rowan held up an index finger. "But." Turning over the sheet, she redrew the chart with greater precision – and with its elements at slightly different aspect to each other. "He throws again, this time—" She paused significantly. "Angling upward." She handed the straightedge to the steersman.

He laid it on the chart. "The area covered . . ." He looked up. "But the path doesn't intersect with the ground."

"Look at the time it takes to fall."

The straightedge swept across the scales. "Infinite?"

"Look again."

A shift. "Zero?"

"The objects never come down."

He leaned back. "That's impossible. They have to come down."

"Of course it's impossible," Rowan said. "Of course they have to come down. Do you see? I've found a situation where our usual methods fail."

Squinting in thought, Arian studied. "No," he said at last. "It's not the method that's at fault. It's the problem. You've set up an impossible situation."

"We don't know that."

"Impossible giants—"

"Or very possible towers!"

The second steerswoman spoke again. "Be hard to build a tower that high."

Rowan threw up her hands. "But we're not concerned with the difficulty here—"

"You can't ignore crucial elements," Arian put in.

"That's hardly crucial—"

"There is obviously," he stated carefully, "something wrong with the problem. We know that the techniques work, but we're getting an impossible answer. It can't be our method that's at fault, so it must be the problem itself."

Rowan drew back. "Arian, that is backward reasoning, and you know it well. You mustn't deny information simply because it differs from what you expect. You're not thinking like a steersman—"

He interrupted, his voice stony. "Rowan, I do not need your instruction in how to think like a steersman."

She stopped short, curbed her temper, then began again. "We know that the approaches handed down to us always seem to work, but we can't always see why—"

"Exactly what I've been working on these years, with my 'backward reasoning'—"

"But there may be different ways to look at it. You've been working from the inside out; but if we can—" She sought analogy. "If we can map the edges we may be better able to see the whole. We may be able to work from the outside in."

The other steerswomen exchanged a glance. One shook her head minutely, but the other tilted her head in Rowan's direction. She obviously agreed but was unwilling to enter the argument.

Rowan prepared to speak again but was interrupted by an arrival at the door. "Rowan? Do you know the Prime is waiting for you?"

She grit her teeth, unwilling to leave battle. "Arian, you must excuse me," she said. She exited with exaggerated dignity.

As she turned toward the Prime's offices, the messenger tapped her shoulder, then pointed in the opposite direction "The garden," the woman corrected, then disappeared on further errands.

When Rowan arrived at the herb garden, the fact of the season's change asserted itself, the blooms of late spring already giving way to those of early summer. A tall patch of knapweed raised shaggy purple heads by the door; the rosemary beside it was past flowering.

In the distance Rowan heard not conversation but music. Surprised, she threaded her way on the flagstone paths to the garden's center.

There stood, among the plots of herbs and flowers, four pear trees, set each in a corner of a patch of marigold. The path between was widened there and curved. At the intersection of the crossing paths stood two low stone benches.

Henra, the Prime, sat on one. Beside her sat Bel the barbarian. They were singing together.

Rowan approached slowly, fascinated.

They were singing an ancient song about a knight lost in a magic forest. Both sang the melody, though Bel added an occasional ornate turn that pleasantly countered Henra's steady note. They reached a point where their words and melody diverged. The Prime interrupted, saying, "I learned that part differently. Teach me how you know it." Bel sang on alone. Her voice was strong and mobile, not deep, but with a husky dark edge to the tone.

Henra then sang her version in a voice clear and pure as fresh water. When she reached a familiar section, Bel joined her again, eyes closed, head tilted back.

As Rowan reached the benches, the song ended. Bel opened her eyes and spotted something among the branches of the pear tree. "Ha! There's one of them!" She leaped up, then scrabbled among the loose stones by the walk. Above her, a wood gnome began flinging down poorly aimed bits of twig, hooting and jeering.

Rowan restrained her. "There's no need to worry. They're harmless."

"Harmless, ha! Look at those teeth!" These the gnome bared yellowly.

Henra was signaling up to him. "Stop, stop. Woman not hurt you. You come down now."

"No. Bad woman, dirty." He spoke in broad emphatic gestures, then hugged himself to a branch, rocking.

"This woman my friend," the Prime told him, but he shrieked fury. The sound attracted the attention of another gnome, who abandoned his inspection of the rain gutter to investigate.

"The gnomes are friendly," Rowan told Bel, but the Outskirter shouted "Ha!" and struggled to aim her stone. A steerswoman on the other side of the garden noticed the ruckus and began to approach.

Henra caught one of the gnome's hands and shook her index finger in his face admonishingly. Rowan clutched at Bel's throwing arm and stepped in front of her, blocking her aim. Outskirter and wood gnome uttered near-identical sounds of frustration.

Abruptly, Rowan and the Prime stopped and looked at each other. Henra began laughing, then Rowan joined her. "I think we're doing similar jobs," Rowan noted. They released their respective charges and helplessly dropped to the bench.

Bel glowered down at them. The gnome leaped to the ground and escaped.

Wiping tears from her eyes, Henra leaned back at last and examined Rowan. The Prime was a small woman, shorter than Bel, and fine-boned and delicate. She had a grace and presence beyond her size, and Rowan, at average height, had always felt huge and clumsy beside her. She seemed half-magical, like an elf out of song, with angular features and long green eyes. Her face was a lined map of wisdom, but age had neither grayed nor grizzled her waist-length hair. Instead, it was laced with silver; no longer plain brown, it was the exact color of smooth sunlit water pouring over dark earth.

"Your friend has mentioned that you've had some trouble," Henra said.

Rowan's mirth faded. "That's right. It's going to take some explaining."

The Prime considered, assessing Rowan's demeanor. She turned to Bel. "If you cross the garden to those doors," she said, indicating them, "you'll find yourself in the dining hall. There are some at breakfast already, and others will be along soon enough. "She smiled. "I think you'll find the company enjoyable."

Rowan followed the Prime back into the cool corridors to her office. Inside Henra seated herself in a massive armchair by the cold hearth. From a stool beside her she picked up a blue knitted lap robe; so deep in the Archives, in the central room, the stone walls were an effective barrier against the warmth of day. Wrapping the robe around her legs, she gestured for Rowan to take the chair on the opposite side of the low wooden table before her.

Rowan went to the chair but did not sit. She felt as if she needed to move. She wanted to pace; she wanted to stride to some open window and view the forested land rolling to the horizon. She wanted her charts, her book, her pen and calipers in her hand – but they were gone.

She saw that the Prime had noticed their absence and was waiting for her to speak. Rowan shifted her weight back and forth. "I was attacked on the road to Donner," she said at last.

Henra tilted her head. "One of the hazards of traveling." She still waited; an unlucky encounter on the road was not, in itself, enough to send a steerswoman back to the Archives.

"It was a wizard's man," Rowan said. Suddenly she felt she could sit, and she did.

Henra leaned back slowly. Her emerald gaze flickered as she sifted possibilities and implications, then fell on Rowan. "The one thing we do not need is the active enmity of a wizard. We take pains not to cross them." Rowan knew that well. It had been stressed in her training, passed on to her, along with an unexpressed, slow-burning anger against the wizards' secretiveness, their refusal to impart information.

Rowan shook her head. "I had no idea I was working on anything to interest a wizard." She pulled out the little leather sack, opened it, and removed the glittering fragment. "I was investigating this." She passed it to the Prime.

Henra studied it, turning it over in her hand, and Rowan began to speak. She described its history, detailed her findings, and gave her justifications for straying from her assigned route. Maps were brought out, and with them spread out on the low table, Rowan sketched the pattern of dispersal, that narrow oval that stretched from the eastern curve of the Long North Road into the heart of the Outskirts. She reconstructed the graph she had made during her conversation with Bel on the road to Donner, and described Arian's indignation at her speculations.

The Prime considered the information, questioning her carefully. At some point a tray of tea was brought in, along with rolls and honey. At some other point, the remains were removed. Lost in the exchange of information, Rowan did not notice the intrusion until Henra graciously thanked the woman, who smiled and exited wordlessly.

At last Henra leaned back in her chair. "And at no point did you encounter any wizard? Or any person known to work with a wizard?"

Rowan examined her memory again, wishing she had her logbook. "Not to my knowledge, not until Five Corners. And those men never spoke to me. Nor asked about me, as far as I know. I think someone would have mentioned it if they did."

"Which means," Henra said carefully, "that they already knew all they needed."

"Exactly."

"Then they know more than we do."

"That's not all." Rowan recounted the dragon attack on the inn in Donner, and Corvus's surprising knowledge of the event. She added Artos's conviction that she was in danger even in Wulfshaven. Artos, and his skill in warfare, were known to the Prime.

Finally Henra sighed. "The obvious solution is to abandon this investigation," she began.

"No!"

The Prime glanced at Rowan, then smiled. "That doesn't suit you."

"We've never been a threat to any wizard. I can't believe this jewel can be that important. It doesn't do anything, not that I've seen."

"Perhaps you haven't seen all there is to see."

"We can't let them limit us!" Rowan was on her feet, pacing. "Isn't it enough that they won't share their knowledge with us?"

"Their secrecy is their strength," Henra reminded her. "If everyone had access to their knowledge, the folk and the wizards would be equal. And if we had that knowledge, it would be free for the asking."

Rowan stopped short. "Then this must have something to do with their power."

"Possibly." Henra turned the jewel over in her hands; it caught the light from a high-set window and flashed, once. "Or, they may see that the course of investigating the jewels will lead you to other avenues, that may in turn lead you to their secrets." She handed the blue shard back to Rowan, carefully folded her lap robe, and rose. "This is a large decision. Let's join the others."

Rowan watched her across to the door. "Do you know what we're going to do?"

Henra turned back to her. "I know what we have to do. I don't know that we will do it."

Rowan and the Prime found most of the Archives' inhabitants lingering over bits of breakfast in a hall whose tall windows looked out to the garden on the one side, to a sweep of woody hills on the other. Bel was seated near the head of the table, and eager questioners on all sides were taking the opportunity to ply her with queries about her exotic background and the customs of the distant Outskirts. The steerswoman at the head shifted her seat in favor of the Prime, and Rowan found a chair on her right, across from Bel.

"There's our wayward child," an elderly woman beside Rowan greeted her affectionately. "It's good to see a young face again."

Bel took in the comment, then looked around the table. "Are there no other steerswomen Rowan's age?"

"Steerswomen begin by traveling," Rowan replied. "The largest part of our work is done on the road and the sea, observing and learning. Most steerswomen travel all their lives."

"Until they get too old," Keridwen put in, from the end of the table.

"Or," Arian added, "until they find some particular area of study which no longer depends on constant fact-gathering."

Bel's glance went to his ring. "You're a steerswoman?"

"Steersman," he corrected. "Yes, there are a few."

"It's not forbidden?"

Several laughed, and Arian snorted derisively. "Most men seem to be satisfied to live by their muscles. Well," he admitted, "to be fair, most men learn to live by their strength early on, and never lose the habit."

"Very few men apply when the Academy is held," Rowan added. "And few of those complete the training. Those who do, manage quite as well as the women. In fact," she said with a nod to Arian, "at present we have more steersmen than ever in our history. Three."

Someone shifted uncomfortably. Rowan looked around the table. "What is it?"

The steerswoman beside her placed a hand on her arm. "Possibly only two, dear. We've lost track of Janus."

"Last year we heard of a ship lost at sea," Henra added, "sailing from Donner to Southport." Southport, Rowan knew, had been on Janus's planned route.

"Was he on it?" Rowan asked.

"We don't know."

Rowan digested the information, then found Bel watching her. "It happens," Rowan explained.

Bel turned to Josef, seated two spaces to her left. "Are you the third steersman?"

He put his hands in protest. "No, not me! A simple groom, beast-tender. Wouldn't be here at all but for the love of my life." He made a nimble snatch at Berry as she passed with a pitcher of water.

Berry made an equally nimble dodge. "As you can tell, my husband learns his manners from the beasts, as well." But she smiled.

"But you're Rowan's age. Shouldn't you be traveling?"

Berry placed a pitcher of water carefully on the table and took her seat next to Josef. "I'm going blind," she explained matter-of-factly.

Bel was appalled. "How awful! But can you still be a steerswoman, blind?"

"If there's a way, we'll discover it," Henra said.

"Work of the mind, that's what you want," Arian advised. "Some huge, rare, imaginative problem."

Berry nodded at him with suppressed amusement. "That's a good idea. Perhaps I'll join you in your math—"

"Skies, no, girl, you're not good enough – *oof*." The elderly steerswoman next to Arian had elbowed him mightily in the ribs. "But it's true."

"Of course it's true," the woman said. "But you needn't beat her with it. She has other strengths."

Henra looked around the table, then spoke to Keridwen. "Where's Hugo?"

"Still in his room, I believe. On chill mornings, he's likely to stay there until noon."

"Tell him to come here, please."

Keridwen hurried off, and the Prime helped herself to another biscuit.

"Hugo has made a study of the wizards," Rowan explained to Bel.

Keridwen returned presently with a frail elderly man, who leaned both on her shoulder and on a walking stick as he approached. He viewed the assemblage. "What's this? A meal at this hour?" He squinted his watery blue eyes at the sky. "Don't tell me it's morning!"

Henra's smile was affectionate. "Come sit by me. I need your advice."

Rowan vacated her chair and pulled another close beside Bel. Hugo lowered himself down carefully. "Ah, now, lady, you don't fool me for a moment. It's my manly companionship you're after, admit it. And more than mere companionship, isn't it true?"

The Prime laughed lightheartedly and spoke as if reciting the lines of a familiar jest. "Now, Hugo, what can you mean? You know you're far too old for me."

"Oh, so you say now! But the gap shrinks, they tell me, as you grow older. A few years from now you'll join me by the fireside, and we'll toast our toes together, and dream of things we might have done. And do a few of them, as well."

Rowan took in Bel's astonished expression, recognizing her surprise as the same that she herself had felt when first seeing the steerswomen behave so informally with each other. She leaned toward the

Outskirter. "We're not an aristocracy," Rowan explained quietly, "and we're not an army, or a religion, either. Whatever doesn't affect our work, doesn't matter."

As if to illustrate the point, Henra made one small gesture, and the table fell instantly to attentive silence. Hugo sat the slightest bit taller, and the wry humor slipped from his face, replaced by the intelligent, waiting expression of the perfect steersman.

Henra spoke to the group. "Rowan was attacked by a wizard's man."

Every face turned to Rowan. In a visible rapid wave, their shock turned to seriousness, and they waited, silently, for more information. Only Josef made a sign; his fist slammed on the table, once. No one looked at him.

Henra continued. "It was one day's travel south of Five Corners."

The elderly woman next to Arian spoke, "You're certain he was a wizard's man?"

"At the inn I saw five Red soldiers. I recognized him as one of that five," Rowan replied. The woman nodded. No one questioned Rowan's ability to recognize the face of a man seen once in passing, as part of a crowd.

Henra turned to Hugo. "Which wizard controls that area?"

He sat quietly a moment, rheumy blue eyes flicking at the action of his thoughts. "That's difficult to say, lady. Olin, north and east of Five Corners, he's Red these days. Or was, as of winter. Five Corners, that's at the limit of his area, as clear as these things can be made out."

Rowan spoke up. "No one seemed surprised to see wizard's men in the tavern."

"With the recent clash, there must be a lot, traveling to their homes. Five Corners is a likely stop for any of Olin's men, returning."

"I didn't know he kept soldiers."

"Ah, yes, well, neither did I, until he sent troops against Corvus and Abremio. It means he must have a keep somewhere, and we've been assuming he didn't."

"Don't all wizards have keeps?" Bel asked.

"No, not at all. Jannik, for instance. All he has is his house in Donner. Mind you, no one's ever been inside." He rubbed his nose thoughtfully. "Now, Olin, he's always been especially confusing. Seen rarely, never in the same place twice, always alone. Often the only way to know he's there is by the sudden appearance of some magical event."

Henra leaned forward, intent. "Might Five Corners be his, these days?"

"Hard to tell. His boundaries have always been especially vague. It's not Jannik's; it might be no one's, or Shammer and Dhree's."

Rowan remembered Artos's complaints. "The new Red holding?"

"Right. They're two, working together as one; I don't understand the arrangement. They're Red." He turned to Henra. "They're the culprits, I believe, or somehow wrapped up in this. I don't know that Five Corners is theirs, but it's possible, and they're the only new variable in the equation." Hugo addressed himself to Bel. "Understand, the wizards and the Steerswomen don't like each other, but there hasn't been violence between us for centuries. We can't get rid of each other, so we tolerate each other. But now a steerswoman has been attacked by a wizard's man—Rowan, could he have been acting on his own?"

Rowan thought briefly, checking over her conclusions. "No. There were five wizard's men at the inn; there are five roads away from the inn. They left before Bel and I did; whatever road we took, we would met one. This was planned."

Berry looked around, as if searching the faces she could not clearly see. "There are other steerswomen traveling in Shammer and Dhree's holding. Why was Rowan attacked, and no one else?"

Henra nodded to Rowan. With all eyes on her, Rowan pulled out the little leather sack, lifted its string over her head, and opened it. "Here's the other new variable in the equation," Henra said.

Hugo took the jewel and scrutinized it while the Prime recounted Rowan's story with perfect accuracy.

"Wizard's make, for certain," he said when she finished. He turned it over in his hands again. "I can't think of any jeweler's process that could do this. Sarah—" He passed the jewel down across the table to the elderly steerswoman on Arian's left.

She peered at it closely. "It's built in layers – the silver-colored backing, then the gem. The lines are etched, so that the metal lies both on the surface and into it." She scraped the edge of the fragment with one fingernail. "The last surface is like very thin glass, but no glass can be made that thin. Strange texture . . ." She passed it diagonally.

The next woman was pale and delicately beautiful, the only sign of her age the silver glittering in her ebony hair. She looked at the jewel carefully, then closed her eyes, rubbing her thumb across the smooth surface. "Oily . . ." she looked at it again. "It's made of oil, somehow, or has oil in it. If fine olive oil were perfectly clear, and somehow made solid, it might be like this."

Sarah took the jewel again, cleared a space in the center of the table, and placed it there, standing to get a better vantage. The other steerswomen shifted and leaned closer. "That's a good point. You can't polish anything to this smoothness. I believe that the top surface was poured on as a liquid, then solidified, somehow."

"Magically," Bel put in confidently.

"Perhaps," Sarah admitted.

The Prime spoke to Bel. "May we see your belt?"

The Outskirter stood to remove it, and it was passed around.

"They were all found in the same place, far in the Outskirts," Rowan explained. "It's the largest concentration I've heard about; I think something could be learned by going there, to see."

"With a wizard on your trail," Berry observed. Josef winced.

"One or more." Every face turned to Hugo. "Think for a moment about Jannik. His control over the dragons isn't complete, but it's almost so. Could another wizard send a spell to break it? Sometimes one or two nestlings can escape and cause trouble, especially the tiniest ones. But Saranna's Inn was – where, the center of town?"

"Not far from the harbor," Rowan said. "Tilemaker's Street."

"And the mud flats are at the edge of town. That's seven miles they had to travel, through the streets – no, isn't there a shallow gully that runs near Tilemaker's Street?"

"That's right."

"And how many dragons were there?"

Rowan counted. "Seven, that I saw myself. More outside, which I didn't see. Someone reported fifty, but the layman's eyes can fool him, in emergencies. At a guess, at least twenty-five, total."

Hugo shook his head fractionally. "I don't believe that can happen."

Bel looked around the now-silent table. "Then Jannik was in on it. Rowan guessed."

"I saw it was a possibility," Rowan said.

Hugo was deep in thought. "Two wizards, cooperating across a line of mutual hatred . . ."

"We need to decide what to do," Henra said.

Arian was surprised. "Decide? One decides when one has options. Where are there options here?"

"Are there none?" She concentrated on Arian. "Very well, what do you see happening next?"

"Rowan continues her investigations. She'll have to be very alert, if she's attracted the wizards' attentions . . ." He trailed off. "But if they're determined, they'll get her eventually."

"Then we must make this move more quickly," Sarah put in. "If we *all* work on it, and if we send more out word to those on the road—"

Berry interrupted. "Then we each become the same threat that Rowan is. And, collectively, the entire order of Steerswomen becomes a threat."

"But if we work fast enough—"

"How fast is fast enough?" Keridwen challenged. "It can't be done instantaneously."

Watching the Prime, Rowan realized that Henra saw an answer, but was patiently waiting for the rest of the steerswomen to duplicate her reasoning; she wanted the chain of thought to be clear in their minds, wanted it to be each person's own possession.

"What is the most basic statement of the problem?" Rowan asked, half to herself, musing.

That was an often repeated phrase in the early education of a steerswoman-in-training, and conversation stopped in surprise at Rowan's presenting it to steerswomen of such advanced experience. But Berry, not many years from her own traineeship, caught the mood. "Investigating the jewels is dangerous."

Henra encouraged them. "Two options, on this level."

"Work in danger," Rowan said, "or abandon the investigation."

Response was immediate, from several corners. "We mustn't abandon it." "We have to learn all we can." "We can't let the wizards rule us." "No one controls us."

The Prime nodded. "That choice is rejected. We work in danger. The options are two . . ."

Keridwen considered. "Accept danger, or change the situation . . ."

"Accepting the danger is accepting death – and incidentally, an end to any investigating," someone noted.

"The first choice is rejected. How can we change the situation?" Henra prompted.

"Find the source of the danger and counter it," another steerswoman offered.

"The source of the danger is the wizards," Hugo noted. "We can't counter them."

"No," Rowan realized. "The source is their knowledge of our actions."

There was a silence. Bel looked around the table in perplexity. Annoyed, she said, "It's obvious. You have to work in secret. Why is that so hard to see?"

"Because it is so hard to accept," Henra replied.

"It is absolutely opposite to everything we do and believe in," Hugo expanded.

She would have to deny information, Rowan realized. She would have to refuse questions, or – worse yet – give false answers.

Henra surveyed every face around the table, then spoke carefully. "Rowan would have to travel to the Outskirts under an assumed identity. No one must know who she is, what she seeks, or that she's a steerswoman."

No one spoke, and Bel looked at them in confusion. "But what's the problem?"

Abruptly, Rowan said, "I won't do it." Faces turned to her. "Lady, I understand, truly I do," she continued, half pleading, "but I can't agree. There must be some other way. To lie, to walk the earth *lying* . . . Humankind needs truth. We all know that; we need it like air and water and food, to survive, to function in the world . . . I'd be like a poison, twisting things every where I went, *hurting* people." She laid her hands against her cheeks and shook her head. "No."

Henra took it all in, considering. "Arian? Would you do it?"

"Me?" He looked up, surprised. "Well, I don't like the whole idea, but I do think it's the best solution. And someone has to do it." Then he smiled. "Oh, you're clever, Henra. Most of the folk don't even know there are steersmen among the steerswomen. I'd never be suspected. But when it comes down to the actual doing of the thing . . ." He thought. "I feel much as Rowan does. I think it would . . . pain me. And my work here . . ." He sighed. "Try to find someone else. Please, exhaust every possibility, and if you find no one, then yes."

Henra nodded, then looked to her left. "Berry?"

She was startled. "What?"

"Would you do it?"

She stared around in stunned disbelief. "Me?" Then, slowly, she said, "Yes . . . yes, send me." She spoke to Henra, her voice urgent. "I'll do it. I'll do anything. I'll lie a thousand times. I'll steal if you ask it. Anything! Please, send me . . ." She gazed up into the sky, her dim eyes bright with tears. "On the road, one last time . . ."

"She's blind," Sarah protested.

Berry turned on her. "I'm not blind, not yet! I can see shapes and colors. I won't walk into a tree; I won't fall off the edge of the road." She addressed them all. "And I know those roads, and I can read a map, held close."

"But she can't observe," Arian said. "And she couldn't spot, say, a jewel imbedded in a cliff. In new territory she could get lost."

The Prime said nothing; she was looking at Josef.

He nodded slowly, then turned to his wife, taking both her hands. "When the time comes for eyes, you'll have mine."

"You'd go with me?"

"No." He laughed a little. "I'd *stay* with you, wherever in the world you may be. You and me, we'll walk under the stars together."

She touched his face and moved close to study his expression. Then she leaned her bowed head against his shoulder.

Josef's eyes met Henra's, and his face was full of calm entreaty.

Henra spoke. "Josef is not a steersman, but with Berry to interpret what he saw, something could be learned. Perhaps not enough, but something. And no one would guess that she was a steerswoman.

"Rowan."

Rowan turned to the Prime.

"You're still the best choice," Henra said. "You're familiar with the jewels, you're highly observant, flexible and imaginative in thought. We would learn the most, if you were the one to go." She held up her hand. "I understand your disagreement. But I want you to consider this: it will be done. Won't you help us do it the best way we can?"

The Prime stood. "Don't answer. Please think. We'll all speak again this evening." The chairs shuffled, and the steerswomen dispersed one by one, until there was only Bel, watching Rowan, and Rowan, silently watching Josef whispering gentle words to Berry.

At last Rowan rose and walked away.

CHAPTER
Ten

"I don't see what the problem is."

They were walking down the winding dirt path that led from the Archives to the riverside below. Oak trees surrounded them, gnarled roots invading the edges of the path.

"Don't you want to find out about these jewels?" Bel continued.

"Yes. But I'm just not willing to lie."

Bel snapped a twig she was carrying and tossed the pieces into the underbrush. "I don't understand you. You were willing to learn about them, even if it put you in danger. But you won't do a simple thing like lying."

Rowan felt a return of the sudden, sharp need that had sent her out of the stone walls of the Archives, a need for a sweep of air that knew no obstructions, for the unbounded sky above her. She walked a little faster, to escape the net of tree branches overhead. "It's not such a simple thing." Of its own accord, a part of her began trying to formulate an explanation, a calm steerswoman's explanation; but the part of her that held the information for that answer was churning with confused emotion.

"Ever since I became a steerswoman – no," she stopped, surprised. "Ever since I was a child . . ." Her voice trailed off, her mind sifting through memories like hands sifting through chaff, seeking a single grain of wheat.

When had it happened, when had she learned to care what was true and what was not? Children lied, they all did, and ranks of casual lies crowded into her thoughts. No, I didn't drop the eggs. No, I didn't tell Father. Yes, I finished all my work.

One single lie stood in high relief, not a great lie, but one that had lasted long into her adolescence. Periodically, she would leave the house and fields, taking some small bit of food, and make the long trek to the farthest of the funeral groves, the last bit of green before the desert took true possession of the land. She would explain that she was going to visit her uncle's tree, and the family would say quietly to each other, "Poor Rowan, his death affected her so badly." But it was not true. She went from a need to see something other than the house, the yard, that dusty path leading to the town of Umber. She knew everything in her world, knew it too well, and there was nothing more that her mind or heart could do with it.

But north . . . Past the groves, there was land no hands had touched. Raw earth, lacking only water, fertilization, and seed. It waited there, waited out the centuries for the slow spread of humankind. It was emptiness to the limits of the sky. At last that view, too, became familiar, but she still returned, without clearly knowing why.

She needed to see different things, change in the land and in the faces of people. But there was a stronger need, one she discovered the day that Keridwen had come to Umber in her own travels. Rowan discovered that the steerswoman *knew* things, and speaking to her, she realized that there was another landscape, one to be traveled endlessly, the limits of which she could never exhaust.

So Rowan and Keridwen had sat together late into the night, Rowan asking first about places, then about people, then about the ideas of people, then about the idea of ideas . . . And Keridwen's answers had grown richer and deeper, as her expression changed from indulgence, to surprise, to interest.

Sometime near midnight Rowan had realized that the aspect of the discussion had changed to that of a conversation between equals; not equals of knowledge or of experience, but of method of thought. They shared a perspective, a deeply rooted way of approaching life. The night ended with Keridwen telling her of the Academy to take place in Wulfshaven some four years from that time. Rowan spent those four years learning to read and write, to do sums, and scrupulously attempting to chart the land she knew, in the hopes of gaining some skill for her training to come.

She had spent her life alone in her strangeness, and had met only one other person like herself. When she joined the Academy, she was like an exile who had returned home.

Looking around, Rowan discovered that she and Bel had arrived at the riverbank and were seated on a rotting log near its edge. The Wulf spread out before them, flat and serene. A thin haze of clouds was moving in from the west, and high above, a mere dark speck, a hawk hung motionless.

"Truth," Rowan said to herself, then turned to Bel. The Outskirter was watching her with concern. She had not intruded on Rowan's thoughts, but was carefully waiting, with true warrior's patience. She knew that Rowan had to follow her own path to her own answers, and that the answers, once found, would be shared.

"If you're traveling down a road, and you ask for directions, and someone lies about them, what happens?" Rowan asked.

"You get lost."

"If you want to know when to plant your fields, and someone lies, what happens?"

"You go hungry."

"If there's a troop of bandits coming, and no one tells you?"

"You die."

"People *need* truth! They need it to be happy, to know what to do, to *live!*" Rowan rose. A single step took her to the water, and she stood with her gray boots mere inches away from the tiny lapping waves as she gazed out at the line of trees on the opposite shore.

"What you say is too simple," Bel said. "Some things are less important than others."

Rowan looked up at the clouding sky, where the motionless hawk still hung. She saw with the whole of her vision equally, and her hearing brought her what her eyes could not see, the shape of space behind her. Lightly moving wind brushed her

120

arms, and damp air floated up from the river before her, against her face and body. She sensed the crushed weeds that lay under the soles of her boots, and the solid earth beneath. She felt the weight of her own body, muscle and bone, connecting her to that earth, the limits of her skin defining the space she occupied. Simultaneous, interlocking, all senses added up in her being to a single perception, a single clear instant. The whole of her surroundings came to her in one perfect moment, all of it real, and all of it true.

"They're going to take it all away," she said.

Bel said nothing.

Some wizard was changing the nature of Rowan's existence. She could either accept an arbitrary limit to her mind's reach, and so be less than a steerswoman, or deceive, and so be no steerswoman at all.

She loved it too much. Less was better than none.

Abruptly, inconsistency caught at her mind: the hawk – it had not moved.

Rowan began to analyze what her senses had brought her. The breeze was from the southwest. Would it be different higher up? There should be a downdraft of cooler air over the river; a hawk would have to beat and circle to maintain the same perspective. The forest was alive with small game; a hawk would have found prey by then.

"Get back," she told Bel, and quickly moved away from the river's edge.

They stopped among the trees, Rowan trying to see the speck through the new green leaves above. Bel had no sword, but a wicked knife had appeared in her hand. "What is it?"

Rowan spotted it. "We're being watched. Or the Archives are."

"By a wizard?"

"Who else can fly?"

Bel peered up. "Will he attack?"

"I don't know. It hasn't moved. Perhaps we weren't seen, or weren't recognized."

Bel nodded. "Then it's watching the Archives. We should tell them."

"Yes. Let's keep off the path." Rowan led the way through the forest, accurately cutting around the twists of the dirt track, first walking, then running.

They entered by way of the stables, breathless from the climb. Inside, Josef was currying Artos's horse, Berry seated on a barrel nearby.

Rowan stopped, trying to calm her breathing. "Berry," she said. "Berry, I'm sorry, I'm going to do it."

Berry and Josef exchanged a glance; then he silently went back to his work. Berry rose. "What made you change your mind?"

"The Archives are being watched. By something that flies."

"It's not just me, anymore," Rowan told the resident steerswomen. They were assembled in the chart room, eight women and two men, some in chairs, some seated casually on the edges of the sturdy copying tables, one standing by the window, occasionally scanning the sky. To one side of the room, Josef and Bel stood watching the proceedings.

"I was thinking about my own life," Rowan continued. "I love the steerswoman's life, and I wasn't willing to change it. But first this restriction, and now this . . . spying . . ." She was standing before the three steps that led to the master chart. She spread her hands in a broad gesture. "How long before we become so changed that none of us are steerswomen anymore? The whole way of life is threatened, for every one of us. I . . ." She paused, shaping her thoughts. "I can't stand for it. I have to try to stop it, whatever it may take. Or at the very least, I have to know why."

Sarah smiled with a teacher's pride. "Spoken like a steerswoman: she has to know why."

There were quiet comments around the room as they consulted each other briefly. Suddenly weary, Rowan sat down on the lowest step and watched them, waiting.

Henra stood and addressed the gathering. "This is no small thing. We all will have a hand in this, I'm afraid, and if someone asks, it would be best if we could refrain from revealing Rowan's mission . . ." She trailed off, uncharacteristically hesitant. Rowan recognized on the Prime's face the same confused pain Rowan felt at the prospect of living with deceit. As Arian had said, when it came to the doing of the thing . . .

Abruptly, Rowan remembered a simple bit of medical knowledge learned from Maranne in Wulfshaven: a poisoned limb is amputated.

"No." Faces turned toward her. "Steerswomen mustn't lie. I have to resign the order."

Shock filled the room, followed by protests. Amid the babble of voices, Rowan felt suddenly empty, a hollow shape of flesh with no center and no identity.

Bel and Josef turned perplexed gazes at each other. Speaking above the noise, Bel asked, "But can't she join again, when her mission is finished?"

"It's never been done," Arian said.

"Not true," Hugo put in, and the people quieted to hear him. "When I was training, there was a steerswoman, named Silva— "

Henra nodded. "Yes."

"She mapped the nearer western mountains," Keridwen supplied.

"That's right. But that was later," Hugo continued. "While on the road in the east, she fell in love with a farmer there. She left us to marry and live with him."

"And he died," the Prime said.

"Pneumonia. But his love was all that kept her there, and she became unhappy. She fostered her children to his sister and came back to us."

"And did very good work," Keridwen added, her eyes on the master chart, where the near edge of the western mountains showed clear and accurate.

The Prime turned back to Rowan, and she was like a woman released from some great pain. "Will that suit you?"

Rowan nodded mutely. She felt distant, as if she had already departed and was on some long unknown road with no guidance.

She looked down at her left hand and saw the silver ring on her middle finger, the band with that odd half twist that made it a thing both mysterious and logical: an object of three dimensions, yet possessing only one face, one edge, folded back into reality by the simple laws of geometry. Without thinking, she removed it and held it in the palm of her hand. It seemed weightless.

More quickly, as if by hesitating she would lose her commitment, she slipped the thin gold chain over her head and let it dangle from her fingers. She looked at Henra.

"Hold on to them," the Prime said, "and wear them again when you can."

Rowan placed them both in the leather sack on its thong, nestling beside the uncanny jewel. Tucked under her blouse, the sack felt faintly heavier, a promise set aside.

Henra sighed, then reorganized herself, efficient. "You'll have to choose another name – and remember to answer to it."

Looking faintly puzzled, Keridwen added, "She should wear a different cloak, as well. We're not the only people who use gray felt cloaks, but each one of us does."

"That green cloak she arrived in," Hugo suggested.

"That will do," Henra agreed. Passing Rowan as she climbed the stairs, she walked to the master chart. "Now, as to her route: she'll have to avoid both Five Corners and Donner— "

"But that's not enough." Heads turned to the side of the room, where Bel stepped forward from her place by the wall. Behind her, Josef crossed his arms and nodded grimly. The Outskirter continued. "She can't just go, and dress differently, and not use her own name. She needs a reason for going, something that no one would think twice about. She needs something else to *be*." She scanned the faces in amazement. "Don't you people know how to protect yourselves at all?"

The accusation pushed past Rowan's weariness of spirit; she discovered herself angry. "Yes, we do," she said vehemently, then with awkwardness corrected her choice of words. "Yes, they do. Steerswomen can protect themselves from bandits and cutpurses on the road. They can protect themselves from wild beasts. They can protect themselves from those who would abuse their good natures. We've never had to, never wanted to deceive."

Bel stood before her, solid and sensible. "Time to learn."

Suddenly, without derision, Josef laughed. "Look at you, a bunch of steerswomen," he said. "You know so much, but the one thing you don't know about is lying." He held up his index finger, like an instructor. "Well, I can tell Rowan how to fool people. The best way to lie is to tell the truth."

The steerswomen looked at each other in perplexity. Bel expanded on Josef's statement. "That's right, you say true things – except, you leave some things out. That way, the person takes what you've said and makes his own conclusions – the wrong ones, because of what's missing."

Josef gave her an affirming nod. "And that's your lie. And the second best way is to tell the truth – something obvious, something the other person knows down to his bones – and add your lie onto it, so long as it fits in."

"The person knows that the part he can check is true, and if the rest makes sense, he'll believe it," Bel said.

"And the last good way to lie is to say nothing. Let the other person guess as much as he likes, and when he's dead wrong," he said with a smile, "you tell him how clever he is."

The group relaxed. The alien concept of deception had been reduced to principles. One thing every steerswoman understood was the application of principles.

More confident, Henra said, "Very well. Without compromising ourselves, we can help Rowan by seeing for her what's unsaid." She gestured. "Rowan, stand up please." Rowan rose and stood before them, the great master chart looming at her back. "Now, everyone, imagine you've never seen her. Try to remove that information from your mind. What can you tell, just by looking at her? What is this woman?"

Rowan waited under their discerning gazes. What was she? Ignoring her present pain, she thought back to her childhood, before she had met Keridwen, when no one around her shared that most basic part of her nature. What had she been then?

Nothing. She felt a return of that emptiness, that blank solitude and unnamed yearning that had characterized her life before. She felt, again, like the child who saw too much, thought too quickly, and had no one who could understand her.

"She travels, constantly, outdoors," Sarah noted. "See how dark her skin is, how streaked her hair. And she travels on foot; look at her stance, and the development of her legs."

"The upper part of her body is not developed," Arian said. "She's not a laborer; she doesn't live by the use of her muscles."

"Her fingers are ink-stained," Henra said. "It's the sort of staining that lives in the cracks of one's hands and can't be removed. She uses a pen, every single day."

"She might be a scribe," Keridwen suggested.

"A scribe who travels?" Arian said. "Not likely."

"Notice how composed she is," Hugo put in, tilting his head in study. "This is a woman who knows she can handle whatever she gets into. And see how she watches us? She's thinking, and she's used to thinking. She's used to figuring out for herself what to do."

"That spells steerswoman to me," the dark-haired woman noted.

"Try to put that out of your mind," Henra said.

Rowan listened to the information, considering the clues as if they applied to some stranger, grateful for a problem to occupy her loneliness. A scribe would not travel, not often. Would a clerk? A student?

Berry addressed Rowan. "Say something."

"Say something?"

"Anything, just speak. Describe the weather."

Rowan looked out the window. "It's a beautiful, cloudless day. It's comfortably cool, but the sunlight coming in heats the stone floor. I can feel a draft from the warm air rising." She realized that she had noticed more than the average person would, and had supplied the information casually. She would have to stop that.

Hugo made a wry face. "Well, by that voice, she's educated."

"No," Berry said. "Or, not necessarily. In the north, they have that careful manner of speech, even among the uneducated. And the crispness of her consonants, and the rhythm, that confirms it. She's from the north, past the western curve of the Long North Road. Far north, I'd say, from the sound of her vowels. I think she's from one of the farthest settlements, by the Red Desert. I'd place the town nearest as Umber."

Bel looked at Rowan in amazement. "Is that all true?"

Rowan winced. "Exactly."

Henra was disturbed. "That's far too precise. She advertises her origins."

"But Berry's using a steerswoman's ear," Arian said. "Would the average person notice this?"

Everyone turned to Josef. "Average person, eh?" he said wryly. "All right, well, she sounds a little . . . foreign, but not so much. I wouldn't think twice. Say it again?" Rowan repeated the sentences. Josef nodded. "Maybe educated. Sort of . . . stiff."

"Bel?"

"You all sound foreign."

Henra nodded. "Perhaps that will do, then. As she'll be traveling in the south, it may be sufficient to simply admit she's from somewhere in the north. Bel, take Rowan's place for a moment."

They exchanged places, Bel eyeing the group with suspicion. Then she stood before them, a solid, wide-legged stance, strong arms relaxed, hands comfortably by her sides. Her chin was tilted up in unvoiced challenge.

Rowan looked away briefly, filling her eyes with the gray of stone walls, clearing her mind of preconceptions. Then she looked back, with a fresh point of view.

She saw it immediately, and her voice and three others spoke together. "A warrior."

"Undeniably," Henra admitted.

"A solitary warrior," Hugo amended. "One not used to regimentation."

"And she'll be on the road," Berry pointed out. "A traveling warrior; that means a mercenary."

Rowan took that information and tried to integrate it with what had been said about her own appearance, feeling a touch of surprise, as if she had expected all her steerswoman's abilities to vanish with her ring and chain. She speculated. What would bring two such people together? Why would they travel? What would be their relationship?

It fell together with the perfection of a discovered truth. So perfect, and yet so untrue; it was like an immense joke, and she laughed, bitterly. The steerswomen looked at her in amazement.

Rowan spread her hands and addressed the group. "I've got it."

CHAPTER
Eleven

He had killed a man, his first week on the road.

He was a little surprised at how calmly he had done it. He had killed him as simply as he would kill a wolf, and it was a wolf, really, a bandit. The gods only knew what the man expected to gain from a boy like Willam; just an easy victim, perhaps. Still, Willam had heard the sound, strung his bow with a mindless speed, and let fly as soon as he saw the knife. He actually had not felt afraid at all.

He was smart enough not to trust to a speed and cold-bloodedness he had only felt the once. But he began to worry about the wisdom of keeping to the deserted back trails. Close to his home village, he had thought it best. He knew he was conspicuous: a big lad with red-blond hair, brown eyes light enough to be called copper by most, and at fourteen years well on his way to acquiring a blacksmith's burly arms and shoulders. One sentence was enough to identify him to anyone he knew, and he surely did not want word to get back to his father. Not that he thought his father might follow. Plenty of young people left home; Will had just left a bit sooner than most.

He had been sorry to leave, and frightened, as well. Strange, how one could be frightened of something big and vague, like leaving home alone, and be calm face-to-face with a real bandit. Maybe that was how it was in life. Willam didn't know.

Those last few weeks at home had been too strange, too busy to allow much time or space for worry: trying to go about his days as normal, doing his work, then spending every spare moment in his shack in the yard, even slipping out at night, to make his preparations. No one bothered him in his shack. There had been enough accidents over the years that people had the sense to stay away. If they wanted him, they always stood at a good distance and called out. They were cautious.

He was cautious, too. He had not been, when he was very young, but experience had taught him harshly – taught him to think carefully, move slowly, control as much as possible. One had to take risks to learn, but he discovered that if he was careful about everything else, then the one risk he took would not hurt him. He could do almost the same thing, over and over, taking just one different risk each time, and in the end he learned what he wanted to know. And he knew it all the way down to its bones.

Other people didn't think like that, he knew; they acted, for the most part, on impulse and emotion. Perhaps that was why what he did was so incomprehensible to them, and sometimes frightening. Still, when they needed something special, it was to him that they came.

But magic did not help him on the road. His bow helped him. And caution.

Caution told him to stay to the back trails as long as he could, then caution told him when it was better to take a main road. Unfortunately, by that time, he was lost.

Leaving his village, he had struck northeast, taking his bearings from the Eastern Guidestar at night, doing the best he could by guesswork during the day. Eventually he met the river Wulf. Actually, he thought he had met it a dozen times; any river he crossed was the Wulf to him, until he reached the next one. When he finally did come to its banks and stood gaping in astonishment at its wild speed and impossible width, he felt more than a little like an ignorant village boy. Bitterly, he reminded himself that that was exactly what he was. However fantastic his mission, however high and mighty his plans, it was best to keep that fact in mind.

A riverman took one of Willam's small supply of coppers in return for a trip across, and Will spent the passage carefully protecting his pack from the spray slapped up from the windy water. On the other side, a careful check proved that the contents were safe and dry.

From there he began to travel due east, and within the hour he was hopelessly adrift in the trackless woody uplands. He beat his way cross-country for a full day until he found a path. It went south, but he took it.

But soon he was no longer traveling alone. He met a merchant on the path, and she had a very good idea: travel south to the main road and try to connect with an east-going caravan. Will did not have the fare, but no one would stop him if he wanted to tag along. Naturally, he would not be under their protection, but it would take quite an attack to really threaten a caravan. Will was glad of the suggestion; perhaps a bit less glad at the company.

As they walked along, the little donkey kicked up a bit, and Willam danced to the left, out of the way of the hooves. Astride it, the merchant struggled with the reins and cursed in quiet aggrieved tones. Will smiled. He liked the donkey, and he didn't like the merchant.

"Attise, can't you control that beast?" the merchant's bodyguard complained. Attise sent back one of her flat glances and said nothing, still maintaining her precious dignity. Willam hoped the donkey would throw her.

"I can't see why he should complain," the bodyguard continued to Will. "Her master used to ride him, and from what I hear, Attise is a feather by comparison."

Willam spoke from the side of his mouth. "Give her time. She'll catch up."

The bodyguard looked at Will in surprise, then threw back her head and laughed. "Ho, Attise!" she called. "Why aren't you fat, like the other merchants?"

"I'm not a merchant," Attise replied in a carefully indifferent voice. "Technically."

"She's a clerk," the bodyguard confided to Willam. "Technically."

It was the bodyguard, Sala, who made the traveling enjoyable. She was cheerful and absolutely straightforward. She said exactly what she thought. Perhaps it was her skill at arms that gave her confidence, but it seemed to be more than that; she was a woman who looked the world straight in the eye.

She reminded Will of a cat who lived in a gristmill in his hometown. The cat, small and solid, all efficient muscle, greeted visitors with benign good nature and loved to be petted and entertained. But its greatest delight was battle; it killed rats and thieving birds with heart-stopping speed and precision, and it was always on watch for more opportunities for murder. Sala was like that, Willam thought: cold-bloodedly amiable. He wondered with a trace of boyish excitement if he would ever have the opportunity to see her in action.

But remembering the cat made him remember his little sister. She had loved that cat, and she would squeal with glee whenever she saw it, toddling toward it on her chunky legs. The cat, perhaps wisely, stayed just out of her reach, friendliness struggling against natural caution at the girl's awkwardness, and the pair would weave their way endlessly about the room, to the amusement of onlookers. She was the only girl in the family, and so bright, so mischievous, a constant amazement. Will's love for the child was total, unconditional.

He had often asked his father if they might find a kitten for her, and he really believed his father was about to, just before that day when two of Abremio's men appeared. Then the girl was gone, kittens were forgotten, and Will was left with only his ever more silent father, a brother too old to feel close to – and a dark, obsessive hatred for the wizard who had stolen the only person he truly loved, confiscating her as if she were some object.

It occurred to Willam that if the people in The Crags and the surrounding villages were more like cats, more like Sala, Abremio could not simply do whatever he pleased.

The people in The Crags were like Attise, and perhaps that was why he disliked her so immediately: he had the villager's disdain for the folk of the city proper. They never said anything directly but always danced around the subject with flowery phrases, looking down their noses at a country person as if he smelled bad but they were too polite to tell him. They were more concerned with how they dressed and how they seemed, than with what they really were, or what they could do.

Attise spoke plainly enough, when she spoke, but she had that same way of seeming to watch and judge a person, and watch and judge herself, as if matching her behavior with some rigid internal standard. It made him uncomfortable. And she was never spontaneous; everything she did seemed planned. Will had the feeling that it was all for show.

For instance, Attise had a map, and a good one. But whenever they came to any crossroads absolutely nothing else would do but that they all stop while she carefully dismounted, drew the map from its place in her baggage, and laboriously consulted it. Why she did not keep it more convenient, or why she did not try to memorize part of the route, Will had no idea. She would study it at length, no trace of confusion or uncertainty tainting her expression, pack it away, remount, and say, "This way," in a voice of absolute authority. The exercise soon became tedious, and Will became more and more certain that she did it only to appear important.

"You shouldn't be so hard on her."

Will came back from his thoughts and found that Sala was walking close beside him, Attise and the donkey some dozen feet ahead. "What?" He had been watching the merchant, and his distaste must have been showing on his face.

"Attise. She's really not so terrible. She's just in a bad situation."

Will glowered at the merchant's back again. "More like she carries a bad situation around with her."

Sala considered. "The problem," she said carefully, "is that she doesn't know how to act."

"You'd never guess it."

She nodded. "That's the idea. She's really just a clerk, as I said. She's used to traveling around in her master's wake, doing his figuring, keeping his accounts. She knows about his business, but she's never had to deal with people, or decide anything. But when her master broke his leg, just when he was about to expand his business— " She paused, looking confused at the complexities of finance. "I don't really understand how it works. Somehow, they have the money now, and they won't have it later . . . I don't see how that can be . . ." She gave it up and shrugged. "Well, Attise knew the right things, and no one else did. So he sent her."

"And you went along?"

Sala shifted her pack to a more comfortable position and tested the convenience of her sword hilt. "I'm for hire. And a merchant doesn't travel alone. Not if she likes living."

Up ahead, Attise was affectedly scanning the landscape, her face carefully impassive. "Well, she doesn't act as if she does," Will said. "I mean, she doesn't seem to enjoy anything."

"She doesn't," Sala conceded. "She's too worried. If the new customers thought she was inexperienced, they'd try to take advantage of her. So she has to look as if she knows what she's doing, and act like a merchant, but she's never had to consider that before. She doesn't know how. And she doesn't like it, not at all. She likes numbers."

Will thought about it. Sala's explanation made sense, a little. If the merchant acted as she naturally did, she would give herself away.

For a moment, the whole thing looked different, as if he had a bird's-eye view. Attise actually was watching herself and putting on a fake manner. It showed, really, when he thought about it.

But did she have to make everyone else unhappy? "She'd probably do better business if she let people like her," Will grumbled.

The bodyguard tilted her head and gave him a lopsided grin. "She has money. She doesn't need friends."

But Willam still did not like the way Attise looked at him. At first, Will had tried to engage her in conversation, but finally gave it up; not that she would not reply, but she didn't seem to encourage it, answering in the shortest phrases possible, with no proper opening for reply. And sometimes she would give him a strange look, a slow calculating stare, as if she were adding things up, then turn away silently. It was Sala with whom Willam conversed.

When they first met, she had asked him where he was traveling from, and he had replied in what he hoped was an offhand manner with the name of one of the towns he had passed through. Over her shoulder Attise gave him that look and then went back to blandly viewing the scenery, and the conversation lagged, then limped in the wake of her brief attention. It was nothing more than one look, but it acted on Willam like a bucket of water over his head. Sala was amused.

133

Somewhat later the merchant spoke up casually. "I've been through your town, with my master. Late last year. Do you know Corey, the blacksmith there?"

Will had prepared for that sort of thing. "No, I didn't often get into the town proper. There was a lot of work on the farm, and not much time for what my dad calls 'foolishness'. But when I was little, my mother sometimes sent me in to the weaver's there. Perhaps, you met him? He's a tall thin man, with dust-coloured hair. Michael." Will had carefully studied the town as he passed through, thinking it would be a good place to claim as his home, once he was far enough from it.

She looked at him. "No." Then she turned away, and Will was briefly disturbed. He could not tell if she had made up that business about the blacksmith just to test him, or if she believed him about the weaver. It gave him a turn; his own father was a blacksmith.

At one of the crossroads they came across a party of tinkers, with racks of wares on display. Attise halted the party and made a great show of examining everything the tinkers had, though her utter uninterest was deadeningly obvious. The tinkers saw this immediately and matched her for bland disdain. Willam found the whole thing tiresome.

But at one point she was studying a beautiful embroidered blouse, and she turned to him almost casually. "What do you think of this?"

The weight of the fabric in his hands, the stiff, intricate embroidery, brought a rush of familiarity to Willam, and a touch of homesickness. It was the work of the Kundekin, the kind of lovely handwork with which those mysterious craftspeople filled their idle hours. But for all its beauty, it was common in their opinion, mere exercise to sharpen the eye and hand. Near their enclave in The Crags it could be got cheaply. It was practically given away, else their closets would be full of the stuff. The tinker was charging twenty times its worth.

Willam felt brief pleasure at seeing such a familiar item, then a small shock when he realized that Attise had chosen to ask *him* about it.

He saw that she was giving him that look again. He said nothing, but she returned the blouse to the tinker. "I believe," she said,

134

"that I'll do better by going directly to the source." Her mouth made a smile, but her eyes did not, and she turned away.

As they continued down the road, Willam's mind was spinning. Attise suspected he was lying, that he was not what he claimed, even knew he was from The Crags. But she was doing nothing, saying nothing. Why? Was he truly so obvious? Was she sneering at him, inside? At that thought Will flushed, first in embarrassment, then in anger. Sala threw him one speculative glance, threw Attise the identical glance, then became lost in her own thoughts.

They made a camp that night in a stand of oak off the west side of the road. Sala efficiently scouted the area, pronounced it safe, and set to making a small fire to dispel the cool of night. Attise settled down to study her damnable map and let her bodyguard arrange their sleeping rolls.

Willam hung back from the fire. It wouldn't do to bring the charms in his pack close to the flames. He was not certain how much distance was actually required, but if he erred, it would best be on the side of caution.

He carried his pack some twelve feet away past a small crowd of ferns and began to pull out its contents. Finding his sleeping roll near the bottom, he spread it out on the ground.

Sala watched in puzzlement. "Here, boy, what are you doing?"

Will looked up sheepishly. "Well . . . I thought two ladies might not like a man to spend the night so close . . ."

Sala laughed in good-natured derision at his manly conceit. "I think our virtue is safe with you. Come here, you'll be glad of the fire later tonight." Will grinned with seeming embarrassment, gathered his gear untidily in his arms, and set it up close to Sala's roll. The charms he left behind, masked by the ferns. He could retrieve them in the morning.

But when he looked up from his arrangements, he saw that Attise had abandoned her study and was giving him that look. "Willam," she said slowly. "Obviously we don't feel any threat from you. But you don't return that regard."

"What?"

She pointed with her chin towards the ferns. "Whatever you left back there will certainly be safer close to hand."

Will was speechless, wavering between denial and disbelief.

Attise tilted her head. "Why don't you let me see it? If it's so valuable, perhaps I'll want to buy it." Her face was blank, but her eyes watched him.

Suddenly he hated this woman, hated her silences, her disdain, her air of superiority. She was toying with him! She believed him not at all, and she had spent the day teasing his lies out of him. It was all a game, to make him squirm for her amusement.

And for that one moment, his fury made him rash. He drew himself up slowly and stood, and let her look at him for a long moment, matching her gaze unwaveringly with his own. "Very well," he said at last. "I'll be glad to show you. Perhaps you will want to *buy* one." He sneered that word, with a sudden release of his helpless anger. "But you'll have to step away from the fire to see them. It isn't safe, otherwise. They're magic, and fire releases the spell."

He knew how events should run. They would be impressed, like the people at home. They might even be frightened; they would try to make peace with him.

But it did not happen that way. Instead Willam suddenly realized, quite clearly, that he was in terrible danger.

CHAPTER
Twelve

Bel's sword was in her hand. She spoke carefully. "Don't move, boy. Not a single move."

Rowan sat, her map abandoned in her lap. Her sword was by her right hand, but she did not take it. She stayed completely still, her eyes never leaving the boy's, her body alert and ready for any change in the motion.

Willam had traveled from The Crags, by his accent, his manners, his recognition of the distinctive work of the Kundekin. She knew which wizard held that city, and he was the most infamous. Appalled, she breathed, "Abremio."

The boy jerked at the sound of that name. His young face was pale, and he trembled, but his beautiful copper-coin eyes did not waver from Rowan's face. At last, through clenched teeth, he said to them, "Do it, if you're going to."

Bel was in sudden motion, and Willam made half a step back toward the ferns, and then she was on him. One hand gripped his shirtfront and swung him off balance; the other brought her sword around. Then he was sprawled, half-suspended from her clenched fist, the point of her sword at his throat.

"I say we don't bother to question him first," Bel said mildly.

Rowan was beside them, her own sword in hand. She stood between the stand of ferns and the locked pair, blocking the way. "Wait."

"He's a wizard!"

Rowan gripped Bel's arm, delaying the thrust that would have followed the words. She said to Willam, "Boy, were you boasting? Tell us, and on your life, you'd better believe I'll know if you lie."

He gasped, astonished. "I'm not a wizard!"

"Then he serves one," Bel said.

"What did you leave in the ferns?" Rowan said; she saw him glance in that direction and hesitate. "You haven't the time to think of a lie. Answer!"

"It – it is magic, but— "

"I knew it!" Bel snarled.

"But it's nothing! It's – it's just— " His face worked, then, as if it pained him to admit the truth. "A real wizard would call them just toys. . . ." He looked up at Rowan, astonished – pleading, and he seemed to be a person unused to pleading. "Please, let me go. I'm not worth his notice."

"His notice . . ." Rowan paused in puzzlement, then began to piece together the evidence of the boy's words and reactions. How must all this look to him?

Bel was equally confused. "Whose notice?"

Then, nodding slowly, Rowan lowered her sword. "Abremio's. Let him go, Bel. He doesn't serve Abremio." She smiled a little. "But he thinks that we do."

Bel released Willam in astonishment. "Us?"

He lay on the ground, rubbing his chest. "I thought, when you named him . . ."

"I thought I was naming you," Rowan said wryly.

"Me?" It came out a childish squeak.

"Who knows what guise a wizard might travel in?"

Bel watched Willam with suspicion. "It still might be him." She stepped around, so that he had a woman with a sword on either side.

Rowan studied him. His panic had eased a bit once he knew they were no minions of that wizard; he was waiting with a combination of confusion and wariness.

She considered the clues. "You're afraid of Abremio's attention. Is he likely to be looking for you? Did you steal something from him, perhaps?"

He sat up, cautiously. "No. He stole something from me."

"What was that?"

"My sister."

"This Abremio steals women?" Bel asked. She directed her query not to Willam but to Rowan, and the steerswoman saw that the boy took careful note of that. Abruptly she realized that she and Bel had ceased to be innocent travelers in his eyes. In acting to protect themselves, they had compromised the only protection they had. There was no longer an easy explanation for their movements. She cursed herself silently.

But what explanation was there for Willam? He had threatened the use of magic and was frightened at the thought of attracting Abremio's attention. "Why does Abremio care about you?"

He thought carefully before replying. "Why does he care about you?" he asked.

He was as cautious as they. Bel smiled despite herself. "We don't know that he does," she replied.

He looked from one to the other. "I don't know for sure, either. But if he doesn't care, it's because he doesn't know I exist."

"You're a danger to him?" Rowan asked.

"No. Not yet." His composure was returning as they spoke. Then an idea occurred to him, and he looked suddenly intrigued. "But you are, aren't you?"

Bel's sword was across his throat again, the guard close under his left ear. "Boy," she said in a perfectly reasonable tone, "I want you dead. My friend," she nodded up at Rowan, "doesn't agree. But she's a sensible person, actually. She won't risk our lives on a kindhearted whim."

"The odds are against you," Rowan pointed out, "unless you can convince us that you're harmless to us."

His fear had returned. "I am!"

"The more we know about you, the better we'll be able to judge that. The less you know about us, the less risk you are."

"Don't ask questions," Bel clarified. "Answer them."

He took a deep shaky breath and looked up at Rowan. "I won't betray you. Because I think we're all on the same side. I'll tell you anything you want."

She considered. It was difficult to believe that this big clumsy-looking boy, so obvious in his deceptions, could represent any direct threat. He looked more than a little foolish, sitting awkwardly on the ground, his possessions scattered about him; the warrior beside him could dispatch him as simply and negligently as she might snap the neck of a snared quail.

And yet—

"The package you left in the ferns contains something magical?" she asked.

"That's right. Charms. They're useful, in a small way. But they can be dangerous, if you're not careful." He held up his right hand for them to see. As Rowan had noticed before, the hand lacked its last two fingers. The underside of the arm was also scarred, as from an old burn, and his right eyebrow was faintly ragged. Abruptly the pattern made sense, and she realized that at some point in the past he had flung that arm across his face to protect his eyes from sudden fire.

"Why were they given to you?" Bel asked.

"They weren't." He looked stubborn, as if he had often had to defend that statement. "I made them."

"You said that you're not a wizard," Rowan pointed out.

"No. Not yet."

"Are you an apprentice?"

"No." He looked earnest. "But I'd better become one, don't you think?"

"Easily said, less easily accomplished," Rowan observed. Wizards sometimes acquired apprentices; but where those young people came from, no one knew. They were never of the folk in the wizard's own holding. They appeared, apparently from nowhere, and more often than not vanished abruptly, never to be seen again. Only very rarely was it possible to make a clear connection between the disappearance of a known apprentice in one part of the Inner Lands and the sudden appearance of a new wizard in some other region. Even in those cases, the apprentice's antecedents were either untraced, or untraceable.

The boy went on. "I have to find a Red wizard. Abremio's Blue; so is Corvus, nowadays. I don't want anything to do with the Blues."

"What makes you think that any wizard would accept you?" she asked.

"Well . . ." Willam spoke grimly. "I suppose he'd have to. It wouldn't do to have one of the folk walking around doing magic, would it? He'd either have to take me in, or kill me."

Bel leaned closer. "Then he'll kill you."

From his position he could not comfortably look her in the eye, but his expression was defiant. "Maybe not."

But Rowan had reached her conclusions. She gestured to Bel to relax her guard, but the Outskirter was wary and did not comply. Will watched the silent argument in confusion.

Rowan casually sat down on the ground next to them, placing her sword across her lap. "You're going to become a wizard so that you can kill Abremio, for taking your sister."

It was an obvious conclusion, but Willam startled a bit when she stated it. Bel gave one delighted "Ha!" and released him again, stepping back to sheathe her own sword. She sat down herself, pulling her cloak under her, and viewed Willam with approval. "Can your magic do this?" she asked.

The sudden change in their mood made him no less uncomfortable. "No," he admitted, studying each of them in turn. Something in Rowan's watching and waiting expression made him amend his statement. "That is, perhaps. If I caught him by surprise. But I can't count on that. And I'd never get him alone. I don't want to hurt anyone else." He spoke with intensity. "That's his way, not mine. And I've never used it to hurt anyone."

"Except yourself," Bel pointed out.

He was embarrassed. "I don't think that counts."

"It's not a game, and no one's counting," Rowan said. "Abremio can do as he pleases." If Willam did join the ranks of the wizards, Rowan suspected that he would soon learn to do as they did.

"But – they're not all like him!"

Rowan gestured vaguely; it seemed to her that it was only a matter of degree. But she admitted, "He's the worst of them."

"Stealing women?" Bel asked. "What does he do with them?"

"Children," Rowan corrected. "Of both genders. And no one knows." Before leaving the Archives, she had spent two intense hours with Hugo, as he briefed her on the known details of the six major wizards. Hugo had learned in his own travels that Abremio occasionally sent a pair of soldiers to confiscate an infant or a young child from its family. It occurred rarely enough to seem a unique event to the folk involved, yet often enough to form a habit recognizable to someone who observed widely. "Was there something different about your sister?" Rowan asked Will. Often, though not exclusively, this was the case.

He was puzzled. "No . . . small for her age, perhaps. She spoke early and walked late, that's all. Why do you ask?"

But to answer would be to admit a larger scope of knowledge than she was supposed to possess. As had often happened on this journey, she found nothing she could safely say, and so said nothing. It was the worst sensation, to close the lid on her knowledge, a wrenching unpleasantness. She set her mouth in a grim line to keep from speaking and looked away, trying to control her instincts.

"I wish you wouldn't do that!"

She turned back and found Willam glaring at her in fury.

"You – you treat me like I'm stupid, or like I'm nothing. But I can figure things out for myself. I know that you're both spies, from a Red wizard."

Bel and Rowan exchanged a startled glance, then Rowan seized the idea and turned it over and over in her mind.

It was the perfect answer. It explained all their actions: their original deception, their reaction to Will's claims of magic, their attack on him, their unwillingness to explain themselves. Will had assumed that they served a Red wizard because of their fear of Blue Abremio.

They did not have to lie at all; it was deception by silence. Without a word passing between them, Rowan and Bel agreed on their new identities.

As spies, they would hardly admit to being spies. They both sat simply looking at Willam, waiting for him to realize this. Eventually he did, and grudgingly let his temper cool.

"We're not enemies," he pointed out. "I hate Abremio, I don't want anything to do with any Blue wizard. I'm looking for a Red. So, we're on the same side."

"It would be a good idea if you forgot that we're anything but a merchant and a mercenary," Bel said. Rowan could not help but smile; the statement was perfectly true on every level, yet served only to reinforce the credibility of their new deception. Even her smile, she realized, added to the effect.

"I won't give you away," Will assured Bel, and included Rowan in his glance. "But, well . . . maybe we can help each other."

Bel looked at Rowan. "It might be a good idea . . ."

Rowan's humor vanished. "I don't like it."

"But if his magic is any good— "

"We don't know that it is." Rowan was reluctant to have anything at all to do with magic, but as the supposed servant of a wizard, she could not admit to that. She hoped Bel could follow her reasoning without prompting.

But Bel turned back to Willam. "Show us this magic, then," she suggested.

The boy hesitated. "But you don't want people to notice us . . ."

"And it would attract attention?" Rowan asked.

He nodded. "It's rather loud, most of the time."

"You can't do it quietly? Put a spell of silence on it?" Bel wondered.

"There's still a lot about it that I can't control." He rubbed his damaged right hand, an unconscious, musing gesture.

"What does it do?" she asked. "What do you use it for?"

He looked a little sheepish. "I can dig wells. And help clear boulders and stumps from new farmland."

"The boulders vanish?"

"No . . ." He searched for words. "Sometimes they break apart. Sometimes they just . . . leave. Very fast."

"How is that dangerous?"

He looked at her darkly. "It's not good to get in the way."

"I believe that's true of every sort of magic," Rowan said.

But Bel was delighted. "It sounds very useful," she said, ignoring Rowan's interjection. "I think this is a good meeting. I'm sure we can help each other."

"No!"

Bel and Willam looked at Rowan, startled.

"I don't think it's a good idea at all." She wanted to say: If the wizards are ignoring their own lines to cooperate against us, if every wizard is our enemy, then we do not want one of their fledglings at our side. We don't know enough about them; we don't know why they act as they do. This boy wants to learn their ways, and their ways are all against us. We would never know when he might turn.

She could say none of this. All she could say to Bel, in Willam's presence, was: "Think about it."

Bel shook her head, a broad emphatic gesture. "If you find a perfectly good sword by the side of the road, you don't throw it away."

"What if you suspect it's cursed?"

Bel replied, stressing each word, "You use what comes to hand." Will nodded, watching Rowan for a response.

Rowan took a breath, trying to calm herself. She turned to Willam. "And how would we help you?"

"You take me with you," he said. "And when we return to your master, you tell him about me."

"A recommendation?"

He nodded.

"And what makes you think we carry any influence?"

"Perhaps you don't. But it's better than me just showing up on his doorstep. And if I really do prove myself . . ."

"Where's the harm?" Bel asked. Rowan saw that Bel was trying to suppress amusement. "*If* we have the chance, we let it be known that Willam helped us, and that he'd make a good apprentice."

Willam was waiting for Rowan's answer, his face open, sincere, eager, guileless . . . and for a moment, she cared about him and what might happen to him. "Will," she said honestly. "You shouldn't become an apprentice. I hate to think what it will do to you. No good will come of it."

Something in her expression reached him, and he was taken aback, suddenly uncertain. Then she understood; it was her sincerity. Never before had he seen sincerity in her face, and it broke her heart to realize that. "Trust me," she said to him, knowing she had never given him reason or evidence to trust her.

"My sister . . ." he began.

"Do you realize you're not the only one?" Rowan asked. "He didn't single you out; it's simply something that he does, periodically. Does that make any difference to you?"

"No . . ." he said at last. Then he became more certain. "Maybe it makes it worse. And it's not the only evil he does. I've seen how he works, a bit. I lived near his city, The Crags – but you knew that."

Rowan called into her mind a detailed map of that area. Willam's village had to be on the near side of the drawbridge, far enough from the city proper that he had not acquired its involuted manner of speech, but near enough that pronunciation of individual words was the same. He had lived close enough to the city to be familiar with Kundekin handiwork, and that eliminated the farther-flung villages under the city's direct influence. Also, he had been near enough to enter the city on occasion and see Abremio's daily manner of rule at first hand.

She hazarded a guess. "Oak Grove."

He stopped short, disturbed. "That's very close. Langtry." He went on. "Anyway . . . I guess I have to stop it, if I can."

She nodded, comprehending. "You've been working on this for a long time."

"A long time . . . working so hard . . ."

"Attise." It took Rowan a moment to remember that that was her name. "Maybe we *can* help each other." Bel said it simply, watching Rowan's expression, and it occurred to Rowan that the statement might carry more than one meaning.

"You're from the new holding, aren't you?" Willam asked. "The one they fought the war for, with those two wizards together?"

"Shammer and Dhree," Rowan supplied without thinking, then realized that her reply would be taken as an admission that he had guessed right.

"Do they have an apprentice?"

"No." She sighed and spoke to Bel. "If either of us has the opportunity, we'll put in a good word. That's the only promise we can give." It was a true statement, as true as she could make it, and still it carried in its heart a hundred unspoken lies.

But it satisfied Will, and he laughed with happy relief.

CHAPTER
Thirteen

"I would very much like to see what he can do," the steerswoman said.

Bel looked back at Willam, who was chatting with one of the caravan's mounted guards. The man was riding a rather bedraggled horse, and extolling the romance of his lifestyle, with expansive gestures and more than a little condescension.

The boy ambled along beside him, with his odd, distinctive gait. His strides were slightly longer than his height would suggest, and he walked smoothly and jarlessly, as if he were carrying a load of eggs in his pack. It seemed easy and natural.

The donkey trotted along beside them in cheerful high spirits, due simply to the fact that it was no longer carrying Rowan. It had protested being ridden from the first, and now that it carried only her baggage and Bel's pack, it seemed to feel that its little universe had been restored to rightful order. Its bad temper had completely vanished.

Bel added to Rowan's statement. "Without attracting attention."

"He did say it was loud."

"I wonder what sort of noise it makes?"

"I can't imagine." Like the donkey, Rowan had been restored to a more natural mode – she was walking. Her clothes were not the best for such exertion – the wide split skirt hissed around her legs annoyingly, and the boots were too new to be comfortable – but she walked, and felt easier in her mind for the swinging familiarity of it.

There were two main roads running east and west in the Inner Lands. One, the Shore Road, stretched east from Wulfshaven and eventually ended in Donner; but it was an ill-kept route and wasted many miles by laboriously tracing the northern shoreline of the sea. It served mainly to connect the little villages each with its neighbor. Only by happenstance did it form a continuous road with both ends terminating in major towns.

But the Upland Route, which they had chosen to take, was centuries old, a good and dependable route east. It crossed the Wulf some miles north of Wulfshaven, dipped south to the city itself, skirted the hilly country that ranged down from the north, and traveled northeast and then due east to Five Corners. It was part of the major caravan route, and from Five Corners transported goods could continue in several directions.

But that town was too likely to recognize Rowan and Bel from their earlier visit. They planned to leave the caravan long before that point and wend their way across country and along less direct roads to the Outskirts.

The day had turned warm early on, and both women had added their heavier outer clothing to the donkey's burden. They walked in the midst of a faint haze of road dust raised by the travelers ahead of them. Rowan breathed it in as if it were sea air.

She was using her resurrected sense of freedom to engage in her normal activity: she was finding things out. Denied the direct approach of questioning the travelers closely, she was utilizing a combination of close observation and the normal degree of idle curiosity she might be expected to display as Attise. Her restrictions took on the aspect of a game, and she ranged up and down the caravan's length.

A pair of point riders headed the line, on hard-worked, scruffy ponies. A horse-mounted scout periodically came into view in the distance, signaled them, then disappeared again.

A charabanc drawn by a team of donkeys came next, carrying the well-to-do who did not wish to exert themselves unnecessarily. A party atmosphere suffused the group of strangers, but Rowan found them disinclined to indulge in idle conversation with a walker. She recognized their origins by their accents, and rightly identified one narrow gentleman from the upper Wulf valley as escort to the six oxcarts of tin ingots that followed a few spaces behind. Tin was mined in the hills of the upper Wulf, by one of the two known enclaves of the mysterious Kundekin, and the man's sentence structure showed the influence of long conversation with those normally reclusive people. Rowan speculated to herself on the effects of so large an import of tin on the metal-poor economy to the east.

The carts were followed by a handful of young horse-mounted travelers, all of a group, jesting with one another. They chatted freely but superficially and seemed more interested in a series of pranks played by one of their number. The most frequent victim was a lone Christer pilgrim, an attractive target due to his air of blind self-confidence and his unvarying reaction of dull puzzlement.

In all, some twenty wagons and carts made up the main body of the line, interspersed with riders and walkers. Some, like the tin importer, were planning to travel all the way to the junction at Five Corners. Others took advantage of the caravan's protection for local trips, the fee for such participation being minimal. Still others traveled with the caravan for some significant segment of their journey, separating again when necessary; Rowan and Bel belonged to this category.

Rowan watched Will for a moment. "I wonder how one comes to be able to work magic."

The Outskirter was surprised. "Everyone knows. You're born with the talent."

"Young Willam doesn't seem particularly remarkable."

"Ha. You can't tell just by looking."

"Making it easy for anyone to claim magical talent."

Bel shook her head in mock aggrievedness. "There you go again, doubting. You doubt that the moon ever existed, you doubt the gods, you doubt the cards, and you doubt magic. Is there anything you don't doubt?"

"Quite a lot," Rowan told her, laughing despite herself. "I don't doubt that some things people believe are true, and some are false.

And I don't doubt that there's some means to tell the difference."
Then she admitted, "But I sometimes doubt that I possess the means." They pulled abreast of an oxcart loaded with beer kegs, and the conversation was forced to end, lest the drivers overhear.

The guard turned away to patrol, and Willam caught up with the women. "He says that last year at this time, the caravan was set on by bandits right here." Under his concern, Rowan detected a buried trace of wild boyish curiosity.

"Then it won't be, this year," she decided, knowing that bandits who worked in groups tended to keep distinct territories and so had to vary their tactics. Will managed to look both relieved and disappointed. "Not at this location, that is," she added, and his expression became too mixed to interpret.

He was distracted by the group of walkers just ahead of the beer cart. Four men and a young woman had been trading turns pulling a two-wheeled luggage cart. Three of the men now positioned themselves between the poles and jogged in time, moving the cart closer to the front of the line, their exertions aided by the cheerful "Hup, hup" and handclapping of the woman. Their remaining companion strolled along at his ease, in parody of haughty condescension.

"What's in the cart?" Will wondered.

"Instruments. They're musicians."

Will watched them depart, then wandered back to study a farm wagon carrying a load of provisions and a silent, sad-eyed family of four.

Bel scanned the line ahead and behind, then shook her head in amazement. "Things go differently in the Outskirts."

"I imagine so."

"Everything here is so easy – and comfortable."

Rowan was taken aback. "Not at all. If these people traveled each alone, they'd certainly be robbed."

"What about steerswomen? Aren't they robbed?"

Rowan paused to form a reply that would not betray her connection with the Steerswomen if overheard. "They carry little. And what they have of value – that is, information – is free for the asking."

"So they're not molested?"

"Yes, but rarely. So I hear."

Bel considered. "So these travelers band together and they're safe."

"Safer," Rowan corrected.

"The Outskirts are never safe."

Rowan wanted to ask her for more details, but decided it would seem too odd. Instead she satisfied herself with reviewing the information she had gleaned from Bel in previous conversations, trying to organize it in her mind. Bel noted her preoccupation and turned to amusing herself by trying to keep track of Willam's wanderings. Presently a pony cart doubled back from the head of the line, and a lunch of dried meat and bread was passed out to those whose payment had included the service. The day wore on, pleasantly enough.

"So." Damaine, the caravan-master, pulled up beside Rowan. "Only as far as Taller Ford, hey?" He was a slim, energetic man, dressed in bright red linen trousers, a square-cut sleeveless shirt, and a broad-brimmed hat. His dust-brown hair was tied behind the nape of his neck.

Rowan raised her voice to be heard over the creak of the beer wagon. "I'll be heading south, and then east. To Alemeth."

"Alemeth!" He blew air through pursed lips. Then his eyes glittered. "Silk!"

"That's right."

"Then you'll need transport for your goods." He began to calculate.

"We'll probably go by sea, once the deal's established."

"It's off the regular lines." He had a good knowledge of his competition's habits.

"We may hire our own."

He threw up his hands in mock distress. "Think of the expense!"

"Think of the convenience!" Rowan laughed.

"No, now, where are you based?"

They entered into a cheerful discussion of the relative merits and costs of the competing modes of bulk transportation. Rowan found her mathematical ability coming into play naturally, and was able to calculate rates and mileages with offhand ease that startled

151

Damaine and gave him occasional pause. The conversational give-and-take was both lighthearted and cutthroat. Soon Rowan realized, with some surprise, that this occupation was one she could be good at, and even enjoy. She and the caravan-master ended up laughing in admiration of each other's expertise.

One of the guards up ahead hallooed, waving his hat at his master. Damaine acknowledged with his own signals, then cupped his hat behind one ear to catch the explanation. Walking down among the cart noise, Rowan could not make out what was said.

"Hmph." Damaine turned to her. "Did I see you writing letters last night?"

She nodded. "Yes, keeping my master posted." In fact, the letters served to report her movements and any new information to the Prime. Arian had provided Rowan with a deviously clever mathematical cipher that permitted her to conceal her information economically within very few paragraphs. There was no particular reason at this point to suspect her letters might be intercepted; she had detected no sign of scrutiny since she had left the Archives. Still, it was a reasonable precaution.

The address to which she sent them was a nonexistent one far in the upper Wulf valley, ostensibly her point of origin. But to reach t' it area, her letter would have to pass through Wulfshaven itself, and a notation on the address suggested it be routed through the offices of a small herring fleet. Such interim destinations were common with letters traveling long distances, trusted to the hands of a succession of strangers. However, one of the clerks in the offices was a failed steerswoman who had maintained friendly relations with the residents of the Archives. The plan called for her to reroute the messages.

Rowan had managed to send one communication from a small village the travelers had passed through on the road south to the caravan route. It consisted merely of assurances that she had met with no problems yet. How long it would take to reach its destination, Rowan had no idea.

She had spent the last few evenings enciphering the news of her and Bel's encounter with Willam. She said to Damaine, "When we reach the next town, I'll see if I can find someone going west who might be willing to carry a letter."

"Well, you won't have to wait," he replied, gesturing up the length of the caravan. "There's a steerswoman up ahead, coming this way. You can pass the letters through her."

Rowan's thoughts froze, then went into a flurry, trying to guess who it might be. Who was on this road; who was traveling west at this time?

And how could Rowan avoid meeting her?

She thought of Janus, assumed lost, and she hoped desperately that it was him. But Damaine had not said "steersman". She resisted the temptation to ask Damaine if it was a man or a woman approaching. Steersmen were so rare and notable that it was unlikely the guard ahead would simply use the general term. Also, she reminded herself, as Attise she should not care which it was.

She tried to let none of her thoughts reach her face. "Good," she said to Damaine. Steerswomen were frequent and reliable letter carriers. To refuse would have been to be conspicuous.

Somewhat later, she crossed the line in front of the beer cart and joined Bel and Willam, who were idly chatting with the Christer pilgrim. Will glanced in annoyance as she gestured Bel aside. Since he had decided they were allies, he took mute exception to their excluding him from any consultations, but he never protested, for fear of losing their indulgence. Bel handed him the donkey's lead and stepped back behind the wagon with Rowan.

"There's a steerswoman up ahead."

Bel tilted her head. "And she'll recognize you?"

"Almost certainly. There aren't that many of us, and the older ones, the ones I haven't met, are working the limits of the Inner Lands far from here. Very likely, it's someone I trained with."

"And she won't know anything of your doings."

"It will take some explaining. And, there's the chance she'll give me away before I can explain at all."

Bel nodded. "Then you'll have to avoid her."

"Exactly."

Bel scanned the length of the caravan. "There are enough people for you to lose yourself, if you know when she's passing by. I'll scout ahead and warn you."

"And you'll give her a letter." Rowan explained the custom to Bel. "I'll have to step aside to add a note and to address it. Then you can run it up to her."

Bel smiled at a happy thought. "Let's have Willam do it. It will make the poor fellow feel useful."

Rowan could not help laughing. "That's a good idea."

They rejoined Will and the pilgrim. Rowan pulled from her baggage the folio of letter paper that she carried in place of her steerswoman's logbook. Bel picked up her conversation with the Christer and gestured for Will to stay with her as Rowan stepped to the side of the road.

There was no time to melt sealing wax. Rowan made do by folding the paper several times over and tying it with a bit of ribbon. She spit onto her ink stone, mixing a bit of powder, and addressed it, propping the folio against her knee.

She had to hurry back up the line to reach Bel and Willam, waving the paper a bit to dry the ink. She wondered briefly if she looked too undignified at the moment to be a proper merchant.

"Will."

He turned to her.

"Here, be careful of the ink. I need you to run up ahead and pass this on to a steerswoman who's coming this way."

He opened his mouth to speak, very probably to ask why she did not simply wait until the steerswoman reached her. Rowan gave him a warning look, and he closed his mouth again. In the presence of the Christer, he could not ask for her justifications. Resigning himself to his mysterious mission, he shifted his pack to a more snug position, tightened one of the ropes that served as a strap, took the letter, and headed off.

He did not exactly run, Rowan noticed, but extended his stride to a smooth ground-devouring lope. Piecing the clues together, she decided that fire was not the only thing that might threaten the safety of the charms in his pack.

The pilgrim noticed. "Is there something wrong with his legs?"

"I don't know," Rowan replied.

The Christer looked after the boy, then began to hold forth with a long, boring, and largely spurious list of medical recommendations.

It was half an hour later when Will rejoined them, by the simple expedient of standing still as they caught up to his position. "She's going to be camping with the caravan tonight. I thought you might like to know."

Rowan was taken aback. "What?"

The pilgrim had left their company, and the boy felt free to speak. "She fell in with the musicians up ahead. I think she's a musician herself."

The name spoke itself before Rowan could stop it. "Ingrud."

He was surprised. "You know her?"

She managed to prevent herself from explaining further and lapsed into one of her silences. Bel took over. "Let's say we know of her. And that we have to avoid her, or at least Attise does."

He glowered. "I wish you'd told me."

Rowan turned on him. "What did you do?"

"Well . . ." he began defensively. Ahead, a few heads turned in their direction at the loudness of his protest. He continued, quieter but vehement. "Outskirswomen are good sources of information. You can ask them anything, and they have to answer, no matter what. I thought— " He stepped closer and spoke still more quietly. "I thought, with what you're doing, you'd want to know something about what the land is like farther up this road. And a merchant would want to know, anyway."

"She's going to come looking for me?"

"I told her you had some questions . . ."

Rowan threw up her hands in exasperation, furiously turned away to calm herself, turned back before she could, and pointed one finger a bare inch from his face. "Don't do that," she said in a low, vicious voice. "Don't go off making plans for us on your own initiative— "

Angry, he spoke louder. "Well, if I knew a little more about what you're— "

Bel slapped his shoulder once, very hard. Caught off-stride, half-turned, he stumbled, and Rowan stepped out of his way—

—then abruptly countered her instincts in panic and stepped back in to grab him—

—and countered instinct again to change her sudden clutch into a smooth interception, a catch with some give in it. Like catching a tossed egg—

She ended with both knees on the ground, one arm across Willam's chest, the other gripping his left shoulder from behind. His right arm was flung around her neck, a fistful of cloth on her back clutched in his half-hand. His left arm was thrown forward, to ward off the ground or to cushion his fall.

They froze. Willam held his breath. Rowan waited.

Eventually she said, carefully, "Is anything going to happen?"

He looked at her, eyes wide. "No," he replied. He sounded not at all certain.

Bel stood to one side, puzzled, but the look on their faces had stopped her from offering help. Instead she intercepted two little girls, locked in deep converse, who were about to trip over the pair.

Rowan cautiously helped Will up. Speaking close to his ear, she said urgently, "Can't you do something to make those things safer?"

He gazed about with a stunned expression, like someone amazed to be alive. "No," he said. "I mean, I don't know. I was never able to find out."

She urged him into a slow walk. They began to drop back as their fellow travelers continued at a steadier pace. Bel tugged the donkey back into motion and fell in with them.

"If the charms are this dangerous, perhaps you should get rid of them," Rowan said.

He shook his head, partly in dissent, partly to clear it. "I don't know that the spells would have escaped. *Sometimes* they do, if you drop them. Not always. It's just hard to be sure. I've never carried so many at once. If one releases, they all will, this close to each other."

Bel had caught the substance of the conversation. "What would have happened?"

Shock and guilt on his face, Willam looked up the line of travelers and wagons, then down it, then at the surrounding landscape. It

156

came to Rowan that it all would have been affected in some terrible way. "Nothing good" was all he said.

Bel looked pleased. "Then you ought to be more careful. A good weapon should be treated with respect."

He nodded vaguely, then came back to himself. "The steerswoman," he said.

It took Rowan a moment to remember that he was not referring to her. "Ingrud," she amplified. "I'll try to keep out of the way tonight. When you or Sala see her, tell her that I've changed my mind. She'll be too occupied to think much of it."

Rowan sat in darkness on the edge of the camp, on the far side of the charabanc, her back against one tall wheel. The team of donkeys that had pulled it during the day were contentedly grazing around her and tugging at their staked tethers, her own beast among them. Behind her, travelers and drivers were gathered into cheery groups. Some were dancing.

Listening, Rowan identified the instruments: a pair of three stringed viols, a bass flute, a bodhran, and a banjo, all led in a mad swirl by Ingrud's squeeze-box. The music was an ancient dance tune, "Harrycot Fair". Nearby, someone was trying to dredge the nonsense lyrics from memory and making a bad job of it.

Rowan sullenly tossed a pebble at one of the donkeys. It fell short, and the animal ambled over to investigate, on the chance that it might be edible.

The music stopped, to scattered applause and appreciative comments. It did not start again, and the voices picked up their conversations. Apparently the musicians were taking a rest.

Someone approached. Rowan looked around the wheel to see Bel wandering in her direction, the very image of nonchalance. Beyond, in a circle of chattering people, Rowan caught sight of one energetic figure topped by a wild cloud of smoky brown hair.

Rowan turned back and waited. Her donkey, appetite satisfied, came over to her and lowered itself to the ground. Shifting to one side, it found that the length of its tether was just sufficient to allow it to lean its head against her knee. It did so, and heaved a little happy sigh.

Bel sat down beside her, eyes reflecting the light leaking under the charabanc. "I like her. She's an interesting person."

"I wish I could talk to her." Rowan and Ingrud had their differences and were perhaps not the best of traveling companions; yet somehow, despite their talent for annoying each other, they had forged a friendship during their training. It was an odd friendship, one that seemed to require equal doses of distance and proximity.

But now Rowan felt a need as compelling as hunger. She needed to see Ingrud again, to find out how the road had treated her. She wanted to compare notes with her, to read each other's logbooks, to reminisce about their training and share dreams of further roads ahead.

Instead Rowan was sitting in darkness, listening to Ingrud's music in the distance.

"I think you'll need to talk to her," Bel said. "She's carrying one of the jewels."

Stunned, Rowan turned to her. "You're sure it's the same? Did she show it to you?"

"She's using it as a brooch for her cloak."

Rowan felt a sudden chill. Ingrud was carrying a jewel in plain sight. And whoever had tried to strike at Rowan was looking for a steerswoman with a blue jewel—

"She's in danger, and she doesn't know it." She shoved the donkey aside and rose to peer past the charabanc toward the firelight. Ingrud was no longer in sight. "Can you get her over here, alone, on some pretext?"

Bel considered. "She's too popular at the moment. I'll wake her from sleep later tonight and tell her there's something she should see."

"She won't trust you," Rowan said. "Not even a steerswoman would go off into the dark with a total stranger. Not on this road, not in this season."

Bel thought a moment, then smiled. "I'll bring Willam. She likes him. He's been plying her with questions all night."

158

"Questions?"

"Yes." Bel laughed. "He seems to have a lot of them. He acts as if he wants to know everything about everything."

As Bel made her way back to the firelight, Rowan felt an odd stab of jealousy. She thought: He should be asking those questions of me.

CHAPTER
Fourteen

"The merchant Attise, isn't it? You're having no problem, I hope."

Rowan looked up at the mounted guard, trying to affect an air of dignified distraction. "No, there's no problem, thank you. I needed to think, and I thought a bit of a walk might help matters."

He shook his head indulgently. "Oh, that's not a good idea, merchant. Wandering off in the dark by yourself. With all the noise we made tonight, every thief and cutthroat for miles around is surely headed this way. And possibly arrived. We're one of the first caravans this year, and they've had a hard winter, I think.'

Rowan knew that to be true. "I trust your excellent patrolling."

He laughed. "Best of the lot, that's me. Still, it's good to be safe. You'd be wise to take yourself off to sleep."

Only a solitary thief could manage to slip into the camp. Rowan carried a sword, and believed it unlikely she could be caught by surprise in these circumstances. "My bodyguard will be joining me shortly."

His face brightened. "Sala! Now, she's certainly impressive. And knows her business well. A fine soldier, and a fine woman, too, I think. She could probably teach me a thing or two. I wouldn't mind wrestling her, any number of ways, if you catch my meaning."

Rowan suppressed a grin. "I'll tell her of your high opinion."

He considered. "You do that." He turned his horse and moved off, a musing, contemplative expression on his face. Rowan turned back to her own thoughts.

The first thing she'll do, Rowan thought, is shout my name. Then she'll ask why I've left my route. Then she'll wonder why I'm dressed so oddly . . .

Rowan would have to speak first, she realized. She needed to find some way to prevent Ingrud's quicksilver emotions from giving Rowan away to whoever might still be awake to listen. But she could not think of what to say or do, and then she heard people approaching and knew she had run out of time.

They were speaking, Ingrud's tone dubious, Bel's reassuring, as they came around the side of the charabanc. Will followed in their wake, suspicious of Bel's behaviour and Rowan's change of plans. Rowan moved back to prevent the light from catching her face too soon. She waited until the trio reached the point where the wagon completely blocked them from the rest of the camp, then stepped forward. "Ingrud . . ."

She had been wrong about her friend's reaction. Ingrud's narrow, foxy face quickly showed first surprise, then delight; but when she took in the strange clothing, she stopped short suddenly. One glance showed her that Rowan's steerswoman's ring was absent.

To Rowan's amazement, Ingrud burst out in dismay, "No! Not you, too!" She turned to one side in helpless outrage and pounded her own right leg with a fist. "This can't happen again!" Angry, she stepped forward and shook her index finger in Rowan's face. "I will *not* be put off this time! I'm *going* to get an explanation!"

Rowan pulled the hand down, tried to calm the steerswoman. "Ingrud please, not so loud . . ."

"You and Janus have a lot to answer for— "

"Janus?" Rowan shook her head, then dismissed the non sequitur. "I'll tell you anything you like, but please, we mustn't attract attention."

Puzzled, Will said to Bel, "They do know each other. I asked the steerswoman, and she said they didn't."

Bel was distracted by an approaching guard. She stepped forward to reassure him. "They're old friends," she explained when he

161

pulled up. "I'm sorry about the noise, but you know how it can be when old friends meet . . ."

"You are going to explain this!" Ingrud asserted, oblivious to everything except Rowan. "Janus can do what he likes and be damned for it, but you're my friend . . ."

Rowan realized with astonishment that Ingrud was close to tears. Abruptly ashamed for she knew not what sin, she held out her arms to her friend. Ingrud went silent, and then Rowan found herself embracing a helplessly weeping woman. "It's all right," she tried to reassure her in the midst of her own confusion. "I can explain everything. It's all right . . ." She looked up over Ingrud's shoulder at the guard. "I – I'm afraid my little joke went badly," she extemporized. "I shouldn't have tried to surprise her."

The guard relaxed a bit and looked to Bel for confirmation. "Really, there's no problem here," Bel said. "We're sorry we bothered you." He nodded, said something to her that Rowan could not catch, and wheeled off.

Ingrud calmed at last, and Rowan managed to get her to sit on the grass beside the charabanc. The steerswoman insisted through her tears, "You had better tell me what's going on."

"I was about to ask the same of you," Rowan replied. "What's the matter? And what's this about Janus?" She found a handkerchief in a sleeve pocket and gave it to Ingrud.

Ingrud pressed it across her eyes, as if she wished to blot out the world as well as her tears. "He's left."

"What do you mean? I'd heard he was missing . . ."

"No, he's left, he's quit!" Ingrud looked up. Light from under the charabanc played across her face. Her agitated hands worked at the handkerchief. "I met him in Deaver's Well last autumn. He was traveling with a band of tinkers. He's not a steersman any longer!"

Rowan rocked back as if from a blow. "He's resigned? But why?"

Ingrud shook her head widely, smoky curls moving across her shoulders. "He wouldn't say. I asked him, and he wouldn't tell me. He wouldn't tell me where he'd been, what he'd been doing . . ." She closed her eyes again. "He refused to answer any of my questions. So he's under our ban. I told him so. He said he didn't care."

"Incredible . . ." Rowan groped mentally, searching for some approach by which to understand what she was hearing. Steerswomen had left the order before, for many reasons, internal or external. But to resign without explanation, without that simple courtesy to one's fellows; and worse, to place oneself under the Steerswomen's ban by refusing information . . . Small wonder Ingrud had been so upset on seeing Rowan without her ring and chain. It must have seemed that the impossible had happened twice, and this time to a better-loved friend . . .

But while one part of Rowan's mind was filled with concern for Janus and confusion about his motives, another was casting about, seeking connections and finding none. She said, half to Bel and half to herself, "It probably doesn't have anything to do with us."

Bel nodded, satisfied, but Ingrud looked up.

"I don't know what Janus was doing, Ingrud," Rowan continued. "I had heard that he was missing, that's all."

"And what about you?" Ingrud's face showed a mixture of anger and concern.

Rowan hesitated. "Will." He was startled by her sudden attention, then squinted suspiciously. "I think the steerswoman will need her cloak in a moment."

"You're trying to get rid of me," he accused.

Bel nudged him. "Of course she is. Now do as you're told."

With ill humor, he complied.

Rowan gestured for the Outskirter to sit beside her. "This is Bel," she told Ingrud, and then proceeded to deliver a rapid concise explanation of the jewels, the evidence of wizards' interventions, the Prime's decision, and her own mission.

Ingrud interrupted her then. She looked carefully into Rowan's face, studying her expression. Ingrud's tilted eyes were a lovely mixture of brown and green. Rowan remembered them as always filled with merriment, but now her gaze made Rowan shy back. "Are you still a steerswoman?" Ingrud asked quietly.

Rowan drew a breath and expelled it slowly, calming herself. She found that it was difficult to say. "Technically, *temporarily* . . . no."

Ingrud looked dazed, incredulous. "I hope all this is worth it."

"I think we're in a great deal of danger. All of us, the whole way of life."

"It seems impossible."

Rowan leaned forward to stress her point. "The wizards are putting restrictions on us. They've never done that before. We can't permit it; who knows how far they'd take it, if they had that power over us?"

"And what's so special about these jewels? What magic can they hold?"

"None that's visible. They seem to do nothing at all. I've carried one for over a year, and it's had no effect on anything, that I could tell. Bel's carried hers for over ten years. And you carry one yourself, so Bel tells me." Rowan pulled the little sack from around her neck. Her ring and chain jingled faintly against each other as she pulled the jewel out and handed it across. "Is this the same as the jewel on your brooch?"

Ingrud studied it, then looked up in amazement. "This is the source of all the problems? Of all these ridiculous schemes?"

"Ridiculous schemes? Ingrud, that's a poor phrase— "

"This is nothing!" She held it up to Rowan and Bel, and it flashed dimly in the starlight. "It's a decoration, a trinket!"

Bel was studying Rowan, waiting for her response. Rowan found herself growing angry at Ingrud's behavior. "Then," she said, "it's a decoration that can't exist, and a trinket that comes from nowhere."

"Don't be ridiculous. They're perfectly normal." Ingrud handed the blue shard back to Rowan. "And I know where they come from. I've been there."

CHAPTER
Fifteen

Willam sat on the edge of a stonewalled well in the little town square, seething in fury. A promise is a promise, he thought, even for a spy. Attise was not going to lose him so easily.

For the hundredth time Willam wished that Sala had been working alone, or with someone other than Attise. Sala would have stood by her word, Will was certain. Although, he realized, Attise had not actually promised to let Will stay with them – she had promised to help him if she had a chance. What she thought of as "a chance" she had left undefined. That was exactly the problem when dealing with her; her words, her meanings, kept slipping around, twisting and wriggling like tadpoles.

Of course, that was an asset for a spy, and it explained why Attise was in charge. Sala was likely too honest and straightforward to do well without someone like Attise directing their work. After all, spying was a nasty business, even for a good cause.

But it had been a cruel trick. Willam had walked a full morning with the caravan before he realized that Sala and Attise were missing. Attise had calmly sent him to the head of the line after breakfast, supposedly to distract Damaine while she and Sala spoke to one of the guards on some important subject. He had not noticed that they were gone until noon, and the thing was, they *had* been talking to the guard, and the important subject was that they were leaving the group early. Attise had not exactly lied to him, not this time.

"Likely you're looking for lodging?"

Will, watching the meager traffic in the village square, had been so lost in internal complaint that he had not noticed the villager coming up from behind. His road-sharpened suspicion was alerted. He didn't like people who approached in ways designed to go unnoticed.

But it was unlikely that he would be robbed in full daylight in the center of town. "Maybe. But there's no inn here?"

The man made a sound of derision and made a gesture with one hand; the other held a cloth-wrapped object, open at the top. "Town like this? Not enough business. But I've got room, if you want it. Reasonable." He lifted his package, which was revealed to be an open jar of some sort of liquor; he took a long draught from it.

Will was extremely reluctant to associate himself with the man. He looked around the village square. Immediately visible along the high street were a tannery, a bakery, a smithy – he felt a warm familiarity at that – an unidentifiable shop whose sign was at the wrong angle to see clearly, and a row of small dwellings. The street wound off north through what looked like pastureland. The only cross street seemed to dead-end in both directions.

Very likely he could find someone to give him sleeping space in return for work, or he could doss down in one of the pastures, if no one minded. But the man before him was the only person to approach him in the hour or so that he had been sitting on the edge of the stonewalled well.

It struck him as a little odd. Perhaps the village had had more than its share of bandits, or perhaps the war had passed over them, and the people were wary; but if that was so, why was this one fellow so interested? It felt wrong.

But he had to talk to someone. He turned back to the villager. "Do you have room for three?"

"Three?" The man's face acquired a calculating look.

"Three people. And one donkey. I'm supposed to meet some friends, or rather, I'm trying to. We got separated on the way. They have't arrived, have they? Two women, one of them a mercenary?"

166

The man blinked. "Mercenary? I'd have heard." His avaricious expression was replaced by a thoughtful one. "There was a steerswoman came through two weeks ago."

That was Ingrud, Will realized. "No, that's too long ago. My friends might be three days ahead of me, no more."

"No, there's been no one."

They had to have passed through the town, unless they had cut across country. Perhaps they had attempted to do that, gotten lost, and had to double back; Attise was so obviously hopeless with directions. They could easily be behind him. "Well," Will began to figure. "I don't have any money myself. One of my friends was carrying all we had." That should keep the man on the lookout for Attise and Sala. "I guess I'll have to sleep in a field. Though I wouldn't mind spending the night indoors, for a change." He allowed himself to look disgruntled. "If my friends arrive tonight, we'll be able all three to stay with you. If you're willing to come find me . . ." The opportunity to charge lodging for three instead of two insured that Will would be told when the two women arrived.

The villager considered. "Rain tonight," he observed.

Will peered at the sky as if this was news to him.

The man wavered, then said grudgingly, "Miller. Talk to the miller. Might be there's a shed to shelter in."

Will beamed. "Well, thank you, friend. That's kind of you."

There was a shed, but there was no miller; gone for the evening, Willam assumed. He let himself in and found a collection of empty sacks and a pile of lumber. The sacks made good bedding, and he found himself more comfortable than he had been for a long time.

Lying in the gathering dark, he took the opportunity to review his plans. If he could not find Attise and Sala here or farther up the road, he would just have to take himself to Shammer and Dhree alone. He knew from the steerswoman that their keep was somewhere north of here. Once he got near that lake Ingrud had mentioned, someone would know where the wizards were, or at least in what direction to look. He wondered briefly how two wizards could share one holding, then dismissed it as their own problem.

167

But that Attise. He shifted in annoyance. He kept trying to do well by her, but she was so secretive, so deceptive, so close-mouthed. How could you deal with someone like that? How did Sala manage it?

Likely Sala was no spy at all, but just what she seemed: a mercenary, a hireling. But she actually seemed to like Attise, though he could not see why. Perhaps because she, at least, knew what Attise was up to, was in the spy's confidence. He seethed. If he knew as much as Sala, maybe he could get along with Attise better, but she would not give him the chance.

He hated being kept in the dark, being pushed around. It was an easy, cheap thing, to push people around. All one needed was to be stronger, or to be smarter, or to know something that could be used on people. But it did not give one the right.

He knew how easy it was. He had pushed the other children around, when he was a child. He was always bigger, always stronger than the children his age, and some who were older. He was the leader by right of strength, and he was never afraid of anything or anyone. He soon learned that he could make the others do exactly as he pleased; and he had enjoyed it, he remembered, with more than a little guilt.

But he had stopped doing that sort of thing, stopped it when someone else bigger and stronger than him, stronger even than his own father, had taken from him the one thing he loved the best: an innocent, helpless, beautiful little girl. He could still hear her shrieking, still see her struggling against the soldier as he held her before him on the great horse. And the other soldier's sword against his father's chest . . .

And the memory of that day had driven him, with cold hatred, past what he had thought was possible: nurturing a tiny chance discovery, cautiously, thoughtfully, through reason and experimentation, into an unsuspected power.

No one had the right to use strength against the innocent. When he was a wizard himself, he would make sure no one ever victimized anyone again. He had to, *because* he was strong. Because he could work magic.

He reached one hand to the reassuring bulk of his pack, then turned over and slept.

Something in the small of his back gave him a sudden shove. He rolled, tried to get loose from the sacks, and ended up half standing, knife in hand, back against the wall.

In the dim light from the cracks in the wall, a figure was squatting beside his pack. "I can't figure if you're abysmally stupid or abominably clever." It was Attise, her voice heavy with weariness.

Will did not relax. It was dark in the shed, they were alone, and for all their traveling together, he still did not know this woman. "You tried to lose me."

"Yes, I did, and made a poor job of it, I can see." She sighed in exasperation and rose. "Come on."

He managed to stand. "Where are we going?"

"To Carroll's house."

" 'Carroll'? "

"Our host. Let's see what – what Sala can make of you."

She strode off, leaving him to scramble his possessions together.

She led him to a small cottage that seemed more a small hill of ivy than a dwelling. The leaves pattered and trembled in the drizzling rain.

As they entered, a rotund woman looked up from setting the table in the front room. Her black hair was pulled back severely from her face and bound in a single greasy braid, and her shapeless clothes had seen too much use and too few washings. "That him?"

"Our wandering lad," Attise confirmed. Her carefully affected voice covered her annoyance.

Sala entered from an adjoining room, carrying a kettle for tea.

"Willam!" She was delighted and put down the kettle to clap him on the shoulder.

"I'm sorry I got lost," he told her, trying to look sheepish.

"No harm done; we're all together again." She beamed up at him.

The housewife seemed satisfied. She gestured at the table. "Well, have some breakfast, then, or maybe it's lunch – who can tell the hour in this weather?" she grumbled.

The travelers seated themselves and made an attempt at casual conversation with the woman. This proved futile in the face of her continuing diatribe against her husband, delivered in monotonic segments as she moved to and from the kitchen. "I know he's at Miller's again, deny it as much as he likes, drinking that brew old Grandfather Miller makes, coming back at all hours. Useless he is, or next to it. No skill, no money—" She raised her voice a bit. "And no children here either, if you haven't noticed." She grunted disparagingly. "Useless."

Attise attempted to redirect her conversation. "Well, we're certainly grateful for the lodging . . ."

"Hmph. No skin off his bum; I do all the work, not that we can't use a few coppers. I tell you . . ." She wandered off, still muttering, and a long pause followed until it was clear that she intended to remain there.

Sala went to the window and peered outside. Attise passed Willam a bowl of cold stew, yesterday's by the look of it. Will set to with a wooden spoon and a chunk of black bread, and found that his hunger made its flavor incidental.

"How did you find us?" Attise asked him.

He spoke between mouthfuls. "I knew where you were going. Ingrud told me."

"Ingrud?"

"That's right. You kept me away from her after you talked, I guess because you thought I'd ask about what you said to her. But before that, earlier that evening, I talked with her a lot."

Oddly, Attise looked a little regretful. "Yes, I remember."

"Well, I asked her where Shammer and Dhree kept residence. She didn't really know, because all that's new since last she was in these parts. But from what she'd heard from the people coming back from the fighting, most of the action was taking place near someplace called Lake Cerlew. I asked her how to get there. It's north, and this was the first northbound road I found when I doubled back."

"And you assumed we were going to Shammer and Dhree?"

He nodded, tearing off a piece of bread to soak up the last bit of stew. "Where else would you go? But I didn't think I'd actually catch you up."

Sala turned from the window, pulling the shutters against the rain. She wiped mist from her face with one hand. "You didn't catch up with us," she told him, shaking water from her fingers. "We doubled back." She sat down next to Attise.

"We left the road, circled the town, and entered from the north," Attise told him. "We wanted to prevent anyone from connecting us with the caravan. We're claiming to be traveling through from Morriston, between here and Lake Cerlew." She turned to Sala. "And now he arrives in town, coming from the south, telling everyone he was with us."

Willam stopped eating. With a strange thrill, half fear, half excitement, he realized that this was no mere stop along the way. Attise and Sala had intended to come here; there was some job, some mission they had in this town; and if he could help them, somehow, their recommendation would carry more weight with their master.

"People haven't been very curious," the mercenary pointed out to Attise. "Perhaps those who spoke to him won't be the same as those to whom we gave our story."

"It could be awkward." Attise considered carefully. Watching her face, Willam could sense her sifting through possible explanations, alternative deceits.

"This wouldn't happen, you know, if you didn't keep me in the dark," he said.

Attise looked at him as if he were speaking in tongues. "What?"

Rain hissed in the dirt of the street outside. "You're always deciding for me. You never let me know what's going on. If I knew, I wouldn't make these mistakes. I could *help* you."

She seemed unable to find a reply. After a moment with nothing forthcoming, Sala took over. "The less you know, the less danger you're in. And we abandoned you because we like you, and we don't particularly want you to die. If you stayed with us, one day you'd follow us into a trap."

Attise found her voice. "Perhaps today."

Will was shocked, then thrilled, then wary. "Here?"

Sala disagreed. "If anyone wanted to harm us, they would have tried already," she said to Attise.

"Assuming they know I'm the right person. They certainly don't — yet."

"Perhaps the whole thing is innocent. Perhaps Ingrud was right. She's not a fool, you know." Already, Willam realized, it had happened again; he was once more mere spectator to some incomprehensible exchange between the two mysterious women.

"She's a steerswoman," Attise conceded.

"There you are."

"No. The conclusions one reaches depend on the information one has. She may have been fed deceits." Attise drummed ink-stained fingertips on the table, considering.

"Then let's assume that she was, and that you're right, and there's nothing in this town for us. Let's go on our way."

Attise said nothing, but sat thinking.

"What you're going to do will identify you, just as if you shouted your name," Sala noted.

To establish his presence in the conversation, Will said, "Your right name."

Attise's blue-gray gaze flicked in his direction. "True." She tilted her head to the sound of someone dashing across the street at a staggering run, escaping the drizzle, and turned her attention back to her bowl an instant before the door clattered open. Their host entered, and proved to be the same fellow Willam had met by the well. Faintly weaving, the man discovered the trio in his front room and regarded them with a certain amount of foggy confusion.

"No, one shouldn't make assumptions of that sort," Attise spoke up, fabricating a conversation to continue. "One region's commonplace is another's rarity." She gestured with her spoon at Willam, marking him the recipient of her opinions. "Even a dreary little spot like this one; I have every intention to visit the shops and manufactories before we leave. The possibility always exists, and nothing's so satisfying as cornering the market on some lovely item that your competitors will never be able to obtain."

Will glanced at Carroll, then tried to play along. "As long as people want to buy it."

"Exactly." She nodded. "To be desirable, any product should be either beautiful, or rare, or uniquely useful. Better, some combination of the three."

172

He made a wild guess. "And there's shipping cost."

Her smile seemed genuine. "Of course. The smaller, the better."

Will began to enjoy the game, until he saw Sala's expression. She had her back to Carroll and so was free to let her face show her thoughts. She disapproved. She glowered at Attise. It came to Will that when a mercenary disapproved of something, it was something dangerous.

There was a noise: "Ah!" It was a nasal sound of discovery and confirmation, and it came from the kitchen. Carroll's wife swept in with a display of self-righteous dignity, a shrewish expression, and a wooden ladle, which she brandished at Carroll. "Look at you, this early in the day, *and* in front of guests!"

Immediately, with perfect grace, the man corrected his posture, composed his expression, and stood regarding her coolly. Will, who had seen many persons drunk, marveled at his control. "Woman," Carroll intoned in a dignified voice. "You do carry on."

His wife gathered herself for a reply, then wavered. His act was perfect. She began to doubt.

He crossed his arms, perhaps a trifle slowly but without difficulty. "Tend more to your work, and less to your—" He paused to choose the exact word. "Intrigues," he finished.

She squinted up at him, then turned the squint on the others in the room, as though suspecting them of collusion. Attise watched with bland disinterest. Sala studied the pair as if she anticipated a sporting event. Will contrived to appear stupidly puzzled.

The woman made a throaty sound of disappointment and left the room. Carroll sniffed wetly.

Turning to his guests, he greeted them gravely and inquired after their comfort. Attise looked aside, as if wishing to find a polite way to express her opinion, then gave it up. She pushed out a chair. "Why don't you join us for some tea?"

The man looked toward where his wife had gone, then glanced back at the door. He stepped to it, pulled a little cloth-wrapped jug from a hiding place behind the brick doorstop, and brought himself to the table. "Well, thank you, I don't mind at all." Seated, he laid one finger aside his nose conspiratorially and added a bit from the jug to each cup, hesitating only momentarily before Willam's.

Will found that the stuff evaporated on its way from the front of his mouth to the back, and he coughed. Carroll nodded gravely at him as if he had expressed some deep insight.

Attise tried to draw the man into conversation, but he seemed far more interested in replenishing his cup, and he replied vaguely to questions about the types of local handicrafts. Yes, there was a tanner, a weaver, a potter, a silversmith. Yes, they did fair enough work. Eventually Will, who had politely drunk three cups of the fiery tea, discovered an urgent need to visit the outhouse and excused himself from the stilted conversation.

The back yard was as shabby as its inhabitants, unkempt, with a large trash heap tucked in one corner. Will thought it was a shame; the house itself was lovely, old stone and ivy. But as he looked about, he noticed that the adjacent yards all had their own piles of odd discards, items not useful for compost or fertilizer.

As he emerged from the bushes that discreetly screened the outhouse, he heard a crash of pottery. Carroll was standing by the trash heap; he looked up suspiciously as Will approached, then relaxed as he recognized the boy, taking rather long to do so. Will glanced down and noticed the liquor jug on the pile, smashed, and several more of its mates, some new, some of them very old indeed. He laughed to himself and leaned toward Carroll confidentially. "Your secret is safe with us." The man regained his careful dignity and wandered off on his own mission.

When Willam reached the front room, Attise and Sala were in deep conversation, listing the different types of shops Carroll had mentioned. Will found his chair and picked over the remains of their meal.

Pulling her purse from inside her blouse, Attise inspected the contents. She passed some coins to Sala. "Get a few supplies, from as many different shops as possible, and see how much gossip you can collect in the process."

"Are you going to try our hostess?"

Attise looked toward the kitchen and winced. "I'm not certain I can coax her away from her favorite subject. I'll check a few of the other shopkeepers, in my role as a merchant. The weaver, perhaps, or the tannery."

"To begin with," Sala noted.

"Of course." She looked in her purse again, seemed to calculate, and was displeased with the result. She returned it to its hiding place.

"What about me?" Willam asked.

"Stay out from underfoot."

"That's stupid," Sala said vehemently.

Attise looked at her in surprise.

The mercenary continued. "If you must go about advertising your presence, at least try to confuse them. If this is a trap, then they're expecting a woman traveling alone. They may not have caught up with the fact that Willam and I are with you. If you keep him by your side, you might throw off some suspicion, and they may be slower to realize what's afoot."

"I'd rather work with you," Willam said to Sala.

"I don't need help. I'll be doing the easy part. She's the one who's jumping into the fire."

"If there is one," Attise commented. "And that's what we need to discover."

They passed the tannery by, but tucked between two houses Attise found a potter's, little more than a ramshackle shed. The front was constructed of ill-sorted planks of varying ages and colors. No door was visible, but a merry whirring was heard from inside, and Will and Attise made their way around the side to an opening that had been created by the simple expedient of removing several planks from one wall.

Outside the rain had stopped, but the single room inside was dark and dank, save for a shaft of weak sunlight that descended from the ceiling, where a section of the roof had been levered up and propped with a pole.

In his patch of sun, the potter was happily at work, humming a little tune, a lean, fair man with wild curly hair. He spared the visitors a friendly glance; then a second, speculative; then, surprisingly, a third, amused. "Give me a moment," he called, and braked his wheel.

"Well, strangers." He turned on his stool and leaned, elbows on his knees, to examine them with twinkling blue eyes. "Are you lost? Looking for directions? You can't have come in here on purpose!" Will noticed that the lower half of one leg was missing, replaced by a long wooden peg.

Attise laughed a bit. "Actually, I did." She introduced herself and Willam. "I'm a merchant, passing through on business to the south. I thought it might be useful to examine the local wares. Occasionally one can find something worth transporting, something unusual, perhaps, or fine work."

"Fine work?" He leaned back and laughed out loud. "Well you certainly won't find any of that here." He made a sweeping gesture to indicate his workshop.

Attise eyed the rickety shelves and their contents with an expression almost apologetic. "I'm afraid not." She was acting more natural, Will noticed, easy and friendly, without her usual, close-watched stiffness.

"No, cheap and sturdy, that's my stock-in-trade. The things I make are easy to replace, and people break them without a second thought. Sometimes they do it just for fun. In fact, around winter solstice I make a hundred plates, just for the folk to smash at midnight. You could never eat off those plates, but they do make a lovely sound."

Watching Attise's reactions, Will noticed that she and the potter seemed to have some natural affinity for each other. He wondered if she planned to seduce him. Spies often did, he understood, for information.

But Attise inclined her head politely, with a cheerful smile. "Well, I won't take any more of your time." She glanced up at the little skylight, checking the hour, then stopped, curious. "That can't be very efficient."

"It isn't," he admitted ruefully. "But then, neither am I, and it suits me well enough. When the sun moves, I move too. It's a good excuse to take myself off for a bit of friendly conversation and a pot of brew."

"But there's no tavern in this town."

"No, but we manage well enough. Old Grandfather Miller supplies the brew, and the best conversations are always found in your neighbor's kitchen."

"There is that," she said. "But it makes it harder on the stranger. After days traveling, a brew and a conversation are things to cherish."

He made a wry sound. "It's all local gossip, local intrigues; you'd find it boring, I'm afraid."

"Not at all. If you travel long enough, everything feels local."

"There is that," he said, and at that phrase, he and Attise suddenly looked at each other in mutual astonishment and spoke simultaneously. "Where are you from?"

They laughed together, and she went on. "You're not from here?"

"No, not at all. My town was Denham Notch, on the West Road. It's far north, off the western curve of the Long North Road."

"Where the West Road turns from northwest to southwest."

He clapped his hands. "You know it! I thought you might. Skies above, you're like a fresh wind off the desert. I knew I liked you as soon as you spoke. Where's your town?"

"Terminus, at the other end of the road."

They were going to reminisce, Will realized; bored with the conversation, he took himself off to one side to examine the potter's ware. Attise and the potter kept chatting like old friends.

"Terminus! I've been there a dozen times when I was a point rider on a caravan. That was before this." There was a thump as he slapped his peg.

Behind one of the shelves, the wall was stone, not wood; the outside of the adjacent building, Will realized. He reached behind a row of pots and touched the wall. Pulling back his hand, he found it coated with a damp powder. He smelled it, then tasted it.

"But I never saw you there," the potter said to Attise.

"I'm hardly memorable."

Will turned back. Attise had found a seat on a workbench and was swinging her legs cheerfully. "You know," Will began, and the potter turned back, a little annoyed. "This stuff that's growing on your walls, it'll get on your pots."

177

The potter eyed him. "It does, sometimes."

"Well, I could scrape it off for you. You should do that, once in a while."

Speaking to Attise, the man said, "Your lad's getting bored. Why don't you send him off wandering for a bit?"

Attise was watching Willam with that sharp, too-intelligent gaze. "No," she said. "He tends to get into trouble if he's left to his own devices."

Will tried to look sheepish. "Really, I don't mind doing it for you. It'll keep me busy."

They exchanged glances, and the potter shrugged. "Suit yourself." He turned back to Attise. "No, I would have remembered you." Willam could hear the smile in the man's voice.

Will found a potsherd and another stool and, moving the items from a high shelf, began scraping the stones, using a broken jug to catch the powder. The conversation behind him wandered haphazardly. Willam soon finished his first section, replaced the pots, and began on the next.

"Did you find it to be true?" the potter asked Attise at one point. "Aren't the people friendlier in the south?"

Attise made an affirmative sound. "I think it's the desert that does it to us. Life is so fragile in the north, you have to work so hard, live so carefully. It makes us cautious."

"Well, I never regretted settling down here. There I was, stumping my way north off the Upland Route with my mind full of misery, and these people took me in. They didn't know a thing about me, but they made me feel like pure gold. You won't find a finer town than Kiruwan."

"Have other strangers settled here and found the same thing?"

There was a pause. "Well." Willam heard him shift. "No other strangers have moved in. No, everyone else is native."

Willam abandoned his stool for the third shelf.

"Perhaps you can advise me. Is there anything in this town that I might find worth buying?"

The potter took his time in answering. "There's Lena, the weaver. She does some interesting things. And you might try the jeweler."

"A small town like this can support a jeweler?"

"Well." There was a rustle and thump as he stretched his legs. "He makes most of his money as a silversmith. But we do have enough people coming through in winter to make his other work pay. I suppose you might find something you can use." He did not sound very enthusiastic; possibly he had a grudge against the man.

Will heard Attise jump to the floor. "Then I'll look in on those two. Thank you for your help, and the conversation."

"I enjoyed it." He sounded a little regretful.

"Willam." Will turned to see Attise beckon. "Let's go."

"But I'm not finished."

"He's a hard worker," the potter observed. He was looking at Will a little differently; Will could not identify the change.

"Can't I stay for a while?"

"I don't mind," the man began, but Attise interrupted.

"No." She was studying Willam, and it suddenly occurred to him that nothing he had been doing had missed her notice. "I think I need him with me."

Outside, Will detoured to carry the broken jug out back to the trash. Once out of sight, he dug out his grubby handkerchief, poured the powder into it, knotted the ends, and discarded the jug.

They found Lena, the weaver, plying her shuttle in a little room completely filled by the bulk of her loom. She listened to Attise's requests grudgingly, then conducted them into a second room, where bolts of cloth were stacked haphazardly. Attise duly inspected the work, but Will could tell she was not really interested; and try as she might, she could not draw Lena into casual conversation.

It came to Will that visiting the weaver's was mere distraction. Attise was marking her time, waiting for something to happen. There were too many things Willam did not know, too many events outside of his control. And the caution he had learned so dearly from his spells began to prick at him. If there was danger somewhere in this town, he – and perhaps even Attise herself – was walking into it blindly.

179

CHAPTER
Sixteen

"Are you learning anything?"

Attise looked up at him. "Nothing to speak of." They strolled down the street together in silence for a while.

Will slipped to Attise's opposite side, to avoid the muddy gutter. "Well, what are you looking *for*?" But he expected no real answer.

She stopped before a tall-windowed shop. "Perhaps this." Stepping across the gutter, she entered, pausing at the door to motion Willam to follow.

Inside, tall shutters had been pushed wide open, and the broad room was surprisingly bright. The walls were covered with shelves displaying plates and cups of silver and pewter. Toward the back, the room opened further into a workshop with benches and a small unlit stove.

Standing near the windows were a number of dark wood cases, lined with velvet of different colors to offset the varied contents to best advantage. A hasp on the front of each case suggested that they could be locked, although lids and locks were not in evidence. The velvet was dusty in some cases, worn in others, new in a few.

Attise scanned the shop, then strolled idly to the first case and examined the contents. A collection of red and pale-green stones set in silver was displayed on yellow velvet. Will reluctantly found himself fancying an openwork ring of subdued elegance.

"Well, here we are, then, here we are!" A little man bustled in from the rear of the shop. He was of Attise's height, with a high forehead, dark hair, and a beard of more gray than black. "Lovely work, that, lovely work. Some of my best." He approached and indicated an item. "There, you see? Delicacy, that's my specialty. You won't find many who can manage work like that." He seemed delighted by his own expertise.

"It is lovely," Attise admitted.

"Oh, yes, and," he held up one finger, "if silver's too dear for your purse, I can do much the same in pewter." He bustled over to a second case, sifted through its contents casually, and came back with a dusky twin of Will's ring, with a paler stone.

Attise took the ring and studied it. By now Will knew her conceits from her genuine reactions, and he realized with some surprise that she was keenly interested. "Where do you get the stones?" she asked the shopkeeper.

"Ah. Well." He drummed his fingers and pursed his lips. "Garnets from the schist in the local hills, lots of that, as you can see; but people always underestimate its versatility, don't you agree? Peridots, they're from the north, and someone came in last year with a lovely chunk of tourmaline – never saw anything like it, and I think you'll agree I've put it to good use . . ." He wandered to another case.

Attise turned to Will. "Isn't your mother's best dress blue? Or was it violet?"

"Ha, ha." The jeweler shook a finger at her. "Now, you can't fool me, not in a town like this, tongues wagging all the time. You're not idly passing the time. You're a merchant, and you're inspecting my goods to see what you can use. Well, I'm more than glad to help you, and I'll even give you a hint: volume discount is a distinct possibility, yes. Especially with these garnets. Really, I can't seem to get rid of them."

Attise replied with careful casualness. "But garnets are so . . . common, in so many places."

"Oh ho." His brown eyes crinkled, and he bounced on the balls of his feet. "The unusual," he said expressively, then paused for effect like a showman.

181

He stepped back to a cupboard against the wall, unlatched it, and pulled out two small trays covered with black velvet, which he carefully placed on top of a display of garnets. Then he stepped aside to view the reaction.

Will's response was an involuntary "Oh . . ."

"Incredible," Attise breathed.

The works displayed were all constructed of larger and smaller panels of a rich gem. Shifting light fragmented the color into every shade of blue, in shapes that reminded Will of frost flowers on the surface of frozen water.

Each panel, large and small, was embellished with silver inlay: intricate geometric patterns, emblems, and in some cases even landscapes. One necklace of startling beauty showed scenes from a hunt: in the center panel, a stag, wild-eyed, leaped a rushing brook, hounds in pursuit, all perfectly depicted in tiny silver lines.

"What's the stone?" Attise asked. "And how do you manage to cut it so thin?"

"Oh, now . . ." The jeweler pursed his lips. "I'm not about to let that little secret out, am I?" He indicated the trays emphatically. "There's no one else who can do that work, no one but me. And of course, the more rare something is . . ."

"Of course." Attise's mouth twisted, and she examined the hunt necklace again. "But these silver lines . . . are they filigree? It doesn't seem possible."

"Well . . ." He surrendered to a need to boast. "No, they're not constructed at all. You see," he leaned close and pointed at the stag, "I etch the patterns, with a tool of my own devising – very fine as you can see. Then I set the gem in a wash . . ." Attise shifted her attention to the man's face, listening intently as he explained. "The wash is an adhesive, and when it dries, well, I polish the surface of the gem, just a bit, and the adhesive comes off the surface and stays in the etches."

Attise thought a moment, then blinked. "Then you pass it through a wash of molten silver?"

The jeweler clapped his hands and laughed. "Well, there you are! That's exactly what I do! And the silver stays in the lines."

Attise nodded distractedly and ran her index finger across the face of one panel. "And you seal it with . . . is this a varnish?"

"Something like," he conceded. "More of a gum, really . . . now wait, wait a bit." He came to himself and shook a finger at her. "Here, now. I can't go telling you everything, can I? That's not good business."

She laughed. "No. Not at all. Forgive me, I have some interest in the craft." She turned back to the display. "I might find some customers for such work. Do you manage to sell many?"

"The process is tricky," he admitted reluctantly. "I find I have to charge more than people hereabouts and coming through are willing to pay. Except for the smaller pieces; actually, some of those move quite nicely." He indicated a group of brooches and a trio of tiny pendants. Too small for scenes, they were decorated with simple geometric designs.

Something about the brooches jogged Willam's memory. Abruptly, he remembered that Ingrud had worn one as a clasp on her cloak. He was about to comment, but stopped himself when he could not recall how Ingrud's known movements would intersect with Attise's pretended ones.

"What about these rings?" Attise asked the jeweler.

The little man winced. "Not at all popular, I have to admit. A bit of an error on my part. People don't seem to like to wear them where the gem touches their skin." William touched one experimentally and found the oily surface eerie and unpleasant.

Attise sifted through the rings and found one with a simple but striking design. She began to slip it on her middle finger, then stopped and shifted it to the third. "I see what you mean," she told the jeweler. "But they do serve as a good example of your technique." She turned to him. "I'd like to give this some thought."

"Of course, of course! Mustn't rush into things, but I don't have any doubts, my work is unique! Still, think, and come back later. Take that ring to keep, if you like," he waved his hand. "No charge, call it a sample. Just as well to be rid of it, actually." He tapped his cheek thoughtfully. "Now, if you come back, make it the evening, if you don't mind. I have a little something to do; in fact, I ought to leave now."

"Business?" Attise asked nonchalantly.

"Ho ho!" He bounced again. "Business of a personal sort. A lovely little lady, housemaid down at the first farm up the main road. It's her afternoon free, but she never goes far, her mistress is an invalid, very devoted, she is. Now, if you want to talk sooner, you come there, ask for my Ammalee. Don't worry about interrupting, business before pleasure . . ." He bustled off closing and locking cases, then pulling the tall shutters in. Attise looked long at her ring, eyes narrowed in thought, oblivious to all else, until the jeweler hurried them out and locked the door.

They returned to their lodgings, Attise in a black, silent mood, impervious to questions. Back at the ivy-covered house, they found Sala sitting on a bench in the sunlight with a group of small packages and a disgruntled expression. "I never met such a closed-mouthed lot. You'd think I was a criminal, the way they brushed me off. I could hardly get them to do business."

Attise tested the grass, found it too wet, and settled down beside Sala. "What did you get?"

"Some cheese, dried meat, and hardbread." Sala, catching Attise's amused look, gave a wry half smile, and continued. "No gossip, no details. The war hardly bothered them. They've had no contact with wizard's troops. The potter moved here ten years ago. Everyone else has been here forever."

"We did a little better. Here." Attise slipped off the ring and passed it to Sala. The mercenary studied it with suspicion.

"It's the same."

Attise nodded.

"Ingrud was right?"

"No." Attise thumped one knee in frustration. "No, it seems— " She moved her hands as if there were something between them. "It seems as if it ought to fit, but it's all too facile." She dropped her hands. "I talked awhile with the potter. As it happens, he grew up near the place I did, and he was quite open with me, for a while." Sala was interested, and Attise made to continue, paused, then looked significantly at Willam.

He bristled. "I'm not going anywhere."

"Will— "

"I do whatever you want, but you never tell me anything. You're just using me— "

Sala interrupted. "Of course we are. And you're using us. It seems fair to me. Now go away."

"But I could help you better. And maybe you could help me better, too, and easier, if I knew what was going on." He turned from one to the other, Sala's face stubborn, Attise's full of weary exasperation. "Maybe you think I'm not much, but I'm not stupid, I can see things too. Why did the people stop being friendly?"

"What?" Sala was taken aback, but Attise watched him closely.

"The potter said that people here were friendly to strangers, but they weren't friendly to you, or to me. The jeweler was friendly to Attise, but the weaver wasn't." Calmer, he sat on the wet grass and looked at Attise intently. "It's something to do with that jeweler. Something important is going on here, isn't it?"

Attise hesitated, then said, "I hope so."

"You don't know for sure?"

"Not yet."

"What will you do if you find out there is?"

Her mouth twisted. "Run away."

"And report this to Shammer and Dhree?"

The women exchanged glances; then Attise took a moment to think. She leaned forward. "What did you take from the potter's shop?" Sala looked surprised at the change of subject, then watched Willam with renewed interest.

Will was not surprised at all. "There's some stuff that grows on stone walls, and in caves. In Langtry, we had a lot of it. People had to scrape down their walls regularly, especially in cellars."

"And?"

He knew what she wanted and shrugged uncomfortably. "And I use it in my charms."

"What does it do?"

With great reluctance, he said, "It works with the other things in a spell, one of the spells I know."

Attise said nothing else, but sat watching him, waiting.

"I don't think I should tell you anything else," Will said at last.

Willam noticed with some surprise that Sala was looking at Attise as if concerned for her. She touched the merchant's arm to get her attention. "Don't press the boy. I think it's a good thing. The more magic the common folk know, the better matters will go for everyone."

Surprisingly, Attise made no protest against the comment, but only stirred uncomfortably.

Suddenly Willam noticed that Attise was tired – no, exhausted. She seemed weak and worn, and her expression bleak. She turned away. "Willam," she began, not looking at him. "I'm sorry that you think I'm being unfair. It's not my doing, it's the situation."

"You mean that because of your mission, you get to push me around."

Her voice was flat. "I don't mean to push you. I simply do what I need to do. It's because I don't do what *you* want me to that you have a problem. Now, please leave for a while, so that Sala and I can discuss this."

Watching her, Willam slowly recognized again what Sala had pointed out to him once: that this woman was doing something against her own will, acting in a way that she hated. Sala had meant it differently, but now he realized it was true in a deeper sense. Somehow, in some important way, Attise was helpless.

His anger evaporated, and what was left, surprisingly, was pity. "If you don't like working for Shammer and Dhree," he said, "why don't you quit?"

She closed her eyes and shook her head, and Willam could not tell if that meant that she could not quit, or that she could not tell him why, or that she did not want to talk about it. He began to wonder if it was possible to quit the service of a wizard, if it was permitted at all. Perhaps Shammer and Dhree would do something terrible to her if she tried. Perhaps they were no better than Abremio – maybe there was no difference between the behaviors of Blue and Red. But that could not be; there had to be some difference.

Suddenly he wished, truly and sincerely, that he could do something to help Attise. Without preamble, he said, "When I'm a wizard, I won't do this to people."

She understood. But she turned back, and amazingly, he saw pity for him on her own face. "When you're a wizard," she told him sadly, "you'll do what wizards do."

The front door thumped open, and a thin voice demanded, "Have you seen him?" Carroll's slatternly wife stormed out, fists on her hips, glaring up and down the damp sunlit street.

Startled, Attise looked at her once, blankly, then rose and turned aside to deal with her own dark thoughts.

Sala exchanged a glance with Willam. "Meaning your husband?"

"Who else? Slippery devil, saying he's off visiting, saying he doesn't know where the money went." She whirled on them, shaking her fist vehemently. "All the good coin you gave me, gone! Never drinks, doesn't touch a drop, he says! Well, I'll catch him at it, one of these days, and when I do he'll be as gone as the moon. I tell you . . ." She wandered back into the house, muttering, leaving a large silence behind her.

Will tried to find something to say, to recover from the unresolved, interrupted discussion. Something comradely. "I'd drink if she was my wife."

Sala glanced at Attise's back and played along. "Never marry. Or marry someone more entertaining."

"Or smarter; you'd think she'd have it figured out by now. I guess she doesn't look at the trash heap much."

"Trash heap?"

Attise had turned back and was looking at him as if he had said something astounding.

He paused, puzzled. "That's right," he told her, confused. "Out back. There's a dozen broken jugs in the trash. And some not very old, either. She doesn't have to try to catch him at anything – those jugs tell the story themselves."

Attise looked at the house, then the other houses, with a faintly stunned expression. "This town doesn't have a communal trash area."

He could not tell if she was asking him or telling him. "No," he confirmed. "From the yard, you can look along the whole row of houses— "

But she had swept into the house, through the front room, past the still-grumbling wife, and toward the hall to the back door. Will hurried after. "Where's Bel?" she asked when she saw he was still with her.

That was Sala's real name, he knew; but Attise only slipped and used it when she was excited or upset. The mercenary caught up. "Here."

As they emerged from the rear door, Attise turned left, ignoring the trash heap Will had mentioned, and hurried on, intent.

"What's the matter?" Will asked. They had crossed the back garden and were passing through the next yard. An elderly woman emerged from a chicken coop and stared in bleary confusion as they swept past.

Attise made an offhand apology to her and continued on to the next yard. "Either nothing, or everything," she said to no one in particular.

"What do you mean?"

But she was absorbed in her urgency and did not reply until Sala repeated the question. "Contradictions. That's what's wrong with this town." Attise stopped and scanned the area. "We have a saying," she continued distractedly. "'There are no contradictions.'" She spotted her goal and hurried on.

"Who's 'we'?" Will asked Sala, but she waved him silent and followed Attise, fascinated.

To Will's amazement, they stopped by a pile of trash behind one of the shops. Sala peered at it while Attise stooped and began rummaging through, heedless of the dust and dirt.

"What are you looking for?" Sala asked.

"Nothing specific." Attise pulled out a pair of wood laths connected by an odd rusty hinge and examined them closely. "But I shall be very interested in what I do find." She dropped the laths and was briefly absorbed in the study of a tangle of string. The mercenary dropped down beside her and watched as she extracted from the tangle a short white splinter.

"Contradictions," Sala hazarded, "between what you know and what Ingrud said."

Attise kept the splinter and moved to another side of the heap. "And," she said, poking at some potsherds, "between the way the people of this town act, and what they tell us." She found a boat-shaped piece of dark wood as long as her hand, cracked down its length. She stopped and gazed at it, lost in thought, then looked up at Sala and Willam as if surprised to find them there. Hefting the wood, she studied the shuttered windows at the back of the shop. Will realized that the shop was the jeweler's, and as he watched Attise, he found himself reminded of the careful, thoughtful expression Ingrud had worn when he had asked her questions.

"What sort of trash does a jeweler leave?" Attise asked.

Sala paused in surprise. Then, inexplicably, she laughed. "Not the sort you have there?"

Puzzled, Will recognized one item. "That's a shuttle, a shuttle from a loom."

Attise had returned from her thoughts strangely lighthearted. She grinned up at him, and he found the expression incongruous on her face. "That's right," she said. "And this," she held up another item "is half of a bone needle, broken." She pointed at parts of the heap. "Rather many bits of string and thread, too short to be of use." She reached in, pulled out a potsherd, and indicated it. "Stained on the inside; that's from dye." She dropped the items and stood, dusting her hands. "Until very recently, the jeweler's shop was held by the weaver."

"He moved his shop?"

"I think that if we ask, we'll be told that he didn't. He's a recent arrival. And here's the proof." She pointed with her chin at the heap.

"But," Will said, "the potter said he's always been here. Was he lying?"

Attise nodded.

"What happened to the weaver?" Sala wondered.

Attise pointed down the row of shops. "She moved onto the cross street, to that new house on the end. It's not a proper shop at all; it's not set up correctly. It's just a dwelling, pressed into use." She turned back to the jeweler's. "He took this one because it's one of the oldest buildings in town, supporting the claim that he's always lived here."

"But why would the people lie?" Willam asked.

"Why does anyone do anything?" Attise replied. "To make their lives better, or to prevent them from getting worse."

Sala nodded. "Rewards or punishments."

"In this case."

"The jeweler is a wizard's man."

Attise held up a cautioning finger. "And we mustn't let on that we know."

"And this was all designed— "

"To convince me that I'd been mistaken. That I'd been . . . chasing the moon."

Sala laughed a little. "We have that saying, too."

"That surprises me not at all."

Will looked from one woman to the other. They ignored him completely.

"And here we stand in full daylight, in sight of the back windows of the jeweler's shop," the mercenary said.

Attise was amused. "He's visiting Ammalee, who is a housemaid for an invalid living at the first farm up the main road." Will remembered the conversation.

"So his shop stands empty."

The merchant made an airy gesture. "Convenient for us to break into and discover all sorts of fascinating items pertaining to the making of jewelry."

"Which you'd recognize?"

"Some. Not all, because of his 'secret process'— "

"But they'd be the sorts of things that make sense."

"Exactly. It would be the *sorts* that were important. Items unidentifiable in specific, but recognizable as to type."

"To someone used to thinking that way . . ."

"Such as myself."

The jeweler might be a wizard's man, Attise had said. "Are you going to kill him?" Will asked.

They turned on him in surprise. "No," Attise told him. "We're going to act naturally, and leave here."

"And report to your masters?"

A quick glance at each other, another glance toward the shuttered shop, apprehension on their faces, and suddenly it was as if a toy house of twigs collapsed inside Willam, revealing something hidden within, something startling. Everything was changed.

He said in slow amazement, "That jeweler was sent here by Shammer and Dhree themselves. You don't serve them at all."

190

They faced him. Attise was wearing her watching-and-waiting look, but, strangely, Sala was standing as if ready for sudden action, dark eyes full of danger. A memory came to him unbidden: when he had first met these two, it had been Attise who had saved his life.

She spoke. "Willam, if you want to find Shammer and Dhree, follow the main road north to Lake Cerlew. Make your way along the shore to the east; someone there will know where to send you. I don't recommend you approach the jeweler. It's best you're not connected with us."

Sala listened in growing astonishment, then turned on her. "You can't mean that. We mustn't let him go!"

"It will take him some time to reach the wizards. We can vanish into the woods."

"It's too risky."

This was impossible. Attise, whom he hated, was trying to save him from Sala, his friend.

"I won't have the boy hurt, Bel. He's innocent. And you said it yourself: the more magic the common folk know, the better things will be for everyone."

By that statement, Willam identified another change, but it only added to his confusion. "You don't serve a Blue, either. You – you don't serve any wizard at all."

Sala narrowed her eyes and shifted, but with a gesture Attise asked her to wait. Attise turned to the boy, spreading her hands in a wide gesture of honesty. "Willam, I'm not a spy. I'm a steerswoman."

"No," he said immediately. "Steerswomen never lie."

She nodded, and her mouth twisted a bit. "True. Say, then, that I'm a lapsed steerswoman. I was one, until the time came that I needed to lie, to save my life. I'll be one again, when that time is past." She shifted uncomfortably, but her gaze remained steady on Willam. "The wizards want me, Willam, all of them. They're hunting me. Don't betray me."

And then he finally realized that it had to be true. Ingrud had recognized her, had been distressed, had talked about that steersman who had quit the order. Attise had needed privacy to explain something to her. And Attise sometimes knew things she should not, recognized connections invisible to others, and pieced things together in a way unlike other people. Nothing was as it had seemed.

To a steerswoman, lying must be like torture. Attise must have been dreading every day, suffering through every conversation with a stranger. It would make her quiet, so that she would not lie unless she had to. It would make her angry, to go against her training so. And she would be bad at it, as bad and as transparent in deceit as Attise was.

And it had to do with wizards. Attise was in danger from the wizards; she was somehow a victim of theirs.

The steerswomen never used their knowledge or their intelligence to hurt people. They knew more than anyone except the wizards, and they never used it to control, never tried to have power over others. They were not like most people.

They only cared about learning and discovering, and they shared their knowledge joyfully. In that they were as innocent and direct as children. Willam knew well the evil of using power against the innocent. He had been helpless that time; this time, things stood differently.

Attise was watching him intently, without annoyance, without anger, without fear or discomfort, without deceit. She was watching him like a steerswoman, but her eyes held a question, and a steerswoman's questions had to be answered.

"I won't tell anyone about you," he said. "I won't betray you. I'll help you, if I can." And he could, he realized, perhaps better than anyone else. He lifted his head a bit higher. "But, tell me, lady . . . tell me all about wizards."

CHAPTER
Seventeen

It was as easy as laughter, as natural as breathing, as joyful as the swing in her step on the road. Attise the reluctant merchant fell from her mind like a muddied cloak, and Rowan felt right in her heart for the first time in what seemed like a lifetime. It did not matter to her that she walked in danger; it only mattered that she could speak and act freely again, and that the power given to her by her training and nature need not be hidden like some secret sin. The one true concern she had was that she might die before the puzzle was solved, and that would be tragedy indeed.

To protect the hope of an answer: that was the goal, the duty and the pleasure. She felt it with more urgency than even the need of preserving her own life. To stay alive served the goal.

And in the meantime, as she and her comrades clambered alone, up and down the hilly countryside, she was doing what her spirit had designed itself to do. She was answering questions.

"Since as far back as the Steerswomen's records reach, there has always been a wizard resident in the city of The Crags. This probably accounts for the heavy-handed control Abremio holds; The Crags has never been without a wizard. It depends on its wizard to a degree not found in any other holding. Its politics depend on his decisions, and its workings depend on his magic. How long this situation existed before our records, we don't know.

"We do know that sometime thereafter, a wizard became established in Wulfshaven, on a far less formal basis. The logbooks of the first steerswoman, Sharon, make some oblique references to the event. In fact, it was clear that she approved of it."

"More fool she," Bel muttered. The Outskirter fussed a moment with the frogs on her cloak as the wind picked up and whirled it around her legs. She had never resigned herself to the loss of her own piebald cloak, left at the Archives because of its conspicuousness.

Willam looked at her, then checked Rowan's reaction to the seemingly heretical statement. But Rowan merely nodded.

"Yes. Sharon herself said that, over and over, at a later date. A lot of her logbooks are filled with complaints about her own misjudgments. But humans aren't infallible, and conclusions depend on the knowledge at hand."

She gathered her information and continued. "So, those two holdings are the oldest. For many years there were only two wizards, and believe it or not, there was no animosity between them."

Willam was puzzled. "But they fight all the time, now."

Rowan held up a finger. "That's not quite true. They fight periodically."

"Same thing."

"Not at all." Rowan was annoyed at this twisting of facts. "Get your information right. They clash, regularly. In a large way, once a generation. In a small way, several times, and you can count on two shifts of alliance each generation." Rowan found that the information that Hugo had given her at the Archives was falling more clearly into place in the retelling, and she reminded herself that such was often the case.

"So. That's how matters remained, for nearly two hundred years. Around that time, the lands around the Greyriver began to increase in population. As the town at the river's mouth became an important port, dragons appeared, first in small numbers, then greater." She noticed Bel's sidelong glance and continued. "At the same time, two new wizards established themselves. One took residence in the port and immediately took the dragon problem in hand. No one contested his holding, least of all the townspeople, and the town even took its name from its first wizard."

"So there was a wizard Donner who did what Jannik does now?" Bel asked.

"Who's Jannik?" Will queried.

"The wizard in Donner," Bel supplied. "He controls the dragons there. Or doesn't, depending on his mood."

The boy turned his wide copper gaze back to the steerswoman. Despite herself Rowan felt a shift in her breath. Those eyes, so strange in color, were so beautiful. He was a beautiful boy, and would be a handsome man one day soon.

"But which wizard is after you?" Willam pressed.

Rowan had explained her mission to him. "We don't know for certain. But there's good reason to suspect that it's Shammer and Dhree."

"And that's where we are now, in their territory." He seemed to give the fact careful consideration.

"Possibly."

He nodded grimly. "Good."

"There's no reason to be pleased about it."

"I agree with him." Bel was a few steps ahead, and Rowan, perturbed, moved up to where she could watch her friend's expression.

The Outskirter continued. "I'm tired of this. I don't mind danger, but I don't like it forever waiting just out of sight. I want to see it face-to-face, or I want it to go away."

"It will go away," Rowan assured her, "when we reach the Outskirts." She smiled a little. "Then you'll only have your old familiar dangers."

"I'll be glad to see them," Bel admitted. She looked at the sky and at the track ahead. "And it's time we found a place to spend the night." The Outskirter lengthened her stride and pulled ahead on the trail.

The steerswoman watched a moment, then returned to her explications to Willam. "Now, the second wizard, a woman, claimed the upper Wulf valley. The area was largely uninhabited at that time, and she lived, for the most part, the life of a recluse— "

Will interrupted. "But what do they *do*?"

"Do?"

"What kind of magic? Is it different for each wizard?"

Rowan considered. "Not really. Any specialities they favor seem to be based on their situation. Jannik in Donner has control of the dragons, but there's no indication that another wizard couldn't do the same. Corvus, in Wulfshaven, has knowledge of the movements of sea creatures and the weather, but he's based in a major seaport, where those things are of vital interest to everyone."

He brooded a moment. "Abremio seems to be able to do anything."

"So I hear. I'll ask you about him at length, in a bit," Rowan said. "You have firsthand knowledge."

"But I've never seen him do what I do."

"And what exactly do you do?"

He hesitated. "Well, I've told you . . ."

"Yes. Rocks and tree stumps. Digging wells." She spotted Bel, who had wandered off the path ahead looking for a discreet campsite. They exchanged waves, and Rowan led Will toward the Outskirter. "You've told me what it's for, or at least the use you put it to. But how exactly do you do it?"

"Well, I place the charms around the object, or under it, or in a hole . . . Then I have to put fire to them. That has to be done from a distance— "

"How? Magically?"

"No," he admitted, embarrassed. "I tried that, but I can't make it happen. I use a burning arrow. Or sometimes, a sort of path made out of straw, or crumbled bits of another charm."

"And then?"

He shrugged uncomfortably. "When the fire reaches the charms, the spell releases."

"And it's not good to get in the way," Rowan added, remembering his earlier description.

"That's right."

Rowan nodded. "How do you make the charms?"

He did not answer. Rowan stopped and turned to face him, one hand on his arm. He avoided her glance, looking pained and unhappy; it was an expression she had seen before, on a few other faces.

"Will," she said, "I'm glad you're traveling with us. I like you. And I think that on this journey, I can use all the help that I can

196

get." She paused. "I'm not a real steerswoman at the moment, but the time will come when I shall be again. You can refuse to answer me now, but you can't forever."

He stuttered a bit. "I know that. It's just – maybe I won't be able tell you anything, not ever."

"How so?" Ahead, Bel hailed them again, but Rowan ignored her.

"Well . . ." His face worked with thought. "There are some things the wizards don't ever tell the folk. About how their magic works."

"There are many things the wizards don't explain," Rowan conceded cautiously. "The reasons behind their actions, their shifting allegiances, and the workings of their power."

"And we don't know why."

"Correct."

"But that's just it!" He swallowed. "We don't know why they hide those things. Maybe there's a *reason*; maybe it's the right thing to do. Maybe it's something people shouldn't know."

Rowan said nothing, but let him work through the problem alone. On the horizon, the westering sun cut below the heavy bank of clouds that hung above like a flat ceiling. For a moment the world turned gold and dove-gray, and a fine drizzle fell briefly, then ceased. One part of her mind noted that there must be a rainbow somewhere over her right shoulder.

"This magic I can do, it's just something I figured out for myself," Willam went on. "There was nobody— " He struggled for a moment. "There was nobody wiser than myself to tell me what it means, or what to do about it. I just don't know enough. Maybe it would be terrible if anyone else knew how it worked. Maybe it's terrible that I know."

"And how am I to judge, without information?" Rowan said.

He shifted the pack on his back and used both his hands in a wide, pleading gesture. "Lady – Rowan, I'm going to be a wizard someday. When I am, if I find that they're keeping their secrets for some mean reason, I promise you that I'll tell you everything, anything. But until I really know it's safe, please, don't ask me to do something that might be bad." He dropped his hands, looked stricken. "I can't do anything that hurts people."

He stood before her, a tall boy, bigger than his years, strong for his age, more intelligent than his peers, possessing some secret power – and begging her, humbly, to not make him hurt anyone.

"You'll be a poor wizard," Rowan said. "Or, you'll be the best of them." She turned away and walked toward Bel's waiting figure.

He caught up with her in two long strides. "You won't ask me again?"

"I'm going to think on this awhile."

Bel had found a clearing a few paces off the south side of the trail. A damp circle of ashes showed where some previous traveler had camped, months earlier. A tangle of low birches surrounded it, and Bel was using the branches to create a rain fly from the merchant Attise's cloak. She had refused to abandon it when Rowan returned to using her own gray felt cloak, declaring it to be too useful.

"We'll need a fire tonight, with this damp."

Rowan scanned the sky and decided that the mist would continue to midnight without converting to a proper downpour. "If we can get one going at all, we might be able to keep it all night."

Bel was digging in her pack for the trail provisions purchased in Kiruwan. "If we can find dry wood after all that rain."

Rowan and Willam foraged through the underbrush and managed to acquire a pair of stout damp branches, which Willam cracked methodically and effortlessly across his knee. A handful of dry twigs and needles from the lee of a lone fir tree was the best that could be found for kindling, and Rowan plied her flints doggedly, creating a series of merry little blazes that guttered dismally against the logs. As she tried with one last pile of needles, Willam spoke up reluctantly. "Let me try."

Rowan eyed him a moment, then rose, slapping the damp from her trousers.

Willam went to his sack, opened it, inserted one hand, and felt inside carefully. What came out was one package, the size of his fist, wrapped in oilcloth. Rowan moved closer to observe, and Bel watched him cautiously from across the clearing. He spared the Outskirter a single glance, then studied Rowan, his face unreadable. Perhaps it was a surrender of sorts, or a bargain: he could not tell her, but it seemed that he was going to show her.

The package unrolled to reveal a layer of wool, and nestled in it, separated from each other, were three objects wrapped in paper. Willam removed one, carefully rolled the others back into the oilskin, and replaced it in his pack, which he carried to the edge of the clearing and secreted behind a weedy tussock.

Returning to the fire site, he seated himself on the ground. Rowan dropped to the ground beside him.

The paper was secured by twists, which he casually undid. Inside was a quantity of black gravel that faintly glittered. Taking a pinch of the gravel between his fingers, he crumbled it to powder onto the logs, creating a thin line along the surface of each. Rowan noted that the lines continued from each log to the next, creating a continuous network, then recognized that the lines formed a hexagram. The final arm continued outward from the heap, ending a foot outside the first circle. There Willam arranged Rowan's little pile of needles, adding one more tiny pinch of the black gravel. He paused a moment, studying what remained in the paper; he had used less than a third of the quantity.

Finally he twisted the paper closed again and methodically returned it to its place in his pack behind the tussock. When he returned, Rowan wordlessly handed him her flints, and he gestured her back, doing it twice before he was satisfied with her distance.

With his back to her, she could not clearly see what he was doing, but from the sound it seemed nothing more than striking sparks into the pile of kindling. He tried three times; then there was a sudden hiss, and he stepped back quickly.

A line of sparking fire fled from the kindling, sped to the logs, and raced along their lengths, spitting madly. There was a group of sudden quiet noises from the wood, like gasps, and one log abruptly split down its length with a loud *crack*. Rowan was aware of a sharp, acrid odor.

Flame flared, faded, leaped again, and then the fire settled down to blaze in earnest. Bel fearlessly strode over, kneeled by the fire, and peered at the still-sparking wood. "Can you make anything burn?"

The boy watched her broodingly. "No. I can't burn stone. But I can break it. It's easy."

"Is that when it becomes noisy?"

"Yes. Very. And dangerous."

Rowan moved to Bel's side. Each log, she saw, was burning individually, along the line the gravel had traced. Using the toe of her boot, she rearranged the wood so that the flames better fed each other.

Bel looked up at her. "Are you going to ask how he did it?"

She shook her head. "No." But she sat up long that night in thought, watching the fire.

They spent the next day following the narrow trail down one ridge and up the next. The land began to open, and deep in one valley the travelers came across an abandoned farm, with a burnt-out, ruined cabin. There was no sign of the previous inhabitants, but when they crossed a fallow field they found a low hill of violent green, such as grew where corpses were buried. Rowan considered the extent of the mound and calculated. "More than those who lived in that house. I suspect this was a battle site."

"That definitely puts us in Shammer and Dhree's holding?" Bel asked.

Rowan shrugged. "That depends on which side won this particular battle."

The past winter and now the spring had claimed the land for wilderness, all the shouts and the clash of arms lost in the past as though a hundred years had gone. Only the mound remained, its shape unnatural, its green too bright, feverish. The travelers stood silent for some time, each lost in thought. A fresh light wind rose, and the grass shivered, then rippled like the shining surface of a rising wave. The valley was a bowl of clean sunlight, quiet, and when Bel shifted the creak of her gear was a sudden, strange, human sound: an intrusion.

Willam studied the scene grimly. Bel looked about, faintly puzzled. With a gesture, Rowan led her friends around the edge of the mound, and they continued east.

They soon left the farm behind, and their spirits lifted again. Rowan could ignore, briefly, the sensation that danger hovered somewhere, like a high hawk, too far to see.

She studied the land about her, comparing it with the few maps she had. As Attise, she had allowed herself only the sort that the common folk usually carried: copied from those of the Steerswomen, but by a less exacting eye, with less detail, excluding information not of interest to the average traveler. Rowan made corrections and additions, and found satisfaction in the routine.

With deception and manipulation abandoned, the three travelers had learned to be at ease with each other, and the going was enjoyable for itself. Rowan amused herself watching Bel's reactions. "Everything keeps changing," the Outskirter commented. They were moving along a rocky ridge, among stands of young pine.

"How so?"

"The Outskirts are much the same everywhere. The only differences come when you get closer to the Inner Lands, like the approach to Five Corners. But here, you'll have one kind of tree for a while, then pastures, then flat land, like the mud flats in Donner. Every place is different, with different kinds of life."

Rowan nodded. "Certain terrains encourage certain types of vegetation and certain types of animals."

"There aren't many different animals in the Outskirts. It's the goats and us, for the most part."

"And the goblins."

"Yes. And the demons. And insects."

They continued in silence for a while. Halfway up the ridge, the view was clear to the north, and the two women paused. Half a mile away, pines gave way to maple, which carpeted the hills to the horizon. Far off, a line of silver indicated a distant lake.

Bel looked up at the sky, as if expecting it, too, to be different from the Outskirts. "The Inner Lands seem to go on forever."

"They don't," Rowan told her. "They end to the north, just past the land where I was raised. It's red earth there, and no one's been beyond it yet. There are a few mountains visible to the west. I often wondered about them. They're probably an extension of the same range that runs north from The Crags."

Bel puzzled that over, trying to piece together Rowan's picture of the world. "And what lies west of those?"

Rowan looked dissatisfied. "No one's been there to report. Or perhaps some of Abremio's minions have gone, but they haven't given out any word." She mused for a moment, then continued. "The southern shore of the Inland Sea is inhabited, too, but not to any great distance. The vegetation gets odd farther south, and it's hard to introduce anything useful. It might be a worse version of what you have in the Outskirts."

Bel nodded. "Goats." She adjusted her pack and began to continue the ascent, tugging the reluctant donkey's lead. "You need goats about if you're going to spread the greengrass. They'll eat anything."

Rowan followed, sidestepping on the steep ground. "They can't eat redgrass or blackgrass."

The Outskirter looked back. "Of course they can. Our herds do it all the time. We couldn't survive if they didn't."

"It must be a different type of goat." With dust from their scrambling rising around her, Rowan's mind filled with speculations and calculations. "That might explain a great deal. It might even be one of the reasons the Outskirts keep moving."

Bel was puzzled. "Moving? How can they move?"

Pausing to brace herself against a splintered tree trunk, Rowan gestured out at the far horizon. "East. The Outskirts have been shifting for hundreds of years, and the Inner Lands spreading behind them. You can trace the shift by comparing the maps at the Archives. Some thousand years ago, this was the Outskirts." Bel took a moment to peer about in plain disbelief. Rowan laughed. "It's true." She continued. "Your goats might do well in the south. What a difference that could make to the people there . . ." They continued on silently for some time, the steerswoman lost in thought.

Bel watched her with amusement. "You're going to be writing a lot tonight again, aren't you?"

"What?" Rowan came back from her preoccupation with difficulty. "Yes, I suppose I am." Since Willam was in their confidence, she openly treated her folio like a proper steerswoman's logbook, crowding the pages with her close, eccentric handwriting.

"Don't you sleep anymore?"

"Too often, and too long," she replied distractedly.

Will came back up the trail to meet them. Like a ranging puppy, he had the habit of "following from in front", as folk called it; he would lope ahead, just out of sight, double back to check their position, receive some unspoken confirmation recognized only by himself, then wander off again when his curiosity got the better of him. Generally Rowan simply swung along at her own efficient pace, with the ease of the long-distance walker, and Bel ambled beside her tirelessly, taking a step and a half to Rowan's one.

"I flushed some turkeys up ahead," Willam informed them breathlessly when they reached the ridgetop. "They didn't go far. I'm sure I can get one for our dinner."

Rowan grinned. "That's a good idea. You give it a try."

Since she had dropped her disguise, the change in her relationship with the boy had altered astonishingly. She often wondered how she had ever found him difficult. It had seemed before that he was always in the way, always had to be considered and planned around – a mere nuisance. She had never understood what Bel saw in him.

But now she saw what Bel had seen: a big healthy lad, strong and intelligent, always trying to please. He was by nature cheerful, yet when Rowan answered questions he was all attention, wide copper eyes focused on her face in utter concentration. She began to learn the style of his intellect. Less quick, less flashy than the sharp minds she knew among the steerswomen, Willam tracked down her ideas doggedly, winning his understanding more by single-minded persistence than native talent. Once understood, the information the steerswoman imparted became like rain on dry ground; it soaked in deep, and made something grow—something he could use, either to nourish himself, or to turn into a weapon in his private war.

The change, she knew, was only in herself; she was relieved of deception, and her mind was free to work on its familiar paths. She recognized for the first time that lies worked damage in two directions.

Willam had strung his bow and was giving more of his attention to the tops of the trees than to the path he was walking. He stubbed the toes of his oversized sandals.

"Shall I take your pack?" Rowan volunteered. "I wouldn't want you to fall with it again." She laughed. "I don't think my nerves could take it." The donkey was carrying hers and Bel's.

"If you walk carefully," Willam replied reluctantly. "You can't stomp down on each step the way you do."

His demonstration of the previous day had impressed her. "I've seen how you carry them."

He surrendered the surprisingly heavy pack and jogged ahead. Rowan, in odd high spirits, amused herself by imitating his walk. There, she thought, now I'm carrying magic. But it was mere words; she felt no different.

All that remained, she reminded herself, was to get to the Outskirts. No wizard intruded there, and in the anonymity of the ranging tribes, she and Bel could make their way to Dust Ridge and see what might be found. There lay the greatest concentration of the jewels; so beautiful, so mysterious—and so seemingly useless.

The detour to Kiruwan had taken them off their projected path. They were north of the Upland Route, and Rowan was leading the trio due east. They would cross the Long North Road well north of Five Corners, which suited her well, as it was the area she had covered immediately following her training, and so was intimately familiar with it.

Willam planned to part with them when they crossed the Long North Road. He would follow it, either south to Jannik, or north to Olin's holding. Rowan had suggested Jannik, despite Will's dislike of Blue wizards; Jannik had a known home, while the location of Red Olin's keep was still a mystery. Additionally, Olin was the most capricious and peculiar of all the wizards.

Up ahead, Willam had left the trail and was moving cautiously and quietly among the trees. Rowan and Bel dropped farther back and finally stopped, not wishing to alert the game.

The boy was out of sight when Rowan heard the soft sound of the bow's release. High to the left, the branches of one tree shivered, and amid the drumming of wings, four birds burst from the greenery, leaving one behind, thrashing in the leaves.

Willam was standing at the foot of the tree when Rowan and Bel reached him. "It's stuck," he said disgustedly. "Can someone give me a boost?"

Rowan looked up and spotted the bird, impaled flapping on the long arrow, lodged among the close branches. "You're a good shot." She carefully set his pack on the ground, and by climbing on her shoulders, Willam was able to reach the lowest branches. He clutched one and swung himself onto it, then continued up nimbly.

Bel watched dubiously.

"There aren't any tall trees in the Outskirts," Rowan said, remembering.

"No. There are a lot nearby, where the Inner Lands meet the Outskirts." Bel tilted her head for a better angle. "But I've never seen anyone go up one. He looks like one of those wood gnomes."

Far above, invisible among the leaves, the boy gave a cheerful whoop. "I can see past the next ridge from here! Wait . . ." Twigs rustled, and a few moments later the turkey fell to the ground at Bel's feet, quiescent. She inspected it, very pleased, then found a leather thong to tie its feet to her belt. It was a good-sized bird, and Rowan found herself speculating about nothing more esoteric than the nearness of dinnertime.

But shortly she looked up at the treetop again. There was no sound or sign from Willam. Disturbed, she called up to him.

His voice came down. "Wait . . ."

Beside Rowan, Bel was instantly alert.

"Someone's coming," Will said, and his next words were masked by the sound of his rapid descent.

"How many?" Rowan called as he came nearer. "What sort of people?"

"It's soldiers." He hung from his hands and dropped to the ground. He was disheveled and panting, with bits of twig and leaves caught on his clothing.

Bel had dropped her pack. She stood with one hand resting as if casually on the sword hilt by her right shoulder. Rowan unconsciously did the same. "How many were they?"

"Six, lady," Willam replied between gasps. "I counted six. And horses."

"The soldiers were mounted?"

"No, only two horses, with packs."

Bel was grim. "There's a blessing. We'd have no chance at all against six mounted soldiers." The Outskirter took it for granted that the strangers represented some threat.

"Have we a chance against six walking soldiers?" Rowan felt momentarily disoriented. Was it mere coincidence? Or would their peace be lost, so soon . . . "How were they dressed?" she asked Willam. "What were their weapons?"

"Swords, all. No spears. And cuirasses."

"Did they wear sigils?" Bel asked.

"Too far to tell. But their surplices were red."

Rowan calculated. "Shammer and Dhree, or possibly Olin; it might be either."

Bel's dark eyes glittered. "They're coming for us."

"We can't know until we see how they react." But internally, she was certain.

"That may be too late."

Rowan scanned the area: rocky land, gnarled underbrush, and the overhanging oaks. "How far away were they?"

"Half a mile, I make it," the boy told her.

Bel nodded with satisfaction. "What's our plan? It'll be a job to fight them. We might do well to avoid them, this time, and act when we're better prepared. We're fewer, we're forewarned, and we're more mobile." She caught Willam's astonished look. "Sometimes," she told him, "it's wiser to run."

"I'll follow whatever's decided." He turned to Rowan. "Lady? Are we going to run?"

Abruptly Rowan discovered a strange fury in herself, and an undeniable call, something that had built unnoticed during those short days of peace. She inspected the anger as if it were a phenomenon of nature, amazed—and then not amazed but comprehending, and finally agreeing with it in both logic and emotion. She reached her decision.

"No," she said, then looked down the path, eyes narrowed. "Not this time. Not anymore."

CHAPTER
Eighteen

In the failing light, the smoky fire gave more heat than illumination, and a single thin black line stretched straight up from it, absolutely still in the unmoving air. The chart and papers spread before the gray-cloaked, hooded shape were barely visible in the shadows of the trees, the figure unmoving, as if lost in thought. Nearby, a little donkey was tethered; the curious swiveling of its ears was the only motion in the camp.

Not a leaf rustled, not a sound was heard until a high voice shouted, "*Now!*"

Three men ran forward past the camp, turned, and stood with swords drawn, blocking the way back up the path. More soldiers, two women and a man, jogged up to the fireside and ranged themselves behind the seated figure.

There was a pause; no one moved or spoke. Eyes narrowed in suspicion, the squad sergeant stepped forward and prodded the figure gently with the point of her sword.

Rowan pushed back her hood and turned to look up, backlit by the fire, face shadowed. "Yes?"

The sergeant struck an arrogant pose, her sword point on the ground, both hands braced on its hilt. "No good to resist us, lady. We've come to get you."

Rowan calmly glanced at the squad arranged around the clearing, then nodded. "I see." Adjusting her cloak about her, she rose and faced them.

"I think she has a weapon under there," one soldier said.

The sergeant gestured her squad members closer, one of them pausing to untie the donkey. "Pass it over, then, lady. You've got to come with us."

There was no fear in Rowan's face, only the calm alertness of a steerswoman. She paused, then said carefully, "I'm sorry to hear you say that."

To the right, a tiny blaze flared, and the sergeant turned. Suddenly bright flame ran hissing along the ground, ran like a wild living thing, sped across the path, and twisted back behind Rowan. It shaped some image that burned in the eyes, a mystic diagram, a work of magic. They were surrounded by glowing, burning lines.

The sergeant's throat sprouted a bright wet shaft. She staggered, fell.

The donkey brayed and twisted, and the soldier grasping its lead was tugged off-balance onto his knees. A second arrow appeared in the ground, inches from his foot. Regaining his feet, he drew his sword, turning just in time to see Rowan's blade an instant before it struck across his eyes and drove into his brain.

Bel ran from cover across the lines of fire, and her sword met another with a sharp ring. Her opponent was confused by the eerie fire, but at that familiar sound regained his reflexes and returned the attack with terrified fury. The Outskirter laughed.

Rowan dodged an overhand blow and dashed to the far side of the hexagram. A female soldier, eyes bright with reflected flame, turned on her. Rowan parried once, then moved left to avoid a thrust coming from behind.

Bel's man took two steps back, and Will's arrow caught him high inside the thigh. Bel moved forward and swung, striking at the same point. Her blade reached bone, then she twisted it out. He fell, wailing, trying to block the severed artery with one fist. She abandoned him.

And suddenly the numbers were even.

Rowan parried with all her strength, studying the woman's style, searching for some weakness, some opening. She sensed the movement behind her again; the man was maneuvering, trying to keep her pinned between two opponents. She dove, then pulled to the right. She knew Willam was behind her in the shadows, and she heard him shifting to get clear of her. He tried for the soldier beyond Rowan's pair and missed.

That man was occupied with Bel. The Outskirter worked deftly, almost nonchalantly.

Rowan scrambled back; heard Willam retreat. She feared that her male opponent would turn and attack Bel from behind, but the Outskirter found one spare instant and used the strategy herself. Her blade struck Rowan's man across the back. He was shielded by leather, so no blood was drawn, but some bone broke and his right arm was disabled. He switched hands deftly and turned on his attacker.

Rowan was alone again with the female soldier. She angled right, and Willam ignored her and ran to the left around the now-guttering hexagram.

The woman was huge, muscular, adept—and far too good. Rowan, overmatched, constantly retreated before her, trying to angle her motion to bring her foe around to Bel's side.

Will was staying out of the action, as instructed. But he watched desperately, looking for an opening.

As the hexagram faded, there was a fizzing flare beyond Bel; the boy was providing more illumination. In the new light Bel shot a glance at Rowan, and they exchanged one mote of information: the steerswoman shook her head; the Outskirter nodded.

Under the distraction of the flare, each turned, moved across five feet of open ground, and exchanged opponents.

Willam wavered, confused. He had been told to spare the soldier Rowan fought, but now she was fighting two.

The swordswoman towered over Bel like a giantess, and Bel had to double-step back to stay out of that long reach. She did not try to match force for force, but dodged and twisted, using her own heavy sword against her opponent's as a fulcrum for her movement.

Rowan tried to concentrate her attentions on the injured soldier, but found herself driven back by his partner. She had to prevent them from separating to attack from two sides, and so kept stepping back and to the left. When the injured man broke away to circle her, she recognized the moment and shouted, "Willam!" She did not hear or see the arrow's flight; she heard the impact and a man's cries, and saw him stagger back into her field of vision. He had been struck but did not fall, the shaft protruding from his chest. He clawed at it.

Bel's adversary was undone by her own advantage. An overhand blow at the length of her reach was met by Bel's sword and left her the slightest bit off-balance for a mere instant. Bel pivoted forward, dropped down under the woman's long arms and, with her back on the ground, drove her blade up beneath the edge of the cuirass and into the soldier's stomach. The giantess writhed once, then toppled like a tree.

Will's victim had stumbled, dazed, to the edge of the clearing. He had three more shafts in him but stubbornly refused to die.

Rowan fought a simple holding action on her man. The rhythms of movement came to her like a drill, and she doggedly followed it, while he followed his own, in a dance of reflex and training.

But in a moment when she had circled right, he saw the whole of the clearing before him, and there was panic in his eyes as he realized that every one of his companions had fallen. He made half a dozen errors in his fear. Rowan took advantage of none of them.

Willam finished his stubborn victim by simply stepping up and slashing his throat with a hunting knife.

Bel pulled herself from beneath the body of the female soldier. She wiped the blood from her eyes with her fingers. "What a mess," she commented in a mildly aggrieved tone.

Will moved closer to Rowan and her opponent, not interfering but watching with interest. In the midst of parries, the soldier spared the boy a glance of terrified incomprehension. Rowan continued the drill.

Bel retrieved her sword. Seeing her approach, the man turned to break and run, but Rowan dropped and clutched his right leg, then scrambled away from the wild sweep of his sword as he spun back.

Bel swung at him without aggression, and he reflexively met the blow. Behind him, Rowan regained her feet, took careful aim, and struck the side of his head with the flat of her sword. He sank to the ground.

She dropped her sword and leaned her hands against her knees, breathing heavily.

A crashing and stumbling in the undergrowth told her where the donkey had fled. In the distance could be heard the frightened cry of one of the soldiers' horses. Rowan gestured to Will, and he set off after the animals.

Bel inspected the soldier. Between gulps of air Rowan called, "He's not dead?" The plan had called for Rowan to identify and single out one member of the attacking squad, the one possibly most tractable. Rowan had frankly assumed that it would be a woman; fighting women tended to be smaller than men, and so relied more on intelligence. The steerswoman had hoped for someone more intelligent, more reasonable than the average soldier. But that huge swordswoman had been beyond Rowan's ability to hold.

"He's alive." The Outskirter rolled him over. "We'll need some rope."

Rowan's racing pulse recovered. "Yes. I believe we'll find that one of those horses is carrying some."

When the soldier awoke he found himself bound, arms to his sides, ankles together. He was propped up against a boulder by the rising edge of the clearing.

The scene of the ambush lay before him, his comrades lying in their blood – at Bel's suggestion, they had not been moved, to create a stronger effect upon the mind of the captive. Black lines showed where the strange fire had run, and there was a thin acrid odor piercing the smell of blood and dust and sweat.

Two women stood before him. One was small and sturdy, a brilliant swordswoman who had felled the best fighter in the squad, a woman twice her size. The second was unimpressive, mild-looking but for eyes that watched too closely, saw too clearly, and seemed to understand too much.

The steerswoman squatted down beside him. "The first thing we need to know," she said, "is who sent you."

He mustered a brave front. "You're getting nothing from me."

"Don't be a fool!" She rose and gestured to the carnage in the clearing. "None of this was our choice. We have no quarrel with you personally. Answer our questions and you can go on your way." At that Bel glowered, but held her peace.

"I'm not stupid, so I'm not talking."

"You're stupid if you'd rather be dead than alive."

"Going to kill me if I don't talk? Lot of good it'll do you."

Rowan paused to consider the statement. "An interesting point."

Bel could contain herself no longer. "You can't mean to let him go!"

"No. Not after all this. He'd run straight for his master, and we'd have the whole situation repeating. We can't hope to ambush the next lot."

"If we can get him to talk," the Outskirter pointed out, "he won't dare go back to his master." She turned to the man. "Do you understand? You can live if you choose to."

He was a long time answering. "You don't know wizards."

"You'll have a chance."

He seemed about to reply, then stopped and shook his head.

Rowan tried again. "If you won't tell us who, will you tell us why?"

He glanced at their faces, looked away, and said nothing.

Willam arrived, leading two restive, wild-eyed horses. He took in the scene with his wide coppery gaze but did not interrupt.

"And now we have a problem," Rowan said dispiritedly.

Bel crossed her arms and tilted her head at the man. "I think it's obvious. If he won't answer, we'll have to make him answer."

It took Rowan a moment to get Bel's meaning. "You mean we should force him to talk?" She felt her stomach twist. But the Outskirter was right; it was, in fact, obvious.

Defending oneself against attack, attacking those who planned harm – those were easy to justify, as direct and clear as killing an animal for food, or protecting oneself from rain and cold.

But, interrogation enforced by pain . . .

"I wouldn't know where to begin," Rowan said; but as soon as it was spoken, she realized it was not true. A smattering of knowledge; a few facts about anatomy arranged themselves of their own accord, and presented to her a framework for action. It would be very easy, she realized, to cause the man pain and damage, without endangering his life. She could do it. As a steerswoman, she felt a moment's incongruous pleasure in recognizing a field of information she had already possessed, unknowing. But it was not information that she was happy to discover.

Bel shrugged. "I know what to do."

The facts of the situation again ordered themselves before Rowan, doggedly presenting the same conclusion. "No. I can do it." However much her friend might be involved, Rowan was the source and reason for the fight. It was her responsibility. This dirty job was her own.

It slowly dawned on the soldier how serious was their intent. He looked from one woman to the other in growing astonishment and finally fixed on Rowan in disbelief. She leaned forward, speaking reluctantly. "Your last chance, friend. Who sent you, and why?"

He was pale. "What're you going to do?"

They altered his bonds, first freeing his left hand, bracing it against the top of Bel's pack, then securing it in place, palm up. He struggled desperately and quieted only under the influence of a choking hold from Bel, held long enough to bring him to the edge of fainting.

Rowan took a moment to regather her determination. She pulled out her knife and examined it reluctantly, testing its edge, wondering if she would ever be able to use it to eat again. It came to her that, quite sensibly, she would.

Shaking his head to clear it, breathing in heavy gasps, the soldier spoke to her. "You, you're a steerswoman."

"That's right."

"It's a bluff, right?" His voice quavered in desperation. "I mean, you lot, you're not that sort, are you? You steerswomen, you're supposed to be, supposed to be . . ." He ran down.

"Supposed to be?" Rowan prompted.

He swallowed. "Well . . . good."

She digested his words. "Last chance," she said again, and felt on her own face a mirror of the panicked pleading that she saw in her victim's. Bel watched her sidelong.

Rowan looked at the knife, looked at the soldier, looked up at the sky. She drew one shaky breath and stepped forward.

Bel's hand was on her shoulder. "Wait."

"No." A mote of anger sparked in her. She dared not interrupt herself, but knew she must act in the momentum of her decision.

Bel grabbed one shoulder and pulled her around to face the other way. She spoke quietly. "Get out of sight."

"What? Why?"

"Because you're no good!" Bel hissed. Then she continued more calmly. "A torture victim's mood is just as important as the pain. You're sorry for him, and he knows it. You don't want to hurt him."

Rowan turned to her blankly. "I don't."

"Well, I do!" Her eyes blazed. "I *hate* him. I'll be glad to see him suffer. And he's going to suffer, not because of you or because of me, but because he made an evil choice, to serve a wizard who means us harm."

Rowan attempted to formulate a reply, but Bel pressed on. "When you start cutting him, you'll want to stop, and he'll want you to, and you'll know it, and he'll know it. It'll be back and forth between the two of you. You'll look for any excuse to stop. He'll use that against you." She stopped and glanced once at the man. "Let me do it. I'll take him apart and enjoy it."

"It's my job."

"The job belongs to the one who can do it best." The Outskirter's gaze challenged her, but as Rowan watched, her friend's expression changed to reluctant sympathy. "Rowan, cold blood's not for everyone." She jerked her head. "Get out of sight."

The horses had quieted, and Rowan had no desire to upset them again. She led them down the path, until it curved and the clearing was out of sight, tethered them to a stout fallen tree, and turned away to where the path's edge sloped down to the ravine below.

An outcropping of rock stood a few feet down the slope. Rowan climbed down and found a seat, looking north across the darkening landscape. Northwest, a lake caught the failing sunlight, a single silver line in the distance, like a sword.

From up the path there came an odd sound, like the cry of an unidentifiable small animal. The horses shifted nervously.

The evening was clear, and to her right the Eastern Guidestar hung like a beacon, twenty-five degrees up from the eastern horizon, forty degrees south of due east. Unseen over her left shoulder, the Western Guidestar stood, much higher than its partner and dimmer at present.

The sounds in the distance became more continuous.

She felt a strange combination of relief and shame. The responsibility was hers, and she had abdicated it, and deep inside she was glad to do so. It made her feel somehow unfit; it rankled.

The noises became appalling, inhuman.

Bel was right; the job was best done by one best suited for it. And yet—

She tried to distract herself. She realized that it would take a problem to lose herself in solving, something useful, confirming her own skills. She sifted, searching, the soldier's voice a weird music behind her thoughts.

The jewels – irritating, frustrating, apparently *useless*, yet still the fulcrum on which all these events pivoted. But the information was too slight and too familiar. More was needed for further thought to be effective.

She wanted something more technical and involving, something with information and principles to grasp and work with. That incidental paradox that she had argued with Arian about . . .

An object flung with great force from a high tower, at a certain upward angle: by using straightforward techniques known to any steerswoman, by taking them further than anyone had before, Rowan had seemed to demonstrate that it was possible for the object never to strike the ground.

It was quite obviously false. Things simply did not happen that way. And yet, why would the techniques work in other circumstances but fail in this one? She reconstructed the details of the problem in her mind, and the events in the distance, the strange sounds, and her own shame faded from her awareness.

She recognized that there was an interrelationship between the height of the tower and the force of the impetus. The higher the tower, the less force was necessary. At a great enough height, one needed merely to let go of the object, and it would fall away, never quite reaching the ground; slightly lower, and it would reach ground eventually.

The shorter the tower, the more force was needed, until eventually the object could be flung by someone standing at ground level. But the force required was impossible, immeasurable – and she reminded herself that "impossible" and "immeasurable" were not the same idea. It was patently impossible to construct a tower high enough – she knew too well the restrictions on the variables involved – but the force of the impetus was merely immeasurable.

She had a feel for the quantity, however; she could *imagine* it, in principle, but not with precision. She disliked this. It was too vague.

And it left her with the same glaring contradiction that had so outraged Arian at the Archives: no matter what the numbers said, objects did fall to the earth.

But did they? Every single time?

Approach it from another direction. What does not fall?

Birds flew, by some technique known to themselves. Wizards were said to fly and could make things fly, possibly by the same means. Clouds floated, but they were vapors, like steam, mere fogs risen above ground level. When she had been a child, she had dreamed of tying a rope to a cloud and being lifted into the sky. She imagined herself a child without knowledge, looking at the world as a child did. Would a child be surprised to hear of objects that did not fall?

Not at all. The sun did not fall, nor the constellations, nor the Guidestars. Children, and for that matter, most adults, took that as given.

But the sun did not fall because it was no object moving across the sky. In fact it was the stable center of the universe, and the world moved about it in a great circle, spinning improbably on its axis. Rowan remembered how amazed she was when she had first learned that. But once known, it was easily confirmed, by any number of methods.

The stars were far suns, or so tradition said. But this was unprovable. In any event, they were immeasurably distant.

The Guidestars hovered forever in the sky. They did not fall, but neither did they move. They hung immobile on the celestial equator and seemed to shift only as the traveler below changed position on the world's surface.

They were neither far suns, nor immeasurably distant. Their height was easily calculable from their apparent displacement when viewed from different locations on the world. Though they were very high indeed, if they had been suns the world would have been aflame from the heat of their proximity.

But they did not move.

She noticed vaguely that there was silence from up the path, had been for some time, and that Willam was seated beside her. The boy was shaking, rank with sweat. Rowan ignored him and returned to the seduction of the problem.

Reason and reasonableness were at odds. Something was wrong, either in the calculations, or in the formulation of the problem, or in the principles by which she understood the world.

And that was the possibility that Arian had overlooked. The error was not necessarily in the calculations, nor in the construction of the problem.

She checked the numbers over and over, trying to quantify the vaguenesses, to identify and limit the areas of missing knowledge. She kept reaching the same results: it might be true. It might be possible for a falling object never to reach the ground. And more: under certain conditions, it might actually be *impossible* for it to do so.

At some point she realized that Willam was gone, and in retrospect remembered that he had risen, stepped to one side, vomited, and returned up the path.

The sounds in the distance began again.

She was briefly taken by nausea at imagining the nature of those proceedings, and in her single-mindedness she found herself annoyed at the interruption. Of their own accord, her thoughts slipped back into the fascination of reason.

What would actually happen, taking the calculations as valid? Precisely, how would an object flung to that height behave?

It would move away into the distance, past the horizon. And then?

If it never reached the ground, it would simply continue, completely around the world. Eventually, it would come back

217

into view from the opposite horizon, crossing the point where it had started.

No, not quite – because the world would have turned a bit in the interval.

This made the computations more complicated. Annoyed, she altered the orientation of the object's path, from north–south to west–east, on the equator, to minimize the effect of the world's rotation. It helped.

Abruptly, in a leap of reason, she flung it higher, far above the minimum height necessary for an unfalling object—

She came to her feet and spun to seek the Western Guidestar hanging motionless above her—

And was face-to-face with Bel. The Outskirter had spoken.

Rowan shook her head in momentary confusion. "What?"

Bel repeated, her face showing vast dissatisfaction. "It's no use," she said. "I think he's under a spell."

"He won't say anything?" She vaguely recalled a wild, weeping voice in the distance, and that it had spoken at length.

"It isn't that. He talks. He's even eager to. But he just doesn't make any sense. You'd better hear it yourself."

As Rowan approached, she looked once at the state of the man's hand and arm, then kept her eyes to his face. Unfortunately, her observation and memory were too good. The sight stayed with her, against her will; and then she chose to remember it, and recognize and accept the results of her actions.

Bel dropped one hand on the trembling man's right shoulder, in a gesture that seemed almost friendly. His head snapped up, and he looked at her, wild-eyed. "No! That's all there is, I swear it, I don't know any more!" His skin was white, slick with sweat.

"Of course," Bel reassured him. "But just repeat it for the steerswoman, there's a good fellow."

He looked at Rowan and began to speak, urgently, desperately. As she listened, Rowan felt her scalp prickle.

What she heard was not the incoherent gibberings a man might make in delirium. The sounds were organized, inflected like speech, and the look on the soldier's face reflected the meaning he believed them to carry. The pattern of inflection teased the ear, mimicking reason – but not one of the utterances matched any single true word. The effect was uncanny.

At the end, his communication slipped into comprehensibility with a plaintive "That's all, please, I'd tell more, but that's all they told me."

Rowan stood helpless, sick with horror. Somehow, this was the most appalling result of magic she had yet witnessed – worse than the casual death of Reeder's boy, crueler than the orchestrated slaughter of innocent people by a swarm of dragons, stranger than Willam's eerie traveling fire. This man's very will and sacred reason had been twisted by some wizard, twisted for a purpose incidental to his own life.

Rowan crouched down beside him, studying his face. He avoided her gaze, his breath hissing behind clenched teeth.

"Listen," she said carefully, trying to sound kind and reasonable. "I'm sorry, but there's a problem here. We believe you're under some kind of spell." He screwed his eyes shut, ignoring her. "I know you think you've told us something," she went on, "but you haven't really. It's an illusion."

He looked up at her, and a small sound escaped from the back of his throat. Realization grew on his face, and with it the terror that the evening's events were not finished, that there was more to come.

"Perhaps there's some way you can get around it?" Rowan said. "Can you approach it from some other direction?"

A strangled cry escaped him, and then he was speaking again, in a high pleading voice – all sounds with no sense.

"No, wait," Rowan told him. "It's no good. Try to calm down . . . start with something simple."

Beyond hearing her, he cried his desperate monologue.

"Try to tell us your name," she suggested, and touched his shoulder, attempting, irrationally, to comfort him.

He tried to writhe away from her hand, twisting at the ropes. His left arm slipped slickly in its bonds, raw flesh and bone tangling against rope. He uttered a gurgling cry and fainted.

Bel let out a gust of air. "Well."

Rowan sat back on her heels and was silent for a long time. Finally, she nodded.

"What happens now?" Willam asked. He was as pale as the soldier.

Bel made to answer, but Rowan stopped her with a gesture. She spoke to Willam. "Get me some cloth. The spare linen shirt from my pack should do." He hurried to do it.

Bel came closer, suspicious. "What are you going to do?"

Rowan found Bel's knife. "To start, I'm going to bandage this arm." She cut the ropes that held it, carefully disentangling them from the muscle and tendon.

"You're not going to let him go?"

"That is exactly what I am going to do." She took the shirt that Willam handed her and began tearing strips.

The Outskirter rounded on her. "Are you insane? Don't you know what will happen?"

"I think I have a good idea." She gestured Will to bring a waterskin.

"But he didn't betray his wizard, and now he knows it. There's no reason for him not to return to whoever sent him and say that we hadn't been stopped."

"Very probably that's what he'll do." Seeing that the soldier was regaining his senses, Rowan instructed Will, "Give him some water. No, don't untie him. I'm sorry, friend. I'm helping you, but it will still hurt."

"They'll know where we are!" Bel leaned close to Rowan's face. "They'll know where we were, they'll know where we're going, and they'll find us in an instant!"

"They'll have the information to do so." Rowan took the skin from Willam and poured water over the hand and arm. The man shrieked and fainted again.

"Rowan." The Outskirter spoke seriously. "You've always seemed a sensible person, if inexperienced— "

"Thank you." She did not have needle and thread to stitch back muscle and skin, but she noticed that Bel's work had been very clean and efficient. The hand would be useless, but the man's life was in no immediate danger.

"But this is pure madness. It's nothing less than suicide." The soldier groggily came to again and startled at seeing Bel's face so close. She stepped back, annoyed. "Rowan," she repeated, and waited until the steerswoman looked up. "I don't care to die."

"Good. Neither do I." Rowan turned back and continued the work, noticing that she was learning more about the anatomy of the human arm than she had previously known.

Bel said nothing more.

Rowan finished the bandaging, untied the man, helped him to his feet, gave him a bit of food and water to take, and led him to the head of the trail. He stood, swaying and trembling, looking about in disbelief. Rowan gestured with her chin. "Go on."

Behind her, Bel made a wordless sound of rage, and the soldier stumbled, turned, and left down the trail at a staggering run.

Bel set loose a flurry of curses. She stormed back to her pack, flung off the ropes, and dragged it aside as Will watched in amazement. "It's impossible, it's insane, and I'm having no part of it." Her movements were jerky with agitation. She pointed back up the rising path. "I am going *that* way. I'll probably get lost, and I don't care, because I'd have a better chance of survival. I'm *not* following you to suicide."

Rowan stepped over to one of the bodies of the slaughtered soldiers and examined its trappings. Without looking up she asked Will, "What do you think?"

He glanced from one to the other, confused. "I – I don't know. I'm glad we didn't kill that man; it's not his fault he's under a spell, but . . . Lady, I think we *should* have. It would have been safer . . ."

"I didn't think you could be so stupid!"

Ignoring Bel, Rowan pulled the helmet from the corpse's head and studied it, thinking.

"I can still catch him," the Outskirter said through her teeth.

"No."

"Rowan— "

"Here." She tossed the helmet to Bel, who reflexively caught it. "Does it fit?"

"Fit?"

Rowan turned to the boy. "Will, are you any good at tracking? I know how to do it, but it's mostly theory with me. I expect you've tracked game before . . ."

"Yes."

Bel turned the helmet over in her hands, watching Rowan with suspicion.

The steerswoman stood. "I'm sick of running, and I don't care to dodge any more attacks. I want to find out who's responsible." Her mouth twisted. "And since our poor friend couldn't tell where he came from, he will kindly lead us there."

Bel stood stunned. Then slowly, she began to laugh. She tossed the helmet into the air, caught it, and pulled it down on her head. It fit.

CHAPTER
Nineteen

"How do we get in?" Bel wondered.

"The same way every guard gets in."

The cliffs were a riot of raw stone and wild levels. It disturbed Rowan; her maps showed the lake as smaller, the cliffs smoother and slightly farther north. This area had been *made* this way, made recently, and by magic.

One arm of stone reached out into the lake; its far edge probably marked the limit of the original cliffs. Now, rock rose sheer from the waters to cradle the pale gray walls of the fortress. The perimeter seemed to be constructed of massive single blocks, one for each of the six faces. Rowan could think of no source for such stone, no way to quarry it, and no way to transport it. In the dawn light it seemed more like ceramic than rock.

Without a doubt, the fortress belonged to Shammer and Dhree.

Rowan and her companions had tracked the wounded soldier for two days, until a heavy storm had battered the forest. When it had cleared, they found that all traces of his trail had been eradicated. By continuing in his last known direction, they came across indications of the original squad's outward-bound passage, but no sign that the survivor had returned that way. The three agreed that the man had likely died in his attempt to return home, victim of hunger, weather, and his weak condition; but the trail left by the horses and people of the outgoing squad was still readable. By following it backward, the travelers eventually found a north-bound road that finally led them to the lake shore.

"Will, we need you to stay here." His face darkened, but Rowan forestalled his protest. "I'm not trying to exclude you. You're our last line. If we don't come out in three days, you have to head back to the Archives. It's important that the Prime know what's happened. Will you do it?"

He nodded reluctantly. "I guess it makes sense. But you had better tell me all about any magic you saw, when you come out. I'll wait here and keep the horses ready."

"Good lad. Do you still have the map?"

"Yes." He pulled it from his shirt. "What's the route to the Archives?"

She did not look at the map, but kept her eyes on the fortress. "Follow the cliffs along the west shore of the lake until it turns north . . ." Rattling the parchment, Willam puzzled over the chart as Rowan continued, reciting the complicated directions precisely, with off-hand ease and only half her attention. ". . . and when you reach the Wulf you should be able to get passage to the Archives. There's a landing; most of the rivermen know where to find it." She turned to him. "Is that clear?"

He looked a bit bemused. "Yes."

She took in his expression, then laughed. "Attise the merchant wasn't very good with maps, was she?"

"No." He made a wry face. "I used to wonder if she wasn't a bit thick."

"I was afraid that if I showed any skill at all, I'd show all of it. I was truly bad at pretending."

"And here we go," Bel said, "into the middle of it, pretending all the way."

The two women were dressed in attire removed from the corpses of the soldiers they had slain. The outfits were not truly uniform, save for the leather helmets, cuirasses, and the red surplices. The individuality of the remaining equipment allowed Rowan to risk retaining her gum-soled steerswoman's boots. To the casual glance they were not remarkable, but they provided better traction than leather soles, and they were silent.

"I've had practice since then," Rowan said.

They had been watching the fortress since the previous day, observing the visible movements of guards on the perimeters, and the entry and exit of supplies and personnel.

From the front entrance, a railed causeway led along the rocky arm to the road at the base of the cliffs. The end of the causeway was closed off by a barred iron gate set in a stone arch. Each party entering was in the company of a soldier. At the gate, the group would pause; the soldier would step up to the right side of the arch and do something unseen from Rowan's angle, and the iron bars would swing slowly open to admit the party. The bars moved with no visible human intervention.

Rowan took a moment to review what she knew about the recent war: the cursory tale Artos had given her, and the incidental information gained from Hugo as he outlined the present status and attitudes of the known wizards. With her knowledge of the lands involved, and logic to fill in the blanks, it would have to suffice. She gestured to Bel and began to clamber down the tumbled rocks to the road below.

The arch of the gate was mortared stone, the iron bars as thick as Rowan's wrist and completely clear of rust. It was new, as new as the changed landscape.

Rowan walked to the right of the arch as if familiar with procedure. Temporarily shielded from the sight of the guards at the other end of the causeway, she took a moment to examine the stones.

At eye level, one block had been replaced by a small square brass door. A turn of the little handle opened it easily. Inside the back surface was faced with ceramic, with a recessed circle in the center, decorated with a complex pattern of copper lines.

Rowan sighed, relieved. "Simple enough." Bel ignored her, occupied with keeping the reactions of the guards at the keep's entrance under observation, while simultaneously trying to project an air of nonchalance.

The women had carefully searched the possessions of the soldiers they had slain. Each had carried a small wood-and-copper disk, like a talisman or amulet, embellished with unreadable runes. The steerswoman removed hers from a pocket built into her confiscated sword belt and fit it into the recessed circle.

There was a quiet sustained tone, a single deep musical note, heard but faintly. Of its own accord, the heavy crossbolt slid aside slowly, and the gate swung inward. Bel froze and stood watching it as a cat might have watched a dog, her lips peeled back from her teeth.

Rowan came to her side, looking down the causeway. "Expect magic, Bel."

A cool updraft from the lake below countered the heat beating down from above. The women walked along the smooth-surfaced road through an atmosphere that seemed to have no temperature, no real presence.

Four guards manned the entrance to the fortress proper. Three stood in proper soldierly stance, watched by the fourth, who stood at his ease, viewing everything with an overseer's disgruntled disdain.

The guards could not be expected to know every single soldier in the wizards' employ; the purpose of the spell at the magic gate certainly was to prevent entry by unauthorized persons. Rowan gave the men a casual acknowledging nod as she and Bel passed by and turned to the left. "Easy enough," Bel said under her breath.

"You there! You two!" They froze.

The senior guardsman stamped after them in outrage. "Look you, if you've *both* got the amulets, you're *both* supposed to use them. You know that – it throws off the tally."

Rowan thought quickly. "She doesn't have one." If the amulets were used to get into the fortress, then only people originating from the fortress would have them. "She isn't from these parts. We pressed her in Logan Falls."

"What? Who's 'we'?"

"My squadron. We're returning from the war."

"You two, alone?"

"We were with Penn's squadron."

"Showing up now?" He stood with fists on hips. "Took your damn time, didn't you?"

"I was sick."

He grunted disgust, then looked alarmed. "No, Penn's squadron, that's the one got in the way of that basilisk, wasn't it?"

"That's right."

He took a half step back. "It's all right," Rowan assured him. "It just turned out to be dysentery. Then we got snowed in and had to wait until spring to travel. And then, well . . ."

Bel spoke up. "We got lost."

He barked a laugh. "Infantry – don't know its ass from its earhole. But look, you been mostly mustered out since then, didn't you hear?"

"Not a word." She tried to catch the style of his speech, to mimic it. "No way to."

"Mph. Should've headed home instead."

"Home where? Mine's pretty well flattened."

"We decided we liked the life," Bel put in.

"Liked it?" He found the idea immensely amusing.

Rowan remembered a comment Artos's regulars often made. "Could be worse. We could be working for a living."

He recognized a standard soldier's sally. "Well . . ." His manner shifted to grudging familiarity. "We've gone and lost a few of the standing, lately. Wouldn't be surprised if you found a place. You look likely, anyhow," he said to Bel. "Go talk to Druin; he's took over for Clara." Rowan nodded as if the statement made sense to her. "Go on." He made a vague gesture to the left and plodded back to his station, muttering to himself.

The two women walked away purposefully and presently found themselves in a small interior courtyard with passages in three directions. Pausing, Rowan carefully placed its size, shape, and orientation within the blank hexagon that was her mental floor plan for the fortress.

"Now where?" Bel wondered.

"I don't know." Rowan's mouth twitched with amusement. "Do you think we should try to report to Druin for assignment?"

"He'd just put us to work."

"True." Rowan examined the courtyard, trying to relate the angles of the exits to the shape of the rooftops she had viewed from the cliffs. "That man's shift has four hours to go." She knew that from her earlier observations. "He'll probably go for his dinner after that, and he may or may not meet Druin in the mess and mention us. We have about four hours before we're suspected."

"That's not a lot of time." Bel tilted her head. "If we did report to Druin, and he took us in, then we'd have as much time as we want, and good excuses to be wherever we are."

Rowan turned back to her friend, amazed and delighted. She laughed, quietly. "Bel, that's – that's *audacious!*"

The Outskirter acknowledged Rowan's reaction with a little self-satisfied smile.

"I would be expected to have some familiarity with the fortress."

"We'll scout around a bit before we show up," Bel supplied.

"That's the answer." Rowan scanned the three passages, then chose one that seemed likely to keep close to the outer wall. "This way." It was large and wide and showed signs of the previous passage of horses. They followed it cautiously through a series of interlinked courtyards, each with side doors; it was likely a delivery route for supplies.

The critical question was: how did the fortress guards normally behave when off-duty? Were their movements circumscribed, and to what degree? Certainly they could not have the free run of the entire keep, but just as certainly they were not simply confined to barracks. Such an existence would be too grim and limited, and the life of the resident guards would be too unpleasant to attract a sizable loyal corps.

There had to be compensations for the work. The only analogy Rowan had was Artos's regulars and the house guards at his mansion. The house guards had an easy job with a certain amount of prestige and were an affable lot, as a rule. The regulars were natural soldiers and enjoyed their alternately ordered and chaotic existence. Gratitude from the townspeople, a romantic image, steady employment, and in many cases a general improvement over their previous existence attracted people to the ranks. The pay was not great, but Artos had more volunteers than he could use.

The house guards were on a wry, friendly basis with the servants and workers, and from that relationship Rowan took her cue.

In one courtyard they came across a wagon laden with small odd-sized wooden crates, where a burly, disheveled man and a slim, pockmarked woman of middle age were occupied with tediously bringing the cargo into a side door. Rowan paused and turned back. "Need some help?"

Possibilities were three: servants were considered of superior rank and would refuse to associate with guardswomen; servants were of inferior rank and would be amazed, possibly frightened, at Rowan's offer; or, questions of rank were inapplicable between the two groups, and the response would be based purely on the freedom of action normal to off-duty guards.

The man ignored Rowan, but the woman looked up with mild surprise, then smiled. "Thanks." She tapped her assistant on the shoulder as he made to unload another crate. Pausing in his work, he watched intently as she indicated Bel and Rowan and pointed from the boxes to the door; then he nodded pleasantly at the pair. He was deaf.

Rowan pulled down one of the crates and hoisted it to her shoulder. It proved to be lighter than it looked. "Where do these go?" she asked. Bel followed her example with an obviously heavier box, behaving as if she considered the work nothing unusual.

The woman indicated. "Through that door, through the room, up the stairs." She paused and winced. "No further, I guess. Wouldn't look good." Attracting the disheveled man's attention again, she attempted to give him a more difficult, complicated instruction. Eventually comprehending, he led the way.

The room was large and long, lined with cupboards and shelves, apparently to store certain nonperishable items, but the crates they were carrying had a different destination. Rowan and Bel were led through a door in the back and up a set of narrow stairs with a landing halfway up, where the direction reversed. At the top was a second landing, and there the man put down his crate, indicated those carried by the women, then indicated the floor. When they complied, he pointed at Rowan and Bel, back down the stairs, pointed at himself, and made a motion toward a short corridor behind him.

Without thinking, Rowan replied in the wood-gnome language of gestures. "I understand. We go down now."

Those particular phrases were simple and obvious, easily comprehensible to an intelligent person; but the formality of the

229

gestures, and the fluid naturalness of their use, surprised him. It was more than pantomime, it was language, and he seemed to recognize something of this.

With a look of surprise and concentration, he repeated a phrase, pointing at himself, then extending his index finger near his right temple. "I understand." He said it twice, testing the moves.

When they reached the lower room again Rowan and Bel found that the pockmarked woman had not been idle. She had carried a number of crates from the wagon to the side door; a simple division of labor was implied that would prevent the workers from jostling each other and speed up the task.

"I'll take the stairs," Rowan volunteered. Bel set herself to shifting crates from the front door and passing them to Rowan at the stairs' foot.

When the steerswoman delivered each crate to the top landing, sometimes the deaf man was there, studying her with shy friendliness. Sometimes he was absent, and she began to catch the rhythm of his work and understand how much time had to pass while he brought each crate down the corridor.

After transferring one crate to his care and pausing until he was out of sight, she dashed down the stairs as quickly as possible. Meeting Bel in the middle of the storeroom, she took the burden from her there. "Try to work a little faster. I need you to be three boxes ahead of me. And see if you can make them light ones."

With Rowan and the man working at one pace, and Bel and the woman outside working at another, it did not take many trips before three boxes sat waiting at the bottom of the stairs. Rowan chose the smallest, hurried up to the first landing, and placed the crate in a spot invisible from above. Returning below, she took a second and managed to reach the top with it in time to hand it to the man above.

Back at the lower landing, she used her knife to pry up the lid of the first crate. The thin wood was held by tacks and offered little resistance. She was able to detach it easily, but temporarily abandoned it to run down for the third box.

Just as the deaf man came into sight, she placed the third crate on the top landing, waved at him, and turned back down.

The box she had opened contained a dozen wooden spools, similar in type to those used for thread, but much larger. Wound around each was a strand of some substance as thick as heavy yarn, in bizarre colors, garishly brilliant. Loosening the end of one strand, she found it strangely stiff. She pulled out a foot-long length and tried to cut it. She was briefly shocked when the knife failed to cut completely through; if she rewound it, the mark would be visible, and suspicious. But a second panicked attempt detached the segment, and she wound it into a tight coil and slipped it into the pocket with her amulet.

Pounding the lid closed caused a din that prompted Bel to peer up the stairs in surprise. Rowan ignored her, finished the job, and brought the box to the top landing to find the deaf man waiting.

Back at the bottom, Bel passed along a somewhat heavier crate. "This is the last." When Rowan delivered it, she could not help speaking to the man again. "Work finished." Those signals were more abstract, and she amplified them with gestures including the stairs, the box, herself, and the man, and a negative shake of her head.

He watched in fascination. Then, with the crate precariously tucked under one arm, he replied. "I understand." He paused, thinking, then hesitantly added, "You go down now."

She grinned at him, charmed by his intelligence, and waved a farewell.

As they left the storeroom behind, Bel asked, "What did you do?"

"I made a friend and acquired a souvenir."

Reassured by their casual acceptance by the woman and her assistant, Bel and Rowan continued their explorations. They encountered storerooms, stables, a smithy, and a woodshop, but no residences. The people they met, though sometimes surprised, never raised protest.

For the first reconnaissance, the steerswoman selected routes that kept them close to the outside wall, in order to gain a sense of the overall shape and limits of the keep, and seek future options for discreet departure. Of those, they found two.

The first was nothing more than a low window in the wall itself, but by leaning over the edge, one could see that the cliffs below were a trifle less sheer than elsewhere, with rocky projections down to the surface of the lake. Conceivably, a person with a rope could lower herself down the face of the wall and scramble laboriously to the water. Unfortunately, the window was in a busy area, and an observer standing nearby would have a clear view of the entire descent; further, the escapee would have to swim to the shore. Rowan was not surprised to learn that Bel lacked that skill.

The second exit was a small gate on the north side, facing the body of the lake. Stone stairs led down the cliffs to a wharf, where a jolly gaff-rigged sailing dinghy bobbed, a pleasure boat. The gate was closed by an iron grille, locked, and equipped with the same brass box found at the end of the front causeway. Possibly their amulets would open it, but she dared not try, remembering what the guard had said about a "tally".

The women peered through the grille.

"That's our best chance, if we need to leave quickly," Rowan said.

"Can you handle that boat?"

"A simple matter."

They retraced their steps to the first courtyard they had found and took a different exit. By asking a passing washwoman, they found the barracks and training area of the resident guard and presented themselves to Druin.

Rowan repeated their story to him, filling it with many details of the action during the war, altered from the point of view of the observers who had reported it to Hugo, to the point of view of a soldier in its midst. She included a certain number of likely soldierly complaints, including invective at the insanity of using a basilisk in close combat. Long before she had finished, she saw Druin's gaze wandering in boredom and knew that she had convinced him of their authenticity.

It took him a moment to realize that she had stopped speaking. "Yes. Well." He regathered himself, attempting to look official, and succeeding in looking harried. "Of course we can use you. Mustering people out, everybody coming and going – confuses things. And this new business; just makes it all worse."

Rowan remembered that he was new at his job. "What happened to Clara?" The guard at the gate had mentioned her as someone Rowan might be expected to know, and so it was desperately necessary to avoid her.

Wincing, Druin looked off to one side and scratched his beard vigorously. Rowan decided that he had fleas. "Not a good story. Had a little run-in with Themselves." He gave the word a capitalizing stress. "Lay low when they're around, that's all. Don't attract attention."

"Can't you be more specific? So we won't do the same thing Clara did?"

Glancing around as if his comments might be overheard, he said, "Could, but I won't. No good chewing it over. Best forgotten." He eyed Bel, with evident approval. "Where'd you get her again?"

"Logan Falls. She did well in the fighting."

"I expect so – you're both here. Shame about Penn. How'd you escape that basilisk?"

Rowan shrugged. "Can't imagine. I expect it didn't notice us, personally, in the confusion. Just lucky."

"Mph. Well . . ." He scratched his left thigh absently, musing, then called out across the yard. "Ellen! These two are yours."

The woman came over, leaving behind a trio of men whom she had been berating for sloppy behavior. At her departure they slinked away unobtrusively. "Good. I'm trying to get another squad together to go after that steerswoman."

Hiding a thrill of fear, Rowan knit her brows as if puzzled. Bel managed to appear innocently delighted at the prospect of a hunt.

Druin was outraged. "What, more? We're too shorthanded already."

"What's this?" Rowan interjected. "We're after a steerswoman? Is she some kind of criminal?"

"Don't know," Ellen said indifferently. "We're supposed to stay clear of them, generally. Always liked them myself. But there's something about this one that's got Themselves all in a bother, and touchy, as well."

"Now, how can we keep proper security," Druin complained in exasperation, "with three-quarters of our people off chasing the moon, I ask you?"

"Don't know. Why don't you ask Themselves?"

"Not me." He made a sound of dry irony, then returned to business. "Well, you show these two around, give them something temporary. We'll see about more search parties later."

Ellen was a big square woman, broad of stomach and blunt of features. Her arms bulked with muscle. Leading the pair through the passages, she studied Bel briefly. "You, what's your name?"

The Outskirter provided her alias.

"Fine. You look competent. Small, maybe, but size isn't skill. You've got something about you, an air, confidence. Bet you could show some of us a thing or two."

Bel acknowledged that with a tilt of her head.

"And you—"

When Rowan responded with her own assumed name, Ellen gave her longer, more careful consideration. "You're smart, aren't you? That's it. You don't look like much of a fighter, not at first glance, but I can tell you're thinking all the time. I'll bet you're good, and I'll bet it's because you can think fast on your feet. I'll assign you together – you're a good combination."

Behind her back, Rowan and Bel exchanged cautionary looks. Ellen was perceptive and a good judge of people; they would need to stay out of her sight as much as possible.

The women's barracks were wide and airy and surprisingly clean. A ten-year-old girl was industriously scrubbing the wooden floor, and she paused to look up with wide-eyed hero worship as the women entered. "Take any free bunk you like; there's plenty." Ellen said to her charges. "Down the hall that way are a few double rooms, for when you need company and privacy at the same time, so to speak. If you consort with the house servants, use their quarters, but tell me ahead of time! Absent from barracks during your sleeping time without me knowing, and that's bad trouble for you."

The Outskirter and the steerswoman selected bunks and stowed their kits, and Ellen continued their orientation. They paid a visit to the armorer, who declared their equipment in remarkably good condition but issued them both ceremonial spears and traded the sword Rowan had taken from her would-be captors for one somewhat lighter. He also gave Bel one of the admitting amulets.

234

He tucked it directly into her sword-belt pocket, causing Rowan a moment's nervousness, but apparently Bel had already discarded the one she had originally carried.

In a practice session under the eyes of Ellen and the resident armsmaster, Bel defeated Rowan three times in such quick succession that the steerswoman was dazed by the Outskirter's skill. Tested against the master himself, Rowan held her own, to his surprise. In a bout against Bel, he declared himself the victim of unorthodox techniques.

Back in Ellen's cramped quarters, the officer scanned a list. "Something simple to start with. Night duty on the northeast wall. You pace the limits, exchange recognition with the guards on the north and east at each end of your walk. If you see someone acting furtive or rowdy, one of you bring him to Druin, the other keep your post. Keep an eye on the lake for any approaching boats. And don't let the servants walk the walls; they try to use them as shortcuts, but they're not allowed." She looked up. "Get some rest; report to the night officer here at dusk. That's all."

"Yes, ma'am," Rowan replied. Then she cautiously ventured, "But I doubt we'd be able to get any sleep the first afternoon we try."

Bel picked it up. "All this is new to me. Perhaps my friend can show me around a bit? We'll stay away from any restricted areas you tell us about."

"No. I want you rested. If you can't sleep, talk or daydream if you like, just do it in your bunks."

In their absence, the barracks had acquired another inhabitant; a guardswoman was fast asleep on one of the bunks, the little scrub-girl seated on the floor beside her, industriously cleaning the woman's cuirass with an oily rag. When Bel and Rowan removed their gear, the girl dashed over to show them the best way to arrange it at the foot of the bed. Bel spared her a grin and a tousle of the hair, which elicited a shy smile but no words.

When the girl left, Rowan moved to the bed-foot and retrieved the coiled strand from her sword belt. Bel came closer to watch.

The strand unwound and rewound easily, retaining whatever shape Rowan bent it in. It was colored fiery orange and dull brown in alternating segments. Scratching it with one fingernail, Rowan found that the orange was its inherent hue, the brown painted on. At both ends its cross section showed a gleaming central core. She could not identify the outer substance, but its feel reminded her faintly of the gum used to coat the boot soles of steerswomen and sailors, though it seemed more rigid. It had no taste.

"Should you put your tongue on that thing?" Bel whispered. "It might be poisonous."

"Whatever its use, it's intended to be handled by humans. If it's poisonous, it's not very, and one lick shouldn't hurt me." Nevertheless, she paused to check for any internal reactions. There were none.

Using her knife, she found that she could easily strip the outer layer, peeling off thin curling slivers. She exposed one end of the core, recognized the color, and again tasted. "Copper," she confirmed.

"But what's it for?"

"It might have any number of uses. It's thin, it's very tough, it holds a shape, and it's probably impervious to weather." She glanced at the soldier across the room, who was breathing heavily in sleep, and continued. "It would be excellent for tying things. Sailors would love it."

"Nonsense. You know it's magical."

Rowan sighed. "Yes. But it's not *doing* anything magical."

"Just like that jewel of yours."

"True." And there was nothing more to be learned.

CHAPTER
Twenty

Despite Rowan's comment to Ellen, they did sleep. The scrub-girl woke them at dusk with an offer of hard rolls and fruit juice.

They found their night's duty uneventful, its tedium relieved by the ribald comments of their counterparts on the north face, as each pair's pacing brought them together. The women managed to respond like true soldiers, with earthy insults. Bel also amused herself by singing quietly as she walked, which Rowan enjoyed. The steerswoman rarely sang when others could hear; her own voice, though true in pitch, was plain and colorless.

To one side, the surface of the lake and the overcast sky merged in a black, featureless void. To the other, the fortress presented observers with an array of cupolas, balconies, and courtyards, and windows lit with gentle lights, most of which were extinguished, one by one, as the night proceeded. Rowan studied the configuration of rooftops as she paced.

At midnight their relief arrived, and the two women made their way to the staircase in a corner tower and descended. Sometime during the shift the wall sconces had been lit, and soft, unflickering light streamed from behind opaque shields. Pausing to examine one, Rowan found that she could not remove the shield. Cautiously she thrust one finger behind and encountered something hard and hot. She pulled back

237

quickly. "These might function like the lamps in Wulfshaven Harbor."

"If Corvus can do it, I suppose Themselves can."

At the first level, Rowan unexpectedly turned aside, went down a short passage, and turned left, the opposite direction from their route back to the barracks and mess.

Caught unawares, Bel hurried to catch up and fell in beside her. "Where are we going?"

Rowan made a gesture. "So far, we've come a bit more than halfway around the keep. I want to complete the circuit, and on a different floor. I noticed something about the layout while we were on guard."

"And what's that?"

They were moving down a wide corridor, with doors on the left and a display of muted tapestries on the right, between light sconces, more decorative than those in the stairway. They passed two servants in whispered conversation, who silenced as they approached and resumed when they had gone by.

"From the walls, it looks like the keep is organized in three concentric hexagons. The outer wall and adjacent buildings, such as we saw on our first reconnaissance – that's the first hexagon." On the left, space opened into a gallery with arched windows. Noticing that the servants were out of sight, Rowan slipped into it, Bel following.

The windows showed an alley below and a rank of buildings across. Past them, the tower joining the northeastern wall to the eastern could be seen. Rowan turned back. "And now we're in the second hexagon."

Bel puzzled over this. "Like rings, inside each other?"

"That's right."

"And where are we?"

They continued down the hall. "The front gate and causeway are on the south. We're now on the east side; counting our movements yesterday, we've gone three-quarters of the way around."

"I see. But I'll never know how you keep direction indoors. What are you doing now?"

Rowan had stopped to look behind the tapestries and found bare stone wall. "There are no doors on this side."

238

"And no windows. We can't even look at the inner ring." Bel viewed her friend sidelong. "And now that's what you want to do most."

"More than that; now I want to go there."

The corridor angled, following the native geometry of the fortress as a whole. Just past the corner, they finally found a narrow door, tucked between two tapestries.

The door was propped open with a wooden block and led to a cramped staircase winding down. Following it, they found another open door; the room beyond was in blackness. Rowan listened for a moment but heard nothing. She slipped in and stood motionless, waiting for the atmosphere and the sound of her breathing to bring her some sense of the room's shape.

Bel paused briefly, tucked behind the door's edge to cover any sudden retreat Rowan might need to make. Nothing happened, and the steerswoman beckoned her in. "No magic lamps here?" Bel complained in a whisper.

"Apparently not."

Light flared suddenly, pottery crashed, and a girlish voice cried, "Oh!" Then she said angrily, "You startled me!" A foot stamped petulantly. "How dare you?"

Rowan fought an urge to run, knowing it would only cause worse suspicion. Bel had dropped the point of her spear to fighting position, squinting in the light, and Rowan laid a restraining hand on her arm.

The room was brilliantly lit, and a slim girl stood by an opposite doorway, one hand flung back, the other steadying her against a cupboard from which some crockery had fallen. She was of Rowan's height but fragile-seeming, and young, no older than Willam. A cloud of dark ringlets framed a face with a small, up-tilted nose, pointed chin, and long dark eyes under straight brows. It was a beautiful face, of that characterless perfection that Rowan always equated with having no face at all.

The girl wore a light silk gown, possibly her nightshift, over which was thrown a hooded cloak of startling beauty. Blue satin folds bright as sparkling water fell from her shoulders to sweep the ground, white satin showing at the lining. The cloak needed no ornament other than its elegant construction and the flare of its movement as the girl stepped closer. She viewed Bel with haughtiness and spoke with sarcasm. "My, isn't she fierce?"

Bel relaxed her posture, and Rowan apologized. "Sorry, child. Instinct and training."

The girl turned her dark gaze on Rowan. "And what might you two be doing here?"

The room was a kitchen. Rowan managed a wry comradely smile. "Possibly the same thing you're doing."

The girl stamped her foot again. "You must speak to me with more respect!"

Taken aback by her outburst, Rowan made to reply, but the girl continued, pacing in anger.

"You guards are all the same, none of you want to treat me correctly. I'm not a servant, remember that, and I'm not one of your cronies." She stepped close and shook her finger under Bel's nose. Rowan caught a faint scent of musk and dried sweat. "You should come to attention when I pass in the halls, and – oh!" She threw up her hands. "Those comments! There'll be no more of that, I tell you. Remember what happened to Clara."

"Miss," Rowan managed to interject, "I'm sorry. Nothing of the sort entered our minds. You caught us by surprise, that's all. No disrespect was intended."

Catching Rowan's tone, Bel spoke up. "And, miss, pardon me, but I'm new here, and I don't know much of anything yet. Please, so I won't make the same mistake again – who are you?"

The girl regained her control and eyed the Outskirter archly. "I'm Liane." She tilted her head, gauging reaction, then turned away and wandered, as if idly, down along the preparing tables. "If you're all that hungry, you may as well help yourselves." A condescending smile was turned in their direction. "Don't worry. I won't tell on you."

They leaned their spears near the door and came farther into the room. Liane graciously indicated the cupboards, and Rowan found a cold leg of mutton inside one.

"And, please, what is it that you do?" Bel continued. Liane's only reply was an expression of self-satisfaction.

The steerswoman had already solved the girl's puzzle, but was at a loss to express it politely. "She . . . holds a delicate and influential position."

Liane laughed and clapped her hands. "I like that! Delicate and influential, that's very true."

Finding a pewter plate, Rowan arranged careful slices of meat, added some bread, and passed it to Liane. Then she cut more casual chunks for herself and Bel. "I must admit, miss," she began cautiously, "that I've always wanted to meet you."

Liane stopped with a slice halfway to her mouth. "Why is that?" A pattern of little bruises showed along one arm.

"It seemed to me that you must be a remarkable person, else— " She spread her hands to include the keep at large. "Else how would you be here?"

The girl looked surprised and gratified, and her expression softened. Here, Rowan thought, was possibly the best source of information they could hope for. Liane was young, naïve, and in a privileged situation. The high opinion she had of herself was at odds with the attitudes of those around her; she was certainly lonely, and possibly easily flattered.

"Understand," Rowan said to Bel, "a wizard could have any companion he chooses. Willing or unwilling, I suppose. The field of possibilities is large."

"Large indeed, and more willing than not. Really, the way some of those people behaved!" Liane fluttered her fingers fastidiously. "Beneath me. *I* didn't try to attract attention at all."

She was altering her speech patterns, Rowan realized, and trying to adopt a form she considered superior. Likely her normal style was more like that of most of the guards. A local girl. "And despite that, you were chosen, from everyone." Rowan tried to sound impressed.

"Oh, yes." Liane sighed ostentatiously. "It was love at first sight, I suppose."

Bel was more dubious. "With which one?"

The girl feigned surprise. "Why, both of them." She gave an arch, self-satisfied look. "They're *very* close."

The Outskirter frowned in thought as she tried to work out the logistics.

Rowan manufactured an envious expression. "Some people are born for good fortune."

"Not all love and fun, I tell you," the girl stressed seriously, slipping into natural speech, then slipping out again. "Mine is an important responsibility! When they're distressed, or out of sorts, when their spells go bad and their plans don't work, who do they turn to?"

There was a large pause before anyone recognized that she expected an answer to so rhetorical a question. Bel surrendered. "You?"

"Yes, indeed! And if I can't soothe them and cheer them up— " She made a wide gesture. "Everyone suffers."

"Are they out of sorts now?"

Her expansive mood faltered. She rubbed her nose with the back of one hand: an unconscious gesture, natural and poignant. "They're very demanding," she eventually replied.

"Is it this business with the steerswoman?" Rowan queried nonchalantly, remembering Ellen's comments.

Liane showed disgruntlement and picked up another slice of meat. "Nothing else. I hate her. Everything's in an uproar, just when we had gotten decently settled."

"We might get sent out in a search squad," Bel volunteered.

"I hope you kill her. No," the girl amended, "that would only make matters worse."

"It's not really fair," Rowan said, trying to voice Liane's own thoughts. "Shammer and Dhree have just fought a dreadful war. I imagine they'd like to rest and enjoy themselves, rather than worry about some fugitive."

Bel discovered her role in the conversation and began to play it. "Not at all," she said to Rowan. "They have a responsibility. If this woman is some criminal, then she ought to be punished."

"I'm sure they have other matters to attend to. How important can one woman be?"

Brooding on her hatred for the mysterious steerswoman, Liane commented distractedly, "It doesn't matter if she's important or not. They still have to catch her. But they don't have to like it."

Rowan stopped short. Implications crowded her mind, each demanding attention. Misunderstanding her silence, Bel tried to carry on the investigation. "If they don't like it, why don't they stop?"

The girl's gaze refocused, and she slipped back into her superior manner. "That's hardly the sort of thing soldiers should worry about. You just do as you're told, and leave the decisions to your betters. Well." She pushed away her plate. "Let's leave the mess for the scullions. It will be a great mystery. Don't you have to report to someone or go and guard something?"

If they reported to the night officer immediately, the lost time would not be difficult to explain away. Nevertheless, Rowan said, "Perhaps, miss, you'd let us escort you back to your chambers?" She thought it likely that Liane's rooms were within the central keep.

The girl smiled charmingly, tilting her head. She had apparently decided that she liked this understanding guardswoman. "Well. That's well spoken, but explaining you would take more trouble than it's worth. However— " She tapped one cheek thoughtfully, amused with her own idea. "I think that tomorrow I'll ask if I might be allowed to have a small contingent of my own, a sort of honor guard? Would you two enjoy a job like that?"

Rowan was astonished. "Very much, miss," she said quite honestly. Bel's grin possibly seemed feral only to Rowan.

"That's good. I'd like it, too." Liane turned away, allowing the cloak to swirl dramatically about her, very conscious of the effect. Pausing at the door, she made a gesture back toward the stairs. "Go on. You're dismissed."

Ascending the stairs, Rowan's steps began to slow of their own accord. Halfway up, she discovered that she had stopped climbing.

Bel paused, looking back down at her. "What's the matter?"

"Nothing. But wait a bit, I need to think. Something Liane said." The conversation had yielded possibly important information, and Rowan stood silently as she organized the implications of three offhand comments.

It doesn't matter if she's important or not. Possibilities were two: the steerswoman was unimportant; or there was no way to determine her degree of importance.

They still have to catch her. There was an impetus to do so that was outside of Shammer and Dhree's control. Possibilities were two: a natural impetus consisting of the real threat she represented; or an artificial impetus.

They don't have to like it. Shammer and Dhree resented the situation. Possibilities were two, and not mutually exclusive: they resented the waste of their resources; or they resented the existence of the outside impetus.

That resentment itself presented two possibilities: it was justified; or it was unjustified.

If their resentment was unjustified, it implied unrealistic attitudes. At least in the two wizards' minds, it was justified.

If it was justified, then they believed she was unimportant, and they disliked acting against their own judgment against a threat they did not see as real. The impetus, then, was irresistible – and artificial.

The steerswoman turned to Bel. "Shammer and Dhree are acting under orders."

She half expected Bel to doubt her and require lengthy justification, but the Outskirter digested the statement, then nodded minutely. "You're certain."

"Yes."

"Who gives orders to wizards?"

Possibilities were two. "Either the decision was made by the wizards in concert, with Shammer and Dhree dissenting but forced to follow the majority . . . or there's some single authority set over all wizards."

"If there were, why would they ever war against each other?"

Possibilities were two. "If the authority exists, either it doesn't care or it approves."

They continued up and then along the second-floor corridor, planning to return to their barracks by completing their circuit of the fortress. As they turned the final corner, they saw in the distance the last member of the squad they had ambushed, the man they had tortured. He was alive.

CHAPTER
Twenty-one

They flattened themselves against the wall.

He was descending an open staircase, moving like a recently risen invalid. His bandages were fresh, his clothes and person clean. A solicitous comrade walked beside him, speaking in low tones.

"If we come this way he's bound to recognize us," the Outskirter muttered.

"I doubt he'll ever forget your face." There was a door by Rowan's right hand. She slid closer and tested the latch. It was unlocked. A tap on the shoulder got Bel's attention, and the two slipped through. Rowan eased the latch silently closed.

The dim corridor they found was warmer than outside, with a faintly muffled feel. Trying to orient herself, Rowan felt a moment's confusion, and then amazed gratification. Briefly, the danger outside vanished from her thoughts. Rowan called her map to mind. "This is it. We're in the center." The ceiling there was lower than elsewhere. Rowan ran her hand along one wall. It was paneled in rich dark wood, kept gleaming by much attention.

"Yes." Bel looked around. "The inner fortress, nestled within the outer one. Do you think he'll come in here?"

Rowan shook her head, thinking. "Possibly not." She made a gesture back toward the door. "That's the part that most people deal with. Official rooms, residences – everything connected with the outside is conducted there."

"Then this is important." They were speaking in whispers.

"But the door isn't guarded, and it stands in plain sight. This area isn't really secret or protected. Perhaps it's just meant to be secluded."

"Or perhaps there's something in here that takes care of intruders by itself."

Fear and excitement fought each other in Rowan. "And that might signify something very important indeed."

"This hall seems normal enough. In fact, it's more pleasant here than in the rest of the keep."

"Perhaps that's its only purpose. The wizards may keep their private chambers here."

"And everyone would avoid them." Bel looked back at the door. "Well, we can't go back out without being seen. And someone else might come in soon."

"Yes." The corridor ran straight for some twenty feet and came to a cross juncture. A single, heavily carved door faced them from the intersection. Rowan approached it cautiously, Bel trailing ten feet behind, watching their back.

Reaching the door, Rowan paused and leaned close. Voices leaked faintly from within. She shook her head once in frustration, then glanced both ways down the crossing corridor. Deserted, with more doors. She added their orientation to her mental map, chose the direction that seemed to have the most options, and indicated that Bel should wait at the intersection.

She took five slow steps, her gum-soled boots dead silent on the carpet, and a door on the right opened. A slight, dark man emerged, his arms full of bundled clothing. Rowan slipped into a more normal pace and made to continue by nonchalantly. Bel stepped back out of sight.

He dropped the bundle. "Say! You can't be in here!"

Rowan stopped and looked about in puzzlement. "Sorry. Made a wrong turn." She turned back.

"You, there!" he called after her. "Stop!"

Rowan ignored him. He called again, then set up a cry for guards. A bustle and clatter grew ahead, and abruptly Rowan's alternatives had vanished.

She was trapped three ways, with the servant behind, the guards ahead, and the door by which she and Bel had entered, with people possibly outside—

She made the only choice she could, and Bel was ahead of her, already at the door. The Outskirter reached for the latch.

There was a faint snap, and Bel spun back as if struck, slamming up against the wall.

A guard-spell!

Rowan felt a hand on her shoulder, turned, and fisted the servant across the face. Then the guards were there, three men, and she was gripped by too many – and too strong – hands.

Bel had recovered her balance and stood weaving slightly, watching dazedly. Rowan wanted to tell her to flee, but it came to her that her friend would do no such thing. One of the guards spotted the Outskirter. "Here, who's that one?"

They must not both be caught. Rowan's mind went into a flurry, then clutched at an inspiration.

She struggled wildly, aiming a kick at the man's crotch. "*She's* the only reason you lowlives caught me. You're all too stupid except her."

One man laughed harshly. "Not too stupid to know there's no women in the inner guard." He called over to Bel. "You! How did you get through that door?"

Rowan spoke before Bel could. She was *chasing* me! Slipped in behind me. She's too damn fast and too damn smart."

"Is that right?"

Bel wavered on her feet. She seemed hesitant, her reactions oddly slowed. The spell, an aftereffect, Rowan thought. Bel, keep up with me!

Bel, beginning to catch on, approached. "That's right."

One of the guards shook Rowan. "So how did *you* get in?"

She ceased struggling abruptly and leaned her face mere inches from his. She made her voice brittle with spite and disdain. "I

247

got in because your pitiful little guard-spells have no effect on *me*."

Someone's grip faltered. "Gods below, she's a wizard."

"No." Understanding grew on the servant's face. "I know who she is. She's that steerswoman."

"What, the one all them squads were sent for? She's here?"

"Yes, I'm here." Her fear lent credence to the sneering anger she feigned. "I've been in the midst of you for days. You wouldn't have caught me at all but for *her*." She jerked her head in Bel's direction.

Her ploy was not working. Bel should have been participating, playing up, filling in the story. Instead, she stood to one side, still dazed, watching with the desperate attention of someone trying to follow a situation suddenly too complex.

Rowan needed a reaction from her, a convincing one, and quickly. Taking advantage of the guard's weakened grip, she pulled half-free, took one step toward the Outskirter, and spit in her face.

Bel went blank in shock and stood for a moment, stunned. A sound grew inside her; then she released a single furious shriek and went for Rowan's throat with her bare hands.

Rowan dodged back into the arms of the guards, and one of them stepped forward to fend off Bel's onslaught. "Ho, hold it there!" He laughed. "They want this one alive, I think."

"Keep her away from me!" Rowan pressed herself deeper into her captor's grips.

"We'll handle the steerswoman, girlie. Calm down!" Bel subsided, looking at the man with a wild eye. "You done good," he assured her. "Probably a promotion in this for you."

"So, we take her to Druin?" The man spoke close beside Rowan's ear. Her heart stumbled. Druin would remember that the women had come in together; the ploy would fail.

"Not this one." The servant approached and viewed Rowan with a self-satisfied, superior air. "She goes straight to Themselves, and no delay." He nodded to Bel. "You come, too."

But when the servant emerged from the room to which they had been led, Bel was instructed to return later to make her report.

Rowan exchanged one glance with her before passing through the door the servant held wide. The Outskirter's expression was stony, with what emotion Rowan could not guess. Accompanied by two of the guards, the steerswoman stepped in to meet the wizards.

When she saw them, her first reaction was: Gods below, they're children!

CHAPTER
Twenty-two

They were not quite children, but they were very nearly so. They might have been twins in their pale, dark-haired similarity. Both were tall and slim, the young man slightly wider across the shoulders; both moved with self-conscious grace, the young woman somewhat more quickly; both looked out from behind identical smooth faces through the same wide-set brown eyes.

The young woman stood by a round oak table, as if she had just risen from one of the two chairs. She wore a blue shift, simple but of beautiful workmanship, as fine as Kundekin-make but without their usual ornamentation. Her thick black hair fell in a braid to her waist. Behind her, a narrow window showed the walls of an interior court, dimly visible in the predawn glow. A lamp – not magical, but oil-burning – stood on the table, soft light falling on a sheaf of papers before her, and on a vase of daffodils. With affected uninterest she watched Rowan and the guards approach.

Her brother, who had just entered through a far door, studied the scene with an air of vast amusement. His hair, the identical color and the identical length, was caught at the nape by a plain silver circle. He crossed to a low chair with its back to the cold hearth and slouched, comfortable as a cat, stretching his long, loose-trousered legs in front of him and steepling his fingers.

Rowan stood between the guards, watching and thinking. She waited for the wizards to speak.

The young man spoke first. "What a lot of fuss she's caused."

"She certainly doesn't look like much," his sister observed.

Rowan could not remain passive. "Neither do you, I must say."

"Speak when you're spoken to!" the young woman spat.

"Yes, do," her brother amplified. Then he smiled slyly. "But tell us what you mean."

"You're very young."

"Are we?" The sister raised her brows affectedly. "How can you tell? We're wizards." She threw out one hand in an airy gesture. "We might be a hundred years old, a thousand!"

It was impossible. Even if a wizard's power could maintain the semblance of youth, voice and movement gave the two away. They were self-conscious, uncertain. They were feigning behavior designed to cover their inexperience. They overcompensated. Life was new to them. They were young.

"You're seventeen, about," Rowan said. "And your brother, not more than a year younger."

"So you think," the girl said archly, but her brother's amusement confirmed Rowan's guess.

"Try and hide something from a steerswoman," he said. "But it's an odd steerswoman, isn't it, who sneaks around in disguise, claiming to be something she's not, infiltrating a wizards' fortress."

"Strange events create strange results."

He raised an eyebrow. "Is that a Steerswomen's adage?"

"No. An observation."

"Ah, yes. Very observant, the Steerswomen." He sank a bit deeper into the chair, his body more relaxed, his eyes more alert. "I wonder what else you've observed, what else you might know. You weren't very kind to our minion, you know." His smile vanished. "I can't imagine why we should be any kinder to you."

Rowan felt a chill, but her gaze did not waver from his. "I'm sorry about your man; but I think that you'll find that sort of thing isn't necessary in my case."

The sister came around the table and leaned back against it, in a semblance of nonchalance. "Meaning what?"

Rowan spared one glance for each of her guards. "Meaning," she replied, "that I won't try to keep anything from you. Meaning that I'll give you any information you desire."

The rhythm of the exchange came to a halt. Her response had been unexpected. Brother and sister exchanged puzzled looks. Finally the young woman said in a light voice, "She's afraid of what we'll do to her. She's a coward."

"I don't think so," Rowan said. "But I'm not stupid. I don't wish to die, or even to suffer, particularly." She smiled thinly at their confusion. "Here." The guards shifted nervously when she reached into the neck of her cuirass; she turned a flat gaze on them, then continued, pulling out the leather pouch where her ring and chain nestled beside the mysterious jewel. As the wizards watched, she placed the ring on the middle finger of her left hand and slipped the chain over her head, its gold glittering against dull leather. "There. Now I'm a true steerswoman again."

She found, with surprise, that her emotions had relaxed, her body stood at ease. In the clutches of the wizards, she was suddenly like a prisoner freed. She was at home again, the home she carried with her. Her mind was clear, and she knew exactly what to do. Facing the pair, she said calmly, "Ask, and I'll answer."

The young man shot his sister a glance. She said stubbornly, "It's a trick," and he turned back, watching with narrowed gaze.

"It's no trick. Steerswomen do not trick people."

"And you expect us to believe it's as simple as that? You don your symbols, and you're suddenly trustworthy?"

"It's not at all simple," she told them. "It only seems so from the outside. And you're free to believe anything you like."

"Impossible," the young woman muttered.

"Wizards are under the Steerswomen's ban," her brother pointed out.

"Not at all. A person is put under ban once he or she refuses to answer a steerswoman's questions, or lies to her." She turned from one young face to the other. "I don't believe either of you have ever spoken to a steerswoman at all, and you haven't lied to me yet. The ban can't apply to you. The only reason I used deceit was my desire to survive. You tried to kill me."

He snorted. "Not us."

"You be quiet!" the girl told him. He raised his brows at her speculatively, but said nothing. Rowan made a mental note of the exchange.

"Once you knew the soldiers were ours, you came here," the female wizard continued.

Rowan shrugged.

"Why? Once you defeated them, why not run?"

Rowan thought. "Curiosity."

The brother was astonished. He threw his head back and laughed.

"It's true," she went on. "I know too little; it makes me vulnerable."

He made a vague gesture. "You know *something*."

"I don't even know which of you is which."

He smiled up at the ceiling. "I'm Shammer." His sister made no comment.

Rowan nodded.

"Very well." Dhree recovered her composure and ostentatiously turned her back, giving her attention to the vase of daffodils. "Then answer our questions, steerswoman." She toyed with one of the golden blooms. "To begin with, why are you being hunted?"

Rowan stopped, stunned. "You don't know." Not a question, a statement.

Dhree carefully showed no reaction. Shammer watched from his chair, head tilted insolently.

If they had sent their soldiers against her, and they did not know why, then her conclusion had been right: they had been ordered to do so. Who could give commands to wizards?

"You seem to be held in low esteem," Rowan hazarded.

"What do you mean?" Dhree asked, controlling anger, and her brother smiled at her discomfort.

"You're being treated like servants," Rowan said.

"If we were held in low esteem, we wouldn't be here at all," Shammer drawled.

Meaning that they were there by permission, that leave had been granted to them, the right to claim and defend their holding. Granted by whom?

"Possibly true." Rowan opened the sack again. "Then perhaps you can make something of this." She passed Dhree the enigmatic chip of blue.

"What is it?"

"It's the reason you were told to capture me."

The wizard took it in her hand, glanced at it once, twice; then, astonishingly, she flung it down on the table. She whirled on Rowan in outrage. "Don't be stupid, steerswoman, and don't play games." She stepped close and glared down at her. Rowan noticed how fine the wizard's skin was, and how clean her hair. She smelled faintly of rosemary. Her voice hissing spite, she said, "Do you really think you can fool wizards?"

The steerswoman was not intimidated. "If you're going to tell me it's a decorative object, I won't believe you. I've been told that already, by someone who was clearly trying to deceive me. I know it's magic."

"Of course it's magic! But it's common, we use them every day, in any number of spells. I could show you a hundred like it— "

"No. Not quite." Her brother had risen and moved to the table; he was turning the jewel over and over in his hand.

"What do you mean?" Dhree hesitated, then reluctantly came to his side.

He indicated. "Look at the coating. It's constructed differently."

"That's your area."

"Of course it is. You're theory, and I'm execution. Well, dear sister," he said, his tone heavy with sarcasm, "theorize."

She studied it, touching it with one forefinger. "Is that coating inactive?"

"Yes, indeed."

"Then it's protective." Her aspect had altered. Gone was the bravado, the venom. She showed the clear concentration of an intelligent mind involved in solving a problem. Other considerations had vanished. Rowan felt an odd, sad touch of kinship with her.

"Protective from what, I wonder," her brother said.

The young woman stared at the jewel, but her attention was turned inward. "Environment," she said at last.

"Ours don't need this protection. And they survive any sort of weather."

"Then a different environment entirely. Desert, perhaps." She looked at him. "You've worked with the Grid."

He shook his head. "They're nothing like this."

Rowan fought to keep her excitement from her face. Information, she thought.

Dhree turned her attention back to the steerswoman. "Where did you get this?"

"That one, from an irrigation ditch in farmland by the eastern curve of the Long North Road. And there are many more, scattered across the countryside in a broad line that runs southeast from there clear into the heart of the Outskirts. If you have a map, I'll show you exactly."

Brother and sister, side by side, gazed at her suspiciously. Then Dhree gestured to one of Rowan's guards, who hesitated, then stepped back to the door to call the servant.

"Maps, Jaimie," Dhree instructed when he arrived. "Covering the lands north of the Inland Sea. The librarian will know which." She paused. "And bring another chair for this table."

It was a strange collaboration.

At times Rowan forgot where she was and with whom she was dealing. She presented her information as completely as if she were speaking to steerswomen, and as long as she was the person speaking, she could become lost in the work itself.

It was only when she felt a question about to escape her that she stopped short and remembered: if she asked a question, they might refuse to answer. On their refusal, she could no longer reply to their questions, and all progress would cease.

And her first question was about the maps.

Shammer took one from the group presented by the servant and unrolled it on the tabletop. At first Rowan could not orient herself to it; it seemed to be a work of art, executed in a style delicate and beautiful, like a watercolor painting. Then abruptly, with a small internal shock, she recognized along the right edge the course of the river Wulf. Southwest she found the city of the Crags, with the fjords depicted in maddening detail. The center of the map was dominated by an immense sweep of mountains, the same that lay on the western limit of all the large-scale maps in the Archives.

And, west of the mountains, *past* the mountains, on the other side of those mountains which no living person had been known to cross:

A string of lakes like jewels on a necklace. A range of weird, twisted hills. A river broader than the Wulf, longer than the Greyriver, writhing northeast to southwest and vanishing at the map's edge.

She stood silent. Her hands hung limp at her sides. She forgot to breathe. She suddenly remembered a long conversation she had once had with a Christer, as he tried to describe to her the sensation of holy epiphany.

And she said to herself: Don't ask them. Don't ask.

Where had the information come from? Who had been there? Who had seen it? How had they traveled?

Who had drawn that map, with so steady a hand, such elegant colors? How precise were the measurements? Were there communities beyond the mountains? Were there wizards?

Shammer released the edges, and the map rolled closed again. "Wrong one." He swept it to the floor impatiently.

Rowan wanted to rescue it and cherish it as if it were a living thing.

The wizard pulled out another chart, read the legend on its outer edge, and spread it on the table. "This one, I think." Dhree tilted her head at it and nodded.

From where Rowan stood, across from the wizards, the map was upside down. That should not have mattered, but the style was so different from that used by the Steerswomen that she was momentarily confused again.

It seemed that the mapmaker considered roads to be no more important than the natural features of the land. Rowan located a brown-and-green shape that she finally understood to be the salt bog, and managed to locate the eastern curve of the Long North Road nearby, dimly marked by a faint gray line. Again she felt that internal shift as the chart became comprehensible.

"Here." She indicated. "There are a number of farms between the Eastern Curve and the salt bog. They're irrigated from this brook— " Astonishingly, one of the irrigation ditches, probably the largest, was marked. "That's where my jewel was found. I began to ask, and then search for more . . ." Dhree handed her a stick of charcoal. Rowan overcame her reluctance to deface the map and drew, from memory, the location of each finding. "And finally, I heard that there are a large number deep in the Outskirts." She drew a narrow oval, encircling the northern findings, sweeping southeast, and terminating in the middle of a huge area colored dull brown. Leaning closer, she found a jagged line crossing the oval at its far end. It was labeled "Tournier's Fault". "That must be what the Outskirters call Dust Ridge."

Shammer made a face. "What a bother, walking all that way, just to see more of something you've already seen."

"It might be important." Dhree knitted her brows in a frown of thought.

"Perhaps you should go there, Sister."

"Perhaps I will, if we can't get any answers from Slado."

Her face impassive, Rowan grasped at the name.

"And how soon did you realize you were being hunted?" Dhree asked.

"It was after I left Five Corners to return to the Archives." She described the soldiers at the inn. "One of them accosted me on the road later. I don't know who controls that area, but the soldiers were Red."

"That's Olin," Shammer told his sister. "Such a stupid man. He always does too much, or too little. Or nothing, when the mood takes him."

"He's insane," Dhree said, half to herself. "Really, that basilisk . . ."

"Still, as she was crossing his holding with her questions, I suppose he's the one who's started all this."

"Maybe not. I can't imagine he'd place any more importance on this jewel than we did."

"The only importance the jewel seems to have," Rowan pointed out, "is the degree of attention it provokes." She took a risk. "I expect Olin was also acting under orders."

Shammer's only response was a twitch of his lips, and the muttered word "Orders."

Rowan trod carefully. "It's interesting. I always assumed that wizards are ones who give orders, not take them."

"Don't become too interested." But both their faces showed the hate they held for the one who gave them orders. They would disobey if they could. And that meant that they could not.

Discussion continued. They dined – a late dinner, or early supper, Rowan could not tell which. The day had dawned overcast, and the shift of Rowan's sleeping time had skewed her usually reliable time sense. The courtyard outside showed no shadows.

Rowan explained that the jewels were a recent phenomenon. "The earliest date I can pinpoint for their appearance is about thirty-five years ago. I have that date for only two of the findings; the others are indeterminate but don't contradict it. And it's interesting that the farms between the Eastern Curve and the salt bog are relatively new. None existed before thirty years ago."

Dhree drummed her fingers on the tabletop. "And why was that, do you know?"

"Demons in the salt bog was the rumor. But only rumor. No one living there had ever seen one."

"That's odd. Demons are never found in the Inner Lands."

Shammer thought briefly. "It's possible. They need salt water."

Rowan puzzled. "But there are none on the shores of the Inland Sea."

A wry smile. "It's the wrong sort of salt."

Rowan put that aside for later consideration.

Eventually exhaustion overtook her, and the wizards decided to consider her information and continue in the morning.

They wondered what to do with her. "We certainly can't keep her in the dungeon. Considering, that is, all the help she's giving us." Shammer spoke as if amused, but behind his air Rowan could still read suspicion and wariness. He was off-balance.

Dhree, musing on the jewel, did not look up. "One of the inner guest rooms. We need bars on the windows, a strong bolt, and an opening in the door for the guard to watch her."

"So we do. That's a day's work on the window for a mason." He pursed his lips, fidgeting with the end of his queue. "I'll do it myself. An hour or so." He departed, humming, possibly relieved to be leaving the theoretical discussion for work more direct and practical. Rowan was left with Dhree.

"What happened to your entourage?"

Rowan was puzzled. "'Entourage'?"

The wizard pushed aside the charts and jewel. "Yes, those mercenaries who fought for you during your attack. Our man reported that his squad was badly outnumbered."

Rowan's mouth hung open for a moment; then she laughed long and without restraint. Dhree frowned.

"Your man," Rowan said when she had recovered, "assumed I would never show up here to give the lie to his story. I had two assistants, no more."

A muscle in Dhree's cheek twitched. "And the three of you overcame our trained soldiers?"

"That's the case."

"Where are your hirelings now?"

Rowan neglected to correct the term and answered only the question. "Not here," she said regretfully, internally limiting "here" to its most circumscribed definition.

"How unfortunate for you."

Her prison was a small, comfortable room luxurious in its appointments. The bed was goose down, with silk sheets and satin coverlet, curtained with lace. A comfortable chair stood by the hearth, where a small blaze had been kindled. Bare spaces on the wall and the off-center arrangement of furniture betrayed the removal of certain items, possibly objects useful to visiting fellow wizards, dangerous or forbidden to common folk. An empty bookcase occupied one corner. Her guard politely instructed her in the use of the magical lamps that illuminated the room; a small brass wheel on the wall by the door, when turned, caused the light to dim and go out according to her wish.

When he left, Rowan settled before the fire, fighting sleep to give herself the time she needed to think. She was a steerswoman again.

She had used that fact as both tactic and technique.

It was a tactic of delay. Co-operating with her captors was buying her time, the time she needed to devise an escape.

And it was a technique of manipulation, far more effective than any web of lies; with every true sentence she spoke, the wizards gifted her, by their reaction and response, with information they would never betray to direct questioning.

Each new fact was like a card, and she sat late into the night, mentally shuffling and spreading them, watching the interlocking patterns appear and dissolve. The branching of possibilities began to narrow, and the patterns started repeating, but she played them, over and over, fighting not only to recognize, but to understand.

When at last she turned down the lamps and took herself to bed, she had managed to reduce all her still-incomplete knowledge down to one fact, true and inescapable: something was wrong, and her whole world was at that moment in the very act of altering. It was changing from something she now recognized as badly misunderstood into something whose new nature she could not even guess.

She slept without dreaming.

CHAPTER
Twenty-three

Except for the fact of being a prisoner, Rowan could find no complaint for the treatment she received. Breakfast was excellent, and the servant who brought it inquired after her comfort during the night. Despite her assurances, he offered extra bolsters, a softer quilt, a finer bed robe; when his list of suggestions eventually worked its way down to musicians to divert her, she stonily called it to a halt and requested his personal absence.

She chose from the selection she found in the wardrobe, grateful at least for the fresh clothing. Presently her door was unlocked, and she was conducted back into the presence of the wizards, and the business was picked up from the previous day.

As their discussions continued, Rowan began to see the inefficiency in the wizards' division of labor. Dhree was quick to follow dense theoretical matters, but when Rowan pointed out practical considerations, she had difficulty altering her ideas to accommodate them. Shammer was able to recognize detail and devise immediate solutions to practical problems; but in questions of theory he first waited for Dhree to reach her own conclusions, then laboriously explain to him.

It was a flawed arrangement, not a true collaboration at all. In every situation, one or the other had to be dominant, and the necessity of communicating across the gaps in their understanding slowed the pace of learning. As the discussion moved from mere fact to speculation, Rowan found the pair more and more isolated in their intellectual corners.

They considered the question of the jewels' distribution.

"As you can see," Rowan began, indicating the narrow oval drawn on the map, "there's a definite direction to the findings, with the largest concentration, I believe, here." Dust Ridge. "This is one of the findings with a date that I'm certain of. Since the opposite end of the trail seems to have the same date"—the farms by the salt bog—"I'm considering the likelihood of a single event or agent being responsible for the entire dispersal."

Dhree frowned in thought. "Such as a man, walking along, throwing the jewels as he went?"

"The path begins on one side of the salt bog. There was another finding not far from the other side, and in line with the first, and with Dust Ridge." Rowan indicated again. "No man could walk through the bog."

"He flew," Shammer said easily. "Only a wizard would possess the jewels to begin with, and flying's no difficult matter for one of us."

"You say the jewels are common. If the wizard in question was using them while he flew, or carrying them, perhaps there was a flaw in his spell, and he fell."

The young man pursed his lips. "He wouldn't use them in a flying spell. They're not strong enough."

Dhree paused briefly, then objected. "It ought to be possible."

"He'd fly ten feet off the ground, at walking speed, with little real protection. Small children could pick him off with stones. But he might have been flying by other means, and carrying the jewels."

Rowan considered. "If he dropped them as he flew, he must have been flying very fast; at Dust Ridge, the jewels hang halfway up a cliff."

Both wizards had difficulty visualizing this. The steerswoman elaborated. "If a man is riding on a fast horse, and he drops a coin, it doesn't hit the ground directly under the point where he dropped it."

Dhree caught on. "He and the coin share the same velocity, until the influence of the motivating force is removed from the coin. It falls, losing horizontal speed, gaining vertical speed." She took a sheet of paper and a pen. "How high up were the jewels found?"

"Halfway up the cliff. I'm afraid I can't be more specific than that." In sudden inspiration, Rowan turned back to the map and found Tournier's Fault. There, along the line marking the cliffs, she found dimly marked measurements. There were no units assigned to the number; were they feet? Miles? But she indicated them to Dhree, and the wizard tilted her head to read, closed her eyes briefly in thought – and then, astonishingly, drew a rough version of the very graph Rowan had used in her argument with Arian, a chart showing the range and interrelationship between possible height, speed, and falling time for falling objects.

Dhree showed the chart to her brother, who used an affected disdain to cover his incomprehension. Dhree was wise to his behavior. She tapped the chart. "Here. The normal falling path was interrupted by the cliff—"

Twisting his mouth, he said, "Tell me what I *need* to know."

In exasperation, she indicated a point along one of the scales. "Here's your range of speed."

He glanced at it once, then shook his head. "Impossible."

"Nonsense! It's just a question of finding a strong enough force—"

"It may be lovely in theory, but it simply can't be done. Forces like that can't be controlled."

"It ought to be possible. If you can find a usable spell, scale up its strength—"

"You can't simply scale things up without considering the effect on the materials and spells involved. In extremes the results become unpredictable."

"If the theory exists, there must be a way to implement it. You're approaching this backward—"

He tilted his chin up. "One of us is."

The course of this argument was very familiar, Rowan noted with amusement, remembering Arian. Seeking a way out of the impasse, she tried the opposite approach. "Shammer." When he turned to her, she continued. "Forget all this for a moment. Suppose you wanted to lodge a cluster of objects halfway up a cliff; try to think of the sort of spell you would use."

Response was immediate. "I wouldn't need a spell at all. Close up, a very good catapult would do the job."

"Imagine that you weren't close up."

He blinked. "Any number of means."

"And I assume that they're all magical."

"You assume correctly." His fingers drummed on the tabletop, and his face acquired the introspective, concentrated look of a person involved in work of the imagination. "I could use a spell that would fling the objects hard enough to leave the ground and strike the cliff. But it's tricky – and dangerous. I'd have to arrange the spell so that it would activate in my absence." He smiled wryly. "In other words, I'd set it up, then run like the devil. With that sort of thing, it's not a good idea to get in the way."

The phrase jogged at Rowan's memory. Where had she heard it? Then it came to her: Willam.

Dhree spread her hands. "Then that's the answer."

"No." He frowned, dissatisfied. "The spell isn't directional – it works in a sphere. The objects would go in every direction: up, down, all around." Reaching across the table, he pulled the chart closer and studied the narrow oval. He tapped it with one long finger. "You wouldn't get anything like this."

An idea occurred to Rowan, and she approached it carefully. "You said that some objects would go up. With a large enough force, I suppose they might never come down again."

The concept amused Shammer immensely, and he laughed offensively. "Silly woman. Everything that goes up, comes down."

But Dhree knit her brows. "It ought to be possible—"

Shammer glowered at his sister, stressing each word. "It can't be done."

Over lunch, they accused her of murder.

"Don't play innocent, steerswoman. You've killed at least two of the regular guard."

"Are they dead or just vanished? Perhaps they took the opportunity to flee your employ."

Shammer's gaze narrowed, and he did not reply. Vanished, then, Rowan concluded, and not due to her.

Dhree picked up the tale. "One man and one woman. They disappeared about the time you were captured, or just before."

Shammer, legs crossed with ankle on knee, flicked a speck of dirt from one soft leather slipper. "I don't like loose ends. It's untidy."

Rowan was about to truthfully assert her innocence, when she stopped short. About the time she was captured? Before? Or could it have been just after?

The missing man, she realized, was the fellow she and Bel had spotted, the survivor of their ambush. Bel would have eliminated him immediately, to prevent his identifying her and connecting her with the captured steerswoman.

And who was the vanished woman? Bel herself, fled? If so, why bother to kill the man? With him dead, Bel could possibly remain a member of the guard, needing only to explain Rowan's absence . . .

Then the answer came to her. The vanished guardswoman was herself, reported missing by Bel, the deed laid at the door of the notorious steerswoman.

"I believe I know who you're referring to," Rowan said to the wizards. She cast about for a true statement. "Violence is unfortunate. I . . . apologize for its necessity."

That seemed to satisfy them. "Violence is a rather simple means to some ends," Dhree remarked.

Shammer indicated to the servant to pour more wine. "One always does what's necessary."

The day passed, but the purpose of the jewels remained a puzzle.

"You said," Rowan prompted, "that you use their like regularly." This was the closest she could come to a direct question.

Dhree caught on. "And that's all we'll say about them."

"It's difficult for me to speculate without more information," Rowan pointed out. "I believe that, together, we may be able to solve this. Since it's as much a mystery to you as to me, it's to both our benefit."

"More to ours than to yours," Shammer commented, "as you'll never have the opportunity to use what you learn." He was seated on the windowsill, enjoying the afternoon sun.

"Steerswomen never use their information," Dhree said with derision. "If they did, they'd be more powerful than they are."

The steerswoman surprised herself by replying heatedly. "We do use our information," she said. "We're not interested in anything as petty as power over others, and if you're planning to kill me or keep me your coddled prisoner forever, then it's pointless and stupid to keep me in the dark."

"A little more respect, please," Dhree said without anger.

Shammer pulled a droll face at Rowan. "I'm afraid you'll get nothing there. My sister is too cautious. Very wise of her, don't you think? But that does remind me—" Stepping away from the window, he came to the table, eyes twinkling. "I think you might find this amusing." He pushed aside the charts and papers, reached into a pouch on his belt, and pulled out a small gleaming object, which he placed before the steerswoman.

It was a tiny silver statuette, as tall as her thumb. The figure was strangely stylized, and it took her a moment to make sense of it. It seemed to be a dancer, poised on one foot, one arm arched high above its head. Its other arm trailed to one side, as if it had been captured in the moment of executing a graceful turn. The figure was otherwise featureless, its gender indeterminate, the oversimplification of form lending it an eerie beauty. The dancer was standing on a flat silver base, from which a silver bar rose, arcing up in a half circle to where the raised hand touched it.

And attached to one side of the bar, destroying the weird grace of the sculpture, was Rowan's blue jewel.

Shammer held up one hand. "Watch." Carrying the figure to the window, he placed it on the sunny ledge, and with a dramatic flourish, stepped aside.

The figure began to dance.

It knew only one move, the completion of that swirl promised by the curve of its back and the sweep of its hands. It spun, slowly, then faster, sunlight glittering off its body.

Rowan watched, appalled and entranced. "Is it alive?"

He laughed with delight and, for once, completely without affectation. "No, not at all! It's magic, dear lady."

Dhree made a noise of exasperation, but her eyes showed admiration and affection. "You're showing off."

"Yes, indeed, and I love it."

He gave Rowan the dancer to keep, so amused was he by her astonishment. Later, back in her comfortable prison, she studied it, speculating and generalizing.

The jewel did finally seem to have a use; in some fashion it imparted life to the silver figure. Perhaps that was the overall purpose of such jewels: to animate the inanimate. What might be accomplished by such animation, what purpose the power might be put to, remained open, indefinite. The jewels might be useful in any number of spells.

The figure stood on her windowsill, innocently graceful, weirdly evocative, dancing in the light of the falling sun.

Through the window, across and below, Rowan could see the guards on the west wall in conversation with another pair, probably their evening replacements. Shortly, the first two left, and the new guards watched with odd interest until they were out of sight. Then the shorter guard shifted her weight, tilted her head up at her partner, and by those two characteristic moves, Rowan recognized Bel.

This section of the perimeter had not previously been Bel's assignment; Rowan wondered if the new arrangement represented the promised promotion. The woman who accompanied the Outskirter was of the tall, broad-shouldered type that seemed to dominate the female contingent of the wizards' resident guard. The two stood casually scanning the area, then consulted briefly. The tall woman stooped to deal with something buried in the shadow of the edge, and Bel strolled to the near edge, to look left and right, then down.

She was facing Rowan's window; the tall woman's back was turned. Rowan tried to signal, using broad gestures, but failed to attract the Outskirter's attention. Turning around, Rowan scanned the room for something more eye-catching.

Shammer's dancer was on the sill. She thought of using the jewel to catch the sun's light, but realized it was too small, and its natural color too dark. On a low table by the hearth were the plate and glass from her dinner, brought in on a silver tray. She quietly moved the crockery and took the tray to her window.

Bel had walked to the corner tower and was returning, carrying what looked like a wooden bucket filled with straw. She gave it to the guardswoman, who acknowledged her with a glance, and returned to her work.

Using the tray, Rowan mirrored the sunlight onto Bel's face. Bel's head jerked up, and she looked to the window, then stepped closer to the edge of the wall.

Had Bel been a steerswoman, Rowan could have conversed with her using the wood-gnome language of hand gestures, exaggerated for distance. As it was, the sum total of Rowan's communication consisted merely of "I am here". What use Bel might make of the information, she had no idea.

Bel did not acknowledge but, appallingly, stepped back and tapped her companion on the shoulder. The woman looked up, and with one hand Bel indicated the steerswoman.

In shocked instinct, Rowan ducked back out of sight. What was Bel doing? Could she gain something by pointing out the prisoner to her new partner?

When she had calmed herself, Rowan looked out again. Both women were gone. She immediately regretted her reflex; whatever Bel's purpose, Rowan could trust her. The important fact was that Bel was still at large, and still in the confidence of the resident guard.

If Rowan could manage to get out of her room, she could find Bel, and both could escape, possibly by water. Willam would have begun on his way to the Archives, if he was following her instructions. She hoped that he was.

Rowan could not count on Shammer and Dhree's continued indulgence. As soon as nothing more could be learned from her, she would be useless to them.

She had only one man guarding her. If he was eliminated, she had a slim chance of making her way out of the inner ring of the fortress—

And then what?

She did not know the usual movements of the inner guards. The only place she could be certain of finding Bel was the women's barracks at the proper sleeping time for those on Bel's new shift. As it was a day shift, Bel would sleep at night. The barracks could easily be full of guards.

Rowan might do better to try to slip away by herself. She disliked the idea, but Bel was in no immediate danger. If Rowan could get out, she might contrive to send a message.

The first step was to get past her guard. Once out, she could make her decisions based on what she encountered.

She needed to get the man inside her room, and alone. And some way to deal with him, once he was inside. She scanned the room, questioning each object: is this a weapon?

Nothing was, so she set a trap.

She lay fully clothed on her bed past nightfall, leaving her lamps dark, letting her fire die, permitting the guard to assume that she already slept. Just before his evening replacement was due to arrive, she rose silently in the dark.

The armchair was heavier than she had guessed, but she could not let it drag as she moved it. Tilting it back, she found its center of gravity and managed to lever it off the ground and lift it, its lower edge propped against her thighs. Walking carefully and awkwardly, she brought it to the side of the door and lowered it painfully to the floor.

A tall coatrack was moved nearby, three feet behind the door's edge. The guard's grilled opening was too small for the rack to be seen through it.

The low rectangular table by the hearth was easy to move, but presented more of a problem; she would need to hoist it over her head and hold it there, adjusting it silently. The chair gave one soft creak as she climbed it, and she froze, fearing that the guard would enter to discover her standing on it, the table clutched in her arms, a pose more than suspicious. She heard the man shift slightly, but he said nothing and did not investigate, apparently dismissing the sound.

The light from the grille did not fall on herself or any of her arrangements. Trying to keep her breathing quiet, she turned the table with its feet in the air and, using her own head as a balance point, slipped the edge onto the door's heavy upper sill. Her calculation had been perfect, and the opposite end of the table came down and rested easily, propped on the top of the coatrack. It would be stable, she hoped, until the swing of the opening door or a blow of her hand struck the rack. Descending, she moved the chair clear of the events she hoped would follow.

Presently the evening guard arrived, and the two men exchanged a few words. Nothing was said about suspicious noises.

Rowan returned to her bed and sat, composing herself. All that remained was to get her guard to enter. There seemed to be only one way to make certain that if he entered, he would enter alone. She balked at the thought, trying to find an option that did not require behavior so – embarrassing.

There was none. Resigning herself to necessity, she rose, stepped to the grille, and stood casually, her own trap looming above her head.

"Excuse me."

The new guard turned, not surprised; he had heard her approach.

She smiled. "I'm sorry, I just can't sleep. I hope you don't mind if we talk?" He wavered, confused, caught between duty and traditional respect for steerswomen. "Talk, lady? What about?"

"Oh, nothing in particular, just to pass the time. It's a long lonely night ahead." She permitted him to see how carefully she studied his face. "What's your name?"

He peered in at her, and she saw wide dark eyes and heavy curls of black hair. He was a handsome man, possibly vain, and Rowan blessed that, hoping it might make her job easier. "Geller, lady."

"Then, good evening, Geller." She inclined her head with facetious formality. "I'm Rowan."

"I know."

She groped for something else to say to keep the conversation moving. "Do you enjoy your work for the wizards?"

He hesitated, then answered truthfully. "Not much, lady. But the war ran over my town. It's work." He was watching her intently.

"Well." She stepped a bit closer. "I wonder, if you would be so kind, could you show me how to work the lamps in here?"

"There's a wheel, by the door," he said, indicating with little jerk of his head.

270

"I'm afraid I can't see it." She did not bother to look, and he saw that. She kept her eyes on his and forced another smile, cringing inwardly.

There was a very long pause. "I shouldn't come in there."

"No one needs to know." Suddenly her embarrassment overcame her, and she dropped her eyes, unable to face him, knowing that the gesture would be misread. "Do I have to be more . . . obvious?" She raised her eyes again. "I can be, if you wish."

But she saw that Geller's beautiful face was screwed up as if in pain. "Lady . . ."

Rowan stopped short. "Yes?"

"Please, don't do this, lady. It's not . . ." He groped for the word. "It's not fitting."

They viewed each other through the grate, he with pity, she with astonishment, then shame.

At last she nodded slowly. "Thank you, Geller," she said with dignity. "You're right. It's not fitting." And she walked alone back to her bed.

When the shift changed at midnight, she attempted the same ruse with the new guard, to identical effect.

The next morning the servant politely brought her breakfast again. She ignored the food, pacing the limits of her chamber. The knowledge she had gained from the wizards nestled like a seed in her brain; the need to pass it on to someone was agony.

The servant watched speculatively, then withdrew.

She could formulate no plans; she could take no action. No decisions were open to her, and there were no means by which to alter her situation. Although they might not yet realize it, she was of no further use to Shammer and Dhree, and they were unable to reveal anything more to her about the jewels. She would have to spend the day with them seeking to learn one last thing: a means to make her escape.

Eventually she noticed that the guards had not arrived to conduct her to the wizards. The morning wore on, and her breakfast dishes were not removed. She questioned the man at her door, but he knew nothing.

It was past noon when her escort finally arrived and brought her along the now-familiar route. Surprisingly, when they entered the wizards' study, the room was empty. The guards did not leave her, and when she spoke they did not reply. When she attempted to make herself comfortable at the table, they indicated that she was required to stand between them.

All her progress in gaining the wizards' grudging confidence had been somehow lost, she realized, and with rising apprehension she prepared herself to face the new situation.

When they entered, Shammer and Dhree remained standing on the opposite side of the room, as if she were dangerous or diseased, watching her with flat gazes of pure hatred. Some moments passed.

At last Dhree spoke. "We'll be rid of you tomorrow."

"That's rather soon." Rowan wanted to start them talking, any sort of conversation, anything to give her some hint as to what might have happened and what she might now expect.

The wizards regarded her as if she had not spoken, but Dhree amplified, seemingly more for her own satisfaction than from any desire to assist Rowan. "Someone's coming to," and she sneered the word, "*collect* you."

Rowan nodded slowly. "Someone sent by Slado, or Slado himself."

There was no reply. Shammer shifted uneasily, as if there was something he wished very much to do with his hands.

Rowan tried again. "If we only have one day left, perhaps we should get down to work. With luck, by the time Slado arrives, you might know as much as he does."

They ignored the comment. As if against his will, Shammer said in a toneless voice, "We've found more evidence of your handiwork."

Her handiwork? What was she supposed to have done? Two disappearances had been blamed on Rowan, both Bel's doing. The one had been mere fabrication to cover Rowan's own absence from the resident guard she had joined; the other was Bel's elimination of the last member of the ambushed squad, to prevent his identifying the Outskirter.

Might Bel have eliminated someone else? To be blamed on Rowan, the deed would have to have been done at the same time as the earlier disappearance. Who else presented such immediate danger?

Someone who had seen Rowan and Bel together, certainly. But the inner guard were a separate corps, and the members of the outer guard whom Rowan and Bel had met were not likely to be introduced to the captive steerswoman and would not connect her with the Outskirter.

Who might have had the opportunity to make that connection? Someone who had seen them together, who might have been likely to see Rowan in the wizards' company – and whose absence might have gone unnoticed for two busy days.

Rowan attempted to dismiss the matter. "Disappearances didn't seem to distress you earlier. As you said, one does what's necessary."

Shammer took four long steps forward and backhanded her across the face.

She fell against the closed door, stunned, dazed. The guard on her left dragged her to her feet with a bruising grip. She staggered against him, regained her balance, and passed one hand across her face to find a split lip.

Abruptly, she understood. "Liane."

Shammer struck with his other hand. The guard on the right prevented her falling, and the two men supported her emotionlessly.

When she recovered, she said, "If Slado is coming for me, I think he'll expect me alive." Some of the words were slurred.

Cold confirmation came from across the room. "Unfortunately."

Shammer, his eyes full of murder, took two careful steps back, then turned away.

Regaining her balance, Rowan composed herself slowly. All advantage had been lost. She tilted up her chin. "So I'll meet Slado. How interesting."

With his back to her, Shammer said, "You'll meet him and die." He gestured. "Get her out of here."

"One moment." Dhree came a bit closer. "I understand that your little game of last night was quite the joke among our inner guard. Pitiful."

"It was the best I could manage."

"I think you'll find that your new guards are, shall we say, above temptation? Still . . ." Her expression turned speculative, interested. "Perhaps you've been a little lonely? Perhaps tonight you could use some . . . company?" She studied Rowan's reaction, eyes glittering cold amusement. "What do you think, Brother?"

"No." He half turned, his eyes blank. "She might enjoy it."

The guard at her door was female, a tall angular woman who watched her with the pitiless eye of a bird of prey. Above temptation, as Dhree had said; the rule against women in the inner guard had been altered.

She tried to clean the blood from her face and clothes, but found there was no water in her ewer. The woman at the door ignored her request, and Rowan did the best she could with spit and a silk handkerchief.

In the evening the guard changed shift, but no food was brought, and the remains of her breakfast had vanished. She sat long at the window, silent, watching the light fade, then the starlight glitter on the roofs and cupolas. And slowly her mind became as still as her body, for there were no plans she could make, no routes to investigate. Options had vanished. Possibilities were zero. She sat in the darkness, unsleeping.

When the shift changed at midnight, her guard was Bel.

CHAPTER
Twenty-four

The Outskirter grinned up through the grille. "I've been promoted."

Rowan stared down at her, astonished, then urgent. "Bel, let's get out. Now."

Bel glanced in both directions, then walked a few feet to peer down the intersection in the corridor. She returned. "Not you."

"Someone's coming?"

"No."

"Unlock the door."

Bel did so, but when Rowan pulled it open and made to leave, the Outskirter stopped her with a gesture. "We have to wait."

"Why?" Rowan spoke urgently. "Bel, I know the layout here now, and you know the internal guard movements. If we can get to one of those exits we found, we might have a chance." Rowan did not know how early Slado or his minion would arrive, or how long she and Bel would need to slip out of the fortress; they had to move, now.

"No, we've got something better. We've got a plan." Bel peered closer. "What happened to your face?"

"Shammer. Who do you mean by 'we'?"

"Willam and me."

Rowan drew a breath. "He didn't leave. He was supposed to leave."

"I needed him here. We've set up a diversion."

Rowan thought rapidly, then shook her head. "There are too many guards here. They won't all run to it, and those who don't will know to head straight for me. I'm too important a prisoner."

Bel smiled rather uncertainly. "You'll be the last thing on their minds. And it doesn't matter if they run to it or run from it, so long as they run. But here— " She reached behind and pulled something from under her cuirass. She passed it to Rowan inside, and closed the door.

It was a bundle of cloth. Rowan shook it out, and a breathtaking swirl of silvery blue spilled from her hands, sweeping the floor. Liane's cloak.

"It'll be a good enough disguise in the confusion," Bel continued.

Yellow light from the grille played on the garment. "It won't work. They know she's dead."

"The wizards?"

"That's right."

"Then they're keeping it to themselves. As far as the outer keep is concerned, she's off visiting. I thought it was odd."

Rowan crushed one handful of satin folds, feeling the weight and beauty of the cloak, thinking of the vain, lonely girl who had worn it. "What is Will going to do? Do we signal him, or he us?"

"Neither. We wait. You have to stand by the window and watch the Western Guidestar. When it goes dark, count one hundred. Then we move."

"And what happens?"

"Something." The Outskirter winced. "I'm not certain what—he didn't explain it well. People will panic, so we'll have to keep our wits about us."

Magic. Aside from lighting fires in wet wood, creating patterns and pretty sparkles in the process, what exactly was Willam capable of doing?

Rowan stepped to the window and studied the stars quickly. The Hunter's shoulder had slipped behind the Western Guidestar. The

Hound's nose would have to approach within five degrees before the Guidestar would wink out. That would be near half past one o'clock. They had more than an hour.

Rowan returned to the door and looked down through the grate. Bel had resumed her position as guard. "I only know the one exit from the inner chambers," Rowan told her. "But from there, there are any number of routes to a few ways out of the fortress. If the confusion's going to be general, we might do well to head for that staircase leading to the dock on the northeast side. We could escape by water."

Her back to the door, Bel shook her head. "That won't do. It's the wrong direction. We go out the main gate, over the causeway."

Rowan's heart froze. "Bel, that's the worst possible choice. We'd be visible for too long. We'd have to deal with the guards inside the gate, and stop to work the spell at the end of the causeway. We couldn't possibly move fast enough."

"It's the only way. It's all arranged. We'll deal with the guards as best we can, and Willam will take care of the spell."

"Can he do that?" Rowan was dubious.

"He says so." Bel spared a sidelong glance over her shoulder. "Shouldn't you stand by the window?"

"In a bit. I saw you, on the wall yesterday. Why did you point me out?"

"I wanted Willam to have some idea of your location."

Rowan stopped short, then laughed. The face of a boy, she realized, was little different from the face of a woman somewhat older than he. With a woman's shaped leather cuirass, the disguise would be impenetrable. "What was he doing?"

"Placing his charms. They have to be a certain distance from each other. He's been working like a madman, making more of them during the last two days."

"Do you think it will work?"

Bel shrugged. "I'm no wizard." She paused. "Rowan?"

"Yes?"

"When those guards cornered us . . ." The Outskirter hesitated again. "You spat in my face."

Rowan was ashamed. "I thought we weren't very convincing," she explained. "I wanted to make you angry."

Another pause. "It worked."

"Do you hold it against me?"

"No." Bel shifted slightly. "But never do it again."

Rowan returned to the window and stood the rest of her watch with the best patience she could muster.

Outside, the day's overcast had long passed, and the stars hung crystalline in a black midnight sky. Between rooftop and turret, Rowan sighted a section of the lake, where small waves scattered the starlight, sending white sparkles dancing on the invisible water. The world seemed to exist in black and white and shades of pale gray, clear and without distractions. On the wall in the distance, seen but faintly, a pacing guardman paused and gazed out at the same quiet scene Rowan was viewing, untroubled, peaceful. Eventually his head tilted up, and he and she saw in the same instant the nightly vanishing of the Western Guidestar.

Rowan began counting, swung the blue cloak about her body, and stepped to the door. "Twenty," she said to Bel.

The Outskirter jogged to the left intersection of the corridor, looked both ways again, and came back.

"Forty," Rowan said.

Bel took a deep breath, released it, and shook her arms to relax the muscles. She seemed calm and cheerful.

It was otherwise for Rowan, and she felt a stepwise increase in tension with every number her mind shaped. "Fifty," she said. "Do we really have to wait this long?"

"One hundred was what Willam told me. I hope you're both counting at the same pace. Is it sixty yet?"

Rowan paused for five counts. "It's seventy." Under the rhythm of the counting, she discovered herself reviewing alternative routes to the front gate; she had information to use, she realized, and that knowledge served to steady her. "Eighty."

Bel pulled the door open, and Rowan slipped through. "Lock it again. It might throw them off. Ninety."

The Outskirter looked up at her, eyes aglitter. "I have a sword for you. I left it behind a tapestry outside the door with the guardspell."

"Good. I'll need it. One hundred."

They followed the corridor, Rowan three steps ahead, wrapped and hooded in Liane's cloak, Bel following behind like an escort. They went left, then right, seeing no one. At the top of a broad stair, Bel stopped Rowan with a touch on the arm, then indicated. Listening, they could hear measured steps and muttered voices below. Two people; one walked away, and the other remained at the bottom, out of sight.

Close to Rowan's ear, Bel whispered, "There's always one guard at that post."

"What's keeping Willam?"

"There's no way to know. That man is inner guard; he probably knows about Liane. I'll have to catch him off-guard. You stay here." Bel paused a moment, thinking, then began running noisily down the stairs, footsteps startlingly loud. "You! Come here, lend a hand— "

"What? What are you doing here?"

Standing silently, waiting for Bel to do her job, Rowan was half distracted by a short, faint vibration beneath her feet. She looked down at the carpet.

"I'm guarding that steerswoman—something's wrong!"

"Wait here, I'll get help."

"There's no time, you'll have to do— "

There was another vibration, stronger; Rowan looked up, and an instant later she heard distant thunder.

"What was that?" And the man made one more sound, a wet choking cough.

Rowan knew what it was. She flew down the stairs to find Bel pulling the point of her spear from the prone man's throat. "Was that noise from the north?" Bel asked. Far off, someone shouted, a long muffled sentence.

"Yes," Rowan replied. Their way to the gate led south.

"About time." Bel abandoned her spear for the dead man's. "Let's go."

Rowan resumed her place in the lead, struggling to maintain a relaxed, casual pace. Halfway to the door with the guard-spell, they were surprised by a bleary-eyed servant who peered from a room in perplexity. "Themselves are up to something," Bel explained, offhand, as they passed. "Go back to sleep." The man gaped at her, then vanished with a look of fear.

Again the thunder rolled, louder. Wordless shouts came from behind, and the two women understood simultaneously that the time had come to run.

As Rowan reached the door to the outer keep, the floor suddenly bucked once, then shuddered, like a ship hit by heavy seas. The air was full of a roaring rumble. Nearby, someone screamed. Pulling the door open, Rowan pushed Bel through, and in an instant the Outskirter handed her the hidden sword.

There was thunder to the north, and the floor writhed unbelievably beneath their feet. Bel was thrown to the ground, but Rowan stood balancing wildly. About her, half-dressed people had appeared, clinging to the walls, crying to their gods and their families.

Abruptly and simultaneously, all the lamps went out. In the darkness Rowan found Bel and dragged her to her feet. Fading thunder left the air filled with shouts; then a crowd of organized footsteps approached, stumbled against the fallen, and reorganized with curses: soldiers. The squad swept noisily past Rowan and Bel, hurrying north.

Bel made an anguished sound. "We have no light."

Throwing one hand against the door, Rowan oriented herself, her internal map twisting in her mind. She exulted. "We don't need it. This is better." She guided Bel's hand to her shoulder. "Slowly."

"We can't see where to go."

"I know the route." She led the way, keeping measured stride, desperately matching her movement with the vivid image in her mind. One of the terrified residents stumbled against her, and she shoved him away roughly.

Pausing, she shuffled sideways, groping with her left foot to find the edge of the stairway she knew would be there. "Down."

A handful of people pushed past them, their voices a chaos of panic. Some took the stairs, stumbling, crying, and they broke around Rowan and Bel like a swirl of water. Rowan clutched the banister and stepped carefully, Bel still gripping her shoulder.

Reaching the bottom, Rowan saw a moving light in the distance, bouncing weirdly, approaching amidst the sounds of many feet. It was another squad of soldiers, their leader carrying a brilliant glowing object: a magic lamp like the wall sconces, but mobile. The beam played across the small crowd, swept once across Rowan, then returned to her. Thinking quickly, she turned her back to them and clung to Bel as if afraid, hiding her sword with her body, letting the light catch Liane's silver-blue cloak.

"The wizards' dolly," Bel shouted above the noise of panic-stricken civilians. She waved them on. "I'll take care of her."

The light swung away. Someone shouted to the growing crowd in an authoritative voice, "Stay where you are. Stay out of the way. It's being dealt with. Stay where you are." Protests and begging questions were ignored as the squad hurried on.

In a sea of babbling voices, Rowan thought furiously. Her dead reckoning had brought them but a few turns from the front gate, but that gate was guarded at the inside. How could they get past?

She could hear the now-buried nervousness in the people's voices, the panic lying just below the surface. None of them knew what was happening, and all were afraid. She briefly felt pity for them, and then an idea came to her.

Drawing a deep breath, she let out a long wailing shriek, feeling Bel startle beside her. "We have to get out!" Rowan screamed. She stepped into the crowd, clutching, and found someone. She shook him wildly, shouting into his face, "It's magic, something's happening! We'll all be trapped!" He tried to twist away in panic, and Rowan heard those nearby begin to echo her words, voices rising.

She shoved her unwilling assistant forward brutally. "That way! The front gate is that way!" Her hands found more people, and she pushed them, shouting, emitting the most bloodcurdling screams she could manufacture.

Panic spread. Rowan quieted herself and pulled back against the wall, out of the way. Someone took up the shout "This way!" and ran staggering, calling others after him. With a goal for their fear, the people fell into loose organization, helping each other as they stumbled toward escape.

Rowan felt sudden fear. "Bel?"

"Here." The Outskirter's voice came from nearby, to Rowan's left.

Relief. "We stay at the back." She found Bel's hand and reoriented herself. "Come on."

The group found its own stumbling way to the gate, and Rowan and Bel followed, more by tracking the sounds than by the steerswoman's skill. A burst of starlight ahead, and a babble of voices, and the crowd met the four startled guards at the gate.

The sergeant had a torch of real fire and grim presence of mind. "Calm down. No one's leaving."

There was a chorus of protests, and Bel shouted wildly, "It's magic, something magic's got loose! It's killed the wizards!"

Rowan took it up. "It's out of control!" She thought that might even be true.

"It isn't," the man replied against the cries of the people, but his face showed that he doubted. His men tried to herd the crowd back, but a woman broke through suddenly and ran down the causeway, one of the guards following, cursing. She threw herself against the spell-locked iron bars at the end, and he gripped her brutally and dragged her away.

A streak of fire flew toward the magic gate and lodged there, spitting sparks. There was a burst of light, a loud *crack*, and the stone and iron flew apart in a hundred pieces. The woman collapsed in a bizarre cloud of cloth and blood, and the soldier clutched at his face and fell, screaming. A shadowed shape ran to the gate from the road.

"Now!" Bel shouted, pushing through the stunned crowd. Following, Rowan broke through in time the see the sergeant's head fall from his body, and Bel's swing, out of control, ending in a bystander's chest. Rowan stabbed her blade in a disbelieving guard's face, wrenched it free, then turned to see the last guard stepping back, stiff-legged, briefly unmanned by surprise. The crowd fell back.

Rowan and Bel ran along the causeway. Halfway across, they were met by Willam; he carried his bow and three arrows, their heads aflame. Stopping, he gave two arrows to Bel. "Hold these."

Rowan pulled at him. "Are you mad? They won't be distracted forever—they may be coming now."

Bel wrenched her away from him with furious strength. "Shut up." Abruptly, Rowan's mind reorganized itself, and she turned to look back at the fortress.

She saw Will's first arrow end in the last guard's chest, and the man clutched at it, shrieking.

The dark towers were outlined by a glow of fire in the north quarter. Ordered shouts and chaotic cries came to her ears. With a look of desperate concentration, Willam set his feet carefully and lifted his head toward the overhang of the main entrance. His burning arrow flew high, slowed, arched, and fell. By its light, Rowan had seen its goal: the window of an observation post, now unmanned. He'll never make that shot, she thought, then knew with certainty that he would.

The last arrow lofted, painfully slow at the top of its flight, then clattered against the sill and rolled in. There was a pause, then flickering light as something inside caught fire.

"*Now run!*" the boy screamed, and the three ran madly, staggering past the pile of bones and raw meat, clambering over the remains of the ruined gate. Just as they reached the road, Rowan felt something like a huge invisible hand smash against her back, pick her up, fling her forward in a crowd of flying rock, and flail her body once against a wall of stone.

She came to with a dark shape crouched over her: the Outskirter. Bel looked over her shoulder. "She's alive." There was no response from Willam.

Rowan sat up and found that parts of her body were numb: her left arm and hand, the left side of her chest, the inside of her right forearm. Her right knee throbbed; her back stung as if scored. As she pulled herself to her feet with the Outskirter's help, the grip of her left hand failed, seemingly because some of the fingers bent backward.

She limped over to where Willam stood silent, at the end of a road that now stopped abruptly at the edge of a cliff. Rowan looked out at the fortress.

The causeway was gone, along with the front entrance and the entire front face. Beyond stood a maze of half-ruined walls, and then standing walls, open rooms clinging to their sides like barnacles, all seen by glow of fire in the ruins of the west quarter, where horses screamed.

As she watched, two of the distant suspended rooms collapsed to the ground like silent sighs.

An immeasurable force, set loose by a boy. A giant fist that smashed, a giant hand that flung stone through the air . . .

"Did you know it would do this?"

He stood silent, expressionless, looking at his work; then he nodded minutely.

Bel came up behind them. "It's a good job, don't you think?" She grinned whitely in a face blackened with dirt and soot.

Rowan touched the silent boy's shoulder and for a moment was amazed that he was mere flesh and blood, merely human. There was no magic to be seen in him. He was only a boy of the common folk, but he had done what seemed impossible. "Willam . . . will you stay with us?"

He turned to her, copper eyes blankly reflecting distant fire. "For a while. Where are we going?"

In this flickering quiet, in the silence after the shock, the world seemed vague, and her mind slowed. She groped for an answer.

"To the Outskirts?" Bel asked.

Of its own accord, information ordered itself in the steers-woman's mind and gave her replies without conscious effort. "I told Shammer and Dhree I was going there. They may have passed it on."

"To the Archives?" Willam suggested.

"I need to get my information to them, but I won't do it in person. If the wizards think I've gone there, they might harm it." Clinging to the framework of her ordered knowledge, her thoughts took shape again, and she knew what to do. "We need a defended position. Arms, and someone to direct them, someone who won't fail to stand by me."

"Where do we find that?"

"Wulfshaven. Artos."

CHAPTER
Twenty-five

The city of Wulfshaven held its breath.

One week earlier, Artos had unexpectedly ordered his soldiers to battle-readiness. Word was sent to those on leave, and they came into town from their furloughs, faces wary and perplexed. The citizens they passed questioned them, but they had no answers to give.

Two days later, Artos called his reserves to active duty, and those men and women kissed their spouses, children, and parents, and set up their encampments on the lawns of his mansion and in open fields around the city limits. The sentries on the perimeter were not concentrated in any one direction.

The day after that, a troop of cavalry was sent north, followed by another of foot soldiers. Their destination was not known, but message-runners sent to their position returned only a day later.

And the next day, word came that Artos was no longer in his mansion but kept residence in the small fort that barracked his regulars.

Daily business proceeded, but with many glances over the shoulder and much speculation in taverns and in private.

In the Trap and Net, as everywhere, speculation was very active and very quiet. Wary glances were directed at the door as each new customer arrived, and when at last it was a steerswoman who entered, one of the drinkers hailed her with a gesture, saying to his companions, "Now we'll learn something, I reckon."

But Rowan ignored the summons and stepped quietly to a corner table overlooking the harbor, where two men with tankards before them sat alone in friendly conversation. She stood without speaking until one of them looked up at her. "I've been waiting," she said then.

The wizard Corvus examined her with a mild gaze. "I rather thought you might be," he admitted. "It must be very boring."

There was a long pause. "Hardly."

He laughed. "Then you are easily amused. Why don't you join me?" He spoke to his companion, whom Rowan recognized as a local fisherman. "Selras, would you excuse us? I believe I have some business with the steerswoman."

The fisherman absented himself politely, but with a perplexed expression. He would have a tale to tell that night, Rowan thought, of a wizard and a steerswoman who against all custom and expectation had business with each other. She wondered to whom he would tell it, and what the ending might be.

She seated herself, sitting carefully on the edge of the chair, one hand before her on the table. The other hand was in a sling, its fingers stiffly splinted, and her face showed the marks of old bruises. She said nothing, but watched Corvus patiently, and he returned her gaze with an identical expression.

The wizard was a man of striking appearance, all darkness, dressed in black and silver. He was tall, lean, and broad of shoulder. His hair was a cap of gleaming black curls, his short black beard silvered to either side. His skin was dark, as dark as was ever seen in people, nearly true black.

Among the folk of the Inner Lands, any shade of skin was likely to be seen, any color of hair, seemingly without rhyme or reason; but that pure combination of darkness was rare enough to be noticed – and to be prized. Women of such appearance tended to cultivate an air of depth and mystery. Such men, being conspicuous, found that high courage and intelligence were expected of them, and so often actually acquired those traits.

Corvus's manner contradicted none of those expectations, and the only lightness in his appearance was the pale sky blue of his eyes.

The two sat for some time. At last Corvus gave a slight smile. "You're forbidden to answer my questions. I'm forbidden to answer the very questions you are most likely to ask. I find myself wondering how this problem can be circumvented."

"I volunteer information, without the necessity of your asking for it," Rowan said quickly. "I ask only questions I believe you're free to answer." Then she waited for his reaction; the entire conversation depended on his acceptance of the conditions. And the conversation had to take place.

He made a small sound of amusement, but his eyes were speculative. "It's an odd technique."

"I've used something similar in the past."

"With Shammer and Dhree, I assume."

She was startled, but managed a grim smile. "You've heard. No one else here seems to have. I thought perhaps I might have outrun my own news."

"My means of acquiring news is, shall we say, less bound by time and distance." He leaned back, and the veneer of casual friendliness he habitually affected seemed to falter somewhat. "Very well. Since the privilege of asking questions is yours, you should begin."

"Are Artos's military preparations necessary?" She was in Corvus's home city, and if the wizards planned to attack her, he would certainly have been told, and possibly would serve as the agent.

"I'd answer if I could, but I don't know what he's expecting."

Despite her tension, Rowan appreciated his ability to adapt to the limitations of the conversation. "The duke expects attack. From what direction, he doesn't know. The source is likely to be one or more wizards."

Corvus seemed to consider. "I know of no wizard who might hold a grudge against Artos."

He was being willfully obtuse, and Rowan frowned, anger and frustration battling within her. "The grudge, as you call it, is not against him, but a dear friend of his. That is to say, myself."

"You seem to have many friends. Powerful friends, I should say." And again he was amused.

Rowan sensed a clue in his words, but could not identify it. She believed she was missing something. Suspecting that a direct question would be refused, she tried an oblique approach. "Power is usually seen as the power that commands others. Of my friends, only Artos has such power."

"Wizards also have that power, and in addition, the power to command nature itself."

She was definitely missing something, something important. "Are any wizards likely to use this against me?"

"We have more immediate concerns."

Her confusion became complete. In the midst of this business directed at herself, was it possible that they would be distracted by other matters? Could she be so wildly fortunate? "If I asked what those concerns were, would you be able to answer me?"

He smiled at the careful logic of her question. "It would depend on the depth of the answer required."

It was a dead end; there was no way to sidle around that response, no way to guess what question he might not refuse. She needed his answers, had to discover whether or not a steerswoman's curiosity would call down battle on an innocent town, cause her friends to die for her, and end her own life by the hand of magic.

She changed direction with one desperate risk. "Has Slado lost interest in me?"

His smile vanished. In the midst of the homely, familiar tavern, he seemed a living shadow of gleaming metal and blackness, and she was sharply aware that the power she feared was present in his person. "No one should know that name."

"Shammer and Dhree were indiscreet."

"Stupid children," he said spitefully. "I was against them from the first."

"Then you're wiser than Slado."

He watched her, all friendliness vanished from his demeanor. "They died, you know." He tilted up his chin and waited for her reaction.

Maintaining her calm, she replied, "Yes, I thought they might have. I'm sorry. They were pitiful, in their way."

"And everyone is wondering who's responsible. We know you didn't do it."

"No, I didn't kill them. But I am responsible."

"Only a wizard could have destroyed that fortress. Whoever it was will give himself away soon enough."

His meaning came to her at last. "You believe that one of your number is a traitor."

"We know it. You'd save us a lot of trouble if you revealed his name."

Rowan was stunned.

Corvus continued. "We now know that all your dangerous cleverness was an illusion, and everything you know about those jewels was fed to you. You were told to look for them." He tapped the tabletop to stress his point, then spoke tightly. "You're serving someone, steerswoman, and it's only a matter of time before we discover who, and deal with him in our own way."

She could not believe her luck. To confirm it, she observed, "So you're watching each other, and I'm simply beneath your notice."

Wrapping his hand around his tankard, he relaxed. She was no danger to him; the threat came from her wizardly master. He regained a measure of his former manner, watching her a bit wryly.

She needed more. "You know about the jewels. Shammer and Dhree didn't. Are you in Slado's confidence?"

He seemed indifferent. "I have my own sources."

"Do you know what the jewels are? Why they're so important?"

His expression grew dissatisfied.

"I doubt your sources will help you there, if Slado chooses to keep the information to himself."

"It's a matter of time," he said again, patiently.

She was dizzy with relief. She looked at the ceiling and looked around the room, unbelieving, her mind a flurry of thought with no outlet. It seemed she was safe, for the moment, and she almost surrendered to it, almost rose and walked out, leaving the wizards to lose themselves in their misguided internal disputes.

But the safety, she knew, was an illusion and would shatter in the end, perhaps under worse circumstances. Better that it shatter now, by her own hand. She turned back to Corvus. "I'll save you time, effort, and strain on your sources. No wizard helped me. No one fed me information. There is no traitor, and I'm even more dangerous than you think."

He gave a short laugh. "That's ridiculous. You didn't destroy that fortress. There's no reason you should care about the jewels, no reason you should take such trouble."

"There were reasons enough. At first, curiosity. Later, because my investigation so interested the wizards."

He shook his head, disbelieving.

"Steerswomen never lie, Corvus. And no wizard could have fed me my information, because I know more about this one thing than any of you do, except Slado." She slapped her own chest, an abrupt, tense gesture. "*I* know what the jewels are."

His brows knit, and he studied her with a narrowing gaze. "Then enlighten me."

"A good choice of word." She drew a breath and began. "Corvus, how many Guidestars are there?"

He did not hesitate. "Two."

"Really? Interesting, if true. I'll rephrase: how many Guidestars were there, originally?" Catching his puzzled expression, she brushed away reply. "Don't tell me, I'll tell you. Four."

She went on, speaking rapidly. "Two is all that we can see, all that we know about. On the celestial equator, immobile, as all can see; but not really, Corvus, not in truth. They do fall, but too high, too fast. They can never reach the ground. They fall in the direction the earth turns, and at the same speed, and so only seem each to hang forever above its one spot on the earth. It's so obvious, isn't it, once it's pointed out?

"But why are there only two? Humankind has never pressed far enough east or west for one of the pair to sink out of sight below the horizon. What would happen if someone did travel so far? I think I know. As one Guidestar disappeared, another would rise on the opposite side. And it would be that way, all around the sphere of the earth; a traveler would always see two.

"That is, until some thirty-five years ago. It's different now. These jewels are part of a fallen Guidestar."

His expression answered her next question without her asking.

"You didn't know," she said.

A hundred speculations crossed his dark face; he shared none of them. At last he said, reluctantly, "Someone told you this."

"No. I only used reason, evidence—" Her mouth twisted. "And a small ability with mathematics."

He made to speak, stopped himself, shook his handsome head in disbelief, and began again. "How—" He corrected the phrasing. "I can't think of any way to bring down a Guidestar."

"Why not the same means by which they were lofted?"

"That was long ago."

She leaned back a bit in pleasure. He had admitted that the wizards themselves had set the Guidestars in place. "You think you don't have that ability any longer? The ability exists, but perhaps you don't recognize it. The force that destroyed Shammer and Dhree, for instance. Shammer himself said it; such things are tricky, and dangerous. And Dhree: she said it was just a question of multiplying the force used. If their two abilities were combined in one person, perhaps that person would find the problem laughably simple." She leaned forward and said quietly, "I wonder if Slado is laughing."

His eyes were on the window and the harbor outside; his mind was miles away. Then he looked at her sidelong. "One can't help but wonder at his reasons."

It had happened, the change she was looking for, the shift in his demeanor. Clutching at the hope, she spoke to him with simple directness. "I'd tell you, if I knew. And I'll tell you, when I do know. It's only a matter of time."

He nodded minutely, and for that space of time, at that one place in the world, regarding that one matter, they had ceased to be opponents. "Slado is playing some game of his own."

"Yes," she said urgently. "And it's a big one, possibly the biggest ever. The Guidestars were originally set there for a reason, and it's not merely to aid navigation." She stopped in mild surprise, then continued in wonderment. "The steerswomen are always taught to be able to navigate with and without the Guidestars. I thought it was for the exercise, but it's something held over from earlier days, isn't it?"

"Very likely." His mouth twitched; then he spoke a bit reluctantly. "The existence of the Guidestars makes one particular category of spells easier to effect."

"Do you need all four? No, I'll retract the question, I doubt if you can answer."

But he did. "Some of the spells in question are simple, and common; for those, one Guidestar would suffice. But there are a few – complicated, and very important . . ." He became silent.

"You don't use those spells yourself," Rowan said, "or you would have noticed the missing Guidestar."

"That's true."

Rowan did not ask who did use them; she believed that she knew. "Would there be problems if those spells were lost forever?"

He squinted in thought, and the squint became a wince. "The effects wouldn't be noticed for some time. Eventually . . . I don't know enough. There could be some very bad results."

"Bad for whom?"

He gave her a piercing look. "Bad for everyone, lady. We wizards do have our uses."

She reached across and tapped his arm like a conspirator. "Then Slado has some purpose more important to him than the welfare of the folk and the wizards. He's your enemy, Corvus."

"All wizards are each other's enemy, in some way," he admitted.

Rowan noticed that the tavern was completely silent. Someone had noticed a steerswoman in conversation with a wizard; now many stood watching, and more had left. Corvus sent a long mild gaze around the room, taking in every face, then made a small gesture – and the rest of the crowd departed quietly. Only the barman remained, standing beyond hearing with nervously shifting eyes. Corvus ignored him.

"That's a useful skill," Rowan commented in amusement.

"Sheer force of personality." He turned back, studying her speculatively. "When I thought that you'd been helped by a wizard, you could have left it at that," he pointed out. "We assumed that you yourself presented no threat to us, and we probably would have left you alone."

"Am I a threat, Corvus?"

"You know that you are."

"Then I'll introduce you to someone even more dangerous. A fourteen-year-old boy, the son of a blacksmith, uneducated, untrained, unable even to read. But able, if he so desires, to shatter a wizard's fortress."

His face went blank with amazement. "A boy killed Shammer and Dhree?"

He had forgotten the rules, and Rowan's only reply was her smile of satisfaction. "It's impossible," he said carefully. "I'd like to meet this boy, but frankly, I don't believe that you know what you say."

"It's the truth. And he wants to meet you; in fact, I promised to recommend him to a wizard, if ever I had an opportunity. I recommend him to you now. He'd like to be your apprentice."

He shook his head. "We choose from among our own."

"A separate people? That's something else we didn't know before. But it's not working very well, is it, if you have to use two wizards for one job. I must assume no one better was available."

"That was Ulado's doing." His expression grew grim at the thought. "It was too soon."

"Not by his lights. Part of his game, Corvus; he wanted that holding established right now, immediately. It must be important to him." Rowan watched the wizard's face change as he internally assembled facts known only to him, to some result that he found deeply disturbing. "I won't ask you what you're thinking," Rowan said. "But perhaps you'll tell me, one day, of your own accord." She rose. "Come. Young Willam has something he'd like to show you. I think you'll find it interesting indeed."

Some ten years earlier, a clever sailing captain had thought to avoid docking fees by bringing his ship past the public wharves, to a private landing up a narrow corner of the harbor. The ship moved slowly, and sounding leads were thrown every five feet of the way; but on a short starboard tack, between one sounding and the next, the hull met a narrow jagged rock, was breached, and the holds filled with water. The ship remained, half-submerged, more decrepit every year, to become the hated enemy of every riverman, confusing the currents and releasing unexpected debris.

Willam removed it.

During his hectic preparations of the previous week, Rowan had been his shadow. She asked no questions, but by some unspoken agreement he abided her presence. She understood little of the proceedings and was annoyed by what she did recognize. They seemed simple processes: distillations and precipitations such as an herbalist might make, but using no plants. At one point she thought he was making tea from some powder, but during the process, when he discovered one hand damp from the brew, he flicked his fingers dry, and the droplets fizzed into sparking flame as they flew.

Now he stood, his bow in his hand, Corvus at his side, on the west bank of the river. The wizard had seen none of Will's preparations but had watched with interest from the bank as the boy scuttled about the wreck, one of Artos's regulars his dazed-looking, cautious assistant.

The day was hot and thick with damp, the sky a white dome of haze. Downriver, the harbor docks were crowded with spectators.

"Is there any danger for those people?" Artos asked.

Will shook his head distractedly. "Not at this distance. I didn't use that much."

The duke was suspicious and uncertain, but did not protest. Behind him, Bel was tending a merry little blaze, three ragtipped arrows on the ground beside her.

Rowan stood, a wide-legged, stable stance, waiting for the ground to become the rolling sea she remembered from the fortress. She had not seen Will's magic at the last violent moment, had had her back to it as she ran. This time she intended to watch.

Willam made a gesture to Bel, and the Outskirter lit one arrow, turned it to even the flame, and handed it to the boy. He stepped up to the water, waded into it up to his knees, and nocked the arrow. With the smooth ease of a true archer, he aimed and let fly in the same movement.

The bolt ended in a pile of straw braced against an afterhouse on the tilted deck, and the straw flared. Will ran back to shore. Bel stiffened, bracing herself, but Rowan stood looser, preparing her body to absorb the motion.

Nothing happened. There was a long pause, and people began to look at each other in perplexity.

"I, I'm sure I did it right—" Willam stuttered. He reached to Bel for another arrow.

Corvus put a hand on his shoulder. "The charm in that straw was the first you set?"

"Yes . . ."

"They absorb water."

"I didn't let it get wet—"

"The air is damp, and you set it hours ago. And even before that, if it wasn't properly protected, it might have drawn water from the air. Are all the charms the same?"

"No. I use two kinds. One releases easiest by fire, and the other by, by a blow, or if another charm nearby is released."

"You use the one kind to activate the other?"

"That's best." They were oblivious to all else, lost in discussion of magic.

Corvus gave a small, almost kindly smile. "But enough heat will release the other sort, too, won't it?"

Willam looked in amazed realization from the wizard's face to the ship, where the afterhouse was rapidly catching fire. He said in a vague voice, "You'd better get down."

Corvus dropped prone with no hesitation, Willam beside him. Artos and Bel exchanged glances and more slowly made to imitate them. The little band of Artos's regulars looked about in confusion, some laughing nervously.

And the spell released.

It was like thunder from the sky, like standing next to a lightning-strike. Time seemed to slow as Rowan's thoughts sped more quickly, and she saw the rapid action with perfect clarity.

Water sped away from the wreck, moving out in a circular wave so violent that it broke in an instant, the stable surface around it like stone by comparison. Spray dashed straight up in a fountain impossibly high.

The ship separated into a hundred pieces, and each piece seemed to flee in its own direction: the bowsprit hurried across the river, the deck shattered and flew up into the air, the sides of the hull seemed to seek earth, pushing the water flat, then down, and Rowan briefly saw the shallow river bottom.

The poop deck became a cloud of splinters that rushed toward her. She turned and dropped to the ground, bits of wood pattering against her back like hail.

There was a long, echoing quiet, and a second wave of water dashed against the shore like a breaker.

Bel let out a delighted hoot and went to pull Willam to his feet. "That was wonderful!"

Artos and Corvus rose more cautiously, and something seemed to pass between them as they viewed each other. Rowan stood up, splinters falling off her to the ground.

Bel was thumping Willam's back, and he took her congratulations quietly, wearing the same expression he wore when he had viewed the destroyed fortress. He looked like a man who had been told some shocking news, secretly knowing that he was to blame.

Corvus took in the group with a long, slow gaze. His eyes ended on Artos. "I suppose, if I tried to kill these two, you and your men would do your best to prevent me."

"You'd have to use some powerful magic," Artos said evenly.

The wizard nodded, and he looked a bit sad. "I don't want to hurt them. Rowan." He turned to her. "Steerswomen are very good at discovering reasons. If there's a reason I shouldn't eliminate you and this boy, it's one that I ought to know."

She did not hesitate. "You won't do it," she said, "because it would do you no good."

He raised his brows in surprise, and she continued.

"Willam and I are nothing special, nothing unique. Killing us would solve nothing." She approached him, her boots pushing splinters into the ground. "That's why I told you that no wizard was helping me; that's why I didn't hide behind your misconceptions. I'm just a steerswoman, Corvus, and a common one at that. Four years past my training, wandering about the world with no better mind than my sisters."

She stood before him, studying his face, urging him to understand. "As long as you wizards thought I was unique, you hunted me. I've managed to avoid you, or escape from you so far; perhaps I can do so for many years. It doesn't really matter; in the end, I think, you'd kill me if you really wanted to.

"But what then? Do you think the Steerswomen themselves are remarkable? Will you destroy the Archives? I don't doubt that you can do so, easily enough.

"But the Archives don't make us what we are. Will you hunt every steerswoman? We're scattered throughout the known world, and we'd go into hiding. It would take a long time, but perhaps you'd destroy us all, yes, and the new ones we'd train in secret."

Looking up into his dark face, his pale eyes, she saw that he was disturbed. "But there's one more thing, Corvus," she told him. "There's Willam."

Bel shifted, eyed Willam, then led him by the elbow to Rowan's side. The three stood together facing the wizard: warrior, thinker, and child.

"He's just a boy," Rowan said. "Of the common folk. All he has is his eyes, his hands, his reason, and his courage. You can't destroy that, and you can't command it. He's not unique, and he's not trained. He's no steersman, he's the son of a blacksmith – but he knows, and I know, secrets you claim for your own. And if it weren't we two, if it weren't now, it would be someone else, sometime soon . . .

"How will you stop us, all of us? Will you break us down to barbarism? Will you kill every son of a blacksmith? Every merchant who uses a simple formula to calculate profits? Every farmer who can add? Every chambermaid who dares to look at the stars and wonder?

"Will you? Then, wizard, who will you rule?"

Corvus spoke, his voice was very quiet. "I don't want to do any such terrible things. I want the world to be as it's always been. It's not a bad world, really, as a whole."

She gave no ground. "The world is changing. You know it and I know it, but neither of us knows why. Watch what happens, Corvus, and when the time comes, choose your side. But remember us, that's all. Remember."

Corvus accepted Willam as apprentice.

It was against tradition, against common and wizardly wisdom. Corvus gave no reason, and Rowan's mind filled with a hundred speculations, each more dreadful than the last. But she satisfied herself at last with the recognition of one simple fact: it was what the boy wanted.

As they turned to leave, Willam stopped, suddenly recognizing his departure for what it was. He paused in realization, then rushed to embrace Bel, his head bending down against hers, and she held him quietly for a while.

When he came to Rowan, he took her undamaged hand in both of his. His eyes were full of amazement and gratitude. "Will I see you again?"

"It might be years. It's a long way to the Outskirts. And no means to guess what may happen between here and there. Or after."

"You're still going?"

Her mouth twisted. "There's something I'd like to see."

He looked displeased, and it came to her that he disliked the idea of her traveling about without his protection. She laughed despite herself, and he became a bit sheepish.

"Well," he said, "I won't forget you, or what you said to Corvus. Don't you forget me, either. I made a promise to you."

It took her a while to remember. "That if the wizards kept their secrets for some mean reason, you'd defy them and answer what I asked."

"That's right." He nodded shakily. "I'll stand by it. You have my word."

The pair walked away, up the riverbank in the hazy air, to the road that led back to Wulfshaven Harbor. Rowan, Bel, and Artos watched in silence.

"Artos," the steerswoman said at last, her eyes still on the boy. "Stay by him. Be his friend. Don't let him forget what he is."

"A common man. So he'll become a wizard with the true common touch?"

"If we must have wizards, that's the kind we need."

They turned away, but for Bel, still watching, her face uncertain. "You're not pleased with this?" Rowan asked.

"I ought to be. I'm not. I'm worried for him. But I do think it's a good thing. A wizard with one of the common folk as apprentice; I wonder how that will affect Corvus?"

"I wonder how Corvus will affect Willam," Rowan countered.

Bel released a pent up breath and looked up at her. "Well, he said he'd help us, one day, and I believe him. We have his promise."

But the steerswoman took a long time in replying. "Wizard's words," she said. "A wizard's promise."

Melanie Rawn
Dragon Prince £4.50
Book One in the *Dragon Prince* Series

The dragon claws were thick as a man's wrist; its leathery wings beat the air like the painted sails of a ship. It circled upward on thermals, bellowing its fury, then hurled down with claws extended towards Zehava . . .

Prince Zehava's family had been custodians of the Desert for as long as the sands spawned fire. But it's true rulers were the dragons, majestic creatures seizing the kingdom's livestock at will and preying on the caravans that dared to cross their dominion.

Zehava had pledged to hunt the dragons to extinction, and his pledge had earned him his death. Now Rohan was Prince of the kingdom, and his respect for the savage lords of the sky was based on more than fear.

For his bride he had taken Sioned, she of the mysterious Sunrunners, whose magic wove power out of light. Together they would change the face of the Desert forever – if their enemies did not destroy them first . . .

'Marvellous . . . impressive . . . fascinating' ANNE McCAFFREY

'Melanie Rawn does for fantasy what Frank Herbert did for science fiction in his classic novel *Dune*' RAVE REVIEWS

'Fun, adventurous, a really good read' MARION ZIMMER BRADLEY

Starscroll £7.99

Book Two in the *Dragon Prince* series

Sioned looked at her son. Enchanted love was in his eyes – exactly the expression that shone on his fathers face when the dragons were around. The gold mattered nothing to either of them; they loved the dragons as part of the Desert, part of their blood.

Rohan, the High Prince and his Princess, Sioned the Sunrunner, had vowed to protect the ways and secrets of the dragons from the dark lords that haunted their borders. But the twisted legacy of the former High Prince is abroad in the land, casting its shadow even from beyond the grave.

An enemy, defeated by the Sunrunners long ago, adds flesh to thought, posing a threat so sinister that steel is powerless against its titanic sorcery. To defeat such forces the ancient wisdoms must be reclaimed; supernal wisdoms hidden within the divine design of the long lost Star Scroll . . .

'Melanie Rawn does for fantasy what Frank Herbert did for science fiction in his classic novel, *Dune*' RAVE REVIEWS

All Pan books are available at your local bookshop or newsagent, or can be ordered direct from the publisher. Indicate the number of copies required and fill in the form below.

Send to: **CS Department, Pan Books Ltd., P.O. Box 40, Basingstoke, Hants.   RG21 2YT.**

or phone: 0256 469551 (Ansaphone), quoting title, author and Credit Card number.

Please enclose a remittance* to the value of the cover price plus: 60p for the first book plus 30p per copy for each additional book ordered to a maximum charge of £2.40 to cover postage and packing.

*Payment may be made in sterling by UK personal cheque, postal order, sterling draft or international money order, made payable to Pan Books Ltd.

Alternatively by Barclaycard/Access:

Card No. | | | | | | | | | | | | | | | | |

Signature:

Applicable only in the UK and Republic of Ireland.

While every effort is made to keep prices low, it is sometimes necessary to increase prices at short notice. Pan Books reserve the right to show on covers and charge new retail prices which may differ from those advertised in the text or elsewhere.

NAME AND ADDRESS IN BLOCK LETTERS PLEASE:

....

Name —————————————————————————————

Address —————————————————————————————

—————————————————————————————

—————————————————————————————

—————————————————————————————

3/87